THE SOVEREIGN'S SECRET

THE SOVEREIGN'S SECRET

Book 3 of The Witchfinder's Well Trilogy

winteranddrew.com

Contents

I

CHAPTER ONE

The Tower of London, July 1575

The gaoler rose from his stool and pointed at the dark stone archway. "The cells you want are that way, sir," he muttered.

He put his tankard of ale down on the table and looked closely at the man who had just walked in unbidden, showing a warrant to see his most high-risk prisoner. The man seemed tall, although it was hard to gauge his actual height as his doublet, hose and cloak were such deep black that he seemed to be an integral part of the heavy shadows. Only his pale, deeply lined face could be seen clearly in the candlelight, set under the shock of grey-flecked white hair that flowed out from under his black woollen cap. The man's close-set blue eyes made the gaoler catch his breath. They reminded him of the hard-edged captains who used to make him squirm as a conscripted fighting man; the ones whose authority could never be questioned.

"This prisoner – he lives still?" the visitor asked, making no move towards the archway. His voice matched his face; deep, gravelly and heavy with long-held authority.

"Indeed, sir, yes, sir," the gaoler answered, shifting his weight from one foot to the other. He paused. "Although I warrant it is by the narrowest of threads."

"How so?"

"He eats very little, by his own choice, and is oft seen letting the rats take the bread and small beer I allow." The gaoler paused awkwardly, but the white-haired man nodded at him to continue, so the gaoler stood a little more easily. "He is clearly in the greatest of pain," he said, "with heavy bruising on both arms and a leg that is broken. He needs must keep the leg still, so he has bound rags around a stick on each side of his shin, which will allow it to set straight." The gaoler paused again, then permitted himself a small smile. "I have told him his fate is to die a traitor's death, and that the same leg, along with his manhood, his guts and finally his head, will all be removed." The visitor nodded again, so the gaoler finished with a little black humour. "If he wants to walk to the gallows then God speed his bones to mend, but I warrant it will be a short-lived victory!" He gave a small laugh at his own joke, then asked, "Master...?" while raising an enquiring eyebrow.

"Wychwoode," the other man answered. "Master Wychwoode. And yes, indeed it will indeed be a short-lived victory."

"I have heard..." the gaoler began, then stopped. Wychwoode

said nothing, so the gaoler took a small breath and continued. "...I have heard him say that his wounds were inflicted by a noblewoman... the one he calls the 'fucking bitch', begging your pardon, sir."

There was a silence, and the gaoler began to think he had gone too far.

"That is indeed God's truth," Wychwoode answered.

"By Heavens, sir...'tis indeed so? A noblewoman?" The gaoler shook his head slowly, "Who broke his leg clean in two, and hit both his arms with such force that the bruising still remains, even to this day? I would credit a lowly woman or one from the stews might do that... but a noblewoman?"

"That is correct."

"Then I see clear why he talks of her with such venom."

The old man narrowed his eyes. "She stopped him in the act of attempting the treason that brought him to this place."

"Then I would surely bow before her, should we ever meet," muttered the gaoler, "while I would have my dagger to hand, for she sounds most dangerous."

"She is a fine and brave woman, fellow," Wychwoode said. "Resourceful, loyal and an upholder of the law. Qualities to be valued. She did what she needed to do."

---o---

Wychwoode fell silent, lost in his thoughts.

This cold stone place seemed to fade away, and with it the swarthy gaoler in the leather jerkin with tendrils of matted black hair sticking to his grimy forehead. Instead he was seeing scenes from a few weeks before, and in particular, the glorious exploits of the very noblewoman he had alluded to; Lady Mary de Beauvais.

Lady Mary standing over the bound and bloody body of the Alchemist, the man she had stopped as he attempted to use the powerful musket he had fashioned himself to assassinate Queen Elizabeth. She had achieved this by beating his arms with an iron poker, then using it to break his leg...

A forest clearing. Lady Mary casually holding the same musket, close by the body of a man she had killed by its power; a neat hole punched in the centre of his forehead, as if placed there with a driven nail...

Lady Mary presenting the supine form of one Lambert Moreton, his spine severed so he would never walk again... Lambert Moreton who had conceived and planned the whole plot; injured from a fall onto his back that she had caused...

He became aware that the gaoler was again talking, and with an effort dragged himself back to the present, and the cold stone jail.

"And the prisoner, sir, the one they call the Alchemist? Are you here to take him to meet the executioner?"

"Nay, fellow," he growled, "for now I must only talk with him."

The gaoler nodded and pointed again at the dark archway, set deep into the stone wall behind him. "Then that is the way we will go, sir."

Wychwoode looked into the darkness. "You will lead," he ordered, "with a brazier to light the way."

Their steps echoed loudly as they passed along the stone passageway, with the glow from the gaoler's brazier making the walls turn a fiery flickering red.

Wychwoode had to stoop to avoid hitting his head on the stone ceiling, and was relieved to make it to a heavy oak door. They passed into another long stone corridor with further archways set into the walls at regular intervals.

Each arch was the opening to a cell; each secured with a barred gate. The bars were covered in a mixture of black pitch and occasional brown streaks – rust or dried blood, Wychwoode was not sure. He permitted himself a curious glance through the bars at the unfortunate prisoners inside. None looked up or even acknowledged his passing; they were all pathetic bundles of rags, sitting slumped in the corner, or, in one case, hanging by the arms from a set of manacles attached to a high wooden post. Then, towards the end of the passageway, they came to a cell with a single prisoner, sitting back on a wooden bench with his head resting on the wall behind him.

As they passed the front of the cell, the man looked up, and for a brief moment, their eyes met. The prisoner scrambled up and staggered quickly to the gate, putting his hands through the bars.

"Master Wychwoode?" His voice was cracked and hoarse, as if this was the first time he had spoken in days. "Is that Master Robert Wychwoode?"

Wychwoode stopped and turned slowly with a look of indifferent enquiry.

"Aye," he said. "I am he."

"By Heavens, sir, you are well met!"

Wychwoode stood in front of the cell, just far enough back from the bars to be out of reach. There was a moment of silence as they observed each other. The prisoner was a tall, heavily built man in his mid-thirties, with a beard that looked as if it had been trimmed not too long ago, but was now somewhat unkempt. He was reasonably well-dressed in the garb of a merchant, although his clothes had clearly suffered from his stay in this filthy cell.

"Have we met before?" Wychwoode asked, with an edge of chill to his voice.

"Yes, yes..." The man nodded briefly. "I came to see you at the Inns of Court a few months ago." He gave a small bow of his head. "Roger Rolleston."

Wychwoode did not answer immediately; he was comparing the dirty man in front of him with the memory raised by the name – the memory coming back of a man whose manner was over-confident to the point of arrogance, and who was there to petition for... what was it? Ah yes – it was for the bond-release of goods from a merchant ship that he had invested in.

"I recall well," he said. "So, what brings you to this unfortunate position?"

Rolleston shook his head. "I was in the wrong place at the wrong time."

"As do most prisoners observe."

Rolleston grimaced. "No, no! This is God's truth, I swear! I was visiting some acquaintances with a view to dealing on a consignment of spices, when the local Pursuivants came to arrest my hosts for Catholic sedition." He shook his head again. "I was accused of being a Catholic simply by being in the company of such recusants, and all my protestations of innocence since have fallen on deaf ears."

"Then you will be brought to trial? That is the proper forum for you to put your case."

"I trust it will be soon, so I can show clearly that I am innocent of all charges."

"Well Master Rolleston, if your case is strong, you will have naught to fear." Wychwoode considered the man before him, clutching at the bars and looking at him with an expression of hope.

"Master Wychwoode, will you intercede on my part?" Rolleston asked.

The older man sighed. If every fellow who had brief acquaintance could call upon his services, he would never have the hours in a day to conduct his business in the law, let alone serve his true master, Francis Walsingham, and above him, Her Majesty Queen Elizabeth. "Nay," he answered with a shake of his head, "I have many more pressing matters. I am engaged on affairs of state as well as with the law."

Rolleston stood back, then suddenly he punched the bar with such force that Wychwoode thought his knuckles must surely be broken. "By Heavens, Master Wychwoode," he growled, "fate has brought you to me, and you are my only hope! I am wholly innocent – I have attended Protestant services with faith and with diligence ever since Queen Elizabeth ascended the throne! I have never missed a service, nor would wish to – go ask!" He shook his hand as if that was all that was needed to clear such pain as the hit would have caused. "Go ask in the parish of Egham, and particularly the church of St. John. The priest there will tell you that what I say is God's truth!"

Wychwoode nodded. "You speak with passion." He considered Rolleston again for a few moments. Maybe he had been too quick to condemn the fellow. What if he did as asked, and used his influence to gain the man's freedom? Then this Rolleston would be in his debt – which might make him useful in future.

It is always good to have resources at one's disposal...

"Very well then, I will ask," Wychwoode said slowly. "If your claim is corroborated, I will see what I can do."

Rolleston gripped the bars again and stared up at him. "I will forever be beholden to you, sir!"

Wychwoode glanced at the man's knuckles, that now had a line of blood running across them. "Indeed you will," he said. "But I make no promises."

As he turned back to the gaoler, who was waiting by another heavy oak door, Wychwoode shook his head to clear thoughts of Rolleston and his troubles. He needed to focus on the man he had come to see, the man known as the Alchemist.

The gaoler silently unlocked the door, then stood back to let Wychwoode through.

On the other side there was only one cell. It was dark, lit by just a thin beam of light coming from a small, barred window high up one wall.

In the corner sat a painfully thin prisoner with spiked hair and a rough beard, wearing only a torn shirt and breeches which appeared to be soiled with his own waste. A chain secured him to the wall, ending in a tight black collar round his neck. Both arms were covered in old yellow and purple bruises, under which faded images could just be seen; images that appeared to be crossed pistols on one arm and crossed muskets on the other. His left leg, blackened and swollen below the knee, was bound by rags and wooden sticks as the gaoler had described.

The two men walked up to the barred gate. The prisoner looked up slowly, his eyes seeming to change their focus from an inner world of pain to the new arrivals.

"Wychwoode," he said tonelessly. "Are you here to stretch me on the rack again?" He pointed down. "I have put my leg in splints and I feel the bones are starting to knit back together. Do you plan to undo all that good work?"

"Nay, Alchemist," answered Wychwoode. "I am not here to put you to the rack again. For as you know, the law has a different – and more permanent – fate for you."

"Ahh, yes. The gaoler here has delighted in confirming to me in great detail what that fate will be. But," the Alchemist looked up, "it has been over three weeks now," he pointed to a regular series of marks scratched into the wall, "and I am still alive."

Wychwoode studied the man. That he had lost weight and was now no more than a set of bones covered by skin was to be expected, for no man would grow fat in this place, and especially not if he used his meagre rations to feed the rats. That he had splinted his leg – this too was to be expected, for why would he not want to give himself some purpose and small comfort, even with the certainty of execution to come? But these were not the topics he had come to discuss. He whispered his instruction to the gaoler, who nodded, and unlocked the gate.

As Wychwoode walked into the cell, the gaoler muttered,

"He is on a short chain, sir, but I would keep my distance if I were you."

"I thank you, good man, for your information and advice," Wychwoode snapped, "but I am confident I can take it from here."

The gaoler nodded. "Yes, sir, yes," he stammered. Then he backed out, closing and locking the gate behind him.

Wychwoode waited until the heavy door could be heard closing further up the corridor, then he walked up to the Alchemist. "Aye," he said, "you are still alive. For now."

The Alchemist said nothing but watched the older man, as wary as an exhausted deer regards the huntsman. Wychwoode moved back to the wall opposite, then leaned against it and folded his arms.

"I came to see your state of health," he said eventually.

"As shit as can be expected," replied the Alchemist, "after what that bitch did to me with her poker; you with your torture on the rack, and what I get to eat in here." He indicated a mouldy hunk of bread beside him, that seemed to move of its own accord. "Full of weevils," he observed. "And the beer stinks of piss. Even the rats have to be persuaded to take it." He shook his head. "No, my health is not good right now – as if that mattered." He shrugged. "But then I'm sure you knew that. Why are you really here?"

Wychwoode went back to the gate and peered through the bars. The gaoler had definitely gone. Even so, he lowered his voice as he came back to the Alchemist. "I wanted to know if you still maintain your extraordinary claim to have travelled here through time, from the year twenty fifteen."

The Alchemist shrugged again. "I still die an agonising

death if I do admit it – you'll burn me as a witch. But if I deny it..." He started to cough; a thin wheezy sound. Once he regained his breath he repeated, "If I deny it... then I get to see what my insides look like." He paused, as if to let the true horror of that sink in, "and your precious Queen gets to see my head on a spike. Either way, I am dead."

There was a silence, then a narrow, calculating look came into the Alchemist's eyes. "Oh, but wait a minute! Wait one minute! It does matter, doesn't it? To you! Oh yes, to you and that bitch Lady Mary de Beauvais... Because I have accused her of being a time traveller as well, and now..." the Alchemist's voice suddenly rose, "*You know it!* Now you *know* she's actually from twenty fifteen!"

Wychwoode remained impassive.

"You have spoken to that couple in York, haven't you?" the Alchemist said. Then a thin smile played around his mouth. "The ones I tied up when I used their room to take a pot at the Queen. They must have heard me and the bitch talking about the future together! So, you *know* it's the truth!" He started to shuffle forward, until stopped by the short chain to his collar. "If I deny it," he said, his voice dropping to a whisper as his eyes burned into Wychwoode's, "then there's no sorcery. I still get ripped apart for treason, but she gets off free as a bird." He shuffled back to release the tension on his chain. "*That's* why you're really here, isn't it? You want me to deny what I told you on that infernal rack, to help make sure your precious Lady Mary is in the clear."

Wychwoode gave a small nod. "I have spoken to Beth and Amos Carter, and they have – reluctantly, I may say, for they hold you in the lowest esteem – agreed with your story.

They confirm that you and Lady Mary talked of the future in a way that showed you both had knowledge of it, and in such a manner that could not be explained by aught except by sorcery."

The Alchemist pointed at his scratches on the stone wall. "So that's why it has been over three weeks! You've been up in York checking out my story." He gave a triumphant grin. "Well, then, let's make this official!"

He struggled to his feet and stood stiffly on his good leg. Wychwoode could now make out the red chafing sores on his neck around the collar. "I am not going to do what you want!" the Alchemist snarled. "I will confirm to everyone that I am a time traveller from twenty fifteen, and therefore, in your eyes, a sorcerer!"

He hopped forward and glared up at Wychwoode from under his brows. "I will shout it from the gallows if necessary, in front of whatever crowd of ghouls turn up to see me die! So, it will be public knowledge! You will have to bring her in!"

He slid back down the wall and once again was consumed by a fit of coughing. "You and your Queen can do what you want with me," he muttered eventually, "but you will have to do the same to that bitch! I said it on that blasted rack, and I'll say it again now. If I burn, then she does too."

Wychwoode shook his head slowly. "I thought as much," he said. "Given the choice of two equally painful deaths, you have chosen the one that means I am bound by my duty to the law, and to my mistress the Queen, to level an accusation of witchcraft against the very woman who twice saved her life. A woman who is even now, to be honoured with a summons to Court."

"Yes, well, all I know is that she stopped me assassinating your beloved Elizabeth and getting money and a title from a grateful Queen of Scots instead. So forgive me if my heart does not exactly bleed for Lady fucking Mary too much."

"She was accused once before of witchcraft, and nearly drowned in a trial by ducking in a well," observed Wychwoode thoughtfully. "Which means this will be the second time she has faced such an accusation."

The Alchemist groaned. "You mean she very nearly died?" He gave a snort of derision that turned into another bout of coughing. Once he had his breath back he said, "That would have saved me so much trouble, believe me," Then he added, "But if she didn't die, didn't that prove the witchcraft?"

"Not at all," said Wychwoode. "For the truth is, God himself took her part." He paused, choosing his words for maximum effect. "As she went down the well, the voice of Our Lord and Saviour Jesus Christ was heard, saying she was his loyal handmaid, and that the witchfinder who accused her was a servant of Satan."

There was a long silence as the Alchemist considered this. Then he gave a slow, knowing smile. "The voice of Jesus?" he said. "Seriously?" He made a short, hollow-sounding laugh. "The voice of Jesus?" He shook his head as he stared at the older man, his breath wheezing at the back of his throat. "And you actually fucking believed it? You have got to be kidding me! She probably had her phone set to play a voice track or something. Easy trick! And she had all you superstitious yokels fooled!" He slumped further down the wall. "The voice of Jesus?" he muttered again. "Give me strength."

"Her 'phone'? What is that?"

The Alchemist gave a long sigh, his eyes burning into Wychwoode's. "It's a twenty fifteen thing. She must have brought it with her. All she had to do was prepare the phone, hide it somewhere and make sure it played the 'voice of Jesus' at the right moment." A smile cracked his thin face. "You check out that phone, Master Wychwoode, and you've got her for blasphemy as well as sorcery!" He laughed. "Oh, it just gets better and better!" This seemed too much for him. Running his fingers under the collar, he once again broke into an uncontrolled fit of coughing.

Once he was able to speak, he said, "You make damn sure you put us side by side when we are staked on that pyre, Master Wychwoode. I want to watch her burn and I really, really, *really* want to hear her scream for mercy as she dies."

CHAPTER TWO

Lady Mary de Beauvais pulled the little girl's head close into her stomacher, so the child's nose was pressed up against the stiff material.

"Mother! I can scarcely breathe!"

Lady Mary smiled as she unpeeled her daughter and held her at arm's length. "My dear, sweet Kat," she said, "I have missed you so much while I was away these many months, that I must hold you to me at every possible moment!"

"Yes, but you must not press my nose like it is a wildflower."

Lady Mary sank to the ground, her skirts billowing out around her, until she was level with her daughter's big brown eyes. "No, I must not, but you *are* like a flower, my precious one!" She placed a stray lock of the girl's hair behind her ear. "You have such beauty! And I cannot credit how much you have grown while I was away!"

"Well, you should not have been away so long, for then I would not have grown so much."

Lady Mary laughed. "Nay, my pretty..." she began, then stopped, as she noticed there were tears now welling up in the little girl's eyes. With a feeling as if a spear had been thrust through her heart, she pulled her handkerchief from her sleeve and gently wiped the tears away. "I am so sorry, Kat," she whispered. "I am so, so, so sorry. I know I said I would only be away a few days..."

"You were gone for such a very long time, Mother," Kat whispered, "I thought for sure that a bad man had crept up on you and you were... you were..." She sniffed hard, and more tears started to flow.

"I know, baby, I know," Mary replied. "But I am here now, and I am safe. I am back to look after you, and to love you." She paused. "Do you know," she said slowly, "some bad men did try to creep up on me, but..." As she said these words, she knew it was too much. The little girl's eyes widened further, and she took a small step back.

"You mean you did face danger, Mother?" she whispered. "Truly?"

"Yes... but..."

Mary stopped again. How on earth could she tell Kat what had actually happened on her journey to York this past spring? How does one tell a seven-year-old that her mother had killed and maimed men, however bad? Yet did she not owe the girl some form of explanation? After all, she *had* been gone for many months.

Or maybe she could make something up?

Mary smiled inwardly. What story could she tell that

would satisfy a seven-year-old's curiosity? Maybe some tale of a cartoon-style baddie would be enough? Then the smile died, and she groaned to herself. Her fib would inevitably be found out. Her son Ambrose had been right there for some of the grisly events, and he would be bound to tell his little sister his own version. Indeed, it was lucky he'd had no chance to do so since they had returned the night before. It would be much better to get a more truthful version in first.

"Yes, there were some bad men," she said. "And do you know what I did?"

Kat shook her head, her big eyes fixed on Mary's.

"Well, there was a bad man who wanted to hurt the Queen. So I struck him with a poker, and he was not able to hurt the Queen anymore."

"You struck him?" Kat whispered. "Did that please the Queen?"

"It did. She said she wants me to join her at Court in London soon, and she wants to ask my opinion on things."

"The Queen said that?"

"Yes."

"The actual Queen?"

"Yes. The actual Queen."

"Oh." Mary waited as Kat digested this information. "And the other men?" she asked eventually.

"There was one who wanted to hurt Ambrose."

Kat's eyes widened. "Did you beat him with the poker too?"

"No, I had a very powerful musket, so I shot it at him, and he let Ambrose go."

"Oh." There was another long silence, while Mary tried to return her daughter's steady gaze. "Was there another man?"

"Well, there was a man who wanted to hurt me. So I threw him off a cliff and he fell onto his back and it broke, which meant he could not walk anymore."

"Oh."

There was a silence as Kat digested this information as well, while Mary dried her eyes again.

"So, my little kitten," she said, tucking her handkerchief back in her sleeve, "your mother had some adventures, and did in truth see off some bad men, but got back safely to you in the end."

"And you will not be having any more adventures, will you?" asked the girl. "You are staying here now?"

Before Mary could answer, a dark-haired girl of around eighteen walked up to them, followed by a tall aristocratic blond man holding the hand of a boy of around nine.

"I thought we would find you both in the gardens..." began the girl, but did not get any further as Kat ran over with a scream of "Livia! You are here too!" then jumped into her arms, sending her staggering back.

"Olivia also returned with us from York last eve," Mary said, standing up and smoothing down her skirts.

Olivia regained her balance and started to swing the child round in a circle.

"Livia! Livia!" Kat shouted into her face as they spun round. "Ma said some bad men did creep up on her, but she beat them with a poker and she shot them with a musket and she threw them off a cliff!"

"So she did!"

"And what of you, Livia?" Kat asked, as Olivia stopped

spinning and lowered her unsteadily to the ground. "Did a bad man creep up on you as well?"

There was the briefest pause, then Olivia smiled sweetly, and said, "No, no. Not at all. I left all the adventures to your mother."

Mary looked away, to make sure she didn't catch Olivia's eye. For a bad man called Lionel Shelton most definitely had crept up on her, and had forced himself on her in the most brutal way. But this was their secret, and would never, ever be shared. She glanced over at the man and boy, who were standing in the shade of a nearby tree. They seemed oblivious to what had just passed between her and Olivia.

She walked over to them. "Art well rested from your first night back in your own bed, after three weeks on the road, Ambrose?" she asked the boy.

He nodded. "Yes, Ma, it was lovely." He looked up at the man. "I told Pa when we first rode up north in the snows that I missed my own bed, and I missed you telling me stories. So it is nice to be home, Ma, truly it is."

"You have stories of your own now, son," his father said, ruffling his son's hair with a grin. "Real boys' adventures that actually happened, not like the mawkish nonsense your mother tells you of the tragic Princess Diana and other made-up tales."

"Really William, let the boy alone," Mary said. "It must have been so frightening for him." Then she added, "It certainly was for me,".

"But Ma," Ambrose exclaimed, "Master Wychwoode told me all! He told of your adventures with Pa before I was born, and he was most insistent that our Lord Jesus himself said you were blessed!"

"Yes, well, we do not like to talk of that, Ambrose," Mary muttered, with a glance at her husband for him to support her.

Sir William nodded, his expression now serious. "Indeed, son, your mother is right. Such matters are not for discussion outside the family."

Ambrose nodded slowly. "As you wish, Father."

"I do mean it, Ambrose, most firmly." William put his hand on the boy's shoulder. "Now, you and Kat may amuse yourselves a while, as I need to talk with your mother."

---o---

"We need to decide on Ambrose's education," William said, when they had walked away from Olivia and the children. "The Grenvilles would have had him for a year or two, and schooled him in Latin, Greek and religion, not to mention how well he was doing at the butts with his archery."

Mary gave her husband a stern look. "Given that the Grenvilles turned out to be seditious Catholics, as well you knew they might be," she left a significant pause so that could sink in, "I am well pleased he was only there a few weeks and is no longer learning religion with them."

William had the grace to look sheepish. "Mary, my love, I have admitted my error, and we have all been through much pain and suffering as a result. I pray you do not keep the subject alive anymore."

Mary nodded. "As you wish," she said, making a mental

note to leave the matter very much alive and open to being re-visited as and when it might suit her purpose. "I would that we make arrangements for Ambrose to be tutored here in his scriptures, as well as in Latin and Greek," she said. "I would not have him leave us again."

"I agree," said William. "I too, have no wish to send him away to another house. It was too painful for us all."

"Good. Then that is settled. We will find him a tutor here." She stopped. "And another thing," she said suddenly. "Kat can be tutored with him. In all his lessons."

William turned back to her, "Now you are being absurd," he said. "Whoever heard of a girl being tutored in such subjects?"

Even though the thought had only just occurred, Mary knew it would be the right thing. After all, why should girls not be as well educated as men? One day in the future they would have equal learning opportunities – why not start it now? And especially with Kat, whose sharp little mind was just crying out to be broadened. Yes, this did need to happen.

But Mary did not answer immediately. Instead, she raised one eyebrow and gave her husband an intense, challenging stare. After a few moments, he coughed and said, "I mean, my love, it is not natural..." Maintaining the stare, she raised the eyebrow slightly higher. He coughed again. "Well, perhaps we could consider it when she is a little older..."

"She will be tutored with Ambrose, now," Mary said finally. "She may have opportunities in life, such as a position at Court. The better educated she is, the better she will be able to secure such a position. And with it a good marriage."

William looked as if he were struggling to assert himself,

then his shoulders dropped. "Yes, of course," he said. "I shall see to it."

Mary nodded. "Good." She walked on. "Then that is also settled."

As they proceeded to the house, Mary's satisfaction was tinged with a small, but niggling sense of unease. Educating Kat fully was the right thing to do – that was unarguable – but it opened up the possibility that her feisty daughter would grow up to have expectations; ones that society was not yet ready to deliver. Not only could that cause her dissatisfaction in later life, but it could also turn her into something of a rebel.

And rebels are people who cause history to change.

This had been Mary's greatest fear ever since she had fallen through a time wormhole into Tudor England ten years earlier, arriving as a confused time-traveller called Justine Parker. Would she cause history to change so much that her own birth in 1988 would be endangered? If so, would she suddenly just 'disappear'? After all, within two weeks she had saved William's life, when history had fated him to die.

This thought had eaten her up inside, and had kept her a virtual prisoner at Grangedean Manor for all that time. That was until she found out there was another traveller from her own time and place who seemed to have fallen through a similar wormhole. So now she had the means of validating her future existence – for if this other time-traveller knew her, and knew her name, then it would mean she had still existed in his time, and had not suddenly 'disappeared'.

So she had ventured out of her safe home environment in search of him, and eventually she had found him.

His name was Rick, but he called himself the Alchemist. Not only had he known her, but he had also presented her with the unassailable logic that nothing could endanger her birth. His explanation of parallel histories made perfect sense, and had finally set her mind at rest about the future. As he put it, her birth was a fact, and nothing she did now could alter it.

However, the future itself – the 21st century one that she knew of cars and phones and computers – that future now existed only in their memories. The potential changes that she had caused by saving William, then by having three children who were never meant to exist, and leaving Grangedean – those meant that a whole new long-term future would now be written.

So even though she no longer feared for her own existence, she could not help but feel concerned when her actions could so clearly have an effect on the future. Who knew what Kathryn de Beauvais could achieve as an educated adult, and her potential to send events in new and unexpected directions?

So even though she knew it was the right thing to do, Mary could not help a small shiver of fear that it was one more nail in the coffin of the 21st century world that only she and the Alchemist had known.

"...Mary, my love, did you hear what I said?"

William had stopped and was staring at her, his hands on his hips and his shoulders back.

"For sure," she replied, then added, "what was it again?"

William rolled his eyes. "By Heavens, woman. I asked if you wanted Jane tutored as well as her brother and sister?"

"In good time, yes. But now she is only five."

Mary walked purposefully back to the house, where they found Olivia waiting for them in the Great Hall.

"Sir William. Lady Mary," Olivia said as they entered, "I thank you for your hospitality, but I must take my leave. I would return to London as soon as I can, to resume my duties as lady-in-waiting to Lady Burnham."

"Indeed you must," answered Mary. "Her Ladyship was most generous in allowing you to journey back with us from York, so we could enjoy your company a little longer."

"But you must stay tonight and dine with us," said William, "for I have invited your father to attend, and half the nobility of the county, to welcome us all back to Grangedean!"

Olivia smiled. "Oh! My father? Of course!" She looked at Mary. "I had not thought I would have the time and opportunity to see him, but if it is such a banquet I am sure Lady Burnham will forgive me one more night!"

Mary put her hand on Olivia's arm. "I am sure she will. So come, let us choose our gowns and have my own lady-in-waiting, Sarah, fix our hair."

---o---

Some hours later, Olivia and Mary made their triumphant entrance into the Great Hall, where all the local nobility and dignitaries were already seated for the banquet, and were starting to get merry on Sir William's finest wines.

A servant opened the doors and announced them, but his voice was lost in the shouting and laughter of the guests. Then William broke off his conversation with the thin, grey-haired man beside him. He stood, and banged his knife handle hard on the wooden table. When eventually he had everyone's attention, he announced, "My Lords, Ladies and Gentlemen! I pray you, make welcome my wife, Lady Mary de Beauvais, and Olivia, the esteemed daughter of my dear friend here, Thomas Melrose." He waved a hand at the grey-haired man. "Please," he raised his goblet, "be upstanding and raise your glasses to these two brave and worthy ladies!"

Everyone got to their feet, stamping and cheering, as the two women progressed up the hall. Olivia glanced at Mary and got a reassuring smile that seemed to say, 'be confident in your yourself, and in your beauty!'

And indeed, they both had good reason for such confidence. Their elegant gowns were made fashionably wide by the latest farthingales, and their waists were pinched in by the tightest lacing. Their hair was pulled back from their foreheads – in the style made popular by the Queen – and formed into the heart-shape that her Majesty so favoured. Their pale faces were softly accentuated by rouged lips and cheeks, and Mary had insisted on applying additional kohl around Olivia's eyes, "to enhance their natural beauty."

Even so, Olivia was relieved once she had taken her seat at the top table and the normal hubbub of conversation had returned. What had all these men been thinking as they stared at her just now? To bed her? To take her by force? She shook her head as she sat and arranged her skirts, then washed her hands in the silver bowl proffered by a servant. No, they could not all be as bad as that despicable Lionel Shelton who had attacked her a few months before. But she could not shake the wariness she now felt around men. If Shelton's assault had taught her one thing, it was now to trust her instincts in regard to them.

"By Heavens," said Thomas Melrose as she pulled a piece of guinea fowl onto her plate, "it gladdens a father's heart to see you again!" He shook his head slowly. "But in truth, it is hard to recognise you! You are such an elegant woman now, not at all the young girl I waved off last winter!" He regarded her a few moments, then he frowned: concern written in every deep line of his thin face. "My dear, I had thought you were in London or Essex with my Lady Burnham, but I understand from Sir William you were on Progress with the Court, and that you were involved in some dangerous actions and adventures... He has said that you showed great daring and bravery. Is this true?"

She inclined her head. "I did only what was necessary, Father."

"Whatever it was, it has made a fine woman of you."

"Perhaps," she answered, as she held up her goblet for wine to be poured by a servant. "But better to thank the good Lady Mary. Without her support and guidance, I am not sure I would have had the strength to prevail."

"Ah, Lady Mary." He nodded. "She is indeed a special person; blessed by the Lord Jesus himself. There was no other woman in this realm I would have entrusted with your safety." He put his hand on hers. "And in truth, it seems my faith in her was well-placed."

Olivia was about to answer, when the doors to the Great Hall were again thrown open, and a tall, white-haired man dressed in black strode in, followed by four men-at-arms.

Immediately the hall was silent.

"Master Wychwoode!" exclaimed William. "You are well met, sir, and most welcome in my house." Wychwoode did not respond, but stared hard at Lady Mary instead. "May I ask the purpose of this visit?" asked William, an edge of concern now creeping into his voice.

"Sir William," Wychwoode growled, his voice low but carrying to all in the room. "It gives me no pleasure, and indeed much sorrow, but I have come on Her Majesty's business." He walked up to the top table. "I have come to arrest Lady Mary de Beauvais."

Mary stood. "Arrest me, sir?" she demanded; her voice surprisingly calm. "On what charges, may I ask?"

Wychwoode gestured to the men-at-arms to come up behind him, until all five were standing before the high table.

"Lady Mary de Beauvais," he said. "I have come to arrest you on charges of sorcery and blasphemy."

3

CHAPTER THREE

Lady Mary de Beauvais said nothing as Wychwoode studied the little jewelled box she kept beside her bed. He tried the lid.

"It is locked. Open it, please."

"If I refuse? It is my private property."

"I have a warrant to search the house for evidence of sorcery and blasphemy. So, I have the right to have it opened – by a key, or if that is not forthcoming, on the point of a blade." He put the box down and studied her a moment. "Mary," he said, his voice soft and tinged with sorrow, "as I said in the hall earlier, I take no pleasure in this."

"Yet you come into my home to arrest me in front of my family and friends, and your men go through my possessions like I am a common criminal?"

"It is the law." He shook his head. "I have no choice."

They were alone in her bedroom, after Wychwoode had

insisted that the search of her most private spaces was conducted by him on his own, while his men searched the rest of the house. William had initially demanded that he accompany them for the sake of propriety, but Wychwoode had been very clear that his interest was purely to gather evidence, and William need have no fears for his wife's modesty. Even Mary had spoken up to assure William she was perfectly capable of looking after herself. Eventually William had accepted this with very poor grace and had marched off after Wychwoode's men instead.

"But you have not yet told me by whom I am accused," Mary began. "Three weeks ago, I prevented the Alchemist from killing the Queen, and now..." she stopped as a dreadful realisation came to her, staring wide-eyed at him. "It was the Alchemist, was it not? It was he who accused me?"

She could see in his eyes it was true. She reached over and put her hand to his sleeve. "Robert," she said softly. "It is good we are alone to discuss this." She paused. "A man who is facing certain death will no doubt say anything to try and save his skin."

He looked down at her. "He might." His gave a slow shake of the head. "I am most sorry Lady Mary, truly I am, but the man has made allegations of you that in all conscience I simply cannot ignore."

Mary removed her hand. "You could try," she said quietly, feeling a bead of sweat start to run down her back. "Do I not deserve that?"

He looked away, as if there were nothing he could say.

"You would believe the word of a traitor over me?"

Wychwoode took a deep breath. "My dear Lady Mary,

he has inferred sorcery, evidenced by talk of future times in front of witnesses… I cannot ignore such things."

"Witnesses?" Then she shook her head in realisation. "Of course! That couple in York, the ones he tied up – they must have heard us talking about the future…" He inclined his head. So it was true. Then another thought came to her. "But you said I was also accused of blasphemy. Talk of the future may be construed as sorcery, but there is no blasphemy in such a thing."

Wychwoode sighed. "Lady Mary, you know I hold you in the highest regard?"

She said nothing, as her stomach started to knot up. Where this would lead?

"I have witnessed your brave deeds and leadership with my own eyes," he continued. "I know such forcefulness in a woman would be seen by many as a form of sorcery in itself, but I also see daily how the Queen shows the same, so I know it has precedence. But…" he paused. "I also have knowledge that you could not be a sorcerer, for you are favoured by the Lord Jesus – as all who were at the nearby well these ten years past heard Him say so clearly. His 'loyal handmaid' I believe he called you."

She stayed silent, letting him continue.

"Yet, the Alchemist has led me to believe the voice came not from our Lord, but from some blasphemous means instead."

So that was it.

The Alchemist must have worked out how the 'voice of Jesus' trick had been achieved. He would have known she would have most likely had her phone on her when she fell back through time, so she had set it up to play the 'voice'. Which meant Wychwoode was looking for her phone to prove blasphemy; the phone she kept locked in the little jewelled box he had just been trying to open.

"When you told the Alchemist of the voice of Jesus..." she began, then faltered to a stop. Maybe she had imagined it. Maybe this was not about her using her phone, but this was all about something else; something she could more easily dismiss.

But Wychwoode confirmed her fears. "He talked of a thing called a 'phone' – which would have produced the voice by sorcery, or by some functional trick, or some such."

Mary looked down, as if to reassure herself the floor of her bedroom was still solid, and not starting to swell like a murderous sea. Then she took a deep breath to try and steady her nerve.

"He challenged you to find it, before he was put to death?" she asked.

"Yes." Wychwoode paused. "But he told me this only two days ago."

"You mean he still lives?" She stared at him with wide eyes. "He has not been executed like Moreton?"

"Nay," he answered. "He remains a prisoner in the Tower of London. He will be put to death very soon, rest assured. But in the meantime, I need to address the allegations he has made, as the law demands. Allegations which have been independently validated."

"Master Wychwoode," she said, trying to keep her balance,

"I have once before been accused of sorcery – an accusation which was not carried through at the time. Must I be so accused again?"

He sighed. "Mary, as the Lord is my witness I must say again this gives me no pleasure, but I must carry it through." He paused. "And you do not question this talk of 'phones' – which leads to me to believe you know what such a thing may be." He looked her hard in the eye, then said the words that turned her stomach to ice. "Mary, do you have such a phone, and did you use it to conjure up the voice of Jesus?"

There was a long silence, as his words reverberated over and again through her head.

'Do you have such a phone, and did you use it to conjure up the voice of Jesus?'

The words seemed to grow louder and louder each time, until she wanted to scream at them to stop, to leave her alone...

'Do you have such a phone, and did you use it to conjure up the voice of Jesus?'

There was nothing for it. To be seen to co-operate might just help, even if only a tiny bit.

She reached into a recess on the carved bed post and took out the key. Like an automaton, she opened the box and handed over her most precious and secret possession.

Even though she had known him for many years and trusted him, he was still at heart a medieval man. So it felt as if part of her soul had been laid bare when he turned her phone over and over in his hand, studying it from every angle and tapping it curiously.

"This is the thing they call a phone?" he asked quietly. She nodded. "And it can conjure up the voice of Our Lord by its sorcery?"

"It is made by the hands of men. It does not work by sorcery."

"Then show me how it so conjures His voice."

Mary shook her head. "I cannot," she answered, "it has no power."

His hands stilled, and he looked back at her. "I know not what you mean," he muttered. "Can you not simply say the necessary incantations?"

"That is not how it works." She paused. The phone had been in the box for months while she had been away. How do you explain a flat battery to someone who has no concept of what a battery is?

"Imagine a water wheel turning a mill stone..." she suggested.

He nodded curiously, so she continued. "If the water does not flow, what happens?"

He shrugged. "The wheel must stop."

"Exactly. It has no energy to turn it. No power."

He nodded again slowly, as if the comparison now made sense. "So this phone – it needs energy to make it function?"

"It does."

"Should it then be held in a mill stream?"

"No." She took out the solar charger and plugged it in. "It takes its energy from the light of the sun."

There was a silence as they both stared at the black screen. Nothing happened.

Mary willed the phone to start up. Maybe he would see that there was no sorcery in it. Although she had to admit that was hardly likely.

"It does not function," Wychwoode said after a while.

"Wait!" she snapped, then added quietly, "please!"

Eventually the start-up screen opened. He was silent as the logo appeared, and when she put in her pin code. Then, when the home screen lit up, he looked at her and observed, "You say this is not sorcery, which would make a smooth black surface come alive with pictures?"

"It is the work of men," she repeated, staring at the screen.

"And it is the work of men that enables this thing to conjure up the voice of Our Lord?"

"Yes," she said in a small voice.

"Show me."

Mary looked up and swallowed hard to try and control her racing heartbeat. "Robert, please do not make me..."

His face was set sterner than she had ever seen it. "Show me, I say."

With a nervous sigh, she opened the voice app, then she paused, her finger hovering over the play button. "If I had not used this," she said, "I would have died down that well."

He shook his head. "Blasphemy is blasphemy, Mary. Better to have died with your immortal soul in a state of grace."

She shook her head. "That is not how I saw it at the time."

She tapped on the play button.

Once again the voice issued the order to the witchfinder Hopkirk to spare Mary Fox, as she had been called then. "Matthew Hopkirk – I am the Lord Jesus Christ and I say before these people that you do not act in my name. Mary

Fox is my loyal handmaiden – she is not now, nor has she ever been, a witch. Matthew Hopkirk, you are a servant of Satan, and I call on you in the name of God my Father, to end this trial now." Hearing it again after all these years, and with the accusation of blasphemy riding on it, made it too painful to bear; and when the voice had claimed to be Jesus himself, Mary could not help but wince.

"There was no intent to blaspheme," she said, breaking the long silence after she closed the app.

"Such is for a court to decide," he muttered. Then in a stronger voice, he asked, "And the men who made such things – in what year do they make them?"

So, with the blasphemy clearly proven, there only remained the matter of sorcery...

"In twenty fifteen," she breathed.

"Speak more clearly, please."

"Twenty fifteen," she repeated. "They are made in twenty fifteen."

He put both hands on her shoulders. "Then Lady Mary de Beauvais, I must ask this question, and I need you to answer me most honestly, as God is your witness, and if there is any hope your immortal soul can be saved."

He took a careful breath, and said, "Are you a traveller through time, come here from twenty fifteen?"

4

CHAPTER FOUR

Wychwoode led Mary back into the Great Hall. His hand was an iron grip on her arm, as if to stop her trying to escape. But he must have known she could hardly put one foot in front of the other without her legs buckling under her. Running would be the last thing she could manage.

His men were there, and at a nod from Wychwoode, they came up to her. Two of them took an arm each, while the other two stationed themselves in front and behind her as close guards.

Apart from the guards, William, Melrose and Olivia were alone. They stood, their faces showing confusion and concern.

"I must inform you," said Wychwoode in a flat voice, "Lady Mary de Beauvais is under arrest, on suspicion of using sorcery and dark arts to perform the most unnatural act of travelling through time itself, from the year twenty fifteen. She is also charged with blaspheming the Lord by causing

His voice to be conjured up using an ungodly tool from the future. She will therefore be taken from here to the Tower, to await her trial for such sorcery and blasphemy."

Olivia went white then collapsed onto her chair, her head flopping to one side in a faint. As Melrose bent over and clasped her hands, William stormed round the table.

"This is an outrage! Robert, what manner of nonsense is this? Mary is innocent of these charges, as well you know! Withdraw this accusation this instant!" His hand went to his belt as if to draw his sword, before realising he was not armed in his own house. Instead he marched over to Mary and pushed Wychwoode's man aside. "Mary, my love," he ordered, "tell them this is untrue!"

She said nothing, but could feel a tear emerge and start roll down her cheek. William stepped back; his face drained of all colour. "You do not deny it?" he whispered. "Blasphemy and sorcery?"

Mary gave him the smallest shake of her head, as another tear emerged.

"Well I do not give it credence!" William shouted. "It is but a misunderstanding – that is all! We will fight against it! We will not let this go its full course." He turned to the older man. "I demand you retract this, this, this – nonsense – immediately!"

"I cannot."

"But we are summoned to Court!" William actually stamped his foot. "Her Majesty will be most angered if we do not attend!"

"I am sorry, Sir William, but that summons is withdrawn."

William scowled at Wychwoode, then looked back at

Mary. "I repeat, this is but a misunderstanding, and we will fight it to our last breath!" He put his hand up to Mary's cheek. "My love, fear not," he whispered. "I will do all I can to end this nonsense. The de Beauvais name will be not tainted by such falsehoods."

She gave him a weak, watery smile, and he moved back, shaking his head.

Thomas Melrose stepped forward. "Come now, Master Wychwoode," he said. He drew himself to his full height and looked the lawyer in the eye. "You know, as we all do, that Lady Mary is a person of the soundest character, who has proven time and again how worthy she is, and who deserves not to be treated this way. My daughter tells me that were it not for Lady Mary, then the life of our dear Queen may well have been lost." He took a step forward. "Yet you put her under arrest for actions of ten years past?"

"Aye, Master Melrose, I do. I am bound by the law."

"For all that every man who knows her can vouchsafe her good character?"

"Which you, and any other man, can do when the matter comes to trial."

Melrose stepped back, his shoulders dropping. "Then in truth, you are resolved to see this through?"

"I am, so we leave immediately," Wychwoode answered. "Lady Mary can take one female companion with her to the Tower." He gestured at Olivia who was now sitting up, her face still pale. "I assume it is to be Mistress Melrose."

He turned back to his men. "Escort these women to the carriage and ensure they are held securely within. We will then take them both to confinement in the Tower of London."

---o---

William accepted some wine from Melrose in one of his finest glass goblets, as he sank into his chair by the fire in the solar. It was an hour or so later, and Grangedean Manor was very quiet – all the guests having been sent home immediately after Wychwoode had started his search of the house, and thankfully before Wychwoode had taken Mary and Olivia away. William had pressed upon the guests the need to keep this matter silent until he had cleared his wife's name. There had been much drunken nodding and muttering, but he knew it was extremely unlikely that this matter would be contained. No doubt it would become the hottest topic in the county, with much speculation on his wife's guilt or otherwise.

Her guilt...

"By Heavens, Thomas," he muttered, staring into the fire, "did you not observe Mary when Wychwoode accused her of travelling through time itself?" He drained the goblet in one go and held it out for more. "She did not deny it, withal. By the Lord's dying breath, she said naught in her defence."

"Nay," observed Melrose as he refilled the goblet, "she seemed accepting of it."

"At least we were alone when that was said," William observed. "All those drunken fellows and their wives did not hear how Mary as good as admitted... that she is a sorcerer." He faltered to a stop and stared silently into his goblet. "Why did she not fight?" he said eventually. "Why did she not call it out for arrant nonsense? For all that in truth, such talk of sorcery itself is nonsense."

"It is believed by many."

"Yet why did she not deny it?"

Melrose gave a small shrug. "For the only reason, Will." He paused and shook his head slowly. "For the reason we both know in our hearts. She believes it to be true."

"That she travelled through time from the distant future?"

"Indeed so."

"But it is not to be believed!" William shouted, slamming his goblet down hard on the table beside his chair, causing most of the wine to slop out. "By Christ alive," he continued, ignoring the red puddle spreading out, "how can any man of a sound mind accept such a thing?"

"She does."

William stared hard at his friend.

"As I see it," Melrose continued, "there are two choices here." He paused, appearing to consider his words with care. "On the one hand, we can accept that your wife has lost her mind, and in her madness, has convinced others that she is a time traveller."

"But why would she do that? Bringing others in on her mad conceit harms no person but herself. And anyway," William bit his lip as he thought, "we both know there is no madness in her. She is more settled in her wits than even you and I."

"Precisely." Melrose nodded. "So then we have the only other choice. That Lady Mary de Beauvais is indeed come here from the year – what was it? Twenty fifteen."

There was a silence as William tried to process this thought.

Of course it was nonsense. For if she was such a traveller, then she would have appeared suddenly, as if from nowhere; when in truth she had told a plausible tale of falling from her horse when riding past. But... Mary was a consummate horse-woman, who could ride any beast and tame even the feistiest of mares, so how would she have fallen? And where was the horse she had been riding? Would she not have insisted on sending a servant out to retrieve it?

No, no... she was not to be doubted. if she said she had fallen, then that was what occurred.

Although for sure, she had not been dressed for riding – at least not in women's clothing. She had been wearing a semblance of male attire, if William recalled correctly. She had been clothed in an unfinished woollen doublet and tunic down to her knees, hose so thin she was all but bare-legged, and boots. And she said she came from Hammersmith, but remarked on this as if such a place was part of London, when as any well-travelled man knows, it is but a village many miles from the city.

William caught his breath. Maybe in 2015 London will have grown so far beyond its walls that Hammersmith will have been swallowed up, as a pike swallows a minnow?

Then he frowned. Was he now starting to believe she could in truth be such a time traveller? That she had not fallen from her horse, but had appeared as if from the air itself? That she was dressed in clothing appropriate to a girl of 2015, not 1565? That she did come from both Hammersmith and London?

To think on it now, her behaviour was always most strange, even to the point of pretending to be a deer when they were alone in his chamber, and dressing as a boy to save his life in the tavern.

In which case, maybe the truth was indeed that she *had* travelled through time...

He looked sharply across at Melrose, and it was clear from the expression on his friend's face that had come to the same conclusion.

"By Heavens, Tom," he whispered, "Can it really be true?"

"I fear so, Will." Melrose answered. "I see you have reached the same understanding as I have. It is the only explanation that covers all the facts of the matter."

William felt his face suddenly flush red, and he stood so quickly that his chair pushed back with a loud scraping noise. "So in truth I am married to a sorcerer come from more than four hundred hence!" he shouted. Then he flung his goblet into the fire, so it flew onto a burning log and shattered into a thousand hissing and steaming pieces. "By Christ's Wounds, Tom, if this is true..." He took a couple of sharp breaths, "If she is indeed such a sorcerer, then she has lied to me all these years! Everything we had together has been false!" He thumped the table hard with his fist. "Why did she trust me not, Tom? Why did she not tell me herself – that I must discover the truth in this dreadful manner? By her arrest in public?"

"Because you would have reacted just as you have this moment, perhaps?" Melrose said quietly, taking another goblet off the shelf and refilling it for William. "And she preferred to keep you in happy ignorance rather than risking your anger?"

"But she has played me for a fool!"

"Belike she has. Although not through malice, I warrant, but through love."

William took a deep drink. For all his anger just now, maybe Tom was right? Could he really blame Mary for her deceit? Maybe it was as his friend had said – that it was for love that she had planned to take her secret to the grave and keep him in happy ignorance? Could she be blamed for that? The Mary he had always loved? The Mary who had always been a good wife and mother to his children?

It was almost as if Melrose had once again read his thoughts. "And do not forget, Will," he observed. "She did save your life in that tavern. It was as if she knew what was to come to pass and was there to stop it."

William sat down and nodded slowly as he stared at the pieces of glass glowing in the fire, the heat now gone out of him.

"She was most insistent I stayed in a cottage in the woods that very night," he observed.

"For sure," Melrose answered. "So she must have known, and was trying to keep you from your fate."

"But she did deceive me, Tom," William said, looking at his friend with wide eyes. "I say again, she never said aught that she was a woman come from the future."

"Yes, but we both know the truth of this. She is a brave, strong and caring woman, wherever she may be from."

"Caring indeed," William said. "You are right, Tom."

"Indeed so." Melrose paused. "And she has ever been a worthy mother, that none can fault in her love for her children."

William turned back to the fire. "The children! The truth of this would destroy them! So we must let them think only that she has been arrested on false charges – no more." William refilled their goblets. "And I must do all in my power to get her home and have such charges dropped, before Wychwoode and his officers..." he stopped and took a deep breath. "Before they put her to trial and..."

They looked at each other, but neither could bring themselves to utter the awful words.

'...and to death'.

5

CHAPTER FIVE

The rooms in the Tower were unexpectedly well-appointed. Mary and Olivia peered into a bedchamber with just enough space for the four-poster within, its frame hung with heavy woollen drapes. Then there was a formal sitting room with a blazing fire already burning in a stone-arched fireplace. This room also contained a couple of high-backed chairs before the hearth, a small writing table, and a *prie dieu* – an oak prayer desk with a sloping top and a kneeling platform at the front.

"I had assumed we would be cast into some sort of dungeon," Mary observed as they were ushered into the room by a yeoman warder, then heard the door locked behind them.

Olivia sat before the fire and kicked off her shoes.

"It is not like you to be so quiet," observed Mary, sitting beside her. "You have hardly said a word since we were taken from Grangedean in the carriage. Do you not have questions for me?"

There was a long silence, as Olivia stared into the fire. Eventually she said, "I have but one question."

"Go on."

Again, a long silence. Then Olivia turned and looked searchingly at Mary.

"Is it true?"

She said the words so softly that Mary almost didn't catch them above the crackle of the fire. The flames danced merrily away in the grate, as if unaware of the significance of the question now hanging between them.

Mary sighed. "Yes," she said. "It is."

Olivia considered this a while, then must have decided that further questions were now needed. "You have travelled through time itself, from the distant future?" she asked.

"Yes. I have."

"Aye, now I think on it, you always had a strange way about you." Olivia said with a frown. "You were so certain that women would one day be the equal of men. That was from your knowledge, not just from hope?"

"It was truer of the world I lived in." Mary paused. "And although there is still much to be done to achieve full equality, essentially yes."

"So all the advice you gave me, that I should be strong and that it is not my fault if a man forces himself on me – that was from your actual experience of things yet to come?"

"Again, yes." Mary put a hand on the girl's arm. "Olivia, I had a different view on this world – a view no person born in these times could possibly have. I wanted to challenge your beliefs; to make you see there are always alternatives." Mary sat back. "And I think I might have helped, just a little bit?"

"Perhaps." Olivia stared into the flames for several long minutes. Then she turned to Mary and said, "The voice of Jesus, that Wychwoode himself told to me and Ambrose up in York – was that not real?"

Mary sighed again. It had been all very well telling the truth about being a time traveller, but to come clean about her deception with the phone? That might place a heavy burden on Olivia if she were called as a witness at the trial. But wouldn't a lie be even worse? After all they had been through together, she owed the girl that, at least.

"No," she said. "I caused the voice to come forth by using the phone. It was as Wychwoode said."

"But causing the voice of Jesus to be heard – that is blasphemy indeed." Olivia shifted in her chair, as if the fire had suddenly become too hot.

"It troubles you?"

Olivia turned to her with a look of sadness. "That it does, Lady Mary. It troubles me for the sake of your soul," she shook her head slowly. "And indeed, for mine as well."

"So what would you have me do?"

"I would have you pray with me for forgiveness," She gestured at the prie dieu. "For then I will know that you are penitent, and can still receive God's grace."

Mary sighed inwardly. As a 21st century English girl, she had never been particularly religious, ever since the occasion when she had been sitting in a school chapel service and the chaplain had been talking of God's love for innocent children. Something in his tone, or maybe it was the way he held himself, made her think that he was simply saying words he'd said a thousand times before and not even thinking about what he was saying. Which meant that she started questioning the words for herself – and finding she had more questions than answers. If God is willing to prevent such things as the suffering of innocent children, but not able to do so, then he is not omnipotent. And if he is able to prevent it, but chooses not to, then he is not good. And if he is neither omnipotent nor good, why should she have to worship him? This sceptical mind-set had set her up for an adult life where religion had no necessary place, and this had served her well in 21st century England. But England in the 16th century was an altogether different place, and she had been quickly accused of witchcraft on the basis of a casual expletive that would not have even raised a modern eyebrow. So she had been forced to adjust her outlook, and accept that an outward show of religious belief was necessary to survive in the Tudor world. She attended church as often as she had to, and had been strict about bringing the children up in the Protestant faith. But her secret scepticism had remained intact, and had made her deeply suspicious of those whose religion was so fanatical that they were prepared to kill for it.

Both Protestants and Catholics.

But for the Catholics she reserved her strongest hatred. Not only had the recent plot to kill Queen Elizabeth been driven by Catholic fanaticism, but one could not ignore the Pope's recent Papal Bull which specifically instructed all Catholics that it was their duty under threat of excommunication not only to disobey the Queen, but actively to seek her death.

Mary knew she was privileged to have seen a different side

of Elizabeth to the stern monarch that everyone else knew. A bond had been forged between them over the dead body of Tom Cobham in a little house in York; a special moment of understanding between the two women. So for the Pope to seek the death of such a woman – a friend as much as a queen – meant Mary would do all in her power to stop that happening.

"Will you come and pray with me?" Olivia asked, dragging Mary back into the present.

Mary stayed still. How could she be honest about such a personal matter? But then again, if a prayer would help set Olivia's mind at rest, however insincerely it was said, then surely the end justified the means?

Mary stood and went over to the prie dieu. "Come, then" she said, "I will pray with you."

They both knelt, squeezing tightly beside each other on the narrow platform. Mary put her hands together.

"I pray to Lord Jesus,..." she began, then stopped.

What should she pray to Lord Jesus? To end this nightmare? It would take one heck of a miracle to get her out of this mess – and anyway that was not what Olivia wanted to hear.

"I pray to Lord Jesus..." she repeated, "to grant me pardon for my sins. For the sin of..." she stopped again.

This felt so wrong.

What was it the religious used to say back in the 21st century? That there are no atheists in foxholes? Well, this was a definitely a 'foxhole', so was she suddenly going to find religion? Judging by the tense knot in her stomach, the answer was 'definitely not'. Mary glanced across at Olivia, who now had her eyes shut and was moving her lips silently. How nice would it be to have that 16th century certainty, the total assurance that there was a god and he loved her...

Love...

In that moment, Mary knew exactly what she should pray for.

"I pray to you Lord Jesus..." she said again, "to grant me pardon for my sins. For the sin of blaspheming you by pretending to conjure your voice..." she glanced across at Olivia, who had stopped her own prayers and was now listening, "and for the sin of sorcery, in that I was sent unwillingly across time itself to Grangedean Manor. But more than both of these, I thank you Jesus from the bottom of my heart that when I arrived there, I was able to do your good work. I was able to save the life of Sir William de Beauvais, then marry him and love him, and by him to bear three beautiful children, whom I love more than life itself. So while I accept that this life may soon be over, I pray to you, Lord Jesus, to watch over my husband and children and make sure they know that I am not a true sinner. To have them remember me as a warm and loving wife and mother, not a person worthy of incarceration and death. To know that I have always loved them and will continue to love them for all time."

Mary felt Olivia shift beside her, pushing herself slightly closer.

"And I pray for Olivia Melrose, whom I have come to love as much as if she were my own daughter. I pray you also keep a watch over her, for she is your good and faithful servant. She is so honest and so true that I am not worthy to touch the hem of her robe, and if I could have but one tenth of her courage and integrity, then I would be content to face my death knowing I am worthy of your love."

There was a long silence, then Olivia whispered "Amen."

"Amen." Mary repeated.

Olivia twisted her body and opened her arms. Mary did the same, and as they knelt on the prie dieu, they embraced with such intensity and warmth that it was as if nothing, not distance, or even death, could ever split them apart.

6

CHAPTER SIX

It was a few hours later and Mary and Olivia were seated by the fire when they heard the key turn in the door. A swarthy man in a leather jerkin with filthy matted hair came in, carrying a wooden tray of meats and wine.

"Mistress de Beauvais?" he said, as he put it on the table.

"Yes?" Mary stood up.

The man bowed low, then stood back and looked her up and down. "I swore I would bow before you. Aye," he continued, "I had thought you would be tall. I can see you might be one to break a man's leg with a poker."

"I see my reputation precedes me," Mary observed. "And how does it concern you?"

"Indeed, not at all," the man replied. "But I wanted to meet the noblewoman who had behaved as a common crone and inflicted such wounding on a man."

"Know your place, churl!" snapped Olivia as she also stood

up. "Lady Mary should not be spoken to with such familiarity by the likes of you!" She paused. "Where is the Constable of the Tower? Why do we not have him to welcome us to this place?"

The man gave Olivia the same inspection as he had given Mary. "And you might be?" he asked.

Olivia drew herself to her full height. "My name is Olivia Melrose."

"Well, Mistress Melrose, we do not currently have a Constable, since Sir Peter Carew left the post some three years since. So I suggest you learn that here in the Tower, I am the gaoler, which means I say as I wish, to any prisoner." He waved his hand at the tray of food. "I am minded to take this away, and bring instead the mouldy bread and small beer we serve the prisoners in the dungeons below. Would that be more to your liking, Mistress Melrose?"

Olivia said nothing, but crossed her arms and sat back by the fire.

Mary said to the gaoler, "You must have spoken with the Alchemist. Is he still here? Has he not yet been taken to his execution for treason?"

The man gave a snide smile in the direction of the back of Olivia's head, then answered, "Nay, mistress. He lives for a few days more, and is yet chained by the neck in my most secure cell below." He paused a moment and smiled again. "Would you like me to take you to him?"

"Oh no!" Mary exclaimed. "I am the reason he is in jail awaiting execution! For sure I am the last person he would see."

"Indeed," answered the gaoler. "He has said things of you

I ought not repeat, for fear of upsetting Mistress Melrose here, and her fine sensibilities." He chuckled. "I just thought it would please you, to see him, is all. Like a dog sees the bear chained to his post, eh?" He nodded at Mary and opened the door. "I will return for the tray in good time," he said, then left.

"Thank you, Olivia," Mary said, after they heard the key turning in the lock. "For taking my part with that man."

"He called you a dog! He is naught but a ruffian, my lady," exclaimed Olivia, her eyes wide. "A cur himself, who should know his place."

"Unfortunately, his place is to keep us locked in these rooms and to decide what we are to eat," answered Mary. "So, although you are right, I fear we must allow him to treat us as he will."

"Indeed, but we do not have to like it."

"No." Mary thought a moment. "But what I do not like, is the fact that the Alchemist is even in the same building as us." She shivered, despite the heat of the fire. "I had never thought I would see him again, and it upsets me to know he is near." She paced away from the hearth then turned back. "I have enough to worry me, with accusations of sorcery and blasphemy hanging over my head, to worry about the Alchemist as well."

"Too true," answered Olivia. "Have you thoughts on how we should respond to these accusations?"

Mary sighed deeply. "I know not," she said. "I had hoped Master Wychwoode would take my side, but it seems not to be."

"He serves the law before his friends."

"That he does."

"But I will speak for you, my lady," said Olivia, coming over and taking Mary's hands in hers. "I will tell how heartfelt your prayers were earlier, and how you have always been so steadfast and true. I will tell all that you are an honest woman now, whatever you may have done before, or wherever you have come from."

Mary smiled. "Then let us hope they believe you."

---o---

It was early afternoon three days later. Mary and Olivia were chatting by the fire as usual, sipping red wine from the gaoler's daily tray, when they heard the key turn in the lock.

"'Tis not time for the tray to be collected," Olivia observed casually. "I wonder who is here?"

Mary put her goblet down carefully and stood up, smoothing down her skirts as she turned to face the door. "Maybe they have come for me," she said softly. "Maybe it is time."

"By Heavens, no!" Olivia exclaimed, standing also.

The door opened, and Mary's heart sank as the tall familiar figure of Wychwoode strode in, followed by the gaoler.

Wychwoode turned to the man and growled, "Begone, sirrah. This matter is private."

When the gaoler had shuffled out, the lawyer gestured for Mary and Olivia to sit. Then he placed himself by the fire, his hands hooked behind his back.

An uneasy silence developed.

Mary shifted uncomfortably in her seat. Had the time really come for Wychwoode to escort her out of these rooms?

These rooms that had become something of a home from home with Olivia's friendship and company these past few days, so that occasionally, just occasionally, Mary had almost forgotten about the reality of the fate awaiting her.

But had it now suddenly become all too real?

She took a sip of wine to try and moisten her mouth, which had now become so dry her tongue felt like a large, gagging ball of cloth. She tried to keep her hand steady, but she could not stop the pewter goblet rattling against her teeth.

Was she about to be taken to her trial?

She gave a small gasp. Or maybe there would be no trial! Maybe they had already decided on her guilt and she would be taken straight to her death! Was Wychwoode here, not to take her to some dusty courtroom, but directly instead to a rough tumbril cart? And from there to some field where there would be a stake set into the ground surrounded by dry wood at its base. And would she then be forced up to the stake and have her hands tied behind it, before some man advanced with a burning torch to... to...

Mary took another sip of wine, and thought she was going be sick.

The old man's gravelly voice forced her back to the present.

"Are you being treated well in this place?" he was asking.

Mary nodded as she tried to swallow the wine.

"As well as can be expected," Olivia said.

"And you are well fed?"

"It is not what we are accustomed to having," answered Olivia, gesturing at the remains of ham and bread on the tray. "But it will suffice."

"Good." Wychwoode paused, observing them in turn from

under his brows. "Now, to business. I am come here this day to take you..." A strangled gasp from Mary interrupted him. She fell back in her chair and her goblet slipped from her nerveless fingers, landing with a clatter on the stone floor by Olivia's feet.

Ignoring the splashes of red wine now staining the side of her skirts, Olivia grabbed Mary's hand and squeezed it for reassurance. She looked up at Wychwoode. "Art come to take Lady Mary for trial, Master Wychwoode?" she asked.

Mary found her voice, and croaked, "Or has that formality been dispensed, and we are to proceed directly to the execution?"

"I am come here this day," the old man repeated, wagging his forefinger on each word, "to take you to neither trial nor execution, although those events sadly remain an inevitable part of your future. I am taking you both by boat to meet someone in his house in the country. Someone who has expressed a wish to meet you before..." he cleared his throat. "Before it is too late."

"I see." Mary took a few deep breaths to try and restore some sort of calm. "And this person – he knows that I am from future times?"

"He does, and he is most curious about you. He wishes to understand you better."

"I see," she repeated. So it was not to be a trial or burning today – that was at least something. She picked up her goblet and poured herself some more wine. Then another thought struck her. "And is he the only one, Master Wychwoode," she asked coldly, "or are my last days to be filled with many such meetings, so that the great and good of the land can all say they met the sorceress from twenty fifteen before she was burned to death?"

Mary felt Olivia squeeze her hand again.

"I cannot answer for others," he answered, "but I am sent to bring you both to meet this man now, so I would you get yourselves prepared and we will depart."

Mary glanced down at Olivia's stained skirts. "Then we will need a little time, to ensure we are both made presentable," she observed.

"I would you both make haste," Wychwoode said. "We need to catch the ebb tide if we are to get under the bridge."

7

CHAPTER SEVEN

The boat proceeded swiftly away from the Tower, heading west towards London Bridge. Mary and Olivia were seated in the stern, facing the eight uniformed oarsmen who were keeping good time from the regular shouts of a coxswain calling the strokes. Wychwoode was seated a little further forward.

Mary looked up as they came towards the bridge. Although she had previously seen it from the bank side, this was the first time she had been able to appreciate its scale and magnificence from the water. It was supported on many thick stone pillars, each with a large foot shaped like the bow of a boat, so the water could flow around. Above the stonework the bridge itself was like a busy street, with buildings along most of its length and only the occasional gap. At the centre was a church, then an arched building, then a drawbridge covering the largest central arch. The top of this building seemed to be decorated with what looked like a number of gargoyle heads, and Mary was just trying to work out what these were, when Olivia put a hand on her arm and said, "The heads of traitors, put on spikes for all to see."

Mary could not help but shudder. It was small comfort that she was fated to be burned at the stake and her own head would not be joining them, but it was still a deeply sickening sight. She looked more closely as they approached the bridge, trying to see if by any chance the Alchemist had now joined them, but could not make out one that looked anything like him.

She looked down to see Wychwoode had made his way back to them.

"I strongly suggest you both take a firm hold," he said. "We will shortly pass below the bridge and be subject to the strong currents and eddies that swirl between the supporting starlings. Many a boat has foundered on the stonework, and lives have been lost."

Mary glanced at the water between the nearest pillars, and she could now see that it was churning and foaming, creating white-capped waves that crashed from one pillar to the other. She must have had a look of concern, as Wychwoode added, "By good fortune, the coxswain has steered this course many times, and has never yet lost a passenger."

As Wychwoode went back to his seat, Mary grabbed onto the rail beside her with one hand, while her other sought out Oliva's and grasped it tightly. She glanced across at her friend and got a nervous grin in return.

"Hold on, then," she muttered, as the boat suddenly pitched forward into the semi-darkness below the bridge, then flung them violently to one side as the bow was pushed towards a pillar. Mary thought her hand clutching the rail was going to be ripped off by the force of it. Then the bow came round so sharply that she was sure they were about to crash, but the coxswain called, "Hold a' starboard! Pull hard a' port!" and at the last second the bow flipped round and headed now towards the opposite pillar. Mary had to push so hard against the rail to stop herself being flung out that she thought her elbow would snap, then the coxswain shouted once more and the bow flipped the other way, and she had to hang on to stop herself crashing into Olivia... and then the welcome daylight came back, the boat suddenly settled, and they emerged safely into the calm waters beyond.

"Art well?" Mary asked, keeping a firm grip on Olivia's hand, but aware that her voice had a catch in it.

"I was so certain we would be pitched out and drowned," Olivia said.

The boat now glided serenely on its way like a contented swan, so it was almost hard to believe what had just happened.

Mary nodded. "As was I," she said, then glanced back at the bridge receding behind them. "In the future people ride through rapid waters such as those purely for excitement, or go on large machines at something called a fun fair, that throw them one way then the next, just as we were."

"Why in Christ's name would they do that?"

"It is so they can be thrilled by the semblance of danger, although there is almost no chance that they will come to any harm."

Olivia considered this a moment. "Is this the women as well?"

"For sure. Girls participate in all these things just as much as boys."

"That is indeed remarkable," Olivia said. "And belike it is a little... unwomanly?"

"By our standards now, yes," Mary answered. "But not by the standards of the future I know."

The oarsmen continued to row in perfect time, carrying them ever closer to this mystery meeting.

Olivia observed thoughtfully, "For sure, it must have been so difficult for you to find your standing when you first arrived here, where a woman is beholden to a man all her life – her father, then her husband."

"It was," Mary said. "And if I had known then what I know now, I might not be in this dreadful position."

"Why, what would you have done differently?"

Mary thought back to her first day in 1565, when she had blundered around like a drunk at a party, casually swearing in front of a superstitious serving girl called Margaret. Looking back, all her woes had stemmed from that one stupid moment; from that one blunder that had ultimately set her on this path to the stake. "I would I had guarded my tongue," she answered. "For there were things that I said and things that I did that marked me out as different, and thus a possible witch. I would I had instead learned quietly how to live in these times before setting forth." Then she added, "But then belike we would not have met."

"For all our adventures together have been hard." Olivia said, giving Mary a troubled look. "We have both slain men, and I have had my maidenhood so cruelly taken. God sees these things, and it will count against me at the final reckoning."

Mary shook her head. "Nay," she answered. "I meant what I said at prayer. God sees that you are a good woman, Olivia Melrose, and that you carry no blame for either of those things." She gave Olivia a weak smile. "I have no doubt I will see Him very soon, so believe me – I will put in a good word for you."

---O---

As they progressed through the calm water towards whatever was their final destination, Mary and Olivia became silent, each lost in their own thoughts.

For all she had joked with Olivia that she would put in a good word with God, Mary felt she should not give up on life just yet. For the sake of her sanity, she was going to have to take each day as it came. And this day she was not to be drowned or tried or burned to death – but simply to meet some curious person who apparently wanted to know more about her.

So be it. Whoever this person was, meeting him could not be worse than a trial – so it would be best to calm herself down, see what this person's interests were, and if she could turn any part of this meeting to her advantage.

Mary lifted her face to the fresh breeze whipping up off the river.

While there is life, there is hope.

She glanced over at the north bank with its shingle

beaches, rickety warehouses and wooden wharfs. It was impossible not to compare this with the 21st century London she remembered; the shining steel and concrete buildings mixing with older classic architecture; St. Paul's Cathedral peeking out above the Millennium Bridge, or the magnificent Somerset House next to modern blocks. But these were all in the future, and now her view was of wharfs giving way to houses, which then grew progressively grander as they came level with the Strand.

"My Lady Burnham's house," Olivia remarked, as they passed a particularly fine half-timbered building with a colourful painted boat tethered to its private jetty.

"Have you got word to her?" asked Mary. "She will be concerned you have not returned after the journey back from York."

"Nay." Olivia paused a moment. "Although I warrant I will be dismissed on return, whether I get word or not." She turned back to stare at the receding house. "She lacks tolerance for tardiness or dereliction of duty, whatever the cause."

Gradually the houses and buildings thinned out, until there was only trees and shrubbery lining the bank. The oarsmen kept time for another half hour or so, and then turned towards a small landing stage on the south bank, close to where Mary thought Putney Bridge might be one day.

With a shouted command from the coxswain, the oarsmen shipped their oars, allowing the boat to bump gently against the stage. Mary and Olivia were helped ashore, then followed Wychwoode up a track towards a large manor house surrounded by majestic elms.

"You are to meet Francis Walsingham," he said over his

shoulder, as they passed a magnificent yard that must have held over fifty stables. "You are to address him as Master Secretary, understood?" The women nodded, as they walked up the steps to the front door, which was opened by a man in black.

Walsingham! The legendary spymaster, who singlehand-edly created a network of 16th century spies and 'intelligenc-ers' that would make even the modern-day MI6 envious. So this was the curious person who wanted to meet her?

As she lifted her skirts and hurried after Wychwoode, Mary had a sudden thought. If anyone in this land, save the Queen herself, could get her off these charges, it had to be Walsingham! If only she could think of a way to make it worth his while to do so.

Resolving to find a way, and with a small flutter of hope rising, she followed Wychwoode and Olivia down a wood-panelled corridor and was shown into a dark room.

It was lit only by a few candles and the light from a small window. There was a large desk in the middle and a table with four chairs in the corner, with several bookcases around the stone walls, each filled with neatly arranged books and wooden trays of documents. The desk had several piles of papers on each side, stacked neatly in ascending order of height.

A man was seated behind the desk, staring hard at them with pebble-black eyes as they came in. He was dressed in black apart from a white ruff; his thin dark face under a black skull-cap ending in a sharply-pointed beard, and his hands arched together under his chin.

Mary glanced at the table, and was horrified to see her

phone sitting like an incongruous paperweight on top of a piece of paper.

The dark man gave a small cough. "Master Wychwoode," he said as he rose and came round the desk. "You are well met." His voice was soft, but with a strong undertone of authority.

"Master Secretary," responded Wychwoode, sweeping off his cap and bowing. "May I present Lady Mary de Beauvais and Mistress Olivia Melrose?"

Walsingham waved at the chairs. "Welcome to Barn Elms. Please be seated. Some wine?" Without waiting for an answer, he rang a small bell. As they were sitting down, a woman's head appeared round the door.

"Some wine for our guests, please Ursula."

While they waited for the wine, Walsingham said, "I am honoured to meet you, Lady Mary, and you too, Mistress Melrose. I have heard tell of your exploits in York recently, and I am deeply grateful for all you have both done to safe-guard the person of Her Majesty, and to bring her enemies to justice."

"Thank you, Master Secretary," Mary replied carefully. "We only did what was necessary for the protection of the Queen."

"Indeed, indeed." Walsingham replied, then he leaned forward and began to study Mary intently. She shifted in her chair under his unblinking gaze, returning it as confidently as she could, while her stomach turned to ice. Being on the receiving end of this man's penetrating scrutiny felt like her very soul was being exposed for his inspection.

Just then the door opened, and the woman reappeared with the wine. While it was being poured, Walsingham sat back, and the moment passed. He brought his fingers together again under his chin.

"Thank you, Ursula," he said, as the woman withdrew. "Now, to the matter in hand." His tone became more business-like. "We have here a very interesting situation." He looked from Mary to Olivia. "On the one hand, we have your exploits in York, in which you and Mistress Melrose have demonstrated your capabilities as dedicated agents to the cause we all hold so dear – as you say, to the safety and sanctity of God's anointed Queen. Then we have, let us say, a counter-situation." He gave a small cough, as if to punctuate the change in topic. "Under the law, you are charged with two counts that both carry the death penalty; in that you are charged with sorcery, on the basis that you are a person born in the distant future, and have travelled here by witchcraft or other black arts."

Mary took a breath, preparing to refute this with her original tale of her time travel being the result of her being a victim of witchcraft, rather than the perpetrator. But Walsingham raised a hand.

"Nay Lady Mary, this is not a trial. I do not expect to hear your defence, for the facts are established and not denied, that you travelled here from..." he glanced down at the paper on the table, moving the phone to one side, "...from the year of our lord twenty fifteen. The means of travel are not relevant, for they are evidence of sorcery however they occurred." He cleared his throat. "And then we have the count of blasphemy, in that you used this thing called a..." again he glanced at the paper, "...a 'phone', to conjure up a voice and words purporting to be those of our Lord Jesus Christ himself, which is irrefutable evidence of the sin of blasphemy." Mary stayed silent as he picked up the phone and studied it, turning it over in his hand and tapping it thoughtfully. "Master Wychwoode tells me it only works when it is shown to the sun, so this has been done." He passed the phone over. "Please demonstrate how it functions, Lady Mary."

Mary pressed the button, and as with Wychwoode there was a pause as nothing happened, then the white logo lit up the screen, casting a strange glow across the four faces at the table. When the start-up was complete and the colourful app icons had appeared, Olivia gave a small gasp.

"'Tis like magic!" she muttered.

"Nay," Mary said quickly, resisting the temptation to kick the girl under the table, "it is the work of men. In my time there are thousands upon thousands of such devices. Everybody has one, and they all work in exactly the same way."

"So they can all conjure up the voice of our lord?" asked Walsingham, incredulity in his voice. "Is your society so godless?"

"No." Mary answered, desperately trying to retain a sense of proportion while explaining a 2015 mobile phone to a candle-lit meeting of Elizabethans. "It is mainly so they can talk to each other."

"But can they not simply talk?" Walsingham asked.

"They can talk over long distances, without being in the same place," Mary explained. She opened the contact app. "See here," she said, showing her list of family and friends. "Here is my mother. I can tap on her name, and her own phone will make a noise to alert her. Then she can talk into it, and her voice will come out here," she pointed to the speaker.

"I can answer by talking into this hole here, and she will hear me. That way we can have a conversation, however far apart we may be."

"And this is not sorcery – that you may converse with your mother despite not being in the same room?" asked Wychwoode.

"Nay – as I have said, it is the work of men."

"And if your mother is not willing to have a conversation?" the lawyer asked. "You have no idea what she may be doing if you are not close to her."

"I can leave her a message," answered Mary. She opened the messaging app. "I can write my message by touching the letters on this keyboard, and it will come up on her phone. She can then reply at a time that is convenient to her." She brought up the last text conversation with her mother and passed it over to Walsingham. "It records all the messages between us. The green ones on the right are my messages and the grey ones on the left are hers."

Walsingham and Wychwoode studied the texts together, their faces lit by the glow from the screen. Walsingham looked up. "This is truly a wondrous tool for passing messages." He pointed at the screen. "What time does it take for these to pass? This one for example – where your mother is concerned you have something called 'clean knickers'? Your response – which does seem to be somewhat less than respectful – how long did this take to appear on her phone?"

Feeling herself blushing deeply, and wishing she had opened a business contact's texts instead, Mary answered, "It is immediate."

"Truly remarkable. Yes, truly remarkable." Walsingham

handed the phone back. "Please return it to its original blackness. We have much to discuss."

While Mary switched it off, Walsingham said to Wychwoode, "If I could have each one of my intelligencers equipped with a phone such as this, I would be able to pass messages and orders, and receive their reports, in the blink of an eye. We would have an inestimable advantage over the Catholics and that devilish woman who still styles herself Queen of the Scots, for all she has abdicated her throne." He looked up at Mary. "Do you have the ability to create more of these?"

Mary shook her head. "I wish I could, Master Secretary, but I have no knowledge of how they are made. And anyway," she added, "there needs to be infrastructure... er... other devices that carry the messages between phones. Without those, you would simply have two phones that have no means of communicating with each other."

Walsingham gave her a blank stare. "'Tis a pity." He paused, his long fingers tapping together in sequence under his chin. Mary couldn't help being reminded of a flower opening and closing. She forced herself to look away.

Then he said, "This 'phone' device is indeed a wondrous piece. Belike it is not the only such thing that is the work of men in twenty fifteen? Perhaps you can enlighten us on what other devices are commonplace in these times?"

Mary drew a slow breath. Where should she start?

"We have many devices that save us time and effort," she said. "We call them machines."

"A machine?" asked Wychwoode. "I understand this to be a functional object, usually used in war." He looked at the two women in turn. "The ancient Romans, I believe, had machines that used tension on a lever arm to propel a rock against fortifications."

"Yes." Mary smiled. Maybe this wasn't going to be as hard as she had thought. "A device that performs a function over and over again, and can be produced in very high numbers, becomes affordable for every household." She glanced at the faces in the candlelight, staring at her in rapt attention. "So, for example, after a meal, the dishes need to be cleaned?"

Olivia nodded. "For sure. The servants fetch a bucket of water and use fine sand and horsetail plants to scour them. It is hard work, but rewarding to have clean platters."

"Well, in twenty fifteen, I would have simply put them inside a machine that looks a bit like a white chest, and the machine cleans them for me, so I can do something else."

"By Heavens," exclaimed Walsingham. "Again, how remarkable!" He was silent a moment. "Does this give your servants more time to do other, more laborious tasks, like washing your clothing?"

"No – I have no servants."

"None to run a household?" Walsingham's eyebrows nearly disappeared under his cap.

"Very few households have servants." Mary paused. "They are not needed. We have a machine to do most things, such as one to wash clothes, another to remove dirt from the floor, or one to keep food cool and fresh."

Wychwoode observed, "I warrant that these machines do every task, in place of servants."

"Indeed, indeed," said Walsingham, with a vagueness that suggested he had lost interest in 2015 white goods. Once again, he silently stared at Mary.

"Now, Lady Mary," he said after a moment, "let us consider something else that fascinates me – to wit, this curious musket fashioned by the Alchemist. It is of course the one that you used to such effect in the Yorkshire forest."

"That I later destroyed in a forge, on Her Majesty's express orders?"

"Yes, that one. You could not have anything more precise than a musket that can punch a hole in the centre of a man's forehead from many hundreds of yards away." He paused a moment, and once again Mary was in the forest, staring through the scope at the man who was holding a knife to her son's throat, holding her breath as she centred the cross hairs on his head, then squeezing the trigger and feeling the gun recoil into her shoulder as the man went down like a ninepin.

"Yet you must have had great faith in the accuracy of the weapon, must you not?" Walsingham asked, bringing her back to the candle-lit present. "Your son was but a few inches away." Then his voice dropped to a low whisper, as he stared down his long nose at her. "Yet you thought not for his safety?"

Mary felt herself flushing; despite herself, her anger was starting to rise. Was he testing her; deliberately trying to provoke her to see her reaction? She took a careful, steadying breath. "I had seen the accuracy of the weapon when the Alchemist fired on Her Majesty and hit Sir Tom Cobham in the back." She held Walsingham's gaze. "I saw it hit my horse Juno in the neck as we took a fast jump over a log." She paused again. "And I heard tell of the Alchemist hitting a coney from a long distance with deadly accuracy. So no, I thought not of my son's safety, for I knew he was in no danger."

Walsingham nodded slightly, and was silent again for a moment. Then he leaned forward, and said, "And your own faith in your proficiency to fire this weapon, that you, a mere woman, had ne'er before discharged?"

"Indeed, Master Secretary," she answered, finding it becoming harder to hold in the anger that was now starting to rise like hot lava from a volcano, "when you are in a situation where there is pressure on you to act, even as a..." she paused, "as a mere woman... you do what needs to be done."

"That may be so," said Walsingham. "Yet the first time you fire this weapon – that you know to be accurate, but which you have never before fired, you are prepared to take the risk to discharge it at the man standing directly beside your child?"

"Yes, I did." And if she had it in her hands now, she would show him just how dangerous she could be...

Walsingham pulled on his earlobe a moment. "I understand why you acted as you did, Lady Mary," he said, seemingly oblivious to the temper she was only just about managing to control. "But I am sad to say it will all come to naught. The law must take its course. You will be returned to the Tower shortly, then arraigned on the charges against you, and once found guilty you will be executed by being burned to death."

That was the last straw. Mary had had enough.

Use the anger. Work it.

Suddenly she pushed her chair back and stood, causing Walsingham to look up in surprise. "For all I have demonstrated my loyalty and value to the Queen, Master Secretary?" she demanded in a voice that echoed off the bookcases and stone walls. "Loyalty that seems to mean naught to you, who profthat to be her servant?" He did not answer, but his eyes narrowed in the flickering candlelight. "As Her Majesty herself said to me, I did her great service not once, not twice, but on five occasions this summer past. Yet you choose to ignore it, because I am a 'mere woman'?" Mary stared down at the dark man. "Master Secretary," she snarled, "you, who questions my motives in protecting my son, and who seems to take delight in my impending execution – you forget I have saved the life of the Queen, and by Heavens, that has got to count for something!"

She breathed hard, then forced herself to lower her voice. "You say the law must take its course, but the Queen you and I both serve – she *is* the law. If she is prepared to pardon me, then I would give my all to protect her, as I did in York." Then she leaned forward with her hands on the table and brought her face down so close to Walsingham that every individual hair of his beard could clearly be seen in the candlelight. "Let me talk to the Queen, Master Secretary. Let me see her, so I can swear my loyalty to her myself." She stood back. "And do you know what I would tell her?" She paused to let him answer, but he shook his head slightly, his eyes wide like a rabbit watching a snake, "I would tell her that letting me go to my death would be a terrible loss to her directly. Do you know why?" Again he shook his head. "I am surprised that I, a mere woman, must point it out, but as we both know, I am from the future." She tapped the side of her head. "Which means I hold great intelligence in here about the things yet to come. I made a study of the history of these times, and I can tell you of plots to put the Queen of Scots on the throne in place of Her Majesty; of the badly-executed beheading of the

Queen of Scots against the Queen's wishes, leading to a sea-borne invasion attempt by Philip of Spain that nearly causes the end of the English throne – and I can tell you of more besides. Can you even begin to imagine how far ahead of the Catholics this will put you? But no – I am a 'mere woman,' and worthless in your eyes, so you ignore this, and choose instead to let the law take its course! Well shame on you, Master Secretary!" She shook a forefinger in his face. "Shame on you for a short-sighted fool!"

Then she dropped back onto her seat, as she continued to hold his eyes, letting this sink in.

"Make me go to my death, Master Secretary, if you must. If the law is so important to you. But will you wonder for the rest of your days what valuable intelligence you will have allowed to die with me?"

8

CHAPTER EIGHT

Wychwoode seemed to be unable to sit down as the boat was rowed back up the river, while a blood-red sun sank slowly in the western sky.

He continually strode up and down the lowered gangway between the oarsmen, before coming back towards the two women seated in the stern, shaking his head in disbelief, then striding away again.

Eventually he stopped in front of them. "I have never, ever, *ever*, in all my years, heard a woman address the Master Secretary in such a manner!" he barked. "I am surprised he did not run you though on the very spot, for being a brazen, wanton, shameless..." Wychwoode shook his head again and stalked away along the boat, before striding back and shaking an angry forefinger at Mary. "What in the name of all that is holy were you thinking?"

Mary looked up at him as steadily as she could. "He was

most disrespectful," she said clearly. "He called me a 'mere woman' – after all I had done to protect the Queen. He made me angry."

"He made... He made...?" Wychwoode spluttered. "Francis Walsingham made *you* angry...? By Heavens!" His mouth opened and closed wordlessly.

Mary sat back on the bench seat, observing the usually calm and lucid lawyer struggling to find words. She had sometimes wondered what it might take to make him lose his customary composure. And now she had found out. Heaven only knew what Walsingham had said to him in private after she had finished her tirade. The two men had stalked off to another room, leaving her and Olivia sitting in an uneasy silence.

Wychwoode glared at her.

"I did not like his tone," Mary said.

"That is not for you to like or dislike!" He leaned forward, so his lined face was uncomfortably close to hers. "You do realise, that your attempt to influence him can only rebound most dreadfully? That he will never allow you to see the Queen, or gain you a pardon?"

"Then I am in no worse a position than I was before," she observed. "But at least I tried."

"No worse? No worse? Oh, yes, your last days will be markedly worse, Lady Mary!" He pointed at Olivia. "I am now ordered to disembark Mistress Melrose at Lady Burnham's house this very evening, so you will be in solitary confinement in the Tower from here on." He stood up. "At least you will remain in your rooms, and not be cast into a dungeon like the Alchemist. Be thankful at least for that." Then he strode back towards the bow.

So now she was to be alone...

Mary took Olivia's hand in her hers. "I am so sorry," she said, "I did not mean for us to be parted. I have very much valued your company these past months."

"And I yours," said Olivia. She gave a small smile. "I admire you for trying, Lady Mary, and for standing up to that man. 'Tis only a shame he would not listen to reason, for it makes perfect sense to make use of your future knowledge."

"Aye," Mary nodded slowly. "But he would not hear it from a hot-headed woman."

"True."

There was a long thoughtful silence between them, punctuated only by the regular splash of the oars and the call of the coxswain. Mary stared across at the river bank, as houses started to appear and the countryside came to an end. Should she have let her anger take hold with Walsingham? Should she have given the dry spymaster both barrels in the way she had? True, she had said what she planned to say – for it had quickly occurred to her that her future knowledge should make her valuable – but should she have let it come out on a wave of anger, or been more measured; more considered? Mary sighed. What was done was done, and as she had said to Wychwoode, she was no worse off than before.

Apart from losing Olivia... In the deep red glow of the setting sun, Mary could see the girl was now struggling to put something into words – something that seemed troubling her greatly. It was not hard to guess what that might be.

"Yes, my dear girl," Mary said softly, "this will most likely be the last time we shall see each other."

At this, Olivia leaned across and threw her arms about

Mary's neck and said with a sob, "I shall miss you so!" She buried her head into Mary's shoulder, and hot tears started to flow. "You truly have been as a mother to me! I have learned so much from you, and all to make me stronger and much more of an adult! And now I know why you have had such confidence to give me, because you have seen things I will never see, and lived in a time where women are the equal of men, and... and... and I cannot bear that I will never see you again!"

Olivia sat back. Mary took the girl's tearful face in both her hands. "Then you must honour me by living your life as I would have lived mine, Olivia Melrose," she said. "By remembering what I have taught you, and by blazing a trail for women in this society."

"I will, I will." Olivia sniffed loudly, prompting Mary to take her handkerchief from her sleeve. "Is there aught I can do for you?" Olivia asked as Mary gently dabbed her eyes. "Any service I can perform?"

Mary thought a moment. "Yes, there are two things I would have you do for me."

"Name them."

"Firstly, I ask you not to attend my execution. I cannot bear to have you see me die in such an awful way."

Olivia sniffed again. "For sure," she said with another sob. "I would not wish to see it either." She took the handkerchief and blew her nose. "And the second?"

"I would have you give my last messages to my family."

"Of course. What shall I tell them?"

Mary thought a moment. "Tell my daughter Kat that I never meant to go away and leave her again. Tell her that I will always love her, that she will be in my thoughts until the very end. Tell Ambrose that I could not be more proud of him, and to keep the stories I told him close to his heart as he grows into the strong and confident man I know he will be. And little Jane..." Mary's voice caught as her throat closed, so she had to stop and swallow hard. "Little Jane," she continued, "please tell her that her mother will always be watching over her, making sure she eats her food..." she gave Olivia a little smile. "And washes behind her ears."

"And Sir William?" Olivia sniffed.

"Please tell William I have loved him ever since I first saw his picture in the 21st century. And tell him I am so, so sorry if I have brought shame on the de Beauvais name. I never meant for this to happen, and all I ever wanted was to be a good wife and mother. I want him to know that he should find a good woman and marry again, so he can have the wife, and the life, he deserves." She swallowed again. "And maybe one day restore the good name of de Beauvais."

The two women hugged each other tightly all the way to the Strand.

9

CHAPTER NINE

Wychwoode was silent as the boat passed under forbidding portcullis of Traitor's Gate, then bumped up against the stone landing jetty. The gaoler was waiting on the steps with a couple of burly yeoman warders.

"Take her to her rooms," Wychwoode ordered.

"And Mistress Melrose?" the gaoler asked.

"She has been disembarked and will not be returning," Wychwoode growled. "Lady Mary is to be kept completely alone and isolated." He waved a dismissive hand. "Now take her, and make sure she is held secure, and does not converse with any person, even yourself. She is a prisoner to be punished rather than to be cared for."

The gaoler gave a sickly grin. "Why, what has the woman done, master, that she is to be so treated?"

"Hold your tongue, man," Wychwoode barked. "That is no

concern of yours. If I hear you have disobeyed me, you will lose your position here. Do you understand?"

The gaoler's gaze slid over to Mary, and he gave an even more sickly smile. "It will be a pleasure, master."

As Wychwoode sat down in the stern, the gaoler indicated to the two warders to take Mary off the boat. They reached across and pulled her none too gently onto the steps. Securing their hold under each arm, they then marched her between them through a stone archway, with her feet barely touching the ground. It all happened so quickly that she did not have the chance to bid any form of farewell to Wychwoode. For all his rage against her this evening, he had been a firm friend for almost all the time they had known each other, and she would have preferred to have said at least one word before parting.

"You are hurting my arms," was all she could say as the warders gripped her tightly. Neither one replied, and if anything, they increased their grip and lifted her slightly higher. This left her hardly able to walk for herself, while it felt like her shoulders would soon dislocate.

"I would you hold your tongue," came the voice of the gaoler behind her. "You do not have your iron poker now, eh?" He was silent a moment. "You will have more to concern yourself than bruised arms in time, I warrant." She could imagine a salacious grin spreading across his coarse features. "And, mistress, it is fitting that your arms are so affected, given what you did to the Alchemist."

"It is 'Lady Mary' to you, churl," she muttered, as they started up a stone stair.

He must have heard this. "Nay," he said. "Your title counts

for naught in here. If I say 'mistress,' then 'mistress' it is." Then he added, "Or maybe just 'woman' will suffice." They emerged onto a cold grey stone passage lit by occasional braziers, with Mary frog-marched by the guards. "And I told you to hold your tongue, woman." He paused. "Or I will have it cut out, so your final days are truly silent."

This had the effect he must have wanted; Mary resolved never to talk to this vile man again for as long as she might live – however long that would be.

They came to the end of the corridor and went through a heavy-looking wooden door into the open air, then proceeded along a moonlit path between two tall buildings. The gaoler came into view in front of her, scuttling sideways like a crab as the warders kept up their pace. "I know not if you have hours, days or even weeks more in my keeping," he said, "but I do know this. I am charged by Master Wychwoode to make sure you are kept silent and alone. So you do as I order without question, and without complaint. Or I will make your last days in this world the most unpleasant you can imagine."

Mary said nothing, staring at the man with burning hatred.

"I will make it so hard for you, that you will beg them to take you to the pyre as a blessed release – do you understand?" Again she said nothing. "You understand?" he repeated. She nodded as best she could, while the guards marched her briskly between moonlight and deep shadows. "Good. Then we are of one mind on this."

They went through another door, up some steps and along an oak panelled passage, with occasional pictures of stern-faced nobles hanging between candle-bearing sconces. Mary recognised the fine plasterwork ceiling studded with embossed Tudor roses; they were coming to her rooms. She waited while the gaoler selected a key from the ring on his belt and unlocked the door. The warders threw her in so roughly that she staggered and almost fell. Managing to steady herself by grabbing hold of the prie dieu, she scowled at the gaoler as he followed her in.

"I also know not what you have done to upset Master Wych-woode, that he has removed your companion and demanded you be kept in silence," he said. "But what e'er it might be, it is enough for me. I hold no care for your well-being, for all that you beat the Alchemist senseless and broke his leg." He walked to the door, then stopped and looked back. "This the last conversation you will have with me, and belike it is the last conversation you will have before you are brought to trial. I will deliver one tray each morn, and we will not converse." With that, he left, locking the door behind him.

Mary stoked the fire back into life, then sank into a chair and muttered, "Good. It is not like you had anything to say anyway."

She stared at the flickering flames, rubbing her upper arms thoughtfully.

So it had finally come to this. Ten years after time-travelling to Tudor England and being accused of witchcraft, was she finally going to be put to death as a sorceress?

She watched the flames starting to lick around one of the logs on the fire. And it would be flames such as these that would curl around her body, devouring it and turning it cracked and black, just as they were doing to this log...

Despite the heat from the hearth, she shivered.

How does it actually feel to be burned to death? To

imagine it would be to die a thousand times before the event – yet to ignore it was impossible.

A piece of the log flared briefly, then broke away and fell into the glowing embers below. Suddenly she could not bear to look at the flames a moment longer.

Getting up, she glanced around the room. The prie dieu caught her eye, standing tall and forbidding, with the kneeling platform at the front. Should she pray for deliverance? She had prayed with Olivia; maybe she should try it again. She knelt on the platform and put her hands together. "Dear Lord…" she muttered. "Dear Lord… Dear Lord…"

Nothing.

She shook her head sharply and stood up. "Oh, for goodness' sake!" she said to the room. "As if that is going to make a difference!"

She went into the little bed chamber, pulled the drapes apart and climbed in, lying fully clothed on the bed. She stared blankly at her feet in their pantofle shoes, peeping out from under the hem of her skirts.

Her feet…

They had been too big for the slippers she had been given when she had first come into Tudor England – making her feel like an ungainly giant, forced to wear her modern-day boots under her first Tudor gown.

Despite herself, she gave a small chuckle. Now her shoes were made to fit her perfectly by the finest shoemakers. She kicked off the pantofles and waggled her toes.

It would be such a waste for fine shoes like these to be burned…

Or would they?

Would she be forced to walk barefoot to the pyre?

Then her feet would be the first part of her to burn – turning black as she screamed in pain...

Mary got up, put her shoes back on, and wandered into the main room.

She turned one of the chairs away from the fire, then dragged the prie dieu over. Resting her heels up on the platform, she sat with her back to the flames.

What would she be doing now, if she had never fallen into 1565 through the wormhole in time? Married with kids? Most probably. No doubt living in some suburban semi, with a husband away on business most of the time. Or was it really business? Maybe he was actually having an affair with some emaciated blonde called Helen from Accounts? What else would he do, now that his wife Justine was fast approaching forty and had lost her figure to childbirth, processed snacks and boredom?

Her mother would drop in occasionally of course, bringing bags of jellied sweets for the kids, staying just long enough to have a cup of tea, complain about her bunions, then be out the door before the sugar high sent the kids into hyperdrive, destroying all in their path around the house.

Her father would sometimes amble in with her mother, make himself a cup of tea and settle in front of the cricket, then get halfway through explaining the rules of the game to her youngest, before being unceremoniously dragged out again to drive his wife home.

It was so sad to think she'd never see them again. Never introduce them to William, or see them burst with pride when they first met their actual grandchildren. Never have her mother tell her to stand up straight ('stomach in, boobs out, Justine!') or have her father tell her to pull herself together, as 'there are plenty more pebbles on the beach, young lady...' when some boy or other had dumped her. 'He was clearly not good enough for you, anyway,' he would add.

They would never see her 'standing up straight' in her finest Tudor gown, her slim stomach most definitely 'in' behind the tightest lacing and firmest stomacher, her hair swept back in the latest style, being applauded by the assembled nobility at a royal banquet, and being welcomed as guest of honour by Her Majesty Queen Elizabeth herself.

They would never see how their little Justine had become the fine Lady Mary de Beauvais, mistress of Grangedean Manor, mother to three fine children, celebrated Tudor adventuress and most recently, saviour of the Queen's life...

And nor would they see the same celebrated Lady Mary in a plain shift dress, being led barefoot from a dirty wooden tumbril up to a stake surrounded by kindling, before having her hands bound behind it and some rough peasant executioner applying a flame, nor hear her scream as the flames licked around her and turned her still-slim body into twisted black charcoal...

10

CHAPTER TEN

A loud snapping sound from a burning log in the dying fire jerked Mary awake.

Slowly she lowered her stiff legs from the prie dieu and bent her knees with a small gasp of pain as they popped in protest, making the sound of a dozen firecrackers.

How long had she been asleep? The dawn light was streaming in through the window – so it must have been all night. No wonder she was stiff.

Slowly she got up from the chair and crept across the room to try and get some feeling into her legs.

She froze at the sound of the key turning in the lock, then breathed a small sigh of relief as the gaoler came in with his customary tray.

He put it on the table, then left without a word.

Mary surveyed the contents of the tray with little enthusiasm. A mouldy-looking hunk of bread sat on a wooden trencher plate, alongside a dirty tankard. She sniffed the contents and decided it was some cheap ale with some unidentifiable grey solids floating in it. She sniffed again, now catching a slight whiff of stale biscuits.

She almost gagged – that smell took her back to the portable loos at a festival she'd once been at. Which meant the most unimaginable thing; the gaoler had most probably peed in her ale. With a grimace she put the tankard down, and decided not to eat or drink. If the gaoler meant her to starve to death, he'd just be doing her a favour.

---o---

By the next day, Mary was too hungry and thirsty to care, and when the gaoler left a new tray of bread and ale, she was devouring the bread before he was barely out of the room.

It left her mouth as dry as an old dustbin. She stared at the tankard. She desperately had to drink, but how could she bring herself to put this foul liquid to her lips?

An idea came to her. She went into the bedchamber and rummaged in her bag. Triumphantly she produced an old wooden bowl that she had brought from Grangedean in case it might be useful, then rummaged again and drew out a spare silk stocking.

Pushing the bowl inside the stocking, she took it into the sitting room, then stretched the fine material tightly across the top. She carefully poured the ale into through the filter into the bowl, trying not to gag again at the sight of the grey, scummy residue it left behind.

Sliding the stocking off the bowl, she surveyed the pale

liquid, then sniffed it cautiously. It did not smell so bad, so she concluded the gaoler had not bothered to foul it this time.

She took a tentative sip. It tasted rank, but the feel of liquid in her mouth was too tempting, and with a small groan she knocked it all back. She felt it gurgle in her stomach and for a brief and worrying moment she thought she was going to throw it straight back up, but thankfully all she did was belch loudly and the feeling passed.

She shook out the stocking and was about to put it back in her bag with the bowl, ready for tomorrow's filtering, when she paused, and studied it. It was a particularly fine silk stocking, and a shame to soil it so badly. Then she shrugged. What use would she have for it now, other than as a filter?

---o---

It was three days later, and Mary had just finished drinking her filtered ale, and belching as before. She had been idly amusing herself by seeing how loudly she could burp after each drink. By now she had perfected her art and was achieving a deep, rolling belch each time.

As she came into the sitting room after returning the stocking to her bag, she heard the door open and close behind her. Assuming it was the gaoler again, she did not bother to turn round.

"Do you put your back to me, madam?" came the voice of a woman. There was something vaguely familiar about it, and she spun round.

In front of her was a slight figure in a hooded cape. As

Mary watched, the woman pushed back the hood to reveal a pale white face under flaming red hair.

Mary dropped to her knees. "Your Majesty," she whispered.

The woman came forward and held out her a slim hand. Mary pressed her lips to it.

"Pray be upstanding, Lady Mary," the Queen said softly. "I am not here officially – indeed only one other knows I am here at all."

"Madam, I am deeply honoured," Mary began. "But…"

"Why am I here?" the Queen said. "And come in the manner of a furtive outlaw?"

"Well – yes."

Instead of answering, the Queen went over to the table and picked up the empty tankard. She sniffed it cautiously, her dark eyes fixed on Mary's, then put it down hurriedly. "You have supped from this?" she asked, her thin eyebrows raised.

"I did, madam."

"You must have had a thirst."

"Yes, madam" Mary said, hoping the Queen had not heard her belching from outside the room. It had certainly been loud enough. "I resisted drinking the foul ale to start, but I had such a thirst I could resist no longer."

"Quite so," the Queen observed. "I was held prisoner here myself you know, as a young girl. I recall well that one is at the mercy of the gaoler for food and drink." She sniffed the tankard again. "Although I fear your treatment is far worse than ever I experienced. This smells most unpleasant. I am surprised you were able to keep it in your stomach," then she added with a smile, "if not the wind it might produce."

Oh God! The Queen of England had heard her burping like an old navvy!

"I...er... filtered it through a silk stocking first," Mary said, feeling her face flush redder than the Queen's hair. "It removed the worst of the... er... solids."

The Queen grimaced, then smiled. "Indeed, you are ever resourceful, Mary. I would expect no less of you." She indicated the chair, still turned away from the softly glowing embers of the fire. "I see you would not look to the flames. Most understandable." She gestured at the other chair. "Please sit with me. We have much to discuss."

Glad to have got off the subject of her noisy stomach, Mary turned the other chair round and waited until the Queen was seated, before sitting beside her.

"I am told you are to be tried as a sorceress and blasphemer," the Queen began.

"So I understand, madam," Mary answered, shocked to hear the accusation that had lived in her imagination these last few days being made painfully real by coming from the mouth of the Queen.

The Queen glanced across at her. "I am not here to interrogate you," she said. "You need have no fear of that."

A small flutter of hope rose in Mary's chest. Maybe, just maybe, the Queen was here to give her the pardon she'd demanded from Walsingham?

"Time enough for that at the trial itself," the Queen continued.

The flutter of hope curled up and died.

It seemed more likely that the Queen was just another

thrill-seeker like Walsingham, looking to satisfy her ghoulish curiosity and meet the sorceress before it was too late.

The Queen tapped her slim fingers on the arm of the chair. "But I must confess I am fascinated with this accusation of sorcery," she said. "I am told you travelled here across time itself?"

Mary nodded. "Yes, madam," she said with a small, resigned sigh. "That is true."

"From a year so far ahead, it is hard to comprehend it can even exist." The Queen paused. "Tell me, Lady Mary, by what name were you known in... the year of Our Lord two thousand and fifteen, I believe?"

"Justine Parker, madam."

The Queen raised an eyebrow. "Justine? Is that a French name?" Mary shook her head. "I see. I feel Lady Mary is altogether a better name, and we shall continue to call you as such, for now." Then she asked, "And in what year were you... will you be... born?"

"In nineteen eighty-eight," Mary answered, staring at her feet.

"So you were twenty-seven when you travelled to our time?"

"Yes." Mary looked up. "But it was not by my will."

"I see," the Queen said. "I have no doubt."

Mary took a careful breath. Maybe she could get the Queen on her side after all?

"I wanted to say as much to Master Secretary Walsingham, madam" she said. "But he would not hear my side of the story."

The Queen gave a wry smile. "Indeed," she observed. "And I hear you called him a fool?"

"I did, madam. And I apologise most deeply. It was my anger talking, not me."

"Oh, there is no need to apologise." Elizabeth smiled again. "Least of all to me." She lowered her voice conspiratorially. "I have thought the same on many an occasion. I wish I had been there to hear it for myself." She gave a small chuckle. "How did he take it?"

"Not well." Mary answered. She bit her lip. "He sent my companion Olivia Melrose away and I am ordered to end my days in silence."

"In truth I was aware of this." Elizabeth said, turning serious. "I have spoken with Mistress Melrose, and she was deeply upset to be parted."

"You have spoken with her?" Mary leaned in and put her hand over Elizabeth's, all protocol forgotten. "Is she well?"

Elizabeth looked down but made no move to withdraw her hand. Mary suddenly realised what she had done. She pulled her hand back to the arm of her own chair as if it were on fire. "Your Majesty," she said with rising panic in her voice, "I must apologise..."

Then Elizabeth did something totally unexpected. She put her own hand over Mary's.

"No," she said, her voice low and intense. "There is no need for you to apologise." She leaned in, her dark eyes never leaving Mary's. "You and I have been through so much together." She shook her head slowly. "Have you forgot how we both grieved over the body of Sir Thomas Cobham in that little room in York? Or how we talked of the life opportunities he had given us both, at the banquet afterwards?" She leaned in further. "I now understand how we formed such a connection, for you are not of this world. You are not like those fawning creatures who surround me at Court."

She sat back, but her hand stayed where it was.

"Mary," she said in a stronger, more urgent voice. "You carry knowledge of times yet to come. I too have secrets I can never share with others around me. Which is why I need someone I *can* share them with; someone such as you. I need your understanding and your counsel."

Then it was if she was no longer a queen, but just another woman; a friend in need, her pale face lined with worry. "I need your strength and your love; by that I mean I need you as someone with whom I can confide, and who will answer with honesty and without seeking favour." She looked down at their hands. "I need someone who will do as you did just this moment, who will put her hand upon mine and not be concerned about protocol – but do this because we are friends who understand and will help each other."

As Elizabeth's words hung in the air, it was clear that there was one massive elephant in the room that had to be addressed first.

"But I am to be tried and executed as a sorceress and a blasphemer," Mary said softly. "What then?"

Elizabeth stood up and paced across the room. "I know, I know," she said, then turned back, her face under the pale make-up still lined with deep concern. "And please believe I cannot simply pardon you, much as I wish to. For the crimes of which you are accused – and will inevitably be found guilty – are ones that raise terror in all God-fearing people. If I pardon you, it will raise questions of my own nature."

Mary gave a small despairing cry. To be so close to a real chance of a pardon – and now it was being snatched away.

Elizabeth crossed quickly back to her. "Nay, sweet Mary, for why would the Queen suddenly pardon a proven sorcerer and blasphemer unless she was enchanted in some way, or shared some of the sorcerer's beliefs?" She shook her head. "I am sorry, but I cannot do it."

Then she paused, before dropping one little word into the space between them.

One simple, hopeful little word.

"*Unless...*"

Mary's head snapped up. "Unless?" she demanded, hardly daring to believe what she had just heard.

"Unless you perform a singular service for Secretary Walsingham, and through him, for me."

Mary suddenly came to the sickening realisation that all that had just passed was simply a means to reel her in like a fish on a hook.

"Oh, right," she said coldly. "Do I have a choice?"

"For sure. You could refuse and would die at the stake as planned."

Mary stood up, and drew herself to her full height, looking down on the Queen. "Then in truth I do not have a choice, do I?"

Elizabeth looked up at her. "I know what you think, Lady Mary, that my words just now were to bend you to my will, and to have you perform such a task, but I would have you know two things." She gestured back to the chairs. "Let us sit again and I will explain withal."

When they had sat, the Queen said, "The first is that I

meant every word I said just now. I value you and I need your counsel as a friend, but I cannot simply pardon you. Yet if you perform this service successfully, then time will have passed, so Walsingham and I can find a way for you to live a long and fulfilling life thereafter, and see out your days in comfort with your family, if that is what you most desire."

"And the second thing?" Mary asked, reserving judgment until she had heard both parts of this plan.

"The second may give you cause for surprise."

Mary raised an inquiring eyebrow.

"Indeed," the Queen continued. "You may have been left with the impression that Secretary Walsingham was much angered by your outburst at his house. But in truth, what you said impressed him greatly. To have knowledge of future events would be most useful, and, for all you called him a fool, he would have you pass on this knowledge in full." She paused. "Yet he also knew that you would not simply give him this intelligence while under threat of death by fire, so he needed to take this threat away and by doing so, bring you into his network of intelligencers."

Mary drew a sharp breath. "You want me to become a spy for Walsingham?"

Elizabeth smiled. "If that is how you see it, yes."

Mary thought a moment. There was one part of all this that still seemed to be shrouded in mystery. "But I know not what is this task you would have me do."

Elizabeth took a deep breath. "You will recall when I first came in, that I said there is only one other who knows I am here?" Mary nodded. She had meant to ask about it at the time, but the conversation had moved on – then it had slipped her mind. "Well, it will not surprise you to know that this other is here now, and will tell you of the task he has in mind. And being privy to the plan will admit you to a very exclusive circle; who are currently only myself, Secretary Walsingham and his man Master Wychwoode." Elizabeth leaned forward. "Secretary Walsingham is in the corridor without, and I will call him in here presently to explain in detail what you must do." She paused. "But I must impress on you that this is most important to me as your sovereign, and it must remain at the highest level of secrecy." She stabbed at the air with her forefinger. "If it becomes more widely known withal, I will deny it absolutely."

Before Mary could answer, Elizabeth stood and opened the door. A dark man in black came in and crossed to where Mary sat.

"My Lady," he said, sweeping off his cap and bowing.

"Master Secretary." Mary stood. There was a brief but somewhat awkward silence. "I must apologise for my outburst at your house," she said.

"Nay, 'tis no matter," Walsingham replied with a thin smile. "Even in the one speech you mentioned several events yet to come that gave us much useful intelligence." He paused. "And cause for concern." He glanced at the Queen, who nodded. "All because I was prodding at your anger to see where it may lead."

"Oh." Mary thought a moment. "Then Master Wychwoode on the boat after – was his anger not genuine?"

"It was not. He was instructed to play the role of a virtuous man enraged, as if a mummer performing upon a stage." He looked at her enquiringly. "I take it he played the part well?"

Mary shook her head in wonder. "Yes he did," she said. "He was most convincing."

"Good." He paused. "Now, your sovereign and I – we would discuss with you the task that needs to be performed, and as I am sure you have been told, in the utmost of secrecy."

---o---

Half an hour later, Mary sat back and looked at Elizabeth and Walsingham in turn.

"You cannot be serious!" she gasped. "You really want me to do that?"

Walsingham nodded. "From what you have told us of the future, it seems the ideal way to avoid such dreadful events coming to pass."

"But it is outrageous!" Mary said. "It will never work!"

Walsingham smiled slowly. "Oh, it will work, Lady Mary," he said. "You will make sure it works."

Then his smile disappeared.

"Or we will commit you once again to trial and certain execution."

11

CHAPTER ELEVEN

Wychwoode had the grace to give Mary a sheepish smile when he entered her rooms a couple of days later.

"Master Wychwoode," she said, in a voice that would have frozen a blacksmith's forge. "Do you come now to apologise for your behaviour after we visited Master Secretary Walsingham?"

He swept off his cap and bowed low. "I do humbly beseech your pardon, Lady Mary, but I was under instruction from my master to make such an act." Then he added, "I took no pleasure in it."

"I would certainly hope not," she said. "For sure I took none myself."

"It was a means to the end," he said. "It needed to seem genuine, so you understood the seriousness of your situation."

"I do understand that now, for all it was most unpleasant at the time." She went over to the table and poured some of the wine that she was now allowed. "Anyway," she said in her most conciliatory tone, "something to drink, Master Wychwoode?" As he took the proffered goblet, she added, "I am fairly sure that, unlike the ale served to me after your instructions to the gaoler, this has not been pissed in."

He took a sharp breath. "The fellow did that?" He sniffed cautiously at the wine, then put it carefully down on the table.

"I warrant he did." Seeing his obvious discomfort, she decided to soften a little more. After all, they were going to have to work together on this madcap scheme. As he sat down by the fire, she said, "Although I will admit you played the part well. Master Shakespeare himself could not have done better."

"Master who?"

Mary cursed herself inwardly – why did she not think? Shakespeare was still a small boy in Stratford. "Oh 'tis no matter." Quickly she poured herself some wine. "Anyway, I believed you, as did Olivia and the gaoler."

He watched her carefully as she took a drink from her goblet, then picked up his own, sniffed it again and took a small sip.

She settled herself in the other chair. Together they stared at the flames flickering around the logs. "If this plan is a success," he observed after a while, "you will no longer need to be in fear of flames such as these."

There was another silence. "If it succeeds, and I no longer face death by burning," she said eventually, "I will in truth want only to live at peace with my family at Grangedean Manor." She looked deep into the fire. "I would have nothing more to do with such madcap schemes."

"Nonsense," he growled.

"I beg your pardon?" She shot a look of surprise at him.

"You fool yourself, Lady Mary." He took another cautious sip of his wine. "You are one who thrives on danger." He gave a dry chuckle. "You would retire to be a plain wife and mother again? Nay, I warrant you would be dead within six months, but of boredom."

Mary frowned as she thought over his words. Was she really addicted to action and adventure? An adrenaline junkie? No, no, not at all. She shook her head. Her idea of an idyllic existence was to be living in peace and quiet, with nothing more challenging than balancing the household accounts and making sure Kat had a new kirtle. That was it.

So why did the thought make her feel slightly nauseous?

"Do you seriously think that it can succeed?" she asked, bringing the conversation back on track.

He glanced across at her, a deep frown on his face. "Do you not?"

"There is much to go wrong."

"Then we must plan most carefully," he answered. "Starting with your name."

"My name?" she asked. "What of it?"

"Oh, come now," he said. "If you will act as a spy, you cannot be roaming abroad in the country as Lady Mary de Beauvais. Not if you want the chance of a quiet life thereafter." He paused. "Who knows what trouble you might cause for others, let alone as part of the plan itself. Would you have those you have harmed turn up at Grangedean Manor, seeking the Lady Mary de Beauvais that has done them wrong?"

She nodded. "So be it," she said thoughtfully. "Perhaps it

is best to be unknown." She looked up. "What name shall I take?"

"Make your choice."

Fighting back an initial suggestion of 'Jemima Bond', she gave it some consideration. Then she brightened, and said, "Something simple and forgettable. How about Anne Carter?"

"Very well," he replied, "Anne Carter it is." He sat back. "Now, Mistress Carter, we come to the other key element of this enterprise. The remarkable musket fashioned by the Alchemist."

She shot him a look of surprise. "The one that was damaged beyond repair at the gorge by Hetherington Hall," she asked, "before being consigned to a forge and destroyed completely, on the orders of Her Majesty?" She paused. "That remarkable musket?"

"Aye. That one." He took another small sip of wine. "I have kept the Alchemist alive against just such a need." He took a deep breath and looked over at her. "We will have him make another one."

"And if he refuses?"

"Then he is to be hung, drawn and quartered, as a traitor."

"And you do not have your musket."

"True."

"So how do you propose to have him comply?"

"We will offer him the chance to be released from imprisonment for the time it takes to construct the new firearm. After the weeks he has spent with only the gaoler and the rats for company, he will welcome the respite."

Mary stared at the old man. "I fear that will not be enough to persuade him," she said. "He will want more."

"Perhaps."

"Especially if you want him to take as much time as he can in the construction," she observed dryly, "then that is a good way of ensuring it."

"We are aware of that," he answered. "So we will need someone to help him in the task, keep him under daily observation, and report on his progress."

There was something in the way he said this, or maybe in the way he glanced over at her, that made her realise just who he meant for the job.

"Oh no!" she exclaimed. "No! No! No!" She turned back to the fire. "I am the last person on earth he would allow to observe him even scratch his nose, let alone help him make a new musket."

"Yet as a fellow traveller from distant times yet to come, who else would be better suited?" He smiled. "I warrant the legendary charm of Lady Mary de Beauvais will work its magic ere long."

"An unfortunate turn of phrase," she muttered, trying to ignore the vision it conjured up of once again being led to her execution.

"I apologise most deeply," he said. "But it cannot be ignored that someone must ensure that not only does he work to our schedule, but that he is also able to function effectively. The man has suffered grievous wounds that must impair his abilities – so he will need assistance. Who better than someone who understands his language and his background?"

Mary pushed her chair back in a rush of anger, and

snapped, "And who worse than the person who gave him those grievous wounds?" She glared at Wychwoode. "It is utter madness! He will refuse to be in the same room as me, let alone have me assist him!"

Wychwoode looked up, his face a blank mask. "May I remind you, Mistress Anne Carter, that Lady Mary de Beauvais is equally under sentence of death? I would advise you to accept this as part of the plan devised by Walsingham and your queen, and concede with good grace." As she slumped back in her chair with crossed arms, he added, "You must find a way to work with the man. That is your challenge, and I would most strongly suggest you accept it."

12

CHAPTER TWELVE

Mary hung back outside the cell gate, drawing warmth from a brightly burning brazier as Wychwoode was let into the dark room at the end of the passageway. The longer she could delay meeting the Alchemist, the better.

She heard the old man greeting the prisoner inside.

"Master Wychwoode," she heard the Alchemist reply, his voice sounding hoarse and thin, although still recognisable. Mary shuddered as the hated sound took her immediately back to the forest after he had shot her beloved horse, Juno. "Once again, are you come to take me to my death?"

"Nay. I have better news, sirrah."

"Better news?" She could imagine the Alchemist's look of sarcastic surprise. "What could possibly be better than being put out of the misery of this place?"

"I am come to take you back to your dwelling in Southwark."

There was a long silence. Then the Alchemist simply said, "Why?"

"We would have you make another of your special muskets."

There was another long silence. "Why?"

"We have need of it."

"And the first one? Can it not be used?"

"Nay. It was damaged by Moreton, then destroyed on the orders of the Queen."

"A pity..." The Alchemist's voice was cut off by a fit of dry coughing, with each racking cough accompanied by the sound of a chain rattling. "A pity that you no longer have it. It would be easier to mend that one than create a new one."

"Indeed," Wychwoode agreed. "But this is the truth of our situation."

"Whatever." There was another long silence. "I do not move very easily, since that de Beauvais bitch hit me with the poker, and you stretched me on the rack. It will not be a quick job to make a new piece."

"You will have assistance."

"Oh." The chain clinked. "I trust it will not be her, eh?" There was the sound of a bitter laugh, ending in another bout of coughing. Eventually the Alchemist's voice rasped out again, "I trust she has already met a most painful end as a sorceress and blasphemer?" He gave a wheezy chuckle. "I trust she screamed very, very loudly as the flames took hold?"

Mary stepped into the cell.

"No," she said softly. "She lives still."

There was a heavy silence. As her eyes adjusted to the dimness, Mary could make out what looked like a thin scarecrow slumped in the corner, a dull beam of light shining down on him from the window like a grotesque stage spotlight. A black chain was secured to the wall behind his shoulder, ending in iron collar disappearing under his long beard.

"Hi, Rick," she said. "Long time, no see."

The scarecrow's eyes glinted as he turned to look up at Wychwoode.

"Are you fucking serious?" he whispered, his voice made all the more menacing by its quietness. "Are you telling me that I have to work with this bitch?" The old lawyer looked down at him with crossed arms and said nothing. "Are you telling me that this evil witch, who should have been burned to a crisp, is not only still alive, but is going to be assisting me in my work?"

"Nice to see you, too, Rick," Mary observed, making her voice drip with irony. "Working together again will be such fun."

"Not in a million *fucking* years!" the Alchemist spat out, crossing his arms and staring pointedly at the opposite corner of the cell.

Wychwoode cleared his throat. "So be it. Then let me tell you what will take place," he said, his voice low and gravelly, as if clearing his throat had made it worse. "At dawn on the morrow I will have you removed from this place and taken to Tyburn. And in case you have forgot, let me remind you again what will happen there." He dropped into a squat, his face nearly level with the Alchemist's. "Firstly, you will be hung by the neck. Then, while you are barely able to draw breath, yet you still live, you will be taken down. After that, your genitals will be removed and displayed before you, although you may not be able to see them clearly, for your eyes will be screwed with pain. But that, sadly, will be nothing to the pain of what comes next." He paused a moment, then cleared his throat again. "You will have your belly opened, your guts severed and removed, then your heart, still beating, will be cut out of your chest, before being burned."

He stood up.

"That, my friend, will be the last thing you see, before finally, merciful death takes you into his arms." He looked up at the window a moment, then turned back to the prisoner.

"But even death will not be the last horror to be borne by your body. For then your head will be removed and placed on a spike for all to see as they step upon London Bridge, and your remains will be quartered and disposed of in pieces."

There was a long silence, and Mary wished she could sit down. But the floor of the cell looked filthy; covered in rat droppings and something that looked suspiciously like a dried human dropping as well. She remained standing.

Wychwoode stared down at the Alchemist. "Or, let me put a different scenario to you," he said quietly. "As before, on the morrow, I will have you taken from this place, but not to Tyburn." He shook his head. "Nay, instead I will have you taken to your own house in Southwark, where you will have the finest bread and ale for a few days in order for your strength to return." He paused, "Or meat pies? I believe you are partial to the pies sold by one Mistress Somerville in the shop close to your house?" The Alchemist gave a tiny nod, despite looking as if he was trying to avoid giving anything away.

"Then you will be provided with all the metal, glass, gunpowder and shot you need to ensure another of your remarkable muskets can be made in the workshop you previously constructed in the outbuilding behind your house, and which has been preserved as you left it." He paused, "Although now it occurs to me that it should not be you who does this work, as not only are you somewhat incapacitated, but you will also need to be secured by a strong chain to the inside of the house." He gave a dry chuckle. "We would not want you trying to disappear into the night, now would we?"

"I can hardly walk, after what you did to me on that fucking rack," the Alchemist muttered.

Wychwoode shook his head. "Nay. You experienced but a single turn of the wheel. Had there been further turns then your bones would have been parted from eachother, and for sure you would never walk again. But I warrant that in a few weeks, your joints will knit together, just like the bones in your leg." He gave a thin smile. "Then you will once again be able to stand and move yourself." He gestured at Mary. "But while you are so... inconvenienced, my thought is that it should be Lady de Beauvais here who will be your hands for this task." He nodded to himself. "She will be quartered in a house close by and will attend on you each day. You will be able to instruct her on each part of the work, which, as you both come from the same future time, she will readily understand. That way the tasks necessary to construct the weapon will be carried out."

The Alchemist drew a sneering breath as if about to respond, but Wychwoode cut him off with a raised hand. "One more thing," he said. "Lady Mary will report each day on your progress to one of my men, who will also be quartered nearby.

And if..." here he gave a piecing glare at the prisoner, "...if she does not report one day – let us say, for example, she has met with some unfortunate accident in your dwelling, then you will be taken immediately to Tyburn, and the first scenario enacted in full."

There was a long silence, during which the Alchemist seemed to be considering his options, giving little snorts through his nose as if to punctuate each thought.

"Seriously? You think this cow here can make a gun?"

"Under your instruction, yes. Now I think on it, it is our best option."

"And if I choose Tyburn over working with...her?" he said, without looking at Mary.

"That is your choice, of course," Wychwoode replied. "Although it does seem a perverse one to me."

The Alchemist's head snapped up, making his chain clink. "Why?" he demanded. "Why perverse? I would only be delaying the time I go to Tyburn anyway."

Wychwoode shook his head. "Nay," he said. "If you successfully perform the service I have set out, then you will be taken to France, Germany, the Low Countries or such continental realm of your choice, given a large enough purse of coin as will set you up in one of their cities, and left there to build a new life for yourself."

The Alchemist's eyes widened in surprise. "You would have me banished with a pardon?"

"Aye, although, I would caution you clearly, that if you ever try to return to England, you will be taken to Tyburn for the full sentence of death as I have described."

The Alchemist rubbed his hands across his eyes a moment, then he looked up and said, "Fine. I will do it. I will not like it – working with her – but I will do it."

Wychwoode breathed out a deep sigh. "Good. Then that is settled. It will be as I said, you will be taken back to Southwark on the morrow." He turned to Mary. "And you are ready to play your part in this, Lady Mary? Or should I say 'Anne Carter'?" He looked back at the Alchemist. "For this will be her identity for the length of this enterprise, and I would thank you, Alchemist, to forget all talk of 'Lady Mary' or even 'Justine', as I believe you first knew her, and use only her new identity, even when alone."

Mary said, "If I must work with him I will. Although I will not like it any more than he does." She looked down at the prisoner. "You had better keep to your side of this, Rick."

He gave her a sickly smile, that was more a sneer. "I will, Mistress Anne Carter," he said. Then he added, "Although you know something?"

She shook her head.

He gestured for her to come closer. Cautiously she bent down until his mouth was by her ear.

"I was always going to agree," he whispered. He gave a small, throaty chuckle. "He had me at Mistress Somerville's meat pies."

13

CHAPTER THIRTEEN

If Mary had expected her working relationship with the Alchemist to be strained, she was not mistaken. The next day they were thrown together in his dingy little Southwark house, and he was as vile as she would have expected.

"Listen, you evil bitch," he began, once Wychwoode's man had secured him to the bed by a chain long enough for him to reach a chamber pot on one side of the room and a small writing table on the other, "we have to make this new gun..." He paused, glaring up at her from under his brow, "...which we wouldn't if you hadn't fucking destroyed the first one, but anyway..." He broke off as a fit of coughing overtook him; each wheezing cough forcing the air out of his thin body, leaving him red-faced and struggling to breathe. "But," he continued, once his ribs had stopped heaving, "we have to make it together. Which means I give you instructions, and somehow, fuck knows how, you are going to make it." He shook his head.

"Have you ever, in your pampered, spoiled little life, actually made anything? And by that I mean something in metal or wood, not a dress or a beef fucking casserole?"

Mary felt her lip curl in response. "Listen Rick," she said, trying hard to keep her voice steady, "I do not want to do this any more than you do, but if we do it, and if we get it right, then there is a chance," she paused, "a slim chance, that we can both get to stay alive. And what is more," she added, "we get our freedom back as well." She took a deep breath. "So I suggest you trust me, give me clear instructions and drawings, the tools to do the job, and let me get on with it."

Which he did. Initially it was with barely concealed bad grace, but as she got more practiced at using the tools in his little workshop in the back courtyard, the Alchemist started to give her his grudging approval. Gradually the number of times he made her go back and remake a part reduced, until one day he actually remarked on how well she was casting and working the metal, as well as shaping the wood.

After a few further days they were able to converse a little more easily, even to the point that he no longer referred to her as 'you fucking bitch' and started addressing her by the name of Anne Carter. After another week he even teased her for having smudges of soot on her nose when she presented a particularly fine casting. It was almost as if the casual working relationship they had once enjoyed in 2015 Grangedean Manor was back, and she found herself almost welcoming his comments on her work – taking pride in his approval.

But more than anything, the fragile bond forming between these two bitter enemies was forged through their shared antagonism towards Wychwoode's man. A man whose combination of arrogance and ignorance meant he was constantly upsetting one or other, or even on some occasions, both of them.

A man called Roger Rolleston.

---O---

At first it had been easy. Wychwoode had introduced Rolleston as his new man, and instructed her to report to him each day at a nearby inn. "It is for your own safety," Wychwoode had explained. "The Alchemist needs to be aware that if he causes some accident to befall you, we will know swiftly, and he will suffer the death of a traitor. That way he will be minded to ensure you are kept in good health, for all you will be dealing with sharp tools and hot fires."

But it soon became clear that Rolleston thought he was working to a wider brief. He had started to appear at the Alchemist's house each day and asking – no, demanding – to see the progress of the gun itself.

The Alchemist, issuing his instructions and providing drawings from chained imprisonment in his bed chamber, had initially ignored this additional imposition. Eventually it had become obvious that Rolleston was starting to see himself as the de facto director of the project. Perhaps it was because the Alchemist was chained and unable to walk, and Mary was simply a woman, but whatever it was, the man had started throwing his weight about and issuing orders, for all they had no benefit to the outcome of the process.

It took a couple of weeks before the Alchemist finally snapped.

"By Heavens, Rolleston, you are an ignorant fucker!" he had yelled one day, after a particularly arrogant comment from the merchant. "You know sod all about this, so keep your long Tudor nose out of it!"

"I know this, you traitorous cur!" Rolleston yelled back, putting his hands on his hips and standing at the end of the bed with his shoulders back and his feet apart, like a Roman gladiator squaring up to his opponent. "I know that you are a filthy little peasant but a step from the gallows for your crimes!"

"And how do you know that, pray?"

Rolleston gave a slow smile. "I was briefed by Master Wychwoode, with enough information to do this work. So I know you are some sort of sorcerer, who was racked for trying to kill the Queen with your self-made musket."

"So you know why we are making another such musket?" Mary interjected with a note of caution. It would not do for this Rolleston to know too much about the mission.

"Nay, that I do not." He transferred his glare from the Alchemist to her. "But I warrant it is for some clandestine purpose of Wychwoode's." He turned back to the Alchemist. "And I doubt very much that Wychwoode has shared such a plan with a traitor such as you."

"Fuck you!" the Alchemist snapped.

"Listen, you Alchemist," Rolleston replied, "if you do not defer to your betters, then you will soon find yourself sprawled at the base of the gibbet, propelled there by the toe of my boot!"

"You are no better than me!" the Alchemist responded,

grabbing his chain as if he would use it as a weapon. "I know full well you were in the Tower as a Catholic traitor yourself!"

"Nay churl," the merchant snarled. "I was falsely accused, while you are a proven traitor and witch, caught in the act of firing your unnatural musket at the Queen." He wiped spittle off his mouth with his sleeve. "You are in no position to pass judgment on your superiors!"

"Not a witch, you fucker," snapped the Alchemist.

"Nay?" answered Rolleston with a twisted smile. "Then where, pray, did you get the knowledge, and indeed the funds, to make your evil musket in the first place?"

"My knowledge is none of your business," answered the Alchemist, "and as for funds, it is amazing how you can earn good money by making household items that no-one has ever seen before and never knew they needed, but now cannot live without."

The Alchemist looked at Mary with an eyebrow raised, as if asking her to step in and take his part.

For a moment she hesitated, captivated by the image of Rick turning out modern-day items for the good wives of Southwark. What had he been making, that had allowed him to build up the money to live on, as well as ultimately to make the gun? Something as prosaic as maybe table forks, previously unknown in Tudor times? Or something more exotic, like a frying pan or a wok? She shook her head to clear the thought, and to concentrate on his request for help.

"I would not have you take such an attitude with the Alchemist, Master Rolleston," she said in a level tone. "He has been offered a full pardon if he helps with this work on the new gun, and that he is doing."

Rolleston stared at her open mouthed. "You would not have me take such an attitude...? You, who he calls a... a fucking bitch?" he asked in a strangled whisper.

"Aye," she replied, with what she hoped was a suitably passive-aggressive smile, "but he is central to this endeavour. So I suggest you learn how to control your temper and leave the Alchemist and me to finish this task without poking your 'long Tudor nose' in." He started to draw breath, but before he could say anything more, she added, "and lest you dismiss me as a 'mere woman', I would remind you that I have the strength and guile of a man – and," she added, pointing her finger closer to his red face, "a much better one than you."

---o---

After a couple more weeks, the gun was nearly finished.

Mary stood in the courtyard and peered through the barrel section, lining it up against a patch of bright sky between the autumn clouds, enjoying the way the light bounced down the smooth metal inside and created swirling kaleidoscopes of silvers and blues. No kinks or burrs. That was good.

She glanced over as Rolleston stepped out of the rickety back door of the Southwark house and came up to her.

She took another long look through the barrel, then lowered it slowly.

"This is completed," she observed. "I am satisfied it will shoot straight and true."

"Good," he answered. "So now you will show me how the whole weapon comes together."

"In good time, Master Rolleston," she demurred. "I must show it to the Alchemist first and have him check all the parts. He is most particular."

"But you have made it to his precise instructions these few weeks," he said, sounding like a small child denied a treat. "Each day you have shown him your efforts – and if he has not been satisfied he has had you rework or remake each part, on occasions many times. So for sure, the final whole will be fit to function to his standards."

Mary took another slow look through the barrel, enjoying the increasingly impatient snorts of the man beside her. It was his own fault; if he had behaved in a more civilised manner then perhaps she would be more accommodating towards him. She lowered the piece again with a small sigh.

"Marry, sir," she said quietly, "for sure it is made to his design, but until he has approved it, then it is not complete."

"So go to it," he snapped. "I am required by Master Wych-woode to arrange for a demonstration of the power of the weapon. He would see it fire and prove itself for range and accuracy."

"Then he must wait until I have tested it first," she said firmly. "I will not demonstrate it to anyone until I am satis-fied for myself it works as it should."

She watched as a red flush crept up from under his lace collar and dark beard, filling his cheeks until they were the colour of beetroot. "By thunder," he snarled, "I have had my fill of your insolence since we have been forced to work together."

Mary took a deep breath to calm herself, becoming aware

that she had shifted her grip on the barrel as if she would use it to beat this boorish oaf about the head, but managed to restrain herself as she strode past him and into the house.

She stooped as she entered the bedroom, then paused to let her eyes adjust to the gloom. The Alchemist was sitting on the bed as always, finishing a meat pie. He took a swig of ale from a tankard and looked up.

"The barrel is complete," she said, trying to ignore Rolleston as he pushed in behind her. "I have held it to the light as you have said, and there are no kinks or burrs within." She handed it over and watched as the Alchemist studied it carefully close to the candle, turning it each way against the light. Then he put it to his eye and peered through, holding the end directly against the bright flame. Eventually he nodded.

"It is good," he said slowly. "I am impressed. Have you checked how it locates to the chamber?"

"Yes," she replied. "It is a little tight; I need to work it a bit more, but it will fit."

He breathed in deeply, which he could now do without coughing, and said, "Excellent." He passed the barrel back up to her. "I suggest you now assemble the whole piece and bring it to me. We can decide if it is ready to be tested."

Mary pushed past Rolleston, then made her way down the narrow corridor to the courtyard, with its little workshop on the far side. She was aware that the merchant was following close behind her, and as she got to the workshop door, she turned and said firmly, "I would you leave me to go in alone. I need to concentrate on the work, which I cannot do with you breathing down my neck."

"I am charged by Wychwoode to ensure the work is done well," he answered.

"No, you are not," she said, tapping the end of the barrel on her open palm to emphasise her point. "You were originally charged with remaining in the tavern and reporting back to Wychwoode that I am safe each day. The fact you choose to spend all your time here is your own decision." She waved the barrel towards his face, and was pleased to see him pale slightly as he stepped back a few paces from the door. "But it is not by Master Wychwoode's instruction. And anyway," she added, "the best way you can ensure the work is done well, is to keep your interfering nose out of it." With that, she marched into the workshop, closing the door firmly behind her and throwing the bolt to secure it.

Once inside, she breathed out a deep sigh that ended in a whispered "and – relax..." before surveying the room that had been her place of work these past few weeks.

Immediately in front of her was the forge – an open grate full of glowing coals that she kept alight at all times. A pair of bellows was secured at its base with the tip just below the grate, so she could work it with her foot to blow in air and raise the temperature sufficiently to melt the metal before pouring it into the sand moulds. Above the grate was a brick chimney, allowing the hot air to escape and preventing smoke build-up inside the workshop.

To the left was the lathe, which the Alchemist had made by adapting the pedal mechanism of a spinning wheel, and which he had geared up substantially with a belt-driven fly-wheel turning a much larger wheel on the side of the lathe itself. This meant that although it took quite some effort to start it off by working the pedals with her feet, Mary could then make the lathe spin extremely fast, and could therefore run her sharpened chisel and polishing cloths along the rest in order to create the smooth barrel and metal stock, as well as the bullets.

On the other side of the grate there was a shelf, on which stood the wooden forms the Alchemist had originally made for each part of the gun. There was the half-barrel form, two castings of which could be welded together and finished on the lathe. Then there were the two half-forms for the firing chamber, a form for the trigger, one for the bolt and one for the bullets. Mary had learned how to embed each form in fine sand to make the mould, with a rod to make a pouring tunnel for the steel. Then she would melt the metal in an earthenware crucible, adding small pieces from offcuts she had been supplied by Wychwoode using his contacts with armourers. She would watch with fascination as the metal started to twist and settle into the crucible, turning from a dirty grey to shining mercury-like silver, and finally into a glowing liquid. Then, once she had scraped off the dirty surface slag to get pure metal only, she had learned how to pour the liquid steel into the mould, break out the piece once cooled, before shaping and finishing it with the rudimentary tools made by the Alchemist or purchased from a blacksmith.

On the other side of the room was the woodwork bench, where she had made the butt and the fore-stock, learning through trial and error how to cut and shape the wood, then polish it with rough sanding cloths and oil it to a fine finish.

Mary unwrapped the completed firing chamber from its

protective waxed cloth and gently applied the barrel to the aperture. As she had said to the Alchemist, it was a little too tight – but that was not a bad thing, as it would give a firm fit. But she would need it to be assembled and disassembled easily, so it had to be just right. A shame she didn't have the tools to cut a screw thread – but unfortunately the Alchemist had explained that this was beyond his capabilities, so a push-fit would have to do.

She roughened the inside of the aperture with a sanding cloth for a few minutes, then tried again. Still too tight. After more sanding and a few more tries, it finally slotted into place. Then she clipped on the two steel retaining strips she had made to hold the barrel in place against the force of the gun being fired, added the trigger, the metal stock and finally the wooden butt. She clipped the sight into place, made from a piece of tubing fitted with two ground glass magnifying lenses obtained by Wychwoode from a maker of spectacles.

She held the gun at its central point in front of the trigger and gazed proudly at the result of her work; a well-balanced, light and simple piece, with smooth, polished metal and a shining, shaped wooden fore-stock and butt. Lifting the gun up to her cheek, she pointed it at the little window and took aim through the sight. Her finger curled round the trigger, as she centred the crosshairs on the beams of an old wooden house across the street. She took a breath and gently squeezed the trigger, then allowed herself a small smile as the bolt slammed against the firing pin with a satisfying *clunk*.

She lowered the gun and glanced across at a shelf on which stood fifty cartridges, lined up in five rows of ten like gleaming little soldiers. Gathering two and putting them in the pocket of her gown, she left the workshop and walked back into the house.

CHAPTER FOURTEEN

The Alchemist turned the finished gun over and looked up, shaking his head slowly. "I would never have thought that you could have done this," he said. "I'd have put money on you doing a cack-handed job that wouldn't work at all, but fuck me, you go and produce this!" He lifted the gun to his cheek and took aim at Rolleston standing against the wall, then pulled the trigger. The bolt clicked and the Alchemist chuckled as the merchant flinched. "Not loaded, mate. More's the pity." He put the gun down on the bed and said to Mary, "Show me a bullet."

She fished one of the cartridges from her pocket and handed it over. He studied it carefully, then, seeming satisfied, he pulled back the bolt to open the chamber and slotted it into place. He casually pointed the gun at the wall between Rolleston's legs and pulled the trigger again.

The report of the gun echoed around the little room like

a thunder-crack, leaving Mary momentarily deafened. There was also an overpowering acrid stench of gunpowder. Rolleston leapt like a scalded cat, as the plaster between his knees exploded in a big puff of smoke and dust. "By Heavens!" he yelled. "Have you taken leave of your senses?"

The Alchemist gave the gun back to Mary, observing levelly, "It seems to work. Now I suggest you test it in the woods to make sure the sight is lined up." He studied the mounting of the tube containing the two lenses. "See how I said to make the mount move?" She nodded. "Fire some shots and move the sight to get it lined up, then pack some soft clay in here," he pointed at the base, "so when the clay sets, you'll have it right." He fixed her with a firm stare. "*Day of the Jackal* – know what I mean?" Mary nodded again, understanding the reference to the film, where the Jackal takes his sniper rifle into the woods and tests the sight by shooting at a melon.

She glanced over at Rolleston, who had turned as white as a sheet. "I know not what is this jackal he talks of," he said in a strangled whisper, "but I know that the madman has fired his weapon at my legs in the most reckless and dangerous manner, and this shall be reported to Master Wychwoode."

Mary shrugged. "I have no idea what it is you are complaining of, Master Rolleston," she said with her most innocent expression. "Surely you were in fact on the other side of the room when the weapon was test-fired into the wall?"

"You would tell an untruth to protect this man?"

"It would be my word against yours, sir," she answered, smiling sweetly. "And as I have earned the trust of Master Wychwoode over these past years, I am sure it will be my word that will be believed."

"Then I would take it to Master Secretary Walsingham."
Mary chuckled. "Big mistake," she said. "Big. Huge."

"Your comment is pretty, woman," observed the Alchemist, appearing to be struggling to keep a straight face.

Rolleston's mouth opened and closed silently several times, then, without any warning, he suddenly turned and punched his fist hard into the wall beside him, with such force that it caused a crack in the plaster, running all the way down to the hole left by the Alchemist's shot. Seeming to ignore such pain as must have been caused, he snarled, "By the Lord's Wounds, madam, I shall not take this lightly. You will regret this, I assure you!" Then he marched out of the room, leaving Mary and the Alchemist staring wordlessly at the crack in the wall.

The Alchemist waited until the front door was heard to slam, before observing, "Fucking nutcase." Mary dragged her gaze away from the wall and back to the man on the bed. "Right," he continued, "back to business. How many bullets do you have?"

15

CHAPTER FIFTEEN

Mary moved her leg wider and settled her position. She was lying on the forest floor, the gun pushed into her shoulder, with her right finger on the trigger and her left hand supporting the fore-stock.

A foot in a black shoe came into her peripheral vision. "I would you take a step backwards, please, Master Secretary," she said, "and stay behind me for safety, as I demonstrate the power of the weapon."

The foot disappeared as Francis Walsingham moved further away behind her.

"You would hit that red apple over yonder, from this distance?" came the voice of the only other person in this quiet forest clearing; a woman with her pale face hidden under a cowled cloak.

"Yes, Your Majesty," Mary answered softly, keeping her breath even as she brought the sight onto the distant apple hanging from the branch. "Do I have your permission to fire?" she breathed.

The Queen was silent a moment, then she said, "Go to it, Mary, I prithee."

Mary stilled her breathing to the slowest she could, feeling her heart rate drop to what felt like no more than a beat a minute, as she moved the crosshairs to the centre of the apple and started to squeeze her finger on the trigger.

As her finger tightened, she couldn't help but think how she had got to this point; the promise to the Queen to go along with this madcap plan; the weeks spent following the Alchemist's instructions to cast and make the gun; the hours in the forest firing the weapon and adjusting the sight before fixing it with clay packing, and now, demonstrating it in front of Walsingham and the Queen.

She forced herself to concentrate on the apple in the sight. Nothing else could matter; nothing other than the round red image in the crosshairs.

She held her breath and squeezed a little bit more.

The bolt slammed the firing pin into the base of the shell and, with the familiar cracking sound, the gunpowder inside exploded, sending the bullet down the barrel at close to the speed of sound. Mary exhaled slowly as she saw the apple in her sight evaporate in a puff of smoke. For a moment she remained still, then she lowered the barrel and rolled to her side, so she could look up at the two observers behind her.

"Your Majesty. Master Secretary," she announced. "You will see that this weapon is accurate at this distance. It is, I believe, fit for the purpose you have in mind."

"Indeed it is," said the Queen. "I cannot be ought but

impressed that it does what we have asked." Mary got to her feet. "And you have manufactured it yourself?" the Queen continued, her thin eyebrow raised as Mary stood before her, "by your own hand at every stage?"

"Yes, madam," Mary said. "I did, from instructions and tools given to me by the Alchemist."

"Remarkable. Quite remarkable." The Queen paused. "You are a talented woman, Mary, and I am most pleased we have had you released from the Tower for this purpose. Let me see the weapon." She held out her hand and Mary passed the gun across. "This is an amazing piece," the Queen said, as she turned it over and studied it closely. "So simple in essence, yet it fires with such ferocity." She gave a small shudder as she handed it back. "I cannot but think of how just such a weapon was aimed at me, and what would have happened if our noble protector Sir Thomas Cobham had not put himself in the way of that ball."

She turned to her spymaster. "Master Secretary, once again we have such a piece in existence, and it becomes a threat to our person if it is ever to fall in the wrong hands." He nodded, as she continued, "so again, once Lady Mary has completed the mission we have charged her to carry out, this must be destroyed, and with it all the tools made by this Alchemist for the express purpose of constructing such a piece."

"It shall be done, your Majesty," he answered with a small bow.

"And the Alchemist himself?" she asked. "Will the full sentence of death for a traitor now be carried out?"

There was an uneasy pause. "He was made a bargain, madam," Walsingham said carefully. "In return for his cooperation and for his instructions to Lady Mary, he was made an offer – for his life to be spared and for him to be sent into exile with enough of a purse to start a new existence." He paused. "But with a stricture to face certain death if he is ever to return to your realm."

The Queen was silent a moment. "It sits most ill with me, Master Secretary, to think that a man who set out to cause my death and to put that Scottish woman on my throne is spared his life."

"It was expedient, madam. He would not have co-operated otherwise."

"And you gave him your word?"

"Through my man, Wychwoode, yes."

"But not with my knowledge or consent?"

There was another uncomfortable silence. Mary could see the Queen was on the verge of issuing a command for the Alchemist to be executed anyway. She carefully placed the gun on the forest floor and bowed to the Queen.

"Your Majesty," she said, "you once told me you valued my honest counsel, and by your leave, I would offer it now."

"Indeed, Lady Mary," the Queen replied, with a look on her pale face that was almost of relief. "What say you on this matter?"

Mary took a breath while she ordered her thoughts. This had to be right. "It is true that the Alchemist set out to cause your death and put Mary, Queen of Scots on your throne," she began. "But it was not done out of Catholic conviction, rather it was done for greed; he thought he would be elevated to a high position and given much wealth by a new regime. So by pardoning him, and giving him money, he is no longer any threat to your person or your throne. Rather, it is to your credit as a wise sovereign that his contribution to this secret plan is recognised – and it is better that the promise made to him in good faith is honoured, than he is torn apart at the gallows."

The Queen observed Mary steadily from under her hood. "You take his part now?" she asked quietly. "Even after you beat him senseless in my defence?"

"Yes madam." Mary said. "I hold no love for the man, as you say, but I recognise that he has done what was asked of him, and he has done it in good conscience. To keep the bargain made with him now would be the honourable and merciful thing."

Elizabeth pursed her lips, her dark, unblinking eyes not leaving Mary's. Eventually she gave a small nod. "Very well. Have the man sent into exile as promised, with sufficient purse to establish his new life. But," she added, "I want him to have a new name, so that no connection can be made with this traitor, and Master Secretary, I want your intelligencers to keep watch on him without his knowledge, so we may know if he ever does aught of concern."

Walsingham bowed, and said, "As Your Majesty wishes."

"And one further thing, Master Secretary," the Queen added. "I would you find some condemned man; one who is already destined for the noose for his crimes, and make the artifice that this is the Alchemist, being executed for the traitorous attempt on my life, and for the murder of Sir Thomas Cobham. For all we have made to keep the events in York this summer out of the records, there will be those who know of this Alchemist and his treasonous crimes. I want it to be clear to them, and to any others who think to commit such a crime that the price of treason is always death, without exception." She paused. "Do I make myself clear?"

"Very clear, Your Majesty."

"Good." The Queen smiled. "Now, pick up your weapon, Lady Mary, and let us now execute this covert plan. There is no time to lose if we are to change the future and avoid all the troubling events of which you have so clearly warned us."

16

CHAPTER SIXTEEN

Sir William de Beauvais marched confidently into the room and bowed low to Walsingham and Wychwoode, sweeping off his cap.

"Pray be upstanding, Sir William," said Walsingham. "Welcome to Barn Elms." He waved his hand towards the table in the corner, where some goblets and a bottle of wine were standing by a single candle.

William replaced his cap and took a seat. Once all three were settled and the wine was poured, Walsingham said quietly, "You have requested this meeting and we have agreed. How may we be of assistance?"

William cleared his throat. If Walsingham didn't know what this was about, then he was either a fool or a liar. Judging by the man's reputation, it was the latter.

"As you know most well, Master Secretary," William began, with a cold smile, "my wife has been arrested on charges of sorcery and blasphemy – yet I know of no trial that has taken place, nor..." he cleared his throat again. "Nor any execution." He took a long breath, then let it out slowly, glancing at Wychwoode as he did so. The old man's furrowed face remained impassive, deeply shadowed in the flickering candlelight. "Sirs, I would know her fate this day."

"Your wife was held in the Tower, pending the trial," said Walsingham. "This you know, and there is no more to tell."

"Master Secretary, I pray you be more understanding!" William blurted out. "She is my wife and mother to my children. We are consumed with anxiety about her! My children do not sleep and cry out for her in the night! I say again, we would know her fate!" A sudden thought occurred. "Was?" he queried. "You said she 'was' held in the Tower. Is she no longer there?"

"My dear Sir William," said Walsingham, his voice so honey-smooth that it set William's teeth on edge. "Your wife is under arrest with the gravest of charges set against her. She will be tried as the law demands, and if found guilty, she will face the appropriate sanction." The corners of his mouth turned up in an approximation of a smile. "I understand this is not what you wanted to hear, but I am afraid it is the truth of the matter."

"And if this trial takes place, although it seems to have been delayed by many weeks, will I be allowed to attend?"

Wychwoode said, "I am not sure that would be wise, Sir William."

"Why? Good God, man, she is my wife! I have a right to hear her defend herself!" He shook his head. "And she has the right to see me there to support her. I must be there!"

"As I say, I am not sure that would be wise."

William clenched and unclenched his fists under the table a few times, trying to release the tension that was now crackling like lightning bolts in every part of his body. He had only been at this table a few minutes, yet already he was being blocked by these men. How satisfying it would be to leap across the table and smash their two thick heads together, then swing punches at each of them in turn, until they begged for his mercy, which he would only give if they agreed to bring Mary to him so he could take her home to her family...

But instead he took a deep breath and said levelly, "Come now, Robert, we have known each other these ten or more years, and have shared many a glass of wine in friendship. How can you be so unfeeling in this matter?" Wychwoode remained impassive, so William continued. "You have said on countless occasions that you value Mary's wisdom and bravery. How do you abandon her now?"

Wychwoode was about to answer, when Walsingham stood up.

"This meeting is finished, Sir William. All that can be said on this matter has been said. I bid you good day, and I wish you a pleasant journey back to Grangedean Manor."

William also stood, but instead of leaving the table, he leaned across and put his face close to Walsingham's.

"Master Secretary, I..." he began, then he stopped. What could he possibly say that would prise open the iron bars that closed off this man's mind? "Master Secretary, I..." he tried again. But no, it was hopeless. "Master Secretary, I wish you good day," he snarled, then turned and left without another word.

It was only as he was striding down the corridor that he realised what he should have said.

"Listen Master Secretary, I wish you never find yourself in my position – find yourself with one you love in mortal danger and beyond your help. For if you do, you will know what it is to feel powerless when your loved one needs you to come to their aid. It is that powerlessness, Master Secretary, that destroys you inside. You, who has power over so many people, I hope you never know what it feels like to have that taken from you. Good day to you too."

---o---

There was a long silence after Sir William had left.

Eventually Wychwoode observed, "As the man says, I have known him these many years. I do wish I could help him, but..."

"But this mission is more important than your friendship," finished Walsingham. Then his voice softened. "I do know that, Robert, God knows I do. But we cannot put this enterprise in jeopardy."

"Indeed no."

Walsingham sat back and put his fingertips together under his chin. "Curious, is it not," he observed, "that we have managed to have both a wife and husband lean across this very table, and seek to lecture me on how best to do my work.?" He gave a little snort of mirth. "Although the wife was considerably more lucid than the husband. When it came to it, the man was unable to give expression to his feelings." He looked up at Wychwoode. "Curious, I say."

Wychwoode nodded. "I felt sorry for him. His anger stopped his mind from working, whereas her anger had the opposite effect."

"True enough." Walsingham parted his fingers and leaned forward. "But enough of that. To more pressing matters. The secret mission."

Wychwoode swirled his wine around his glass, then took a sip and nodded. "For sure. Is the weapon ready?"

"Aye. I saw it demonstrated yesterday in the forest near the village of Clapham. Do you know, it puts our crude and cumbersome weaponry to shame." Walsingham shook his head slowly. "Lady Mary hit a small apple from more than a furlong distant. A furlong and a half, even. It shows the reality of her claims of the accuracy of the weapon." He nodded. "And Lady Mary – she is truly remarkable. If she is indeed from future times, then women are changed, Robert. They are not the same as our women. We are fortunate to have her working for us."

"Indeed," Wychwoode agreed. "It is as I have said before, she has the bravery and resourcefulness we need for this mission."

"And future missions as well, if she wins though this one," Walsingham observed.

"Nay. She says she seeks only to stay home and run her household," said Wychwoode. "Indeed, I am sure if we allow her, she will run home to see her family, even before undertaking the mission."

"If what Sir William said is true, I have no doubt you are correct."

"But this we cannot allow, Master Secretary," said

Wychwoode. "It would put the mission in jeopardy. Who knows what secrets she may reveal?"

"As you say, Robert," said Walsingham. "So we will bring her to my London house at Seething Lane and keep a close watch on her."

"It is for the best, I agree." Wychwoode took a sip of wine. "But let us return to the plan. We are agreed, are we not, that this mission depends on Lady Mary taking a shot at our chosen target from a great distance, using the accuracy of the weapon to ensure success?"

"Aye. That we do."

"And we are fully agreed that a shot is the best way to achieve the desired outcome?" asked Walsingham. "Not a clandestine smothering in the night, or a quiet dose of poison in the food?"

"Yes, the conceit relies on the shot being taken in full public view, so the second part can then be put into motion."

"And if Lady Mary is captured and revealed as the killer?"

Wychwoode shook his head. "It will be regrettable, of course, but we will deny all knowledge. She will be a lone assassin, motivated by religious zeal, nothing more."

"Agreed. And your plan to ensure she gets to the place itself? I warrant she is brave and resourceful, but will be no match for a pack of determined thieves if they come across her on the way. Do you have some four or five men to accompany her?"

"Nay," answered Wychwoode. "This is to be a clandestine journey. To have that many men around her will surely attract attention. I propose one man only – so she will travel easier and faster, and can stay out of trouble more easily."

"If you say," answered Walsingham. "I trust you have a good man for this task?"

"I do," said Wychwoode. "He is perfect."

17

CHAPTER SEVENTEEN

Mary almost dropped her glass of wine as she stared open-mouthed at Francis Walsingham and Robert Wychwoode.

"You are sending *who* with me on this mission?" she asked in a strangled whisper.

"Roger Rolleston," confirmed Wychwoode. "We need someone we can trust to look to your safety."

"My safety?" Mary knocked back her wine and put the glass down, aware that her shaking hand made it quite clearly clatter against the wooden tabletop. "My safety?" she repeated. "The man is an interfering oaf who could not keep a mad dog safe. Why on earth must he come?"

"He is strong and resourceful," Wychwoode answered, his lined face frowning. "He has been briefed, but only on the destination and the need to ensure you are kept secure, not the purpose of the mission."

"And you say you can trust him?" she asked.

"Aye," Wychwoode answered. "I had him released from the Tower after his wrongful arrest for Catholic sedition."

"Yes, he said he was falsely accused," observed Mary. "How do you know he tells the truth?"

"I checked most thoroughly that he has worshipped at Protestant services ever since Her Majesty ascended the throne." He paused. "He was conducting merchant business with a gentleman at a house in Nottinghamshire, when it was raided by some Pursuivants. Rolleston was arrested also, but I am satisfied he was not of their faith, nor in league with them."

It was a week later, and they were in Walsingham's study at his house in Seething Lane, London, where Mary had been staying while the final elements of the plan were being put in place. Her initial demand to visit Grangedean Manor and see William and the children had been firmly blocked. Walsingham had been adamant that she should remain under cover until the mission was complete and had even muttered darkly that it was better for their safety that they knew nothing of her actions. This, and the fact that she was locked in her room every night, had made her extremely anxious. It had taken much reassurance from Wychwoode to convince her not to worry – which naturally had the opposite effect, making her worry all the more. It had also not helped that Seething Lane was only a couple of streets from her recent prison, and she could clearly see the turrets of the White Tower from the tiny window of the small bedroom they gave her on the top floor, making it painfully obvious that her position was still very precarious.

"I have worked with Rolleston these past few weeks," she tried, "and in my opinion, he is most ill-suited to this task." Not to mention how they had parted on the worst of terms after the Alchemist had fired between the man's legs.

Walsingham poured her some more wine. "I accept your reservations, Lady Mary – I mean Mistress Carter," he said as he wiped the neck of the bottle, "but Rolleston meets our needs well; he is a new intelligencer and therefore unknown to the Catholics..."

"Apart from some in Nottinghamshire," she pointed out.

Walsingham inclined his head. "...Apart from those Catholics, I grant you, but in the main, he is unknown. And he has worked with you, so he knows how you operate." He glanced across at Wychwoode, as if seeking reassurance from an earlier conversation. He added, "And marry, my lady, we need you to trust that we have the success of the mission, and your well-being, at the front of our minds."

Mary tried another angle. "Why do I need a man to accompany me at all?" she asked. "Can I not take Olivia Melrose? We have proven ourselves together previously."

"Two women on such a dangerous mission? It is a risk we cannot take," answered Walsingham. "We cannot allow the success of the venture to be dependent on there being no cutpurses or brigands between here and Sheffield." He smiled in what she felt was a distinctly patronising manner. "No. Rolleston's brief will be to ensure your protection on the road, my lady, and to see you safely to the place where you will use the weapon." He paused, still with the sickly smile, "So we would ask you to trust us in this matter."

Mary knew when she was beaten, and gave back an equally sickly smile. "So be it," she murmured. "But I say now, I do not trust the man an inch."

"For sure," agreed Wychwoode. "But he has made a solemn oath to ensure the success of the mission – and that means looking to your welfare."

"He had better," muttered Mary. '*Or I'll have his nuts for earrings*,' she added to herself.

Wychwoode, oblivious to her unspoken threat, turned to Walsingham.

"Now, Master Secretary," he said, "I would we run through the plan one more time to have all parts in good order."

"Indeed, that is most expedient." The spymaster turned to Mary. "Now, my lady, you have told us with your foresight of future events, that Mary, Queen of Scots becomes an increasing thorn in our side over the next few years, and that she becomes an ever more present magnet for seditious Catholic factions, with plots by men such as Babington to release her so she can usurp our rightful queen's throne. You have told us that eventually a warrant is issued for her execution, despite Her Majesty's reluctance to execute another prince anointed by God, and that in the year of Our Lord fifteen eighty-seven the beheading is carried out. However, it is most casually executed," he gave a dry chuckle, "if you will forgive the expression." He became serious again. "And the Queen of Scots dies an unimaginably painful death." He cleared his throat and continued. "This event is then used in part in the following year by King Philip of Spain to validate an attempt to invade this realm with a sea-borne army – and that although this armada ultimately fails, there is much loss of fine English men." He paused, allowing Wychwoode to take over.

"So we have determined that it is best to cut out this canker of sedition now," the lawyer continued. "Thereby saving not only the need to fight the Spanish with their invasion force, but also the plots from taking place around the Scottish Queen. We will take away the focal point of all these events. Your weapon, and your skill in its deployment, affords us the ideal opportunity to cause the swift and painless death of the Scottish Queen, while she is out taking the daily walk she uses to soften the pain of arthritis in her joints. She is currently held by the Earl of Shrewsbury at Sheffield Castle, and you will secure a suitable position to use your remarkable weapon to kill her, and with sufficient accuracy for our purpose."

"May I just point out," Mary interrupted, "that I am not at heart a cold-blooded assassin, and the thought that you see me as one fills me with horror?"

"I do understand," answered Walsingham, "but you must agree that you have previously shown that you are capable of killing in such a fashion, Lady Mary. We are merely harnessing your proven skills."

Mary opened her mouth to reply, then shut it. He did have a point, however uncomfortable that made her feel.

"The Earl has agreed to the plan in the barest outline, although he has none of the detail," continued Walsingham. "Sufficient for now that he has committed to making sure the Scottish Queen walks alone on the appointed day." He nodded in satisfaction. "We will reveal the remainder of the plan to him in due course. This being, that as soon as she falls, and amid the general consternation and reaction to an assassination in plain view, we will substitute the dead woman with a live one who has been trained these many weeks to take on her person and manner, and whose likeness to the Scottish Queen is so far beyond remarkable to be as if God himself has sent her to us. She will be wearing the same clothing as the Scottish Queen, and will have a wound that matches hers closely enough that none will question it – yet the substitute queen's wound will be produced from bursting a bladder of pig's blood, and will be declared not to be fatal. Which is why we need the accuracy of your weapon. Your shot will pierce the Scottish Queen's heart, while the new queen will appear to have taken a hit but a few inches across, to the shoulder. This will, of course, allow her to appear to make a remarkable recovery. This she will put down to God's grace, thereby opening up the second part of the plan.

"What will happen to the body of the real queen?" interrupted Mary. "Once I have..." she paused to steady herself. "Once I have killed her?"

"The body will be taken to a small room near," Walsingham said, "and held securely until it can be given a quiet burial."

Wychwoode then picked up the tale, "Meantimes the replacement, one Frances Barwell, will then become to all intents and purposes, Mary, Queen of Scots. She has been receiving secret daily intelligence from one of our men inside the Earl's household, so she has all the knowledge she needs to maintain the deception. She is a fluent speaker of both the French and the Scots tongue, so she can easily mimic the Scottish Queen's language and manner of speech, and can converse in either as required. Any lapse in memory or any misunderstanding can be put down to the traumatic effects of surviving such an assassination attempt."

"As soon as we have Mistress Barwell in place," Walsingham continued, "she will be taken to a new location to recover, most likely Tutbury Castle, which recovery will be speedy enough that she can very soon travel. Then," and here he gave an uncharacteristic smile, "she will perform the perfect endgame to our plan; she will make it known that that the attempt on her life has made her re-think her faith, and given her cause to convert away from Catholicism to become a true Protestant." He nodded briefly. "And we will also let it be known that the assassin is believed to be a disaffected Catholic – thus giving credibility to her desire to move away from that faith. She will then be brought to London, pale and wounded so she gains the most sympathy, and renounce all claim to the throne of England. A binding legal article will be drawn up to give effect to her decision, and she will sign it. The conversion and renunciation will then be proclaimed throughout the land."

Wychwoode added, "The Catholics will no longer have a person they can champion for the throne, as her son, the nine-year-old boy James, has been raised in the true faith of the Church of Scotland. So they will be forced to live more loyal and holy lives, and we will, with God's good grace, have peace in the realm and less of a threat to the person and throne of our true Queen Elizabeth."

"So we are all of one mind on this?" Walsingham asked.

Mary nodded. Yes, she was of one mind with these men, as she had little choice other than to go along with this in-credible plan. But naturally she had her reservations – there was much that could go wrong, and not to mention the sickening and questionable logic of killing the Queen of Scots now, thereby saving her from a painful death in eleven years' time. Given the choice of eleven more years of life and a painful death, Mary wasn't sure she would choose that option for herself.

Not to mention that this plan would make her into a cold-blooded assassin.

To be a spy was one thing – but an assassin...?

Good," said Walsingham. Then he opened a drawer in his desk and produced an unsealed, folded letter. "Take this," he said, handing it over. "'Tis the final instruction to the Earl of Shrewsbury, appraising him of the plan, or as much as he needs to know, and his part therein."

Mary took the letter and opened it cautiously, then frowned as her eyes skimmed across the page. None of the writing made any sense; it was all in blocks of five characters and none was a recognisable word. She glanced up, to see the two men staring at her intently.

"Aye, it is in code," said Walsingham. "In case it falls into the hands of our enemies."

"And Shrewsbury can decipher this?" she asked, as she folded it again.

"For sure – it is our usual code with him." He paused, and Mary thought he had further information, but was unsure of revealing it. She raised an enquiring eyebrow, and after a moment, he continued. "It has a secret mark that sets it apart from any copies or forgery." He cleared his throat cautiously. "If ever you need to have proof it is genuine, then hold the top left corner to the flame of a candle. If the heat shows forth a secret mark, then you know the paper is genuine."

"And the secret mark is...?" she enquired, then waited as the two men remained silent. "Should I not know this?"

Walsingham paused, then nodded to himself, as if he had decided he could trust her. "The mark of this paper is to have 'GX' – the two letters that each follow my own initials – then a code number. That number will be a high prime number, to wit, one that can only be divided by one or by itself. That way you will know it is not a copy."

"How can I determine if it is a prime number?" Mary asked.

Walsingham smiled. "You must do some thinking," he said. "Can it be divided by two? Then it is not prime."

"For sure," she answered. "That much I do know."

"Then you try three, four, five and seven. If none of those result in a complete number, then it is prime."

She nodded, "Thank you for the lesson in mathematics."

"But you must keep it safe," said Wychwoode, with a small grin at her irony. "I need hardly add that we would not have it fall in their hands, for all it is so encoded."

"And if it did fall into the enemies' hands, and they were able to understand it?"

Walsingham shrugged, "Then naturally we would deny all knowledge of any part of this conceit."

Despite the warmth of the fire beside her, Mary shivered. "And leave me to carry the blame?" she demanded. "Is my name in this, as the person to execute the plan – even as Anne Carter?"

"Not by name, I assure you," said Walsingham. "Neither

that one nor your true name, naturally. Your identity is not compromised by this, even if it is de-coded."

Wychwoode put his hand on her sleeve. "Lady Mary," he said softly. "We would bring you in safe – you have my word." He gave her a half-smile that seemed to offer reassurance.

But Mary was not convinced, and it felt as if the temperature in the room had fallen even further. "I have now seen your play-acting Robert," she answered. "How can I trust you in this matter?"

"By my word, honestly given," he said. "We have known each other these many years and been through much together." He nodded, as if to convince himself as much as her. "So this is my heart to yours. Trust me in this; if the plan fails, I will shield you from blame."

"You had better," she answered. '*Or believe me,*' she thought, '*I'll have your nuts as well.*'

18

CHAPTER EIGHTEEN

Mary settled into her seat as the carriage started to roll forward on the journey north.

As Rolleston sat opposite, she gave him her hardest stare, intended to show just how much she disliked being forced to endure his company.

A few minutes before, they had been taken to the carriage as it stood at the end of Seething Lane, with two horses in the traces and a grizzled-looking man sitting on the open seat at the front holding on to the reins.

The carriage itself seemed well-made; essentially a sturdy wooden box that reminded Mary of a section of a London Tube train with an over-sized curved roof. There was a small door in the middle of each side, with glassless windows all round and thick velvet curtains to provide warmth and shelter from the wind. Inside, there were two bench seats covered with stuffed leather – one facing forward and the other backward, with leather straps beside each one to hang on to when things got bumpy.

Rolleston gave Mary back an expression that was somewhere between a frown and a sneer. "What ails, Mistress Carter? Art sickening for something?"

"In a manner," she answered, grabbing at one of the leather straps as the carriage bumped across the cobbles. "At the thought of sharing this journey with you."

He shrugged. "It pleases me neither, I can assure you." He looked away from her and appeared to study intently the London houses passing by the window.

Mary glanced down at his right hand as it rested on his knee. There was still heavy bruising and scabbed skin on his knuckles. She watched in fascination as he flexed his fingers a few times, which suggested that nothing was broken, despite the force of the punch on the wall of the Alchemist's room.

"By Heavens, what were you thinking?" she asked, pointing at his hand.

He glanced down at it, then resumed his study of the passing houses. "I was much angered," he said, in a tone which suggested the matter was closed.

But Mary was not about to let it drop. If they were going to spend many days in each other's company, then she supposed she ought to know more about this man; about what made him tick.

"Strange to turn the anger on yourself," she observed.

There was such a long silence that she thought he had not heard. She was about to repeat herself, when he said, "That Alchemist nearly unmanned me."

Mary raised an eyebrow. "You flatter yourself, sir," she said drily. "The shot was at the level of your knees."

"Belike," he answered, "but as I say, I was much angered."

"But strange as a result," she persisted, "to cause pain to your own hand."

"Nay," he said, turning back to her, "I felt no pain."

"No pain?" she asked. "How so?"

He shrugged. "I do not experience it at all, as others do."

"Seriously?" Mary gasped. "How so?" she repeated.

"I know not. It is some affliction chosen for me by God, that I do not have this feeling."

"Affliction?" Mary asked, conscious her voice had risen to a squeak. "Surely it is a blessing? I would love not to feel pain."

To be spared the agony of Tudor childbirth not once or twice, but three times – now that would have been a blessing…

"Nay, mistress," he said, the corner of his mouth turned up in a sneer, "I assure you it is an affliction. I can tell tales of grievous wounds received in daily life, that would, in normally disposed people, not have occurred." He paused. "Such as severe burns, known only by a smell of cooked meat… or of cuts received in play combat with swords, known only when my blood splashed across my opponent's arm…"

"I see," she said. "But there must be some benefits?"

"I can see very few." He paused, "Except, perhaps, when I was under threat of torture in that infernal Tower."

"True." Mary thought a moment. "But then, you were not tortured," she observed. "Wychwoode had you released to work as an intelligencer before such a thing occurred. To accompany me on this journey."

"Aye." He turned back to the window, then added out of the side of his mouth, "Which I can assure you is pain enough."

There was a long silence after that. The carriage trundled through the cobbled streets with Mary and Rolleston each staring out of opposite windows at the passing houses and yards.

A blacksmith's forge shone briefly in a gap between two buildings, and Mary saw the smith working a piece of glowing metal with his hammer. She craned her neck round to see more, before the second building closed off her view. How remarkable it was, that just a few weeks ago such a sight would have been of passing interest only – no more than a historical curiosity – yet now she regarded the blacksmith's work with an almost professional eye. How had he cast and cooled the piece? What tools would he be using to finish and polish it? What pride would he take in the final object?

"If this mission fails, and you still live, then you could earn a few pennies as a smith," Rolleston said, giving her an amused look as she sat back in her seat. "Or maybe an armourer's assistant." He gave a dry chuckle. "For if it does fail, then for sure you will no longer have any manner of life – if you even have one at all."

"I have assurances that I will not be blamed if it fails," Mary answered.

"Then you are more of a naive fool than I took you for," he observed. "If you are caught before you have successfully used the weapon you have fashioned – whatever that purpose may be – or discovered after, then you will be blamed for the failure of the operation, and Walsingham for its conception."

"And you also, if you fail in your duties."

He shrugged. "Perhaps. My duty is to get you safely to your destination and back, and I have given my oath upon it. After that, you are on your own. So the failure will be yours and yours alone."

Mary leaned forward and looked him hard in the eye. "Then I suggest we stop this talk of failure and talk instead of success." She paused a moment. "And as you are here, charged with ensuring my safety, I would have you assure me that you have plans for the success of this journey." She glanced away, then back at him. "What if we are attacked by brigands or cut-purses?"

He patted the sword at his belt. "Then I will fight to protect you, Anne Carter," he said, making it sound more like a threat than a promise. "And if I take a cut or two in your defence, then be assured I will feel no pain, and will fight on withal, to win your approval."

"I will take what comfort I can from that," she replied. "Though you will understand I shall keep the gun to hand as well, in case it is needed."

"As you wish."

And not just the gun, she thought. There was another form of self-defence that the Alchemist had patiently taught her, in preparation for her mission.

"What if you're tied up, and your attacker is advancing on you with, say, a knife?" the Alchemist had asked casually, when she had visited him briefly a couple of days before to say farewell, and they were sharing an ale alone in his room. "How will you turn the tables on your attacker?"

"Kick him in the crotch?" she had suggested.

"Maybe, but as I said, you're tied up. Say he comes in close, what then?"

"Not sure," she said. "What are you suggesting?"

He smiled slowly. "Come now, Justine, what do you have that is thick and hard and can cause real damage?"

She raised an eyebrow. "As a woman, I'm not sure what you mean..."

"Don't be daft." His smile broadened. "Your head. Have you never heard of a head-butt; the good old 'Gorbals Kiss'?"

"For goodness' sake," she answered, "I'm not going around head-butting..."

"But you're happy to use a sniper gun?" He paused. "You're being sent on what sounds like a very dangerous mission, Justine, from the few snippets I have picked up. You need to have more than one way of protecting yourself. Especially if you don't have a poker to hand."

"That's not fair, Rick."

"I'm serious." He paused again. "I know we were sworn enemies before, but since we've been working on the same side, and you've been doing what I have told you..." He nodded, as if reassuring himself that his instincts were correct, then he continued, "I've sort of understood you better."

"I'm not sure whether I should be surprised or pleased."

"Yeah, well, whatever..." he muttered. "Look," he shuffled forward clutching his tankard of ale, his chain clinking behind him. "If you're attacked, and you're tied up, then you need to know what to do."

"I will have Rolleston with me when we travel north," she said. "He is supposed to be protecting me."

"Rolleston is going with you?" The Alchemist made a

violently dismissive gesture, causing ale to slop across his blanket, although he seemed not to notice. "Fuck me, you'll need protection from him, not by him! Did you not protest?"

"Of course," she answered. "But Wychwoode did not give me the choice. It's a long journey and they wanted to ensure I had a companion."

"Keep a close eye on that one, Justine," he muttered. Then he added, "North, eh? Any idea where?"

"I cannot say, Rick," she replied. "Sorry."

He nodded, as if he had expected her to say that. "Well, as I say, keep your eyes open with that prick Rolleston."

"I will," she answered. "Although I asked to have my true friend Olivia, who fought with me against your co-conspirator, Lambert Moreton. I would trust her a lot further than Rolleston."

"Yeah. Sounds like that Moreton was a right tosser." He considered her a moment. "Anyhow, let's put that all behind us." He smiled. "But this Olivia – she sounds fun."

"She's very brave, and very loyal. And fearless, too."

"Everything Rolleston is not," he said. "In which case you really do need to know how to give a good old head-butt.

Mary nodded slowly. It did make sense to be prepared, although she hoped she would never need to put this into action. "Okay, go on, then. Show me."

He nodded, tapping his forehead just above his eye "Solid bone, here." Then he went to his jaw. "But thin and delicate here. So what happens if a solid and heavy object meets a thinner, more delicate one?"

"The delicate one breaks?"

"Precisely. So if someone comes in close, bring your

forehead hard onto his jaw. It doesn't take much force if you hit it right; just make sure you carry it through."

"How do you mean?" Mary could not believe she was having this totally surreal conversation, but she asked anyway.

"Listen, if you hit a nail with a hammer, it's easy to 'bounce' it, like so." He mimed hitting a blow that flicked back up at the moment of impact. "All the force is gone because you're not committed to the blow. But if you push through instead, the full force is transferred." He mimed again, but this time carried the blow through without the flick. "So don't go in half-hearted, but full-on. Committed."

"Will it hurt?" She asked the obvious question.

He shrugged. "For sure, you'll have a sore forehead for an hour or two. He, on the other hand, will have a broken jaw." He smiled. "Go figure."

"Well, let's hope I don't need to do a 'Gorbals Kiss' as you call it.

"Yeah." He stared hard at her; his eyes narrowed. "But if you do, be committed."

Rolleston's voice cut across her recollection, dragging her back to the present. "You nod to yourself repeatedly, Mistress Carter." She looked up. "Are you suffering an ague?"

"No." She didn't feel any further explanation was either necessary or justified.

"Yet that was the look of it." Rolleston sat back with his arms folded, as if that was the truth of the matter.

She observed him across the carriage. This was the second time she was travelling north alone with a man in less than a year. How different this Rolleston was from Tom Cobham, her companion from last time. Tom, who had been as honourable and as upright as Rolleston was devious and underhand, had actually saved her in her moment of need and never asked for her approval, or anything in return.

"If a fight is necessary, and God willing it shall not be, then I would you fight for my honour alone," she observed, drumming her fingers lightly on the seat beside her. "A few months ago, a man fought for my honour when I was attacked in a tavern," she said. "He asked for naught as a reward," she paused and held his cold blue eye. "And for that I valued him all the more greatly."

"So if I want your approval, I must not ask for it?"

"Something like that."

He sat back and looked out of his window. "Never can I understand the mind of a woman," he muttered.

Mary let this pass. Instead she said, "And when we arrive, I would you leave me to carry my part of the plan through." Then she also sat back and looked out of the window at the green fields and spinneys that were now rolling past. "I suggest you remain in whatever lodging we have while I undertake the mission, then you can escort me safely back to London."

"As you wish," he said. Then he asked, "And what is our destination? I feel I should know this if I am to protect you on the journey."

Mary thought a moment, then decided to give him one small nugget of information – one that he would be finding out soon enough anyway. "I will tell you this, sir, and no more. We are proceeding to Sheffield, in the county of Yorkshire.

"And what exactly is this mission in Sheffield? You are most secretive."

"And will remain so, Master Rolleston, I can assure you." Mary shook her head. "Believe me, I will not be sharing any further secrets with you."

19

CHAPTER NINETEEN

The evening moon was casting long shadows through the skeletal winter trees as the driver pulled the horses to a stop in the courtyard of a roadside inn. Mary felt the carriage rock as he jumped down from his seat.

The driver's grizzled face appeared at the window. "We stop here for the night," he said in a gravelly voice that sounded like pebbles being shaken in a bag.

"Thank Heaven," muttered Rolleston, "It has been a long journey thus far. I must make haste for the jakes." He leapt out of the carriage and started to run over to the inn.

Mary stepped down more sedately, then retrieved her bag from under her seat and made her way into the building.

As she entered, a large woman with a red face under a stained coif approached her.

"A room for the night, mistress?" the woman asked.

Mary nodded as she put her bag down and stared around the inn.

Like most of those she had stopped in since she had first left the comfort of Grangedean Manor all those months ago, it was a simple, open room with many oak tables and benches, each with a yellow tallow candle. Stairs led off one side of the room, presumably up to the bedrooms. She had stayed in so many such establishments that it was hard to distinguish one from another, but there was something vaguely familiar about this one, and its landlady. Perhaps she had stayed here before? Most probably, when she had previously travelled up to York with Tom Cobham on their mission to prevent the Alchemist in his attempt to assassinate Queen Elizabeth.

Mary gave an involuntary shiver. How different to be staying here again, but this time with a boorish oaf like Rolleston and not with a true gentleman like Tom Cobham.

Then she chuckled under her breath. Tom was indeed such a gentleman, that he had even managed to maintain control when they had inadvertently found themselves naked together after washing in a stream. So when she had ordered him to step away, he had done so – for all it was perfectly clear that it was not what his heart – or indeed his body – had desired.

How different would her life have been if she had submitted to the passion that she had also felt, and had allowed nature to take its course that spring day? Maybe their mission would have taken second place to their feelings for each other, and their purpose for travelling to York would have been lost? And then what? Poor Tom would still be alive today, and her marriage would have been put in desperate jeopardy – and in truth, she could never have done anything to hurt William. Not to mention that the Alchemist would most likely have succeeded in assassinating the Queen, so that English history would have changed forever under the Catholic rule of Mary, Queen of Scots.

But was she, Lady Mary de Beauvais, now deliberately setting out to change history?

It may be that ultimately her mission was to prevent Catholic plots and the Armada by assassinating the Queen of Scots, but either way the future would still be very different. The comforting world of 2015 that only she and the Alchemist remembered would surely disappear into the mist. It would be replaced by some unknown future that was yet to be written; yet to be reshaped by a million new events.

Mary gave a small sigh.

Had she not already started the process by saving William when he was destined to die, then by having three children who were never meant to exist? So what would it matter now if she caused even more changes?

And what of her original fear that if she changed history too much, she would cause her own birth not to happen and she would suddenly disappear? But the Alchemist had convinced her that nothing she could do on this timeline would endanger her birth in a previous one. She had been born in the old 1988, and that was a fact that could not be altered, whatever the new 1988 looked like.

"I have but one room remaining," the landlady was saying, dragging Mary's attention back to the present, as Rolleston joined them, adjusting his trunk-hose. The landlady continued, "It is my best room, well suited to quality travellers such as you and your fine husband here."

"Oh no, we..." Mary began, but Rolleston interrupted her.

"My wife and I appreciate your kindness. I am sure it will be ideal." Mary shot him a look of pure venom, but he continued, "We will have a brief rest before we take our supper, as it has been such a long journey." He smiled at the landlady. "I am sure my dear wife is in need of some stillness after the rigours of the road. Are you not, Anne, my love?"

Mary returned a sickly smile, keeping her anger inside, saving it for later.

---o---

"How dare you!" she snarled when they were alone in the room. "How dare you presume to call us husband and wife?"

"And have questions asked as to why we are not married, yet travel together?" he demanded.

"I do not give a fig for any questions being asked!" she shot back, "I would rather answer questions than have folk think I am married to one such as you!"

"Which would naturally lead to further questions, covering perhaps the nature of our journey, and thence to your secret mission itself." He stood before her with his hands on his hips and his shoulders back. "I would have thought, Mistress Anne Carter," he snapped, "that you of all people would understand the risks involved and the need to avoid suspicion." He paused a moment, then added, "or to prompt folk to recall us later, if asked."

"Whatever!" she muttered, annoyed at the thought he might actually be right. "Anyway," she said, pointing at the floor, "that is where you sleep, as you certainly will not be sharing the bed with me."

He shrugged. "For sure, that is no problem." He gave her a sickly smile. "To sleep on the floor is not a hardship to one who feels no pain."

Mary flounced over to the bed and flopped down on her back. "I do need some rest after the journey," she said, before turning to her side and trying to plump the thin pillow, then giving up and resuming her previous position. "So you can close the door on your way out."

20

CHAPTER TWENTY

A pale beam of autumn sunlight shone down through the thin curtains, warming Mary's cheek and jolting her awake. She gave a small groan and opened her eyes, staring at the rough plaster wall opposite. For a moment she had no idea where she was – searching for the familiar table and chair that usually greeted her each morning while she had been staying at Francis Walsingham's house in Seething Lane. Then she remembered the previous day's travelling with Rolleston; their arrival at the inn and his dreadful assertion that they were married.

She sat up with another groan, and was surprised to note that she was still fully clothed. She recalled she had lain down to rest before supper and had dismissed her would-be husband; she must have slept the whole night in her clothes and missed supper completely. A loud rumble from the region under her stomacher confirmed this. She glanced out of the window. From the height of the sun, she reckoned it was probably around 9am.

She got up, expecting to see Rolleston asleep on the floor as instructed, but there was no sign of him. Thinking that he had already gone down for breakfast, Mary fished in her bag for her hand mirror, pins and comb, then spent a few minutes trying to get her hair into some semblance of order. Her stomach gave another loud gurgle as she glanced in her bag at her travelling pots of make-up. She paused, before closing the bag. Breakfast was the priority, and if Rolleston and her fellow travellers found her natural look too scary, that was their problem not hers.

She took herself down to the tavern and sat at an empty table, looking around the room for Rolleston. There was no sign of him, so when a pretty young girl appeared with plates for another table, Mary beckoned her over.

"My husband..." she began, then forced a smile to cover her distaste at saying those words, "said he would, er... step out a while. Has he returned?"

"Your husband, mistress?"

"A tall man with a dark beard, wearing the garb of a merchant."

The girl's eyes widened briefly, then she said quickly, "Nay mistress, I have not seen such a man." She looked down and muttered, "Meantimes, will you have some bread and cheese to break your fast?"

Mary nodded, and the girl hurried away to serve other guests. Mary again glanced round the room, in case anyone was in some way suspicious and should be noted.

Had Walsingham sent any of his intelligencers to keep an eye on her and Rolleston?

How about the elderly couple in the corner? The old man was squinting in a short-sighted way and the woman had a lazy eye. They didn't look capable of observing anyone.

Then there were the two yeomen whose table the girl was now clearing. They were so absorbed in their own conversation that it was hard to think they were spying on anyone.

Mary felt a hand on her shoulder and looked up, to see Rolleston standing beside her.

"Good morrow, wife," he said, with a cold smile. "I trust you have slept well this night?"

"Do not use that word unless we are in company," she snapped.

He raised an eyebrow and glanced at the room. "I see others around."

"You know what I mean."

"Belike." He paused. "So, wife, I asked a question, and I would have an answer."

"Oh, you would, would you?" she said. "Well, as we are in company..." she paused to give him her coldest stare, "I did, as it happens," she replied, "I must have been very tired, as I slept through supper."

"So I noticed," he said as he sat down opposite. "I thought best not to waken you, so I dined alone."

"I am not sure to be pleased you let me sleep, or annoyed to have missed supper," she said.

"Please yourself," he said with a small smile, as if amused at his little play on her words.

"And where were you last night?" Mary asked, annoyed for wanting to know but curious, nonetheless.

"Were you my wife in truth, Anne," he said with a shrug, "then I would vouchsafe an answer to that question. But, as you so readily point out, you are not." He paused, "So my answer is that it is no business of yours."

Before Mary could think of a suitable retort, the serving girl came over with a plate of bread and cheese, and a tankard of ale. As she glanced at Rolleston, a brief, but deeply guilty look flashed across her face, then she quickly looked away.

"So, mistress, you have found your..." she bit her lip, "your husband?"

"Yes," answered Mary, forcing a cold smile. "I have."

The girl put the food and drink down and muttered, "Something for you, master?"

"Aye, some bread and cheese also, and ale," he replied with an easy smile.

Mary watched as the girl scurried away. Once she was out of earshot, Mary said, "So I think my question is answered, is it not? Now I think I know where you spent the night."

He reached across and broke off some bread from her plate. "Aye," he said as he put it in his mouth, "she is most comely." Then he added, "And most willing in bed."

Mary pulled her plate closer, and said drily, "She would need to be."

21

CHAPTER
TWENTY-ONE

Olivia Melrose stood outside the doors to the Great Hall at Grangedean Manor, fingering her gold necklace as she waited to be admitted.

The servant beside her gave her a curt nod, then pushed them open and strode through. She saw him stop, cough loudly and wait for silence. Once the chatter had died down, he announced, "Mistress Olivia Melrose, Sir William." He stood back and gestured Olivia forward.

She took a deep breath and walked in, conscious that the family at the high table was watching her closely. She had dressed to befit her new status; deciding on a cream silk gown edged with gold thread to set off her pale face and rouged lips, while her dark hair was combed back to give her a fashionably high forehead. She had finished it off with a delicate gold tiara and matching pendant earrings. Hopefully she had judged the look right – grand, but not too grand. Not overwhelming. A look that would have made Lady Mary proud.

As she walked up to the high table, she could not help but notice how different the hall looked in comparison to the home-coming celebration of two months earlier, when she and Lady Mary had made just such an entrance. Then there had been hundreds of bright candles making the room sparkle like a magnificent diamond; now there were only a few flickering stubs in sconces on the walls and a couple on the high table. It made the room seem so much darker, and so much smaller. Maybe God wanted her to realise the difference with last time she had been here, as that was the day that Lady Mary had been arrested and they had both been taken to the Tower.

She looked at the high table, which was the only one occupied – another change from the last time, when there had been long tables filling both sides of the room, crammed with noisy nobility and joyfully drunken friends. Sir William was seated in the centre with Ambrose on his right, then an older lady in a simple brown dress. Kat was on his left, with an elegant woman in her thirties beside her. Beyond her was little Jane, Mary's third child, who was the only one more concerned with her food than with Olivia's approach. Olivia recognised the older lady as the housekeeper Ruth, and the elegant woman as her daughter, Sarah – Lady Mary's lady in waiting.

There was an uncomfortable silence as she walked up to the table, then dropped into a deep curtsey before Sir William.

"Pray be upstanding, Mistress Melrose," he said, "You are

most welcome here." As she stood, she could see how badly he had aged. His bright, twinkling eyes had sunk into his face like pebbles into the bed of a dried-out stream, and his once smooth, clear skin now looked paper thin and lined. Even his beard, previously sandy throughout, was now peppered with grey.

She glanced at Ambrose. She thought he looked older than his nine years, as if the worry caused by his mother's arrest had forced him to miss out on so many precious years of his childhood. It was easy to see how like his father he was becoming; the same eyes, mouth and chin. In a few years he would be the very image of Sir William.

"I came as soon as I could," she said, "Once the Queen gave me leave from her service to attend on you here at Grangedean."

"Aye," he said, giving her a wintery smile, "I had heard from your father that you had been elevated to Her Majesty's service." He glanced down at Kat, who was hanging on to his arm, and added, "We are honoured that one of the Queen's maids of honour has graced us."

Kat gave her a weak smile. Like Ambrose, she looked older than her years. There were frown lines on her pretty little face that had no right to be there.

"Livia, I pray you come and sit beside me," she said, her little girl's voice sounding strangely at odds with the adult tone of her words. "I would you tell me all." How different from last time, when she had thrown herself into Olivia's arms, shrieking like a mischievous little imp, to be flung round in a circle.

Sir William nodded his approval, so Olivia made her way

round the table. A manservant pushed a chair between Kat and Sarah. Once she was seated, the man placed a pewter plate, a napkin and goblet before her, and filled it with wine. Olivia took a sip, then said, "What shall I tell, little Kat?" Although it was clear to her what they would all want to discuss.

"I would know about my mother," Kat replied, staring up with big eyes and biting her lip.

"We are sickened with worry," added Sarah.

"Is Ma still held in the Tower on false charges?" Ambrose asked from the other side of Sir William. "We would visit her there if we could, but Pa says they will not let us."

"We know not as to whether she has been tried, or if she is condemned and executed already," explained Sir William. "They will not tell us anything." He shook his head. "It is wholly unnatural that her family are left knowing naught on such a matter. Every petition I make for information is met with silence and obfuscation. I cannot get a straight answer from any man; not Walsingham or Wychwoode, nor any other I have asked since I spoke with those two directly. I am continually turned away and left powerless in this matter."

"Please, Livia," said Kat, looking up at her hopefully, "what has become of her?"

Olivia put her hand over Kat's and gazed into the little girl's troubled eyes. "I am so sorry, but it is God's truth that I know no more than you. My own questions on Lady Mary's fate have been met with the same wall of silence as have yours."

No one said anything for a moment. Kat gave a small sob, and Sir William shook his head slowly.

"Please forgive us, Mistress Melrose," Sarah said, leaning across and dabbing away the tears that had welled up in Kat's eyes, "but when you sent word you were coming here, we took it that you would be bringing some news of Lady Mary."

"Even bad news would at least let us know what has become of her," added Ruth.

Olivia looked at each of them in turn. "As Christ is my witness, I wish beyond all measure that I could tell you something of value," she said, "but the dreadful truth is that I hoped maybe *you* had news for *me* – that is why I came here."

It was not only that; she had also originally planned to pass on to each member of the family the personal messages that Lady Mary had given her that night on the boat. But now she was sitting beside them and seeing their distress – and with the smallest possibility that Lady Mary was still alive – she knew it was not the time. Those messages would have to wait.

She became aware of a distressed sniff from beside her. Kat said, "Each day you see the Queen – can you not ask her to tell us about Ma?"

"I am so sorry, my little puss, but that is not the thing you ask of Her Majesty." Olivia thought a moment. "I have so recently been elevated to this royal position; I cannot have the Queen think poorly of me for asking too many questions..."

"But Livia..." Kat began, when Sir William raised a hand for silence.

"Mistress Melrose has most clearly set out her situation," he stated. "We cannot demand more of her than she is able to give. The truth of this matter is..." he looked at each of them in turn, "...the truth of this matter, is that none of us here knows what has become of Mary, my wife and your dear lady mother. So we must wait until such times as we are told, and cleave to the thought that no news of her trial or execution means that we can live with the hope that neither has yet happened." He nodded, as if to reassure himself as much as them. "Yes, we will have to wait. Now," he said with a weak smile, "Mistress Melrose is here as our valued guest, and we must give her our warmest welcome and finest hospitality." He pulled himself to his feet and raised his goblet. "I would we raise our glasses to the health of Mistress Melrose, and to the hope that God sends us back our beloved Mary soon."

Everyone stood and raised their glasses except little Jane, until Sarah leaned down and pulled the child to her feet.

"To Mistress Melrose for her welcome presence here this eve," said Sir William, "and to Lady Mary – may God end these false charges against her, and send her safely home to her family."

"Amen," they replied in unison.

---o---

After the meal had finished and Sarah had taken the children up to bed, Sir William and Olivia retired to the solar, settling themselves before the fire.

"Will you stay with us at least a day or two?" he asked, swirling the wine around in his glass.

"That is most kind, Sir William," she replied. "Her Majesty has instructed me to return to the Palace of Whitehall in two days, so I would be delighted."

"Good. Then that is settled." He regarded her thoughtfully.

"I must tell you, it gladdens my heart that you attend us here, as it makes me feel just a little closer to Mary."

She inclined her head with a smile. "As do I also, with you."

"Then we are well matched in this," he observed. "Now pray tell, I must know how it was that you were elevated to Her Majesty's service?"

Olivia took a sip of wine. "It was the strangest occurrence," she began. "I was but a few days after I was fortunately taken back into the service of my lady Burnham, when I was summoned to Court at Whitehall. I was concerned that I was about to be thrown into the Tower myself – belike for my association with Lady Mary – so I said a fond and tearful farewell to my dearest companion Maggie Tyndall, before I boarded the barge. When I got there, I was taken to a chamber where the Queen herself was seated, with no others but Master Secretary Walsingham and Master Wychwoode. Then I was truly afraid, as the last time I had been in the presence of these men, it was when Lady Mary had called Master Walsingham a fool..."

"She did *what*?" Sir William nearly choked on his wine.

Olivia smiled. "She had observed that as a person coming from future times, she had knowledge that would benefit the Queen, and that Master Walsingham should heed this remarkable intelligence before wantonly casting her into the flames."

He nodded briefly. "That is indeed good logic, and just as I would expect from Mary." He paused and frowned as he stared into the fire. "You know, Olivia," he said, "as I said to your father at the time, it troubled me greatly when I learned about her history. I felt most uneasy when I heard that she was born in another time, and angered that she had not trusted me to tell me herself. But," he continued, "I gave it much thought, and I came to see that it did not change the Mary I knew and loved. It did not make her a different person to the girl I married. And indeed, it did make sense of her strange and sudden appearance and her most awkward behaviour when we first met." His intense look as he said this sent a shiver up Olivia's spine. "It made me realise what a truly remarkable woman she is, and how lucky I am to be the man she loves."

"And I too," Olivia replied, finding herself strangely compelled to match his feelings with her own. "She helped me to see how a woman is the equal of a man in many things, and once I knew that she had sight of a future where that becomes so, then it was real for me too." She gave a small chuckle. "Which was in truth, the reason I was commanded to enter the Queen's service."

He raised an eyebrow. "How so?"

"Well, when I was in the Queen's presence, she asked me to tell her how I found Lady Mary's character, and particularly how I believed Lady Mary would act when put under pressure."

"Under pressure?" he asked.

"Indeed, that was Her Majesty's question," Olivia replied. "So I told her God's truth, which is that my lady would always do what is right, however hard it might be, and however much danger it might put her into. Then Master Secretary Walsingham observed that as a woman, she could not be so relied upon. I recalled how my lady would have reacted to such a statement, so I told him to his face that he was mistaken and that my lady had the courage of twenty men. I told him that if I was in peril, there is not another person on God's earth that I would rather have come to my aid." She chuckled again. "I was most forceful, and I swear he physically stepped backwards when I spoke my piece."

"I see. And how did the Queen act on this revelation?"

"For sure, I warrant that she looked on it most favourably. She smiled at me and asked if I missed my lady. I said I was greatly upset when we were parted, and I miss her most dreadfully."

"As do I," he muttered.

"Then the Queen said something I did not quite understand." Olivia twisted her glass as she stared into the fire. "She said that I spoke with the honesty of Lady Mary – and that while my lady was otherwise disposed, she would keep me close by her from this moment on, as my lady's proxy. As one who could give her the same council." She turned to Sir William. "What might she have meant by that?"

He was silent, as he appeared to think this through. Then he said, "Otherwise disposed? That is most singular." He shook his head slowly. "Might it mean simply that she is in the Tower?"

"I thought maybe so. But if the Queen wants her council, she has only to have her brought to court and to ask it. Whether a prisoner or no."

"I agree," he said slowly. "And it would not have been said if she was tried and executed." He gave a small shudder. "So belike she is no longer in the Tower, is still living, but is now elsewhere – somewhere that is secret, as no man will tell either of us where she is or what she is doing."

"I had not thought it," Olivia answered slowly. "But as you put it so, I can see that this could be the case."

He was silent a long while after; the flickering flames reflecting in the sides of his eyes as he stared ahead. Eventually he gave a deep sigh and turned to Olivia.

"I warrant that Mary is out of the Tower, alive – God be praised – and is even now undertaking some clandestine enterprise for the Queen. Her Majesty wanted to know if Mary has the courage to act under pressure – and that suggests a dangerous mission, no doubt dreamed up by that arch-schemer Walsingham."

He got out of his chair and did something Olivia would never have expected. He knelt down in front of her and clasped her hands in his. "My dearest Olivia," he said quietly. "I beg you; I plead with you on my bended knee, to use your new-found position at court to find out what my wife is up to. I warrant that if she is in the gravest danger, then we must do all we can to get her back safely."

22

CHAPTER TWENTY-TWO

If the atmosphere in the carriage had been cold on the journey so far, it was positively frigid after Rolleston's behaviour with the serving girl at the inn. Very little conversation now passed between them, other than was necessary regarding stops for food and sleep, and most of the journey over the next few days was spent staring out of opposite carriage windows at the passing forests and hamlets. Meals at each tavern were taken in an uncomfortable silence; nights were most definitely spent in separate rooms – for Mary had insisted she had no stomach for the conceit that they were married, whether or not others had concerns.

And if Mary had her suspicions about Rolleston continuing his nocturnal activities, she kept them to herself.

So when the carriage rolled slowly to a standstill in the

middle of a forest clearing late one afternoon, it was a few moments before Mary felt the need to break the silence.

"Why have we stopped, I wonder?"

"Belike one of the horses is lame, or cast a shoe," muttered Rolleston, pulling back the curtain and peering out of the window. "Or a stag has blocked our path." He sat back. "I have no doubt we will be on our way again in short order."

Just then there was a whooshing sound, that ended in a sickening thud and a grunt from the front of the carriage. Mary immediately looked out of her window, just in time to see the driver topple slowly from his seat and fall to the ground, an arrow shaft standing proud from his chest.

"By Heavens!" she exclaimed. Her hand went to the door handle.

Rolleston jumped up and pulled hard on her sleeve. "You will stay here," he ordered.

"But the driver is wounded. I must go to him."

"Do not be a fool," he said, glancing out of the window at the body of the driver. "There is naught you can do for him." He drew his sword and opened the door. "You will leave this to me. If there is an archer out there shooting at us, it is best you remain in the carriage."

"Then you have a care," Mary snapped. "Your safety is mine as well,"

He glanced back briefly. "I gave my vow to protect you," he said as he jumped down, then looked back through the window, "and that I will."

His face disappeared, just as an arrow smacked into the side of the carriage, close to where his head had been.

Mary gave a small cry.

There could only be one reason for this ambush – they were going to be robbed!

Another arrow appeared with a whoosh and embedded itself close to the first. She slid down onto her knees.

And then, once the brigands had helped themselves to her possessions and money...

She curled into a small ball on the floor of the carriage.

...No doubt they would have her as well...

She heard Rolleston's sword swishing through the air. "Come out, devil take you!" he yelled. "Show yourself!"

As if that was going to help! The man was going to be shot out there...

Mary turned her head and caught sight of her bag under the seat. "Oh, sod this," she muttered to herself, "I can't just stay here – I have to do something." She pulled the bag out and quickly assembled the gun while staying low on the floor. Fitting a cartridge into the breech, she lifted her hand carefully to the door handle on the side of the carriage away from the arrows and slowly pulled it down.

She emerged at speed, crouching as she ran into the forest, her breath rasping in her throat as she reached the shelter of a large oak.

Trying to ignore the pounding in her chest, she peered back towards the path. Rolleston was standing out in the open with his feet planted squarely and his sword tip raised, looking left and right for the hidden archer.

"Take cover, you fool!" Mary hissed. "You will be shot any second!"

As if to make her point, another arrow swooshed past Rolleston's head and embedded itself in a tree a few yards further back. He turned in the direction it had come, but Mary had already spotted the archer's movement by an oak some twenty yards further up the path. She raised the gun to her shoulder and focused the scope. For a moment she saw nothing but the deeply pitted silver green bark, but as she swung the gun slightly to the right, a shoulder came into view. She followed it down to a hand holding a bow.

"By Heavens, woman, get back in the carriage this moment!"

Ignoring Rolleston's shout, she forced a few more deep, steadying breaths, then raised the gun until it was again pointing at the shoulder. Almost immediately, a sandy-haired man with a face reddened by broken veins stepped round the tree, fitting an arrow to the bow. He started to draw it back.

Mary's finger tightened on the trigger.

Shoot to kill?

Or shoot to wound?

The man had almost drawn the bow string to its full length. She could see the wicked-looking barbed arrow-head quivering under his forefinger.

Mary raised the gun until the man's head was in view, his frowning brow lined up in the crosshairs and one eye closed as he sighted the arrow.

Her finger tightened further.

Then she swung the gun fractionally down and to the right. She shot him in the hand.

The crack of the shot echoed out across the forest, followed by an agonised yell from the archer. The arrow flew high, landing harmlessly behind Rolleston.

Mary lowered the gun. She was about to walk over and

check the archer, when her wrists were suddenly grabbed hard from behind and forced up her back. The gun clattered to the forest floor beside her.

"God's blood, woman!" a strange man's voice hissed in her ear, "you will regret that shot."

"Let me go!" Mary pulled against the unknown assailant's grip, but he was too strong. "Do you know who I am?"

There was a slight pause, then the voice said, "Nay, and by the Lord, I care not."

"What do you want with me?" she said, trying to sound strong.

"I will take from you what I will. What I can carry..." there was another short pause, then the voice added in a whisper, "and what I cannot."

"There is a man with me," Mary said. "He will stop you."

"Aye, there *was* a man," the voice said with the sound of a smile, "but he has disappeared." The rough scratching of a beard rasped across her ear, and she thought she would retch. "I warrant he has seen sense and left you to our mercies." Mary flicked her eyes across to where Rolleston had been standing.

The clearing was empty.

"He would not do that," she asserted.

'I gave my vow to protect you!' he had said. Was that an empty promise?

Of course it was.

The man pushed Mary towards a small tree, then spun her round and pulled her back against the rough bark. She felt some rope being passed around her wrists, and tried not to flinch or make a sound as it was tightened to the point of cutting into her skin. After a moment the man stepped out in front of her.

Her attacker was dark haired, with some grey at his temples and much more in his beard. He was of medium height; dressed in a dirty old wool jerkin and brown breeches.

He drew a sword and placed the tip on her breastbone. "You will stay here while I see what you have done to my companion," he said. Then, with his cold blue eyes holding hers, he traced the sword down her chest to the top of her bodice, so lightly that it did not cut into her skin, before moving it down her stomacher until it was resting on the top of her skirts, pointing at her lower belly. "Then I will return to deal with you." His eyes held hers a moment more, then he pushed the sword tip a couple of inches into the soft material, "Do you understand me well, woman?"

All Mary could do was nod slightly.

"Good." The man sheathed his sword. "Good." He strode away across the clearing, to where the archer was kneeling beside the tree, his bloodied left hand held close to his body.

Mary let out her breath and looked down. The gun was still there in the undergrowth. It was amazing that the man hadn't picked it up. It didn't bear thinking as to what he might do if he decided to examine it more closely.

She tried to hook her toe under the barrel, but her foot would not quite get that far, and all she ended up doing was waggling it uselessly in the air above the gun. Ignoring the pain in her wrists, she inched herself round the tree so she could extend a bit further, but it was not enough.

Muttering curses under her breath, she leant forward to

ease the pressure on her hands, then slid down the tree so she could extend her leg out further, like a crouched Russian dancer. With a small triumphant 'yes!' under her breath, she managed to hook her heel over the gun's breech.

She quickly glanced over at the archer. He was still by the tree, while his companion had his back to her and appeared to be winding some cloth around the man's bloodied hand.

With a small smile of satisfaction that the man's sniping days were probably now over, Mary slowly stood up, inching her hands up the tree to give herself leverage. Once she was fully upright, she pulled the gun again with her heel, until she had it fully hidden under her skirts.

It was not a moment too soon, as the attacker reappeared in front of her, his sword out once again.

"By Heavens, woman, you have done great damage to Nathan's hand." He shook his head. "The ball has passed clean through from one side to the other."

"Good," Mary answered, lifting her head and looking down her nose. "It was his own fault for loosing arrows at us. I warrant he has killed our driver, and would have killed my companion and myself as well, if I had not stopped him."

"You are in no position to argue this matter," the man answered. "Meantime, I will help myself to the contents of your carriage." He gave a cold smile. "A fine lady such as you will have jewels and gowns that will fetch a fair price to compensate for my companion's wound." He glanced back at where the carriage stood, with the driver's boots still visible on the forest floor beyond. "Or I warrant we will simply take the carriage for ourselves, with all contents included."

Mary stared at the man in silent disgust.

"Nay churl, you will do no such thing!" came a loud voice, as Rolleston stepped out from behind a tree with his own sword raised. "Begone, sirrah," he barked, "or I will do to your chest what my lady here has done to that fellow's hand!"

"Fie!" the attacker snarled, turning to face the merchant, "I will deal with you first if I must." He glanced back at Mary. "Then I will continue to attend to your lady."

Rolleston did not answer, but instead took guard, his sword raised and ready.

The man responded with his own guard, and they circled warily for a few moments, as if neither wanted to commit to the first move. The man had a look of fierce concentration, while Rolleston now had a small smile, as if this had all become a bit of a game.

"Come, Greybeard," he called eventually, "make your play, or shall I win by just tiring you out?"

"Nay, fellow," the man replied, "I shall not make it so easy." Then he made a sudden lunge at Rolleston's head that caused Mary to gasp.

Fortunately Rolleston only had to lean away slightly, so that the other's blade passed harmlessly by, then Rolleston made a sudden lunge of his own. Greybeard parried with ease, knocking Rolleston's slimmer blade away. With that, the fight began in earnest.

Mary found herself biting her lip as the two swords clashed at lighting speed; each man turning the other's blade, not only to avoid a thrust that looked potentially mortal, but also to force his opponent to leave his side or his chest exposed.

Each time Rolleston looked in danger her jaw tensed, and at one particularly late parry, she bit her lip hard enough to taste blood.

As the fight moved around the clearing, Mary could see that it was too evenly matched for a quick victory by either man. Maybe it would be as Rolleston had joked initially – the winner would be the one who could simply tire the other out.

But both men seemed to have enough energy for now, keeping the fight going with successive thrusts, parries, blocks and cuts, so that Mary could only watch and hope that Rolleston would prevail.

Eventually she sensed that both were beginning to lose energy. Their swords no longer flashed at high speed and their shoulders were starting to drop.

"Have a care, Rolleston!" she called, as he made a small stumble, but thankfully recovered, before finding some new vitality and driving Greybeard backwards towards a tree. As Greybeard came up against it, she could see an angry frown forming in place of his look of concentration, and he made a sudden lunge that caught Rolleston on the thigh, just below his trunk-hose.

Mary gasped and called out "Rolleston! Your leg!"

Rolleston looked down, then gave a surprised grunt and clasped his free hand to his thigh. The grey material of his hose began to turn red under his fingers.

Greybeard seemed to see his opportunity and lunged forward, flicking his wrist so the blade flew from Rolleston's hand and dropped to the ground. With a snarl of triumph, Greybeard took a further step, his own blade now pointing at Rolleston's chest.

"On your knees, fellow!" he commanded. "Let us finish this."

Mary stared in horror as Rolleston dropped down and Greybeard held up his sword to strike.

Rolleston was going to die – and she was next!

"No!" she screamed; a guttural, primeval drawn-out cry that distracted Greybeard as he moved to strike. This gave Rolleston his opportunity. He grabbed Greybeard's ankle and pulled the man off balance. Greybeard stumbled back a few steps until he hit the tree. As he did so, Rolleston quickly stood, retrieved his sword, then stepped forward and used it to flick the blade from Greybeard's hand.

Unarmed and with his back to the tree, Greybeard was at Rolleston's mercy. He stared down at the blade that was now pressing into the coarse wool of his jerkin, the whites of his eyes showing.

"Do you go to it, fellow?" he said, his voice high and hoarse. "Are you going to finish me now? For naught but an attempted robbery?"

"Yes," answered Rolleston, "I am. Like I would any brigand attempting to rob lawful folk."

Mary screwed her eyes shut, not wanting to witness the sword being driven into the man's chest, wishing she could also bring her hands to her ears to block out the gruesome sound of his death groan.

In the event there was only a gasp, a cough, then the sound of a body sliding down the tree and a thump as it hit the ground.

She cautiously opened her eyes.

Rolleston was standing over the body, his sword covered

in blood. Greybeard was lying face down, with a small red stain growing on his back like an opening flower.

Rolleston wiped his sword on the body's jerkin, then looked over at Mary.

"The archer has run off," he said. "And I suggest we do the same. If the bodies of this man and our driver are discovered, we do not want the hue and cry after us."

"Indeed," she said. "But you had better untie me first."

---o---

It was a while later and they were in a room at a traveller's inn at Stanford, some miles from the scene of the ambush.

Rolleston bent down and peeled back the edges of his hose around the wound. With a look of curiosity, he pressed his fingers either side.

"Let me see it," Mary said quietly. "I may be able to help."

"'Tis not deep, and will soon heal, methinks."

"It needs binding. You do not want it to fester." She paused. "You will not be alerted by the pain if it does."

"Aye. Belike."

"Give me your knife."

He raised an eyebrow. "You would make more cuts to my leg?"

"No, give it to me."

He handed it over, hilt first. She lifted the hem of her gown to reveal the kirtle below, and used the knife to cut away a strip of cloth all round. Then she knelt by his leg and pulled his hose away from the wound, before winding the material round and securing it in a tight knot. "There. It is not perfect, but it will hopefully stop any festering."

"Thank you."

She stood up. "And thank you, too, for fighting for me back there. I do not know what I would have done if you had not prevailed, Master Rolleston."

He shrugged. "No doubt you would have been slain also, Mistress Carter."

"I was so sure you were to be killed when he had you on your knees."

"But it was your yelling that distracted the man," he observed. "So I could turn the fight to my advantage."

She gave a small chuckle. "I have been told before that my voice is loud."

"That it is," he said. "I thought perhaps a cat was being disembowelled."

23

CHAPTER TWENTY-THREE

Rolleston slowed the carriage and came to a stop, calling out to the horses, "Whoa there! Whoa!"

The alarm in his voice made Mary give out a small fearful cry. She held on to the seat and looked around the dim interior, lit by just a trickle of light coming in around the thick curtains. It was the day after the ambush, and they had only been going for two or three hours since finishing breakfast, so there was no reason to stop.

Her hearing was suddenly heightened, expecting at any moment for there to be the whoosh of an arrow or maybe the thud of a crossbow as another set of brigands tried to rob them.

Quickly she reached down to the bag under her seat and

drew out the gun, which she now kept fully assembled at all times. She fumbled for a cartridge and managed to slot it into the breech with trembling hands.

There was silence, so she waited a moment to steady her heart, then pulled the curtain back a few inches with the tip of the barrel and squinted out against the sunshine. "Is all well?" she called out, trying to keep her voice steady. "Why have we stopped?"

The carriage rocked and there was a thump as Rolleston jumped down from the driver's seat, then his face appeared at the window. "No matter," he said with a small grin. "No man is trying to attack us again." He gently pushed the barrel of the gun away, so it was no longer pointing up his nose. "You can put your weapon back from where it came, Mistress Carter. We have stopped for a different reason."

She let out a careful breath. "I am pleased to hear it," she answered, resisting the temptation to chide him soundly for giving her such a scare. "And what reason might that be, pray?"

"Come out and I will show you," he answered.

She put the gun back in the bag, and stepped carefully out into the late-Autumn sun. They had pulled slightly off the track, and were stopped alongside a signpost at a crossroads. One route led to Newark, one to Nottingham, and one to a place called Bridgeford. "Well?" she asked.

"I would show you where I was taken and accused of popery and treason," he said. "It is but a short ride from these crossroads." He paused a moment, as if unsure what to say next. "As I said to you and that Alchemist fellow, I was guilty only by association, as I was there to conduct the business of trade. Belike if you saw the place, you would see that a great injustice was done."

Mary couldn't see anything of the sort; surely a house was just a house, whatever may have happened within its walls? But the look of hope on his face was too hard to ignore, so she said, "I will see the house if you wish, so long as it does not add too much time to our journey."

"Very little," he said with another grin, then pulled himself up into the driver's seat. Mary settled back in the carriage, as he turned the horses and headed in the direction marked 'Bridgeford'.

This path was more rutted and less finished than the main road they had left, so she had to hang on to the leather straps either side of the seat as the carriage swayed and rocked along. "Is it far?" she called out. "This path is most uncomfortable."

"Not too far, Mistress," he called back.

Sure enough, it was only a few minutes later that he pulled the horses to a stop once more, and jumped down again to hold open the carriage door for Mary to step out. They were by some black iron gates set into a red brick wall, which were quite plain; nothing on the size and scale of Grangedean Manor. Beyond them was a medium-sized brick and timber house sitting squat and assured around twenty yards beyond the gate. The path from the gate wound up to the house, then swept past the dark wooden front door, round a small lawn and back to the gate again. Mary thought it looked like it had four or maybe five bedrooms; comfortable, but not particularly special. It had several square-paned windows adorned with thick swirling 'crown' glass, plus two tall brick chimneys rising above the shingle roof. There were similar houses on either side, each a few hundred yards away.

"Oak House," Rolleston said. "Home of Master Antony Brooks."

Mary gazed at the house, while trying to think of something polite to say. "A fine place."

"And as you can see well, 'tis no grand manor, nor a place for the gathering of seditious Catholics, but an ordinary house of an ordinary God-fearing and loyal man."

Mary considered it a moment. "Is Master Brooks also a merchant?"

"He invests in ships, and especially in spices from the Orient."

"So was this the business you had with him?"

"Aye. I have bought many of his consignments. I store them in bonded warehouses at the port of Harwich mainly, then find buyers for smaller parts of each consignment."

"A fine trade," she observed. There was a silence, so she asked, "And was Master Brooks arrested also?"

"Indeed he was, and Mistress Brooks as well."

One of the chimneys had smoke coming from it. "And are they back in residence now, or still held for trial?"

"They are returned here; they were quickly released by the magistrate, as they gave assurances they would observe the true faith hereafter, and were sent back with but a fine."

She turned to look at him. "So why then were you taken to the Tower? Especially as you have protested your innocence throughout?"

He gave a small rueful chuckle. "Methinks I protested my innocence too greatly. The Pursuivants, led by one Silas

Taverner of Nottingham, may God strike him down, needed to justify the heavily armed raid they made on the house. The Brooks family have local standing and were well known to the magistrate, whereas I, an unknown merchant from London, was arraigned because I put up a fight."

"Which you could do without feeling the pain of any hits," she observed. "So you fought on when others would have conceded."

"Precisely."

She nodded thoughtfully. The disadvantages of being unable to feel pain were becoming more obvious. "So what happened after that?"

"The magistrate would not hear my protestations of innocence and had me sent to London, where I was arraigned and thrown into the Tower, accused of being an unrepentant Catholic, and therefore by definition, a traitor. That was where Master Wychwoode found me, and thank the Lord, he had me released in order to serve him and Master Secretary Walsingham. And you too, Anne Carter," he added.

"Yes, and I am fortunate you are practiced with the sword. We were well rid of Master Greybeard and his archer."

He nodded. "Aye."

"Tell me," she added, "where you learned to fight so well? It is unusual for one who buys and sells spices to be so accomplished with a sword."

"Ah," he replied, "but I was not always a merchant." He smiled. "As a young man I wanted to explore the continent, and spent time in Padua, in Florence and in Venice. There were many young Italians there who took exception to me and to my Protestant faith, so I needs must defend myself from their constant attack." He looked towards her, but she could see he was really seeing scenes from his past life. "I vowed I would never again be left at a disadvantage, and engaged an experienced swordsman to teach me. Through him, I learned how to defend myself well." His blue eyes snapped back onto her. "I became the master of any Italian who decided I was no longer worthy to draw breath. I would not be cowed by them, and they learned to leave me alone."

"I see," she said. "And you came back to be a merchant?"

"I met a man in Venice who shipped spices, and I learned his trade – first as an apprentice, then as his secretary. I was able to secure contracts with his suppliers for trade into England, so on my return, I set up my own merchant business." He smiled again. "So there you have it, Mistress Carter. Roger Rolleston, from young man in Italy to merchant released from the Tower by Wychwoode. My life presented to you in full."

"I see. Thank you; most interesting." She frowned as a thought occurred. "And is there a Mistress Rolleston?"

He shook his head. "Nay, I have not met a suitable woman, nor has it ever been expedient to make such a match as the nobles do, for money rather than love." He paused, considering her. "In truth, I have not had the time or inclination to seek a wife."

Not that it stopped him shagging that barmaid, and who knows else besides her...

Mary kept the thought to herself; instead she said, "Thank you again, Roger, for being more honest with me."

"We are on this mission together, Mistress Carter," he answered. "So it is good to be honest with each other."

"True." She smiled, and opened the carriage door. "Now to be honest, I would that we now resume our journey. It is a couple more days to Sheffield, and we do need to make good speed."

She climbed back in and took her seat. A moment later she felt the carriage rock as he also resumed his position in the driving seat.

Then the horses' noses were pulled round, and they headed back towards to the crossroads.

CHAPTER
TWENTY-FOUR

It was a grey afternoon in the Presence Chamber at the Palace of Whitehall, with an early flurry of snow falling softly outside the windows. Inside it was comfortably warm; a roaring fire welcoming the various courtiers, dignitaries and ambassadors who came in a steady procession to discuss matters with the Queen. Her Majesty was seated close to the heat of the fire, while Olivia Melrose and the other ladies were sewing or embroidering quietly to one side. Olivia was bent over her embroidery, working on the tiny stitches that would make a colourful image of Adam and Eve in the Garden of Eden with which to decorate a small jewel-box for the Queen.

Most of the conversations between the Queen and the visitors were on mundane matters so Olivia ignored them, preferring instead to concentrate on her needlework, and on her thoughts.

Since leaving Grangedean Manor and returning to Court a few days earlier, she had been trying to work out how – or if – she could fulfil her promise to Sir William and little Kat de Beauvais to ask the Queen for information about Lady Mary. She had soon come to the conclusion that as she had said to Kat, it would be impossible for her, a newly appointed and lowly maid of honour, to approach the Queen on such a secret and contentious matter. There had, however, been a couple of occasions when she and a few other ladies had been alone with Her Majesty, and it seemed to be the ideal opportunity. The conversations had been light-hearted and inconsequential, so she was almost tempted to go up to the Queen and ask for a quiet word, but each time she had lost her courage and remained silent. This made her feel deeply disappointed in herself. Had she not overcome and stabbed two Catholic men to death in quick order, both twice her size? Yet here she was, unable to ask a simple question of her mistress.

But it was not too hard to imagine how such a conversation might go:

"Your Majesty, I would know of the fate of Lady Mary de Beauvais?"

"I am surprised at you, Mistress Melrose, to be asking questions on matters that are no concern of yours... I had high hopes of you, Mistress Melrose, for your wise counsel in place of Lady Mary... now I am disappointed in you..."

As Olivia bent over her embroidery and concentrated on the pink silk thread that formed the face of Eve, she heard the name of a particular visitor being announced. All thoughts of the Creation vanished in an instant when she looked up to see the tall figure of Robert Wychwoode bow and move forward.

Maybe he could be a potential source of information instead?

Olivia strained to catch what passed between Wychwoode and the Queen, but unfortunately he was whispering directly into the Queen's ear, so Olivia could not make anything out. She did note that the Queen seemed remarkably interested in what he was telling her; listening in total stillness, with her mouth slightly open and her eyes shining as the old man leaned over.

Olivia waited until Wychwoode had bowed once more and left the Queen's presence, before casually asking to be excused herself. On the Queen's nod, she put down her embroidery and walked quickly out.

The old lawyer was striding away down the corridor, his black cloak flapping behind him as if he were a crow about to launch into flight. "Master Wychwoode!" she called.

He stopped and turned with an enquiring look, so she lifted up her skirts and ran up to him.

"I would talk with you, sir," she said.

He regarded her a moment with a frown. "If it is about Lady Mary de Beauvais," he said slowly, "then you must know that I am not at liberty to say aught on this matter."

"For sure it is about my lady," Olivia answered, trying not to snap in irritation. How like him to have known exactly what she was going to ask, and to close down the conversation immediately!

She put a hand on his sleeve, and softened her voice. "But

I must appeal to your nature, sir, and say that there are those who have the greatest love for Lady Mary, and would know of her situation."

"This much I am aware," he answered, "and indeed, I am one of those who holds the lady in the highest regard, but I repeat, I cannot say more." He turned to go. In desperation she grasped his sleeve. He stopped and looked down at her hand. "Mistress Melrose," he said, "you, I also hold in high esteem, following your brave actions in York this spring, but as I have said, this matter is not for further discussion." He pulled his arm. "So I would ask that you release my sleeve and let me go about my business."

"I have but one question, Master Wychwoode," she said. "In the name of Christ, I would you do me the courtesy of giving me just one piece of information."

He gave her a blank stare, that eventually softened into a weak smile. "If you agree to let me go, then I will consider the same."

She took a breath and looked him directly in the eye. "Sir," she said slowly, "I, and her family, would know but one thing. Does she live or is she already dead?"

He was silent, frowning as he appeared to think through his response.

Olivia felt hope rising, for the longer he was silent in thought, the more likely Lady Mary was alive – for if she was dead then he had only to say it. But if, as Sir William thought, Lady Mary was away on a secret mission, then the old lawyer would need to consider his response most carefully. Olivia said nothing herself, leaving Wychwoode the time and space to consider his response.

"Mistress Melrose, I will say only the following," he said eventually. "To the best of my knowledge, Lady Mary de Beauvais lives still."

Olivia's heart leapt at this. To know Lady Mary had not been secretly tried and executed was the greatest of news! But she needed more.

"I thank you, sir," she said. "That will be so welcome to the family to hear," Then she waited a beat, looked up at him with wide eyes and added softly, "But you tell only a part of this?"

He raised an eyebrow but said nothing.

"If this is to the best of your knowledge, sir," Olivia continued, looking away then back up at him in the kittenish fashion that worked so well on the younger courtiers, "then I take it that you know nothing of Lady Mary's current situation? Belike this means she is on... a secret mission and away from contact? Perhaps a secret mission for Her Majesty?"

Wychwoode frowned. "I have not said such a thing," he growled. "And if you say the same, it will be but supposition on your part and viewed most gravely." But he said it like he did not fully mean it.

Perhaps he was wavering...

"Yet Lady Mary herself said to Master Secretary Walsingham that she held knowledge of the future which could be of use to him in his intelligencing," Olivia purred, keeping up her pressure. "So I warrant such a mission would be a way of making use of such knowledge?"

"I say again, this is mere supposition on your part." He paused. "But I will say that you are a most persistent, and astute young woman." Then he smiled again.

So it was true!

Olivia was silent a moment as she considered how best to make use of her advantage and prise further information from the lawyer. What more could she glean that would help her piece together Lady Mary's current situation?

"I warrant Lady Mary would not be alone on such a mission," she began, then hurriedly added, "were she on one."

"Why so?" he answered. "She is supremely capable, as well you know."

"But if she possesses such valuable intelligence, would you and Master Walsingham risk her being alone? If she was not under some form of protection? Belike you have given her a large guard of armed men?"

"Nay, but one man..." he began, then stopped, with a look of shock on his face.

"One man?" Olivia was surprised. "You sent her with but one man? I am aware of her strengths, but one man? Is that all?"

"Roger Rolleston is a capable swordsman and committed to my service, and..." he began, then took a long, slow breath. "You are a most beguiling young woman, Mistress Melrose, and I applaud you for having taken advantage of an old man's good nature." He frowned. "As a consequence I have said much too much, and you will forget it all. Am I clear?"

"Most clear, Master Wychwoode," she said, letting go of his sleeve with a small triumphant smile. "I will not tell a soul."

25

CHAPTER TWENTY-FIVE

Olivia smiled at Sir William.

"I can tell you," she began, her eyes shining brightly in the candlelight, "that your idea was correct. They have not tried or executed my lady, but have sent her on a mission of some sort. I know naught about it, except that it is a deep secret, and for the benefit of the Queen."

They were sitting in the parlour of a small inn on the corner of Pudding Lane and Thames Street, where they had agreed to meet and share any information. Olivia had previously dreaded meeting Sir William if she had nothing to tell him, but now she had good news, she had been counting the hours until it was the agreed time and she could get away from the Palace.

"And what is more withal," she continued, "my lady has

been sent on this venture with but one of Master Wychwoode's men to protect her."

"One man? That is all?" said Sir William with a look of surprise. "It is hardly seemly in a married woman," he muttered with a bitter frown.

"Aye, but I warrant she can be trusted."

"It is not her that concerns me in this matter." He sighed. "Who is this man she is with? I pray to God he will respect her honour."

Olivia nodded. "Master Wychwoode said it was a man by the name of Roger Rolleston."

Sir William sat back. "Roger Rolleston, eh? That is a name I have not heard before. I will need to find out more of him." Then he gave her a weak smile. "Meantimes, I cannot say enough how grateful I am for your help in this matter, Olivia." He regarded her thoughtfully a moment. "You have been able to get information out of Wychwoode, when to me he was like a closed document; folded, sealed and giving away nothing. How were you able to get him to reveal all?"

"Marry, Sir William," Olivia replied with a conspiratorial smile, "perhaps there are some secrets that can only be revealed by the guile of a woman, that a man will never access."

"God's Wounds!" he laughed. "You used the language of love to get that dried old stick to open up? Now that I wish I had set my eyes upon!"

For the first time since she had previously been shown into the Great Hall at Grangedean Manor, Olivia thought Sir William looked a little more at ease with himself. At least he knew that his wife still lived, for all she was sent on some dangerous mission with but one man as a protector. This was clearly uppermost in his mind as well.

"While I am most deeply relieved that she has not been tried or executed," he said, "I am naturally concerned that she is sent on some secret mission, and God only knows what and where this might be." He paused. "God, and that arch schemer Walsingham." He drummed his fingers on the table a moment. "Belike you could make even bigger eyes at Wychwoode, and get more knowledge?"

"I think not," she answered. "He realised he had told me too much already, and begged me to silence. I should not in all conscience have told you any of this."

"Nonsense!" he said. "For sure you would tell her husband. He could expect that. But indeed," he continued, "I will share this with no other, you have my word."

"As I also gave mine," she said with a grin.

"Yes, well, there it is." He paused. "But that does not prevent me investigating this man Rolleston, and seeing if we gain any useful intelligence. I would not leave Mary to whatever dangers she faces, without seeing if I can do aught to assist her."

"Would not Wychwoode help?"

"Perhaps – but as he sent her on this mission in the first place, I am not sure. I should act alone.

"I wish you much success."

Again he drummed his fingers, as if he was deciding whether or not to share something. "But I must tell you, Olivia, I have learned this day that there is another possible source of information we should also explore."

She raised an eyebrow. "Which is?"

"You know the fellow who tried to kill the Queen in York, before Mary beat him senseless with a poker?"

"The Alchemist?"

He nodded. "Well, he is finally to be executed this very day at Tyburn. I have a thought that maybe we could learn something from his last speech on the scaffold. These condemned men often give forth information which can have some meaning to those who seek it, and who know more than the general rabble."

"You would attend his execution?"

"Aye, and you as well, if you are free from the Queen's service for a while longer. You are also aware of the background facts, and something he says may have meaning to you not me."

"It does make me uneasy," she replied. "They do unspeakable things to a man, do they not?"

He nodded. "I know, Olivia, but I have also stood close by and watched as you plunged a man's own dagger deep into his body, before pulling it out and doing the same to another man. So I do not see you as any other young woman, swooning at the thought of violence. I see you as one who understands the ways of men and is able to match them, blow for blow."

26

CHAPTER TWENTY-SIX

Mary rode slowly behind Rolleston through the dark Sheffield streets; the sun mostly blocked out by the high, oppressive, overhanging buildings. Their horses picked their way carefully over the slimy cobbles, taking them through the constant flow of humanity that swirled about them like a fast-flowing stream breaks around a rock.

She adjusted her position on the side-saddle in an attempt to ease the constant rubbing of the stiff pommel on her thigh. It was a shame that they had left the carriage at a travelling inn outside the town's walls, but as Rolleston had said, to bring such a vehicle into these narrow streets would have been madness. She had agreed at the time, but there was no doubt it would have been so much nicer to be seated in the carriage, rather than riding on the uncomfortable saddle he had found for her.

A shout of "'Ware below!" came from above them. Rolleston immediately stopped and held up his hand for Mary to do the same. She wrinkled her nose in disgust as what was clearly human waste dropped out of an upstairs window, landing with a soft 'splat' on the street in front of them. Rolleston seemed unconcerned; merely side-stepping the stinking mess and moving on. Mary put her pomander to her nose as she passed, letting the strong scent of lavender almost, but not quite, block out the smell.

She had just passed it when a young man in a dirty jerkin backed out of a house beside her, appearing to be shouting at someone still inside. Before she could warn him, he stepped back into her path, so she had to pull her horse's head quickly round to avoid trampling him with her hooves. The man jumped out of the way, then looked up at her with a deep scowl. "Watch your step, woman!" he growled, then scurried away and was lost in the shadows below the overhanging floor of the next house.

Mary took another sniff of her pomander. Oh to be back in Grangedean Manor, walking in the parklands in the bright, crisp, clear morning air. The trees would be almost bare by now, with a light silver coating of frost to match the tiny sparkling ice crystals drifting through the air. Or strolling through the little village, being greeted by the farm workers and women with a cheery smile as 'my lady', rather than being called 'woman' by some Sheffield ruffian.

She lowered the pomander. Strange that her longing to be away from this narrow, smelly, unpleasant little street only went as far as her current life in Grangedean. She frowned. Her desire to be back in Grangedean living a life of peace and quiet with her family was deep-rooted, and she had been very clear about it with Wychwoode. But why was she not longing to be back even further; in 2015 in her previous life as Justine Parker? For sure she would rather be anywhere but here, so why not once more in her little flat in Hammersmith, drinking wine and dancing round the kitchen to her favourite music? And Grangedean – why did she long to be there as a Tudor wife and mother, not in her old life as the modern-day girl managing events for visitors?

Mary bit her lip. 2015 now seemed so distant – almost like a dream she could not quite recall. Was she was now so completely settled in Elizabethan times that her original life in the 21st century hardly entered her thoughts? That to be truly happy, she need only be a Tudor wife and mother, enjoying life in Grangedean Manor surrounded by her family, rather than being back in 2015?

Mary sighed. Yes, there was no doubting it; a life of Elizabethan peace and domestic tranquillity with her family – that was where true happiness lay.

Except there was one major obstacle in the path to this idyllic picture...

An act of cold-blooded murder.

Truly, it didn't bear thinking about.

So let's not think about it for now. One step at a time...

Rolleston turned and said, "It is not much further to the inn." He gave a small smile. "I believe it is but a couple more turns and up a hill."

"Good," Mary replied. "I am stiff, and I am most weary of these streets. It feels as if we have been in the saddle for days."

"But an hour, Lady Mary," he laughed, "since we finished our midday meal and left the last place. Naught but an hour." She didn't respond, but shifted her leg slightly to release the pressure from the lower pommel on the back of her knee.

"I am to make for a place called the Crossed Keys," Mary had said, as their food was put before them. "You can remain here."

"I know of it," said Rolleston, as he broke off some bread. "It is atop one of the many hills in the town." He paused, observing her as he chewed. "And you would go alone?"

"I would."

"For all you know not where it is, and will be unprotected?"

Mary thought this through. While she could see the benefit of having him there to guide and protect her, she would prefer him to stay back. But then again, he would be useful in ensuring she got there safely...

"Very well," she muttered. "You may accompany me to the door and see me inside safely. No further. That is all."

"So be it." He looked at her as he broke off some more bread. "And what is your business there?"

"That is not for you to know. Your role is only to get me there safely. That is all."

"Then that I will," he had said. "But first I need to take a piss."

27

CHAPTER
TWENTY-SEVEN

Olivia followed Sir William as he pushed through the Tyburn crowds towards the rough wooden platform, on which stood a crude gibbet with a knotted rope hanging from one end. The two of them received a few curious stares as they moved through the roughly dressed throng; Olivia feeling a little self-conscious in her fine silk gown and with her fashionable hair, but they made it to the front without incident.

She looked up at the platform. A man with grey hair under a woollen cap and a grey beard over his fine ruff was standing to one side, talking with a priest. A muscular man in a black head mask and no shirt stood by a long table, holding a large knife in one hand, and a saw in the other. Olivia took it that he was the executioner.

A thin, sorry-looking man in a torn jerkin was standing on the other side, his hands bound behind his back. This man seemed to be overshadowed by the guard beside him, who was wearing a wide-brimmed blue hat with a white feather, blue breeches and a steel breastplate, and was carrying a halberd with a fearsome-looking polished blade that glowed dully in the grey light. The guard was glaring across the crowd with a deep scowl, and Olivia could not help but shrink back at one point when his eye caught hers.

"That must be the one they call the Alchemist," Sir William observed, staring at the thin man with the bound hands. "Although it looks as if he has healed well from the blows rained down on him by my wife." Olivia studied what she could see of his arms and legs through his ragged clothes, and it did seem that whatever damage Lady Mary had inflicted, there was little sign of it now.

"Aye, 'tis strange," she said, "Lady Mary was clear enough in the carriage on our return journey, when she told us the story of her attack on the man. She said she beat both his arms and broke one leg." She looked harder. "And she said he had painted arms, with images of firing weapons of the future."

"I fancy I do see those," Sir William answered, and indeed now she looked she could see there were crudely drawn images just visible on the man's forearms. "But any bruising has faded to naught," he continued, "and the leg is fully healed." He shrugged. "Forbye, we should not become concerned on the state of the man. His traitorous arms and legs will soon be parted from his body anyhow."

As Olivia nodded agreement, she heard a small snort of amusement beside her, and glanced over at a thin, well-dressed man with a trim beard standing close by. He was staring hard at the condemned prisoner, but she got the distinct impression he was actually listening to their conversation. She was about to ask him his business, when she was interrupted by a shout from the platform.

"Hear ye all!" the grey-haired man called out. He seemed to be the main official in charge, and he raised his arm. When the crowd was silent, he continued, "We are here this day to witness the execution of one Richard Hornby, also known as the Alchemist, sentenced for the act of gross treason against our sovereign queen, Her Majesty Queen Elizabeth, and for the foul murder of one Sir Thomas Cobham." He looked down at a paper he was holding. "Know ye all, that the traitor will be hung, then taken down while he still lives. His entrails in all, then his heart, will then be drawn out before him and burned. Once he is dead, his body will be quartered and dispersed. His head..." and here he glared at the prisoner, "...his head will be placed on a spike above London Bridge, for all to see and know the true price of treason."

The condemned prisoner hung the head in question in shame.

"Bring him forward!" the official barked. The guard dragged the man to the centre of the platform. "What say you, traitor, before the sentence is carried out? If you have aught to say, then do it now."

The man lifted his head and stared around the crowd, who started baying and calling out.

"Traitor!"

"Evil!"

"Die like a dog!"

"But die well for me," the man beside Olivia said quietly.

Again, she glanced at him.

The prisoner on the platform appeared to be about to say something, then he shook his head and looked down, staying silent.

"So be it," the official shouted. "The traitor has nothing to say. Let the execution begin."

The executioner pulled the prisoner over to the gibbet, led him up onto a small stool, then put the rope over his neck.

The priest came forward and muttered inaudibly up at the prisoner as he stood on the stool, then moved away and nodded at the executioner.

"By Heavens, we will learn nothing this day," Sir William said. He put his hand on Olivia's sleeve. "Come dear girl, we should be away. I care not for the rest of this spectacle."

She nodded in agreement. "I have no stomach for it either." As she turned to go, she caught the eye of the thin, well-dressed man beside them.

"Wait a moment," he said quietly. "See, they will hang him to death immediately."

"Nay," said Sir William, who was now close enough to hear this. "He will still live when they draw him."

The man shook his head. "Not this one. You will see."

Despite herself, Olivia turned and watched as the executioner kicked away the stool and the prisoner dropped to the end of the rope. Immediately he started kicking and writhing, his face turning red and his tongue emerging from his lips.

"See," said the man beside them "if they do not take him down now, then he will be dead before they have a chance to draw him."

The prisoner made a few more jerks, then the executioner lifted him by the knees and pulled off the rope, before carrying him over to the table and laying him out.

"They think he still lives," the man muttered, giving a small gesture with his hand to indicate the crowd around them. "But I say he is mercifully dead already."

And indeed, Olivia could see that the hanged prisoner was only making movement when the executioner held his arms or his head.

"He is dead. They are working him like a fucking puppet." said the man. "They offered him an easy death in return for his compliance. That is why he said nothing. They will go through the motions now, for the show – cut him open and take off his head, and all that. Probably got some stooge under the platform to scream at the right moment so these ghouls here think they are getting their money's worth."

"You are very well informed on this, sir," Sir William observed. "Although your course language rather belies the quality of your attire."

"Yes, well, things are not exactly what they seem, are they?" the man replied. "And I have an interest in all this, believe me." He turned away, then stopped and looked back. "I am guessing, you are de Beauvais, husband of Lady Mary." He looked at Olivia. "Which makes you the sidekick Olivia she talked about." He nodded to himself. "So take this from one who knows. If you are looking for the lady, then I suggest you look north."

Sir William was silent. Olivia thought he was deciding whether or not to treat this information seriously. The man clearly knew who they were, so most likely he knew of Lady

Mary's whereabouts as well – howsoever that might be. In which case, his information could most probably be trusted. She glanced at Sir William and gave the smallest nod. He did the same back, then said, "Thank you sir. We do indeed seek the lady. Do you have any more for us?"

The man thought a moment. "I know she was sent on a secret mission for Wychwoode. With an utter fucking tool by the name of Rolleston."

"Rolleston, sir?" Olivia asked. "This name comes up a second time. And you disparage him greatly?"

"I would not trust that 24-carat fucker further than I could nudge him. But they went off together." He gave them a grim smile. "Seek Rolleston and you will find the lady." He paused a moment. "And seek out one called Anne Carter. That is all I will say."

"Again, thank you sir," Sir William said. "You are a good man to help us so."

"Maybe." The man nodded, ignoring the blood-curdling screams that came from the platform. "Maybe not. There was a time when I would have happily seen her burn in hell. But you know what? I was wrong – she is okay, really." He paused a moment. "Yeah, okay." He nodded again. "You make sure she gets back in one piece?"

Olivia said, "We will."

"Good. Now, I have a boat to catch which will take me abroad. Good luck." The man limped stiffly away and soon disappeared into the crowd.

There was a pause, while more screams came from the platform. Olivia said, "What was the meaning of that word he used – 'okay'?"

"I know not. I have never before heard the like," Sir William answered. "But I am guessing it meant 'worthy' or somesuch." He stared after the man, then nodded to himself. "Aye, it fits," he muttered. "It fits." Then he took her arm. "Come, we must be away."

He started to push through the crowd, who let them through without taking their gaze off the spectacle on the platform. "A strange fellow, but well-informed," he said over his shoulder. "I will find out more on this Rolleston. It seems he is the key to discovering the whereabouts of my lady. And Anne Carter." They emerged into the open field behind the crowd. "I would we meet again soon," Sir William added, "so we may decide what is best to be done."

"I have leave again in two days," she answered.

"Good. Then we will convene in the same place as before, at the same time, in two days," he said, just as a great cheer went up. "I warrant they have just lifted the fellow's heart."

"So he dies a traitor," observed Olivia.

"Thus it might appear," agreed Sir William. "For all that appearances may deceive."

28

CHAPTER TWENTY-EIGHT

Mary pulled her horse to a stop below the swinging sign that showed two keys in a cross-shape. "We have arrived," she said. "And I thank you for showing me the way. You may go now – I will take it from here."

But Rolleston dismounted and started tying his horse to the rail.

"What are you doing?" she asked coldly as she dismounted also. "I said you may leave."

"Oh come now," he said with a small smile. "I have come this far; I am not going to abandon you now. Who knows what ruffians there are inside this place?" He glanced at the building's chipped and tired-looking lath and plaster. "It seems most run-down. A single woman walking in alone will be easy prey for any casual fellow who fancies a piece of her." He peered through the grimy windows. "I recall well how you said a man once rescued you from an attack in just such a tavern. Will I need to stand out here and wait to hear you screaming like a wounded cat before I must run in to your aid?"

Mary tied up her horse and peered through the nearest window herself. It did seem dark, although she could just make out a few bare-headed men. "Very well," she said. "You may see me inside and sit at a far distance where you can keep a watch for my safety."

"For sure," he answered. "That makes some sense."

But when they went inside he stayed with her all the way to an empty table.

"In truth, I warrant it is better if I sit here with you," he said brightly, taking a seat.

"No, you shall not," she replied. "Go away. This is a private meeting."

"Oh, come now," he murmured, "look about you. These ruffians are just itching to scratch themselves on a fine lady such as you."

She glanced around, and it did seem he had a point. The rowdy shouting that had first greeted them as they entered had now stilled to an uneasy silence. The majority of the heavily bearded and dirty faces were turned in her direction, and were studying her with some interest.

"Belike they have never seen such nobility. You would be a new experience for them. Unless..." he paused, "unless they could see you were with your 'husband'... Under his protection..."

"Very well," she sighed, recognising when she was beaten. "Very well, you can stay. But you keep silent throughout."

"I will," he answered. "Who are we meeting? I should know, and their purpose, or I may misunderstand the conversation."

"By Heavens, Rolleston," Mary snapped. "I have said I will not share the secret with you. You have got yourself to a position where you are here, very much against my will, and that is as far as you go. Do you hear me?"

He shrugged. "In truth I am intrigued. I have come this far on the journey, and yet I know not the purpose. That has got my interest, and I would know more."

"Well, I am not telling."

"Then I know when I am defeated," he said, standing. "I will take my leave, and with it I will be breaking my oath to keep you safe." He nodded across at a couple of roughly dressed labourers who were still staring at them. "Those two fine fellows over there; I say it will be no more than a minute after I am gone that they are at your table. No doubt they will be offering to show you some fine Sheffield hospitality, if you get my meaning."

"Sit down," she ordered. "You have made your point. I will share my purpose here."

"Good," he said. "Tell me."

"I am to meet a woman named Frances Barwell, to confirm she fully understands her part in the plan."

"And her part is?"

Mary hesitated, then took a deep breath. He would find out anyway once the conversation started with Mistress Barwell.

"She is to impersonate the Queen of Scots."

"Why so?" he asked, looking away as he thought it through, before he suddenly turned to her with a face that had turned quite white. "That incredible musket of yours..." he said slowly, as he appeared to realise the full audacity of the plan. "By Heavens, you will use it to assassinate the Scottish Queen, and put this Mistress Barwell in her place?"

"I did not say that."

"Nay, it was not necessary..." He leaned back. "I see it all now. You have constructed this weapon to kill the Queen of Scots and cut off the Catholics from a credible claimant to the throne..." He nodded. "No doubt this Mistress Barwell will announce a conversion or somesuch. It is audacious indeed."

"I thank you to keep your mouth shut on this, Rolleston," Mary snapped, crossing her arms.

"Oh, you need have no fear on that score. I approve heartily! Any plan that hobbles the Catholics has my full approval!" He grinned. "Nay, 'tis quite brilliant!"

---o---

Frances Barwell was a tall, heavy-set woman with red hair, a long, aquiline nose and small, disapproving lips. Having never met the true Queen of Scots, Mary didn't feel confident to assess the likeness, but she took it on faith that Walsingham and Wychwoode had done their homework – and certainly Frances looked in her mid-thirties, the same age as the Queen.

"You plan to... er... remove the true Queen of Scots on the morrow?" Frances asked in a broad Yorkshire accent, once she had sat at their table and accepted a tankard of ale

"That is my aim, yes," Mary answered. "Will you be ready to assume her place?

"Indeed, I am ready." Her expression softened, then she added in perfect-sounding French, "Je serai comme Mary, la reine légitime des Écossais, détenue par ma cousine Elizabeth contre ma volonté et contre ma véritable prétention au trône d'Angleterre."

I will be as Mary, rightful queen of the Scots, held by my cousin Elizabeth against my will and against my true claim to the throne of England.

Mary nodded. "That's good. She spent most of her early years at the French court, so speaks mainly French."

"You can converse also in the Scots tongue?" asked Rolleston. "The Queen is from that country, so she speaks it full well. You could fail badly in your role if you cannot speak it."

Frances looked directly at Mary "This man is suspitious o me," she said. "I wad nocht hae him doutin me."

There was a silence, then Mary asked, "And the meaning?" – although it did seem fairly understandable.

"This man is suspicious of me," Frances said with a small smile. "I would not have him doubt me."

Mary inclined her head in acknowledgment. "Very well." Then she added, "Forgive my companion, he is a naturally suspicious person."

"I am but concerned for the success of this amazing plan," said Rolleston.

"As we all are," Mary responded briskly. "Now, let us talk of how it will be carried out." She looked across at Frances. "I believe you have not yet been fully briefed?"

"Only that I am to take the place of the Queen of Scots

tomorrow, which role I have been schooled upon in her person and manner, and then I am to renounce her claim to the throne. I know not of the details of how the substitution is to be effected."

"So I will brief you now."

"Please do so."

Mary took a sip of ale to settle herself. "You are to be admitted to a side room in the castle by the Earl of Shrewsbury himself," she said. "It is close to where the Queen of Scots takes her daily walk, and you will be dressed in the same clothes. You are to have a bladder of pig's blood attached to your shoulder under your cloak. When the Scottish Queen goes for her walk, I will take a shot to her heart, so it will be a mortal shot. She will be removed quickly from the scene and her body brought to the room where you are concealed. You will then appear soon after with the blood all about your shoulder, and although appearing to be shocked and dazed, you will say that you are not mortally hit."

Mary glanced at Rolleston, who was listening intently, his mouth slightly open and his eyes shining in the flickering candlelight.

Mary continued, "You will then be taken to the Scottish Queen's chambers. I understand you have also been receiving intelligence on the recent events in her life?" Frances nodded. "Good. Anything you have appeared to have misremembered will be explained by the shock of the assassination attempt." She took another sip of ale. "You will then be taken to Tutbury Castle to recuperate for a day or two, before proceeding to London for the final part of the plan – the renunciation of the Scottish Queen's claim to the throne." She sat back. "All the details of that will be relayed to you by the Earl on the journey."

"A most ingenious plan," whispered Rolleston. "I am well impressed."

"Your praise should mainly go to Master Secretary Walsingham and Master Wychwoode for the plan," Mary observed. "Although I commend your willingness to play your part in this, Mistress Barwell."

"I thank you, Mistress Carter," Frances answered. "I also commend your part in this venture." She nodded again, as if confirming in her own mind the full scope of what Mary was about to do. "To conceal yourself and take a mortal shot at God's anointed Queen – that is an act of true bravery. For all she has abdicated her Scottish throne and is a Catholic, it may be that God will not accept such an act. What if your actions on the morrow condemn your soul to eternal damnation?"

Mary's eyes widened. Wow – that was direct. And a tough one to answer. If she revealed she wasn't concerned because she didn't have a faith, would she lose this woman's natural Tudor sympathy and endanger the whole plan? Or if she said she was prepared to take the risk, was she revealing herself as a reckless heretic?

She sighed inwardly. Truly, religion itself was the culprit here. Setting up one man's faith as another man's heresy created nothing but deep, intractable problems.

Mary took a deep breath. "Mary, Queen of Scots is a heretic Catholic who would have no concerns to take the life of God's rightfully anointed Queen Elizabeth, and then her throne," she said quietly but firmly. "So I, as a follower of the true Protestant faith who has sworn to protect the Queen, and who has already saved her life in the past, I have no trouble in my conscience to do this act. None at all."

She let the heavy silence after her words continue for several moments, then looked at Rolleston and added, "Is that not so?"

He frowned slightly, as if surprised to be asked, then his face cleared and he said, "Naturally, Anne. There is no doubting your intention or your conviction in this matter."

Mary turned back to Frances Barwell and asked, "My part in this venture will soon be over. Yours could continue for days or even weeks until you get to London and sign the papers renouncing the Scottish Queen's claim to the throne. Do you not have a family who will miss you?"

"Nay," Frances answered. "I have been widowed these many months, since my husband Jack Barwell died of a severe fever." She paused. A look of sadness appeared very briefly, before being replaced by her usual neutral expression. "We were not blessed by God to have children, so I live alone. My only sister lives in Nottingham, so I rarely get to see her." She shook her head. "No, God has not seen fit to allow me a loving family, but has instead given me a remarkable likeness to the Scottish Queen. So I do His will in taking her place for as long as is necessary."

"I am sorry about your husband," Mary said.

"Such is God's plan." Frances said, with a small glance upwards, as if to make sure her words were heard in Heaven. "He was a clerk with a master in the law here in Sheffield. So we had a comfortable life, not given to extravagance."

"Is that how you met Master Wychwoode?" Mary asked.

Frances nodded. "He was a visitor to my husband's

employer's chambers one day, when by happenstance I was present. He kept looking at me strangely, and observed that I reminded him of someone." She gave a small chuckle and smiled at the memory. "Then it was as if a ray of sunlight had shone upon him, and suddenly his face lit up. 'I know who you look like,' he said, 'it is the Queen of Scots!' He came up and studied me closely, turning my face this way and that, before he said, 'It is as if God himself has made two copies of the same person! And you are living in Sheffield, where the Scottish Queen is held! 'Tis most uncanny!' So, when he approached me a few weeks past, and outlined to me this audacious plot, he was clear that it was God's will that I am involved, as God would not have given me the face and body of the Scottish Queen if he had no other purpose." She nodded, as if to reassure herself. "So it is with good grace I play my part – as you do also." She stood and held her hand out to Mary. "I will not see you again, I fear."

Mary stood also, and took Frances's hand. "Most probably not."

"I wish you God's grace and success on the morrow."

"And you."

"What will you do now?" Frances asked.

"I go to see the Earl of Shrewsbury, and ensure he is also ready to play his role," Mary answered.

"Then God's grace be with you for that meeting also." Frances smoothed her skirts, stood to her full, imposing height, and left the tavern without a further look back.

29

CHAPTER TWENTY-NINE

Sir William idly swilled his beer around the bottom of the tankard as he waited to meet Olivia Melrose in the tavern as arranged at Tyburn two days previously. He stared into the murky depths as he mulled over the results of his investigations into Roger Rolleston.

His initial enquiries had yielded little; no person he asked had ever heard of the man, which was not altogether surprising, considering that they moved in very different circles. He was beginning to despair of finding any useful intelligence, when he finally had a stroke of luck. He learned that Nicholas Grenville was in London, and could be found at his house in Blackfriars. Grenville was the northern Catholic who had been caught up in the plot for the Alchemist to kill the Queen in York that spring, masterminded by Grenville's errant nephew, Lambert Moreton, and foiled by Mary with her poker. Grenville had been spared from execution, not only because he had agreed to convert away from Rome, but also because Sir William, who had been his house guest at the time, had made it clear that Grenville had been unaware of the plot.

So here was a man with a possible source of deeper information; and who owed him a favour. He had therefore paid Grenville a visit the evening before.

"Rolleston?" Grenville had said, as he poured them both a glass of wine. "For sure I know of the fellow. Self-important merchant who puffs himself up and dresses like a peacock, as a means to satisfy his well-known and constant desire for female flesh."

Sir William flinched. And Mary was alone with this man? That confirmed his worst fears and made him sick to his stomach. Damn Wychwoode for sending his wife off alone with this fellow!

Now, more than ever, he had to go after her.

"Most interesting." he said with a thin smile. "So if I was to seek this man Rolleston, where would I most likely find him?"

Grenville shrugged. "I know not – he could be anywhere. He was held in the Tower until recently, but I heard he was then released."

"Why was he held?"

"He was found in the house of a known Catholic, one Antony Brooks."

"So then, why was he released?" asked Sir William, mentally adding the name Antony Brooks to his list of persons of interest in this matter.

"I know he maintained a story that he was an observant Protestant, regularly worshipping in some church in Surrey or some place, so I warrant the cunning fellow was able to show he was not there on seditious business." Grenville took a swig of wine. "As a merchant, he most likely had some tale of being there on the pretext of trade."

Sir William considered this. "So, he is not a Protestant in truth?"

"Heavens no!" Grenville gave a short laugh. "I will tell you, Sir William, as we have an understanding, but the truth is," he leaned forward with a conspiratorial look; "Rolleston is a confirmed Catholic, as is Brooks, in whose house he was found." Then he sat back. "There, I have said it." He frowned. "But why do you seek him?"

Sir William paused a moment. Given that the mission this Rolleston and Mary were on was secret, it would clearly not serve to tell the truth. So he picked up on something Grenville had mentioned, and he said, "I seek him on a matter of trade; I have invested in a shipment of spices from the Orient. All I know is that he has gone north."

"Ah! He has absconded with your funds, has he?" Grenville answered with an unpleasant wink. "I warrant that is why you seek the fellow." Then he said, "Antony Brooks lives at Oak House at Bridgeford, which means you go to Nottingham, then on a few miles beyond. If, as you say, Rolleston has gone north, you might consider starting your search there."

"But was Brooks not held as well?"

"Nay, I hear he wriggled off the hook like a slippery eel." Grenville laughed again. "He has good associations with the local Justices and would have leveraged those..."

Sir William looked up as Olivia arrived at the table dressed in her riding clothes. He poured her some beer, let her settle herself, then filled her in on what he learned of Rolleston, Brooks and the house in Bridgeford near Nottingham. In telling the tale, he decided to omit the piece about Rolleston being a known womaniser.

"Then we must make haste to this place, Oak House" Olivia said when he had finished.

"We?" he asked. "For sure I shall travel alone. I fear this is not a mission for a young woman."

Olivia gave him a wide-eyed look of surprise. "I warrant my love for my lady is as great as yours, Sir William," she said. "If there is a chance she is in danger, I would not shirk my duty to help..."

"But..." he began.

"...And as you stated when we were last here," Olivia continued, as if he had not spoken, "I killed two men in quick succession before your eyes. I am not just any young woman, Sir William, and I *will* be accompanying you on this mission."

"But..." he said again, then paused. When she stayed silent, he continued, "...will the Queen allow you leave of absence for such time as may be necessary?"

"The Queen understands I have need to return home to tend to my sick father. She has allowed me as long as is necessary to return him to health."

"Oh, Melrose is sick? I knew not."

Olivia shook her head with a look of bemused amazement. "Of course not; it is but a ruse to get time away from Court."

"Oh. Ah, yes, of course," Sir William muttered, as if that was what he had known all along.

"Then I suggest we set off without delay," she said, finishing her beer and standing. I have my horse without, and I am ready."

30

✧

CHAPTER THIRTY

A small, elderly man in black let Mary and Rolleston into an imposing wood-panelled room inside Sheffield Castle, dominated by a roaring fire in a magnificent fireplace.

It was after they had left the Crossed Keys earlier, that Mary had tried once again to get Rolleston to leave her, but he had been adamant that he was coming to this meeting as well.

"Now I know of the plan, what benefit is there in further secrecy?" he had asked, as they walked down the hill towards the castle. "And anyhow, there are many cut-purses and ruffians in these streets. I am sworn to protect you, and that I shall."

"But you have no need to come into the castle," she had tried. "You can wait for me outside."

"Nay, Mistress Carter." He had shaken his head. "Think

you that the Earl and Countess of Shrewsbury will receive a single woman? I doubt it greatly."

Mary had thought the exact opposite, but couldn't think of any way to force him, so they had entered the castle together, and been seen up to this magnificent room by the elderly servant.

Mary looked about her, taking it all in. Above the fireplace was a pair of crossed swords under a red and yellow shield bearing the image of a gold lion standing upright. On either side were imposing portraits; one of a nobleman with a long grey beard that reached beyond the edge of his ruff and was dropping over the edge like the beginning of a waterfall, while the other was of a mature woman with a long, aristocratic nose and red hair. The man looked as if he had deeply resented having his portrait done. His expression was one of pained sufferance as if he was continually telling the artist to 'get on with it'. The woman, on the other hand, looked as if the whole experience was just a bit of fun, as if her natural humour could not be repressed by standing still for such a long time.

The centre of the room was furnished with eight large high-backed chairs around a broad oak table, with further smaller chairs placed around the walls. In one corner stood a large writing desk covered with papers, while the rest of the room held a mixture of occasional tables, decorative pots and a pair of prie dieus. The ceiling was adorned with decorative plasterwork in geometric patterns radiating out from a large central boss that featured the same lion shield as the one above the fire.

The man who had let them in bowed and announced into the empty room, "Mistress Anne Carter and Master Roger Rolleston, madam." Then he reversed out of the door, leaving them standing there.

Mary was just wondering who he had been addressing, when a woman's head suddenly appeared above one of the chair backs, rising up as if pulled by an invisible string. Then the head turned, and Mary realised that she was looking at the woman in the portrait.

"I am the Countess of Shrewsbury," the woman said, as she walked towards them. Mary couldn't help glancing at her face, then flicking her eyes over to the picture to confirm the likeness. "Yes, that is indeed me," the woman said softly. Mary dropped into a small curtsey and found herself staring down at the toes of the woman's silk slippers peeping out from under her gown. "Pray be upstanding, Mistress Carter," came the woman's voice, and she felt a hand under her chin lifting her up. "You and Master Rolleston are most welcome." Mary stood to her full height, which was at least a head taller than the Countess.

"We are come of late from London, Your Excellency," Mary said, "and present our compliments to you and the Earl."

"Indeed, my husband said a woman may come, and would be bringing a message regarding our... guest... the Queen of the Scots," said the Countess. Mary nodded slightly. "Ahh, t'would be a most welcome message if it tells that she is to be moved to the care of another," the Countess continued with a look of tired resignation. "She and her retinue weigh most heavy on our purse, and we get no help from Her Majesty's Exchequer for all our troubles."

Mary gave a weak smile. "I am instructed that the message is for the Earl's eyes alone, Your Excellency."

"Of course, of course," the Countess said, and walked over to a cord hanging in the corner. "You and your companion will take some wine?" she asked, pulling it sharply. A distant sound of a bell could be heard.

"That would be most kind," Mary answered.

"For me, also," said Rolleston.

The elderly man in black reappeared, acknowledged the Countess's request for wine, then bowed and left.

"My husband has been seeing to the Scots woman's retinue," the Countess observed. "I expect him back presently."

"We are happy to wait, Your Excellency," Rolleston said.

The Countess inclined her head in acknowledgment, and said to Mary, "Is Master Carter, your husband, not here also?"

"No, madam. He has other business to attend to." Which was sort-of true enough.

"You must be pained at being parted."

"Indeed I am, my lady."

"But you have the companionship of Master Rolleston," the Countess observed, with an enquiring raised eyebrow.

"Master Rolleston here has been so good as to offer me his protection on my journey," Mary answered.

"Most kind," the Countess answered and turned to Rolleston, looking him up and down slowly, almost as if she were assessing the qualities of a horse she was purchasing. Then she nodded to show he had passed her visual inspection. "I trust you have not been called upon to draw your sword in defence of the lady's person and honour?" She gave a small smile, seeming to show that such things were never actually necessary in her privileged world, but may, of course, happen to others.

"Aye, in truth I did have to do so," Rolleston answered. "Some brigands stopped us on the road, and would have taken our valuables, as well as threatening harm to Mistress Carter. I was able to overcome them with my sword and er... see them off... before any misfortune came to this lady, or to our possessions."

The countess's mouth opened in a small 'o'. "By Heavens, is this true?" she breathed, looking at Mary. "You were attacked?"

Mary nodded. "Yes, madam, 'tis God's truth."

Just then the servant reappeared with a tray of goblets and two bottles of wine.

"I have taken the liberty of bringing a choice of wines, Your Excellency," he said.

The Countess selected one and poured them all glasses. When they all had a glass in hand and the man had withdrawn, then she said to Mary, "You are indeed fortunate that you had Master Rolleston there as your protector."

"Indeed I am, my lady," Mary answered. "And I am most grateful to him."

"Then we must drink to his health, must we not?" The Countess raised her glass. "I commend you Master Rolleston, for your bravery and your presence of mind." Rolleston gave a small bow, as they all drank. "Now, I am sorry, but I must leave you," she said, once they had put their glasses down, "as I have some household affairs that I must attend to. My husband will be here presently, as I know your business is with him." She gave them each a small nod. "Good day, Mistress Carter. Master Rolleston."

There was a silence after the Countess had left. Mary picked up her wine glass and finished off the last few drops, then poured herself another full glass and drained it in one go. "Do not ask me to feel at ease with this situation," she muttered, refilling her glass and draining it again. "To be welcomed as a guest here, knowing what I intend for the morrow – it sits ill with me. Most ill."

"I know," he said, in a tone that surprised her with its sympathy. "It must be hard, knowing what you are charged to do."

Just then the doors opened and a man of around fifty entered, dressed in a black doublet, brown trunk-hose slashed with grey, cream hose and a grey cloak. Again, Mary glanced up to the picture beside the fireplace; there was no doubt this was the same man. Except that where the picture had a look of impatience, the man before them simply looked tired, as if the weight of the world was on his shoulders.

"Mistress Carter?" he asked as he came over and made a small bow before her. "You are well met indeed." He stood to his full height, which was still half a head shorter than her, then gave a weak smile. "I trust Bess has made you welcome?" He eyed their glasses, and poured one for himself. "Those Scottish women will be the death of any man who must shepherd them from one place to another!" He gave a hollow laugh. "Shepherd! I am no such thing when it comes to them, for they are not like sheep, but like cats..." he raised his eyes to the ceiling, "Cats that spit and scratch and do aught but what they are asked..." He looked down again. "You know, all four are also named Mary? It is impossible to address them with any clarity." Then he smiled. "But enough of them. We must harry to our business." The smile faded, and he said, "You have instructions for me, I believe?"

"I do, Your Excellency." She fished in her pocket and handed over Walsingham's coded letter, which he took between thumb and forefinger as if it were white hot.

"Let us see what this says, eh?" he muttered, as he took it over to the desk and broke the seal with a knife. Then he opened it up and smoothed it with his hand, before laying the knife along its side like a paperweight, to keep it from closing again. "Let me see, let me see," he muttered, as he reached for a small leather-bound book and found the correct page. Then he selected a piece of plain paper, dipped a quill in a small ink pot, and hovered over the blank page.

"Oh yes, 'A' is equivalent to 'S'," he continued, as he looked at the book, then back at the coded letter. "Which makes 'T' into 'R'..."

Mary and Rolleston watched as he slowly deciphered the letter, scratching characters onto the blank page as he went. "By the Lord's passion..." he said to himself as the meaning of the code became apparent, "that is most singular, most singular indeed..." He looked up. "Yes, this confirms the outline of the plan that has been shared thus far; that a secret type of musket is to be used that can be accurate from a great distance. I am to secure for the assassin a suitable position overlooking the courtyard so it can be fired upon the person of the Scottish Queen when she steps out on the morrow..." He looked up. "It says not who will be the angel of death who fires this weapon, but am I to take it that it will be you, sir?" He looked enquiringly at Rolleston, who shook his head. "Nay?" He turned to Mary with a raised eyebrow. "Then is it you who will fire this weapon at the Scottish Queen?" Mary nodded. "Remarkable!" The Earl shook his head. "They have sent a woman to kill a woman! Who would have thought it could be so?"

He went back to his sheet of decoded notes. "Yes, yes; I am to bring the new substitute queen to the room beside the courtyard, then burst the bladder of blood... just so, just so... Then I must treat this new queen, who looks and speaks like the original, as if she is genuine, and convey her to Tutbury." He read further. "Oh, but there will be the conceit that the distress of the assassination attempt will account for any lapse of memory." Mary nodded again. "This is most clever – most clever indeed." He looked up at Mary. "So this counter-feit queen, she will renounce the claim to the throne and the Catholic faith? So that no further plots can centre on her in future?" Once again, Mary gave a small affirmative nod. "And I shall be relieved of the burden of keeping the Scottish Queen and her retinue of leeches who suck the blood from my family and my purse every day that God provides?"

"I believe that will be the outcome, Your Excellency," Mary said.

The Earl looked up, and it seemed that some of the weight had already lifted from his shoulders. "Then this plan has my deepest blessing," he said with a small smile, "and tomorrow, I shall play my part in it with God's good grace."

He sprinkled some sand across the sheet of decoded notes, then shook it off. "Then, once you have disposed of the

Catholic Queen," he continued, "I will escort her replacement from Tutbury to London for the renouncement of both her faith and her claim to the throne." He put both papers to one side on his desk. "Come," he said, "we must view the turret where you will be stationed tomorrow, so you can be sure of your angles and distances."

Mary nodded, her head clearing of the wine in an instant. *This was getting real. All too real.*

The Earl led the way out, with Mary close behind. "You really do not need to see this," she whispered over her shoulder to Rolleston as she passed through the doors. "I will meet you back at the Crossed Keys." There was no response, so she looked round, to see he was a few feet further behind. "Apologies," he said with a sheepish smile as he caught her up. "That was a particularly fine Rhenish, so I availed myself of another cup."

"For sure," she replied, then repeated her instruction.

He thought a moment, then nodded. "Yes, I concur. I will see you there presently."

Mary followed the Earl out into the afternoon sun, and as they crunched along a gravel pathway around the castle, Rolleston peeled off and headed out through a nearby gate onto the street.

"Follow me," the Earl said as he strode along the path. "I have the perfect place for the killing on the morrow."

Shit! Why did he have to put it as bluntly as that?

CHAPTER THIRTY-ONE

Sleep that night seemed quite out of the question.

It's not that Mary didn't try. After retiring to her chamber, she was determined to rest and relax so she would be sharp and alert for the awful task in the morning. So she took care to stick to her usual routine – undressing and changing into her nightshift, then cleaning her teeth with the special pig-bristle brush and peppermint paste she had made at Grangedean, before slipping under the blankets and getting 'sleep ready'. This was a procedure she had perfected in the early years of her Tudor life, starting with lying on her back and flexing, then relaxing, all her muscles in turn. She would begin at her toes; splaying them out a few times then letting them relax with a small wiggle, then pulling her feet back and letting them relax also – and so on up through her arms, hands and fingers, ending with the muscles in her neck, mouth and eyes. Not forgetting a quick 'Bewitched' nose wiggle. This usually had the effect of making sure all her muscles were totally floppy, smoothing out any hidden tensions. It also had the effect of making William laugh if he saw it, causing her to have to start the whole routine again. Then, once all the muscles were nice and relaxed, she would roll gently onto her right side, take a few deep breaths and curl into a foetal ball. She would usually be asleep in minutes.

But this night, however much she tried, all her muscles kept tensing up again; making every position she tried painfully uncomfortable.

Tomorrow she would become a sniper, an assassin, a killer. How could she possibly sleep when she was preparing to end the life of Mary, Queen of Scots in cold blood?

She tried to settle on her back.

Did Rick, the Alchemist, have such doubts before he set out to kill Queen Elizabeth? It was unlikely; the man had a free choice and, she suspected, very little conscience. Plus, he was not under threat of death by burning for sorcery if he refused to make the attempt. But did that make it all right? To kill an innocent person because if one didn't, one would be killed oneself? Better to be murdered than to become a murderer?

Mary tried her left side, thumping the pillow a few times to get a head-sized depression into the rough horsehair and straw. It didn't make her any more comfortable.

What about Lee Harvey Oswald? Or John Wilkes Booth? Did they have sleepless nights before setting out to kill

Kennedy and Lincoln? Oswald and Booth... And Chapman, wasn't that the bloke who killed Lennon?

Sirhan Sirhan. Where did that name come from? Mary clicked her fingers and frowned. Oh yes, he was the one who killed Robert Kennedy. And James Earl Ray, of course, who assassinated Martin Luther King.

How did they all sleep, the night before their big days?

Jack Ruby. He shot Oswald.

Oh god! What if there's a Jack Ruby out there for me?

Mary flopped back onto her right side.

Would she be looking over her shoulder for the rest of her life, if it ever became known that the spy and assassin Anne Carter was in fact, Lady Mary de Beauvais? But Walsingham and Wychwoode had promised her security would be assured, and surely the Queen would offer her protection?

But what if it did come out – that Lady Mary de Beauvais was the assassin of Mary, Queen of Scots? Would schoolchildren of the future learn her name and her life story? How would they be taught about her first twenty-seven years – years that had never actually existed in Tudor history?

And what of history itself? The Armada? The Babington Plot? Maybe even the Gunpowder Plot? Such events that would be replaced by new ones in history; ones she couldn't even begin to imagine. All because she was going to centre the Scottish Queen's chest in her crosshairs, hold her breath, and pull the trigger...

Mary sat up with a small cry.

Now she was actually planning her shot, like a truly cold-blooded assassin!

She brought her knees up to her chest and hugged them, rocking slightly on the mattress in the dark. What a dreadful set of events had led her to this point – had led her to becoming this merciless killer...

If only the plot had been simply to kill the Scottish Queen quietly in the night. The Earl of Shrewsbury could have done it, of course; he could have crept into her chamber and dispatched her himself. After all, he disliked her intensely, as she and her ladies were eating their way through his fortune. In truth, he should have welcomed the opportunity. But that was not the plan – the public shooting had been deemed necessary by Walsingham so he could let start a rumour that the would-be assassin was a disaffected Catholic, so making the Scottish Queen's willingness to give up her claim to the throne more credible.

Mary slid back down the bed and tried once again to do her flexing routine, then took several deep breaths to 'lock in' the relaxation.

Think of something else.

Rolleston.

Imagine not feeling pain... She would have traded anything not to have had the screaming agony of childbirth...

If she'd had Ambrose, Kat and Jane in the 21st century, there would have been so many more options...

Gas and air...

Epidural...

Waterbirth...

Is Kat all right? Once again a promise not to leave her had been broken...

She'll probably never want to trust her mother again...

Is Jane eating?

Ambrose? Has William found him a tutor?

William...

William...

Mary drifted off into a dark, dreamless sleep.

---o---

Rolleston picked a piece of crustiness from the corner of his eye and examined it closely on the edge of his nail.

"Did you sleep at all last night, Mistress Carter?" he asked, flicking the tiny thing onto the rush floor.

"Eventually, I must have done," she replied. "I had much on my mind, as I am sure you will imagine."

He nodded. "I do imagine."

"And you?" she asked. "Did you sleep..." Mary paused, as she noticed his eyes were now following a pretty young maid making her way around the room. She changed what she was going to say, "...Did you sleep alone?"

He pursed his lips. "Belike I did. Or belike – I did not."

They were breaking fast in the tavern of the Crossed Keys the next morning. Mary looked at the maid as she bent over a table, her chest barely held in by her thin linen blouse. "I fear she is young enough that you could have sired her yourself, Master Rolleston."

He did not respond to this, but instead he said, "Will you be heading straight for the castle? You have note of the hour when the Scots Queen will be taking her walk?"

Mary sat back and eyed him over her tankard as she had a sip. "I do. She will be taking her walk around noon. I will ensure I am in position around one hour before, so I am ready when she comes out."

"And will she be alone?"

"Yes. Apparently she has very sore joints and does not like others to see her walk."

"Understandable."

"And you, Roger?" she asked. "What is your plan for today?"

"I will take a short stroll around the town now, then I will come back here and await your return."

"Then go to it," she answered. "I would sit here a while longer to gather myself."

"Indeed," he said, standing. "Till we meet after... the matter... has happened." Then he strode across to the front door, pausing only to slap the serving maid's bottom on the way out.

Mary sighed as the girl squeaked and mock-chided him.

Rolleston turned at the door and gave Mary a small wave across the room, then he was gone.

The maid came over. "Some more to eat or drink, madam?" she asked, her face still flushed.

"No, thank you," Mary replied, then added with a slight chill in her voice, "I see you are quite familiar with my travelling companion."

The girl blushed deeper, and stammered, "I beg your pardon, madam, but I thought..."

Mary raised an eyebrow. "What did you think, exactly?"

"That you and he are not... you are not..."

"That we are not husband and wife? Is that what he told you?"

"That he did, madam!" The girl put her hand to her mouth. "Oh, madam, I am so sorry, indeed I am! What you must think of me!" Then she added in a slightly lower tone, "And him…"

"As it happens, he is but my travelling companion, looking to my safety," Mary said, deciding to let the girl off the hook. "He has told you the truth; we are not wed."

"Oh." The girl's colour started to fade back towards normality. "But it has upset you, madam, I can see that." She poured ale into Mary's tankard. "I am so sorry, madam, if you are offended. I meant nothing by it, indeed not!" She bobbed her head and scurried off.

"Nor did he," Mary muttered after her. "Nor did he."

Mary drank her ale slowly. The distant sound of a church bell rang the hour, and she counted ten strikes. Ten o'clock! She finished her ale and stood. She must get the gun and get over to the castle now, or she might not be ready if the Scottish Queen decided to walk early.

With a muttered curse, she hurried over to the stairs and made her way up to her chamber.

32

CHAPTER THIRTY-TWO

Mary wiped her hand on her man's jerkin and put it back on the fore-stock of the gun. The last thing she needed now was sweaty palms. She should have brought a towel or a rag.

Her jerkin was made of leather, and she had added extra leather patches to the elbows to prevent soreness from the hard stone. She was wearing men's breeches and had her hair up under a cap. She had also blackened her face in the approximation of a beard. All this was so she could not only pass as a man – at least at a casual glance – but was also unhindered by voluminous skirts in order to make a quick getaway.

She shifted her grip and put her eye to the scope. A wall that bisected the castle courtyard sprang into view. It had a gate at its centre, topped by a fine stone arch. From this height she could see both sides of the gate – behind it as well as in front. She lined up the crosshairs on the large black door handle for a moment, then idly moved up to the stone lintel. There was the same shield with the standing lion that she had seen above the fireplace the day before. The device of the Earl of Shrewsbury. She swung the scope up to the flag flying above the castle; it featured the same shield. She chuckled softly; the Elizabethans certainly knew a thing or two about branding.

The flag flapped slightly, leading to the conclusion that the wind was blowing from right to left. Mary could see that it was a gentle, consistent breeze at rooftop level; of course, there might be some eddies swirling around the courtyard below which she should allow for. She swung the sight across to find a small tree in a decorative bed and observed the leaves a while. If the tree was any indication, the breeze at ground level was actually blowing the other way; from left to right, although it seemed very slight. Important to allow for it over this distance if she was to hit her target with absolute accuracy.

She shifted her position a little to try and stop her muscles locking up.

This could be a long wait.

She was standing in a damp-smelling circular room in one of the two turrets above the main castle gates, with the only light coming from the single arrow-slit window at the end of a very deep stone sill. She had pulled up a small table for her bullets and a costrel of water, and was using the stone sill as a rest support for the gun. It was a convenient position to fire from, as it was deep enough to support her left elbow as she held the gun. The only issue was her limited barrel movement up and down, which meant her actual field of fire was somewhat limited.

A small motion down in the courtyard caught her eye and she found it in her sights; a servant in Shrewsbury livery coming out of a door and crossing to the other side. She followed him as he walked, keeping his head in her crosshairs for practice, but with her finger well away from the trigger. The thought of accidentally shooting a servant filled her with sick horror.

As bad as shooting the Queen of Scots?

Mary took a deep breath and again wiped each palm, before settling once more in position.

Another servant came out of a door beyond the dividing wall, and she saw him walk up to the gate in the middle, then disappear behind it. She focused on the gate at head height, and was able to pick him up as he came through, getting him neatly in the crosshairs as he walked forwards. He was now coming towards the gate directly below her. She counted the seconds until her limited firing angle was too sharp and even though he was still a long distance away, she was not able to get her barrel to point that low. She reckoned that if the Queen was to walk at the same speed, then the window of opportunity for the shot would be around twenty seconds.

She wondered if the Earl had deliberately sent the fellow out there, just so she could get this information. Did the man know that his every move was being tracked by a hidden sniper? But then, the concept of a distant killer armed with a gun such as hers would be so alien to the average Elizabethan, that it was unlikely he could conceive of the threat he was under. He would be aware of arquebus guns, muskets and crossbows of course – but the accuracy of such weapons was insufficient for a sniper to be as far away as she was.

So, unless the Earl had told him (unlikely), he had been blissfully unaware that a gun was tracking his every move. A gun built to a 2015 design and aimed at him by a time-travelling woman – now *that* he would have definitely been unable to comprehend!

Indeed, if she didn't know it to be true, Mary herself could hardly believe it.

How had she got herself into this situation – and would she have done anything differently? Her original time-travel over ten years ago was unfortunate; she had simply been in the wrong place at the wrong time, and had slipped down a wormhole opened up by the electrical storm. The fact she had her phone with her, and a solar charger, meant she could use it to conjure the 'voice of Jesus' and save herself when tried for witchcraft by ducking in the well. Then saving the life of Queen Elizabeth by beating the Alchemist just as he was about to fire the fatal shot – she had no regrets about that at all. And being forced to undertake this mission under threat of execution by burning – what choice did she have?

Mary put the gun down and stood up, stretching her back until she felt the joints popping. Then she resumed her position, with the sight trained on the door that the second servant had come from.

And she waited.

The clock struck twelve.

Maybe the Queen was not coming out today? Maybe her arthritis was too painful?

The clock struck the quarter hour.

Give it another half an hour, then maybe try again to-morrow?

There was movement at the door. A tall, heavy-set woman in a clean white walking cloak came out, followed by a man in black. Mary lined them up in her sights. The man was the small elderly servant who had let her and Rolleston in the day before.

And the woman...

Mary focused on the distant figure and drew a quick breath. It was uncanny – as if she was looking at Frances Barwell, but fully made up and with her hair done.

Mary watched as the Queen said something to the servant, then he went back into the castle while she turned towards the gate and started walking stiffly. Quickly she was out of sight behind it. After a moment Mary saw the handle turning.

Then it seemed as if reality blurred, pitching her into a dreamlike state, almost as if she were sliding down a slippery slope, unable to grab hold and take control.

The wooden door opened, and the Queen walked through alone, bringing her head right into the centre of the cross-hairs, and Mary's finger trembled on the trigger as the Queen started walking towards her. Twenty seconds was all the time she had available; maybe a few more as the Queen walked so slowly... the Queen kept walking... so it must be fifteen by now, fifteen seconds until she would pass the point where Mary could get a clear shot, so it had to be now, it had to be; now it was ten seconds, so it really was now or never, and then the Queen looked up and it was if she was looking directly at Mary, daring her, challenging her to take the shot; 'take it, take it' she seemed to be saying 'and put me out of my misery! Go on, girl, go on, do me the favour and give me a quick, clean death now rather than eleven more years of unjust imprisonment ending in a painful execution; go on, do it now, I dare you!'

Mary found she was holding her breath as she centred the fine, aristocratic head in the crosshairs, then dropped the sight down to the centre of the Queen's chest, right where the clasp strained to fasten the cloak, right where the heart would be, then Mary heard a small cry of pain, but it couldn't be the Queen because she hadn't fired yet, so *Christ!* it must have been her not the Queen who cried out, and the Queen was still walking; getting closer and closer to the point of no return; six seconds, five seconds...

33

CHAPTER THIRTY-THREE

Mary took the shot.

The cracking sound crashed round the room, reverberating off the stone walls and leaving her ears ringing. It was accompanied by the acrid firework smell of the gunpowder, and a cloud of bitter, choking smoke that burned her throat and made her eyes water.

She blinked furiously down the scope, as the scene unfolded in the courtyard below.

The Queen had been blown backwards by the shot and was lying very still on the cobbles. Her mouth was open with what almost looked like a snarl, as if instead of welcoming the shot, she had actually tried to curse Mary as she flew through the air.

A patch of bright red was growing fast and spreading out from the centre of her chest, turning the beautiful white cloak crimson.

There was a shout and a guard in the Earl's livery appeared at a run, then another, and a third. Together they surrounded the body; one cradling the Queen's head and the other struggling to undo the clasp to the cloak. Several more men appeared, and soon the body was completely surrounded. As Mary watched, it was lifted up and quickly carried to the side of the courtyard, disappearing out of sight.

Quickly she ejected the smoking cartridge case from the chamber, then broke the gun down and put it in her bag. Then she swept the spare bullets and the costrel into the bag as well, before closing and attaching it to her back with its two handles like a backpack. With a quick look round the room to make sure nothing was left, she ran out.

The Earl had shown her the way in and out of the turret room when they had scouted the location the day before. The escape was along the open walkway above the gate hidden from view by the crenelated stone walls; a structure he had called the 'allure'. Then down the steps that were within the other gate turret and out towards the street.

Crouching as she ran, Mary made her way along the allure and pulled open the wooden door at the end. Then she clattered down the stone steps to the door into the street.

Keeping her head down and walking with what she hoped was the rolling gait of a man, she pushed through the Sheffield crowds. She could sense a distinct air of alarm from those around her, and she heard snatches of conversations, with words like 'assassination!' 'a ball to the chest!' and 'blood everywhere!' as the crowds flowed past, mostly heading towards the castle.

Ignoring them, she made for the Crossed Keys where she could clean up, change into her normal women's clothes and be ready to act as if she had never left. Then she could grab her horse and Rolleston, and ride out of Sheffield to the travelling inn where they had left the coach.

And from there – back down south to a grateful Queen and Walsingham.

And an end to the threat of trial and execution?

She reached a junction between two streets, and was about to turn left up the hill to the Crossed Keys, when she caught sight of a pair of armoured halberdiers heading down the hill looking at the faces in the crowd as they passed. Without breaking stride, Mary took the right fork down the hill instead, and increased her pace to put distance between her and the halberdiers.

Were they looking for her? She bit her lip as she picked her way down the cobbles. Maybe. Maybe not. But there was no sense in taking a risk. It was clear from the reaction of the crowds that news of the assassination was spreading like wildfire – so better to assume that these men were on the lookout for anyone acting suspiciously.

Halfway down she saw a grim-looking tavern; a low, shabby building with cracked walls and broken shutters, under a faded sign that said it was called the 'Cock and Bull'. She turned and walked confidently through the door.

Inside it was very dark, with the only light coming from the fire – which suited her purpose admirably. She made her way to the back of the room, trying hard to ignore the smell of stale sweat, woodsmoke and mould. She chose a table close enough to the fireplace to be warm, but deep in shadow. Dropping her bag at her feet, she pulled her cap down and started to watch the door like a hawk.

After a few minutes no halberdiers had come in, or anyone else looking like they were searching for the assassin, so she allowed herself to relax slightly. If she had successfully evaded them, she could hope to be back on her way soon.

A red-faced woman with a dirty cap and apron came over.

"Ale, master?" the woman asked.

"Aye," Mary grunted, turning her head away from the woman's stink, which was noticeable even against the smell of the room.

"Beg pardon?"

"Aye. An ale," she repeated gruffly.

The woman nodded, as if further conversation was not worth the effort, then moved away.

Mary waited until the ale arrived, then allowed herself to sit back and take a sip, her gaze never once leaving the door.

How long to give it before she could reasonably leave? Half an hour? An hour? Would those men continue combing the town for her as long as it may take, or would they call off their search? She decided to give it an hour, then try to get back to the Crossed Keys.

An hour was a long time to wait. The first ale seemed to go down very quickly, as did the second one she ordered, then a third.

So she was no longer watching the door with quite such intensity, and was even dozing slightly with her head down when some men came in and took seats at a table in front of the fire. Indeed, it was only when one of their voices filtered into her consciousness, that she even became aware of them at all.

"A remarkable conceit, that she took only a small wound to the shoulder."

Mary's head snapped up. Right now that voice was as familiar to her as any she had ever known.

Roger Rolleston!

She pulled her cap low, then glanced up from under the brim.

Four men were now seated at the table by the fire. Rolleston was sitting to one side; his profile silhouetted against the flames. Opposite him was a man she couldn't see clearly, as his face was fully in shadow. Then she caught sight of his hand.

His heavily bandaged hand.

She stared hard as he scratched his beard with fingers emerging from the bandaging. She thought she recognised the shape of his head as he leaned forward in front of the fire – last seen... where was it?

Poking out from behind an oak tree?

Nathan, the sniping archer? The one she had shot in the forest? If so, what was Rolleston doing sitting in a dark, dingy tavern with the archer? And if that really was him, then the fellow beside him would be...

Mary gasped and pulled her cap further down.

Greybeard!

What in heaven's name was Rolleston doing drinking and chatting with the archer and how in Heaven's name could he be with a man she had seen him run through with a sword a few days before?

Only – she hadn't actually seen it, had she? She had screwed her eyes tight shut!

She pushed her cap up slightly and looked at the fourth man in the group. At first she didn't recognise him at all, but then he said something, and the low, gravelly voice took her straight back to their journey up to Sheffield. She was sitting in the carriage when he had come to the window to tell her they were stopping for the night.

The driver!

The man who she had left for dead when hit by an arrow!

Mary turned slightly away from them – both to avoid being recognised, and also to have an ear facing them directly, so she could hear their conversation better.

"Has the substitution been actioned?" asked Greybeard.

"Aye," answered Rolleston. "The Barwell woman was slotted in as neat as a ninepin, as soon as the true Queen was taken to the back room."

The 'true' Queen?

"And now?"

There was a pause, and Mary could imagine Rolleston doing his trademark shrug. "She has shown herself as planned and created the conceit that it was but a flesh wound, which she will have dressed in her chambers." Then he added, "And no doubt she claimed to be dazed and confused from the trauma of the shot."

"That was clever," came a voice Mary didn't recognise – so presumably the archer. "To ensure her ladies do not question her memory."

"And it played well into our hands," said Greybeard, "to complete our part of the plan."

"Aye." This was the driver. "The true Queen is recovering well, since we spirited her out of the room where she was left as if dead."

"She is tough, Her Majesty," observed Rolleston. "The breastplate we made protected her from the shot, but the force of the ball still sent her flying to the ground. She said she thought she had broken her head on the cobbles, but by the grace of God, she was able to walk away from the room later."

"We must be thankful for the assassin's accuracy with that musket," said Greybeard. "Not only did the shot find our bladder of blood with unerring precision, but it also hit the Queen in the middle of the breastplate, where it was strongest. Think if she had missed, and say hit the Queen in the head, then we would be in a very different position."

There was silence, then Rolleston said, "So I would we raise a toast to the woman whose blind ignorance and accurate marksmanship has made our Catholic plan so successful!" There was the sound of tankards being thumped on the table, then a pause as they drank. "To Mistress Anne Carter. Without her our plan would have been as naught!"

Mary stiffened, feeling as if a cold wave had broken over her and her whole body was made of ice; completely numbed. What more could these traitors; these vermin, say now?

She hadn't heard the half of it.

Rolleston continued, "Do you know, I thought she would never be one to carry out the attack on the true Queen. I did not think she had the strength to do it."

"Or the courage," observed Greybeard with a dirty-sounding chuckle. "I thought she was going to shit herself when I tied her up and threatened her in the forest."

"She had the wit to hide her strange musket beneath her skirt, did she not?" observed the archer.

"I agree," answered Greybeard, "but that played into my hand well, for I must let her keep it so she could use it for the assassination. I would not have wanted to question her over it, as a real brigand would."

"You are correct, Antony," said the archer. "Although I would you had taken it off her before she wounded me so grievously in the hand."

Antony? Mary almost looked round. Did that mean Greybeard was the investor Antony Brooks? Now she thought about it, he did look a bit dapper for a highwayman. His beard was too neatly trimmed for a start. How had she not seen that?

"She was like a frighted kitten before a snake," said the driver.

"Until I came to the rescue and fought for her honour," Rolleston laughed. Then his voice changed, and he muttered, "And you opened up my leg like a piece of mutton, Antony."

"Come now," answered Greybeard. "It is no different from when we were boys and you hit me in the head with your catapult."

"Yes, and as I recall, you knocked me to the ground with a wooden sword."

"So I reckon we acquitted each other equally." Greybeard paused. "Then and now."

"But that was not part of the plan for the ambush, was it?"

Rolleston continued. "Make it look like show – flashing blades and every cut parried; that was what we agreed." There was a silence, then he added, "Make her think I was her saviour."

"You made as if you had killed me while her eyes were shut, did you not, good fellow?" said Greybeard. "That was enough, I venture."

"For sure. In truth, it was fortunate I had plenty of blood flowing from my leg to smear all about my blade and on your back," said Rolleston. "That was a nice touch."

"There you have it," said Greybeard. "Had I not opened your leg, we would have not been able to pull that little trick."

"Anyhow, it all worked well in the end," interjected the driver. "Did you not say that after the fight and your sad tale before Antony's house, that she bent more easily to your will? So in the end she told you all, enabling you to insert our plan into hers?"

"Almost true," answered Rolleston. "the rescue and the tale helped, but I had to lead her in a few more steps to tease out the full plan." He chuckled. "Your two ruffian friends made most convincing would-be rapists in the Crossed Keys, Nathan. That was what finally convinced her to let me stay and learn all."

"Indeed," answered the archer. "Although I had to ride hard to get to the message to them, once you told me it was to be the Crossed Keys," he gave a short laugh. "It was hard to ride one-handed." He held up his bandaged hand. "How did you get away from your lady?"

"No more than any man would say – I told her I was taking a piss," said Rolleston.

There was a silence, then the sound of an empty tankard

hitting the table. "We should be going, as we have ground to cover this evening," said Greybeard. "You have the letter and the Earl's note in plain words that proves the plot, Roger?"

"I do." There was a rustle of papers, "neatly purloined from the Earl's desk last eve, when my lady thought I was taking a last glass of his Rhenish."

"I have never known you to pass up a glass of wine, Roger," said Greybeard, a smile in his voice.

"Nay, old friend," answered Rolleston with a chuckle, as there was the sound of something heavy being placed on the table. "I took the unopened bottle also."

34

CHAPTER THIRTY-FOUR

It was many minutes after the men had left that Mary was able to move a muscle, such was the shock of learning just how much of a fool she had been.

A stupid, blind, trusting fool!

How had she not seen that Rolleston had been playing her like a bloody harpist? Oh yes, he had known exactly which strings to pluck in order to win her round; the 'knight-in-shining-armour-battling-for-her-honour' thing – that came from her little anecdote on the first day in the carriage – when Tom Cobham had saved her from a would-be rapist. And then trotting out the 'I-was-an-unjustly-accused-innocent' sob story... so clearly designed to tug at her naturally sympathetic heartstrings.

And so clearly an evil, calculating lie! He was, and had always been, a treasonous Catholic, determined to replace Elizabeth with the Queen of Scots.

He must have planned the whole thing in league with Brooks and the others. All that business of spending the night in the beds of serving girls; he probably spent most of the night plotting with his friends. And she, Mary, had tut-tutted, dismissed him as a sexual addict and slept like a log. Meanwhile, they were downstairs, working it all out.

To start with, they had planned the fake ambush, with the driver being hit – but clearly not killed – by the arrow. Mary shook her head. No doubt he had been wearing a thick leather vest under his jerkin as protection – just like the Queen of Scots.

A cold snake of anger suddenly squeezed itself tightly around her gut as she recalled Rolleston's words that morn-ing, dropped casually into the conversation. "I will take a short stroll around the town," he had said, "then I will come back here and await your return."

A short walk to the castle, more like – to prepare the Queen for their plan to save her life, and to fit their armoured breastplate!

The devious, scheming sod!

Mary clenched her fists so hard that her nails nearly broke the skin.

The Queen had stepped out for her walk much later than usual – no doubt as she was having her armour and bladder of pig's blood fitted.

And hadn't Mary played her part to perfection, doing ex-actly what the Catholics had wanted and planned for her?

Hadn't she just..?

Oh yes, their plan was even more devious than Walsingham's – especially as it used his scheme as their start-point...

Mary forced herself to unclench her fists, and to take a deep breath.

So, they have the Queen of Scots. What happens now?

The damned woman would be gloating over her freedom and travelling triumphantly towards London. And what's more, she would be able to travel openly, thanks to Frances Barwell so conveniently 'covering' for her in Sheffield.

On the way she would be presented to as many Catholics as possible; stirring them on to support her cause. There would be forces raised, as Catholic landowners, emboldened by the sight of the woman they believed to be their true queen, pledged their militias and the men in their service. No doubt the word would also be going out to the Catholics in the north, still smarting from the failure of the Northern Rebellion a few years earlier.

Walsingham's coded letter and the Earl's translation would be presented as proof of the plot, bringing not only the committed Catholics to her side, but also those so-called Protestants who still secretly believed in the old ways of worship. Damn Rolleston for sneaking back and stealing them off the table before the Earl had thought to lock them away.

Damn the unfeeling bastard to hell!

With a growing Catholic army behind her, the Queen of Scots would become an unstoppable force, sweeping towards London to claim the throne. At best she would take it unopposed, and at worst there would be a bloody battle, with many lives lost on both sides.

None of which would be happening if she, Mary de Beauvais, had not been such a stupid, trusting, bloody idiot, revealing the plot when she had been sworn to secrecy by the Queen herself...

Mary took another deep breath, forcing herself to calm down and consider how this would play out.

When the new queen was crowned as Mary II – what then?

Of course, she would restore Catholicism.

Once again every man, woman and child in the land would have to immediately and uncomplainingly change the daily practice of their religion. A wave of priests would miraculously appear, emerging from their foul-smelling hiding holes like bears from hibernation, or triumphantly stepping ashore from exile. They would replace the Protestant clergy in every place of worship, from the smallest chapel up to Canterbury itself. Anyone suspected of having an English bible would be open to an accusation of heresy; liable to be arrested and have their home searched. An open charter for petty jealousies to flourish and for society to split apart like a busting balloon.

Philip II in Spain would look on with approval, no doubt offering to help 'catholicise' England by sending over the Inquisition – and with it would come the terrible burnings and martyrdoms that had so characterised the first Mary's reign twenty years before.

And Elizabeth?

Mary put her head in her hands.

Thanks to her utter stupidity, the poor Queen was going to be faced with the one thing she had justly feared: the loss of her crown to her Scottish cousin.

And not just her crown. For how would the new Queen Mary treat her rival, who had kept her imprisoned for many years in castles that were so damp and drafty that it had given her painful arthritis, and then tried to have her killed by a secret assassin?

Mary stared blankly into the fire, and it seemed as if she was back in her rooms in the Tower, with Elizabeth putting a hand over hers.

"I need your understanding and your counsel..."

And what had that understanding and that counsel given to Elizabeth?

Imprisonment and almost certain death.

Mary felt as if she was about to throw up.

She took a further deep breath and stood, clutching the table for support.

"This is my mess," she said to herself. "My own stupid, stupid fault. So what now?"

She steadied herself and looked into the fire.

"I have to stop them. Whatever it takes, at least I have to try..."

Or die in the attempt?

Yes!

She ran out of the tavern and headed back into town.

---o---

A few enquiries later, she arrived at the market square, and found a horse dealer in one corner.

He was a tall, bald man with one lazy eye and the other constantly roving independently around the square as he talked.

"A horse for you, young master?" he asked, when Mary had stated her needs. "For sure. I have the finest beast right here."

Mary eyed the sorry-looking horse standing alone behind him. "Is that the only one you have? I need to ride at speed on the most urgent business."

"Aye, it is the only one. Trade has been brisk this day, with talk of the Queen of Scots being shot. There are those who wished to be away from the town at speed and sought a beast on the spot." He gave a small chuckle that was more of a sneer. "But, Master, the good news for you is that like all fine dealers, I have saved my best till the last." He gave her a yellow-toothed smile. "He is a worthy beast I tell you, and will take you far without complaint or tiring, at a trot, an easy canter, or even at a gallop."

"And you have a saddle, a bridle and reins?" she asked, deciding she had little choice, if she wanted to be away quickly.

She had decided against going back to the Crossed Keys for her own horse, in case any of Rolleston's men were watching it. They would no doubt be expecting her to go back there – and it was only by good fortune that she had overheard them in the Cock and Bull and avoided it.

"That I have young master," the dealer said, without either of his eyes quite meeting hers.

A few minutes later a price was agreed – which was more than Mary wanted to pay, but considerably less than he had first asked. She handed over the coins from her purse and the deal was done. Then she swung up into the saddle, gathered the reins and made her slow way out of the crowded market square, then out onto the streets of Sheffield and the road south.

35

CHAPTER THIRTY-FIVE

Mary urged the horse through the narrow streets out of Sheffield, surrounded by crowds who seemed to have little care for the rider in their midst with an increasingly urgent need to get past. They seemed more content to gather in shocked huddles, no doubt sharing increasingly salacious stories of the assassination attempt at the castle.

As she rode, Mary began to think the horse dealer had deliberately sold her a stinker. Far from being eager to move, it plodded along without any sense of urgency, and although it would have been difficult to proceed any quicker through the milling crowds, Mary could sense the horse was not particularly eager to speed up. It was like driving a large car with a tiny engine.

A bread seller with a barrow of loaves suddenly stopped

right in the middle of the road and started to sell a loaf to a woman a grey coif, causing Mary to slow the horse even more and plod round.

"Have a care, man!" shouted the trader, looking up. "You would knock over my barrow and spoil my loaves!"

Mary did not respond aloud, but muttered "moron" under her breath as she continued past them.

Once she got moving again, Mary reviewed her plan. The first stop had to be the traveller's inn a couple of miles outside Sheffield where she and Rolleston had left the carriage. Assuming that the Scottish Queen would want to travel in some comfort after her various ordeals, it seemed reasonable to suppose that they would stop to collect the carriage. Indeed, it made sense that Rolleston had wanted to leave the carriage there, as it would be available for their journey south once they were away from Sheffield.

Mary urged the horse into a gap in the crowd and looked up. The town gate could just be seen ahead. The sooner she could get clear of all these blasted people, the sooner she could make some speed – and maybe even catch Rolleston and the Queen at the inn.

With that hopeful thought, Mary rode out of the gates and into open countryside.

Once she had a clear road ahead, she squeezed her legs to try and get the horse up to the 'easy canter' promised by the dealer.

Unfortunately the horse had other ideas, and reacted to her instructions by slowing its walking pace. "Oh come *on!*" Mary snapped, digging her heels in. But her normal empathy with horses didn't appear to work on this beast, rather it seemed to take pleasure in doing the exact opposite of what she wanted. The more she urged it, the slower it went. So in the end she stopped flapping around on its back like an angry swan, and instead tried not urging it at all. However, this seemed to be exactly what the horse had really wanted all along, and it settled itself into a leisurely walk.

So by the time they finally ambled into the yard at the traveller's inn, Mary had used every swear word she knew at it, and had even made up a few new ones as well.

She slid from the horse's back and looked it hard in the eye.

"If England falls to the Catholics, you useless, brainless donkey," she hissed in its ear, "it will be your fault. Do you hear me?"

The horse whinnied and raised its head, then bared its teeth at her, as if to say that it was all her fault and nothing to do with him. "Come on, you pathetic piece of dog-meat," she continued, dragging it into the stables.

The inside was dark. Unlike many of the inns she had stopped at, which just had a high roof supported by a single wall on one side and stout wooden pillars on the other, these stables were a secure, dry, four-walled building, giving the horses real protection from the cold winds. The only light came from the door and gaps in the wall boards that threw random beams of light around the building.

Once Mary's eyes became accustomed, she could see that there was a large hay bale at one end, and beside it a blackened wood water-trough about the size of a modern bath. The smell of sweating horses and their waste was overpowering, so she found an empty stall as fast as she could, tied the horse to the rail, then walked back out into the fresh air of the main yard.

The first thing was to see if the carriage was still there, which would mean Rolleston and the Queen would likely be there as well. If not, then she would have to think again...

Mary started looking around for the familiar shape. There was a chance she was not too late. Rolleston had probably not been too far ahead, as he would have needed time to get the Queen away from the castle, tend to any injuries she had sustained from the shooting and the fall onto the cobbles, then get her onto a horse and out of Sheffield. No doubt they would have had just as much difficulty getting through the crowds as she had. Although they would have made more speed once they had hit the clear roads.

Damn the dealer's slow, plodding horse!

There was no immediate sign of the carriage in the court-yard, so she ran round to the back of the stables, hoping to see it standing there, solid and real. But there was nothing other than some weeds, a bale of hay and a few barrels.

With a muttered curse, she went back to the yard, just as a bright-eyed old man poked his head out of the stable door.

"I be the ostler here, young master," he said. "Is that your horse put just now in yonder stall?" he pointed back into the stables. She nodded. "Shall I have some water and hay for it?"

"Thank you," Mary replied, resisting the temptation to suggest a humane killer would be more appropriate, and trying to make her voice sound as gruff as she could.

She was about to walk into the inn to ask about Rolleston, when she had an idea. She followed the old man back inside.

As her eyes adjusted again to the dim light, she could see he was putting hay in front of her horse. He then went to the water trough and scooped up a pail, which he carried back and poured into the horse's own trough.

She cleared her throat. "I am seeking some companions who may still be here," she asked. "Can you tell me if they have departed already?"

The ostler came out of her horse's stall, wiping his hands on his apron. "I will certainly try, master," he answered. "Picture them to me."

"A tall man dressed as a merchant, an older man with a grey beard, a thickset man and one with a wounded hand. They would have had a tall red-haired woman with them also."

"Oh aye, master," he said with a smile. "I recall them well. They left in a fine carriage but half an hour or so ago..."

Half an hour! If only that lazy old nag had gone at a reasonable pace, she might have caught them!

The ostler was continuing. "...The merchant – I heard one call him Rollwood or similar, and he called another Antony, I think it was – this Rollwood, he gave me a farthing for my care of his horses. The lady said not a word, and indeed she seemed quite unwell – so they had to help her into the carriage." He paused. "Most strange, I thought it, for when they helped her up, she seemed greatly dismissive of their assistance, as if she was a noblewoman, for all her lowly attire." He frowned. "Now what was her name? They called her Mistress somesuch, as they helped her into the carriage." He thought some more. "...Mistress Anne C-something, it was."

"Carter?"

The ostler smiled happily. "Aye, master, that was it. Mistress Anne Carter was her name. That was it."

Oh, really?

REALLY?

Rolleston was going to pay for that little joke!

She fished in her purse for a farthing, then took a deep breath. "But half an hour since they left?" she asked, handing it over.

"Much obliged, master." He bit the farthing, then pocketed it. "Maybe more, maybe less. If your horse is fresh, you will soon catch them."

Mary looked back at the dealer's nag, chewing on its hay. As if knowing it was being discussed, it turned and eyed her moodily. Even at its freshest, this horse would never go fast enough. She would need to find another, and quickly.

She glanced across at the other stables. There were five further stalls, with a horse's hindquarters visible in four of them. If only one of these others was her ride, rather than the obstinate mule she had come here on...

"Yes," she said. "Thank you for your help."

He nodded, and as he turned to leave, a man walked into the light of the doorway. Standing there silhouetted, all Mary could see was that he was reasonably tall and well-built, with a rakish cap and his hands on his hips.

Rolleston?

The man moved into the building, and one of the random beams of light picked out his body like a searchlight. He was wearing a fine brown doublet with gold edging, yellow trunk-hose split with brown and gold, black hose and a leather garter. Then he walked forward again, so the beam of light moved up to his face. Mary let out the breath she must have been holding. She had never seen this man before.

"You, ostler," he snapped. "Is my beast ready? I ride out in but a half hour."

"Yes, master," the ostler replied, looking towards a well-built chestnut mare in the furthest stall. "I will have her saddled and ready most presently."

"And you have brushed her well? Mane, tail and coat?"

"I have that, master."

"And her hooves, have they been oiled?"

"Indeed they have."

The man drummed his fingers on his sword hilt. "Good. I will be having my ale and pie in the parlour, and will be back before the half hour."

"She will be ready in good time, master, my word on it."

The man did not reply, but marched out of the stables and could be heard striding across the cobbles to the inn.

Mary turned back to the ostler. "I thank you, good man, for your help." She walked to the door and stopped. "My horse requires but hay and water – that is all."

Then she walked over to the inn herself.

---O---

The familiar smell of sweat and candle smoke replaced that of horses as Mary entered the parlour of the inn; a smell so strong that she could almost taste it. Taking a seat, she looked around for the horse-owning man, and spotted him a few tables away. Now she could see his face more clearly in the light of the candle on his table, she could see how he could be mistaken for Rolleston, if a little older and a little rougher around the edges. Indeed, he seemed to have the look of a yeoman about him, rather than a man of the high-status that his clothes suggested.

"Another fraud," she muttered under her breath. Then she put her hand to her mouth as a dreadful thought occurred, and she murmured, "Am I becoming an Elizabethan snob? Oh, goodness. I do hope not!"

She looked round to see if anyone had heard, as there was not much noise from the few travellers sitting at the various tables. But they were nursing their tankards of ale and plates of bread and cheese or pie, and chatting quietly. A dog was working the tables for scraps, running from one hand to the next with its tail wagging. After a moment it approached Mary.

"Sorry old chum," she said softly, "nothing for you here." The dog, which looked like some form of long-legged terrier, put its paws up on her lap and examined the table, as if it didn't quite believe her and had to check for itself. "See?" she said, "nothing there." The dog gave her a disappointed look, then jumped down and bounded across to the next table.

Mary looked back at the man, to see that a pretty young serving girl was just bringing a tankard of ale and a steaming pie to his table. As the girl leaned over to put them down, Mary saw the man put his hand up and grab at her chest. The girl froze. Then he smiled at her, as he moved his hand slowly up to her collar, before working it under her linen chemise like some dreadful burrowing insect. Then, as Mary watched in sick fascination, he slowly slid his hand down, until she could see it was clearly cupped around the poor girl's breast.

"Good firm duckies, my girl," she heard him say with a sneer. "If I was not so soon leaving, I would have a proper look at them..." He withdrew his hand and with his eyes still fixed on the girl's, he brought his palm up and sniffed at it. "...And maybe more."

The girl pulled her collar back up, as if by fixing her clothing she could undo what had just happened, then she scurried away without responding. It looked to Mary as if the girl had experienced this kind of behaviour many times before from such a man, and even if it was not unexpected, it was certainly disgustingly unwelcome.

After she had gone, the man took a deep swig from his tankard and smiled to himself as he started to eat his pie.

Mary sat back and shook her head slowly. What a total *prick*. Just like Rolleston – another heartless, misogynistic example of Elizabethan manhood.

And just like Rolleston, she was not going to let this go unpunished. It was going to be a pleasure to kill two birds with one stone; as not only was she going to steal his horse – for the sake of Queen and Country, naturally – but she fully expected this would bring the heartless sod down a peg or two when he found it gone.

Mary reckoned she only had a few minutes until the ostler had the man's horse saddled and ready. And judging by the speed the fellow was now wolfing down his pie, he would be heading out at about the same time. So she had better move quickly herself.

She got up and slipped outside, then hurried over to the stables. Peering round the doorway into the dim building, she could just make out movement by the man's horse. Then there was the sound of a hand slapping a horse's neck.

"There, girl, there. You are quite the one, are you not, my lovely?"

Mary heard a rustle of straw, then the sound of footsteps coming towards her. Quickly she moved round to the side of the building and flattened herself against the wall. She waited a few seconds, then peered round. The ostler was heading away towards the inn; no doubt to let the man inside know his horse was ready.

Mary slid into the stables and went up to where the mare was standing, fully saddled.

"Yes, you are quite the one, aren't you?" she said as she stroked its neck. "But now you are going to be mine. I shall call you Justice. Do you like that, Justice?" The mare gave a small whinny. "I will take that as a 'yes', shall I?" Mary lifted the stirrup. "Now, Justice, I need to make sure we fit each other well. Your previous master had quite long legs." She shortened the stirrup, then went round to the other side. Justice moved over slightly, giving her more room. "Thank you," Mary said as she adjusted the other stirrup, "I think we are going to understand each other brilliantly." Then she slipped her finger under the leather girth strap. "Nice and tight," she observed. She undid the halter rope and led Justice out of the stall. A mounting block was standing to one side, so she pulled it over with her foot, then used it to swing herself up and settle into the saddle. "Right, my girl, let's go."

She squeezed her heels and Justice trotted out of the

stables, just as the front door of the inn opened and the mare's previous owner came out with the ostler.

"Oi!" he shouted and started to run towards her.

Mary put her head down, gave a firm kick and flicked the reins. "Come on, girl!" she urged, and there was no delay or sluggishness in Justice's response. With a neigh and a shake of her head, she was off like a Derby winner coming out of the stalls. As they passed through the gate at the end of the courtyard, Mary glanced back over her shoulder. The man was skittering to a stop on the cobbles, then snatching off his cap and flinging it down in anger.

"Forget him now," Mary said. "We've got a queen to find!"

She put her head down again, lifted her bottom like a true jockey and galloped out onto the lane heading south.

36

CHAPTER THIRTY-SIX

Justice was as fast and sure-footed as the dealer's horse had been slow and ponderous, but after cantering for over an hour, it was clear that she was starting to tire. So when the road went through a small village, Mary slowed her to a walk and started peering around in the growing darkness for a horse trough. She found it by a small green, and let Justice enjoy a long and necessary drink.

Eventually the mare lifted her head from the water, but left it hanging low as she fixed her dark liquid eye on Mary.

"You are tired, aren't you, old girl?" Mary said as she ran her hand down Justice's damp neck. "You've been running hard, and I am pretty sure we will have got closer to those blasted Catholics, but you do deserve a rest." Then she added, "Just a short one, mind, as we must press on. We need to get there as soon as possible, and that means tonight."

Without re-mounting, she led Justice toward some

flickering lights on the other side of the green. "Look," she said, as a swinging sign became visible above the door of one of the buildings. "A tavern. I could do with a drink as well."

The tavern was a sad-looking tumbledown; a single-storied, timber-framed building, with cracks in the walls and a thatched roof with gaps that suggested it would be far from watertight in the rain. There were two windows on each side of the front door, all with dirty and crooked shutters. As she walked up through the small courtyard towards the door, she spotted a horse rail to one side, so she walked Justice over. There was a long manger by the rail, containing a few sparse bundles of hay.

"Look, Justice," she said, trying to sound bright for the horse's sake, "you get to have dinner as well!" She tied the horse with a rope long enough to let her reach the hay, then went inside and sat at a small table by one of the windows. There was a clear patch in the glass where she could see Justice across the courtyard by the light of the rising moon. The mare had her head down in the manger and seemed to be chewing contentedly.

Mary chuckled. It was good to keep an eye on Justice; heaven forbid that someone might try to steal her.

A serving girl came over, and Mary ordered a pigeon pie and ale. They arrived shortly, giving off a delicious, warm, comforting smell. She breathed it in deeply, triggering a sudden memory of being back in the Great Hall at Grangedean Manor having supper with William and the kids...

Oh to be back there in reality, in place of this shabby, dirty, run-down little tavern in the middle of nowhere, and to be with her family instead of being alone...

Mary shook her head in frustration. Now was not the time to descend into self-pity.

She cut into the pie, and this time the smell actually made her mouth water. She took a piece of meat. It was nothing like the pies that came out of the Grangedean kitchens; indeed, Ruth would never let the cook produce anything like this, but right here, right now, it was just what she needed.

Shortly after this, when the food and drink were settling comfortably in her stomach, she sat back and found herself giving a long, deep, chest-stretching yawn.

In truth, it was not surprising she was tired. It was incredible just how much had happened in the space of one day. Mary closed her eyes.

What a day it had been...

After a particularly bad night's sleep, she had tried – and it seems, failed – to assassinate the Queen of Scots; uncovered the Catholic counterplot; stolen a horse and ridden like a demon through the dusk after the Queen of Scots in order to... what? To kill her properly this time?

Mary gave a deep sigh. Somehow it didn't seem like that was a good option anymore. Somehow it seemed like the failure of the first attempt was a sign that maybe she wasn't cut out to be a cold-blooded assassin. Had it been in truth a lucky escape – when she'd pulled that trigger and not actually killed the Queen?

But then, if she didn't kill Mary, Queen of Scots, Walsingham's plot would fail, Elizabeth would probably be deposed and executed, Catholic-inspired terror would stalk the land – and if Walsingham didn't have her burned at the stake, then Mary, Queen of Scots most certainly would.

There was no doubt that bringing forward the death of one woman would save countless other lives...

She pushed with her foot at the bag she had put under the table and felt the reassuring weight of the gun inside. There was no doubt that she, Lady Mary de Beauvais, had both the means, and the motive, to make sure that finally, that death would happen.

Could she do it? Could she once again pull that trigger, knowing that fate had stepped in previously to prevent her actions having a lethal outcome?

Mary opened her eyes and let out a long, frustrated breath.

That was a decision she would have to face if she caught up with Rolleston and the Queen of Scots.

When she caught up with Rolleston and the Queen...

Because if she did not catch up with them, then her only option would be to watch Elizabeth be deposed and killed, and know, in whatever time she had left before Queen Mary had her found, arrested, tried and executed for treason, that it was all her fault. That she had a chance to put things right, and failed.

She could not – she must not fail!

Mary stood up, knocked back the last of her ale, then grabbed her bag and left the tavern.

37

❧

CHAPTER
THIRTY-SEVEN

The signpost at the crossroads swept past so quickly that it took a moment for Mary to realise that it was the one that pointed to Nottingham, Newark and Bridgeford. She pulled Justice up so sharply that the mare dropped her hindquarters and almost reared up, as she struggled to come to a stop. Finally Justice was standing still, her flanks heaving and her head tossing, steam rising into the moonlit sky from her neck.

Mary turned the horse round and they trotted back to the signpost.

"I am sure it was this one," she muttered, "although it looks quite different at night." She peered at the moss-edged wooden signs with their crudely carved lettering looking very black in the light of the moon. "Yes," she said, "it is definitely the right one." She wheeled Justice round to the direction of 'Bridgeford'. "Come on," she urged the mare, and they set off down the rough path.

The glow from Oak House was visible even before she got up to the gate; it was lit up like a Christmas tree with candles blazing in all the windows, giving it a cosy warmth that was quite at odds with the potential threat of its inhabitants.

Once Justice was tied securely to a tree out of sight of the house, Mary dropped to the earth by the gates and peered through. Oak House was only around twenty yards away, so she didn't need the gun's scope to see clearly who was inside.

Rolleston, Brooks, the archer and the driver were in the parlour, standing by the fire with glasses in their hands. They seemed to be very pleased with themselves; she could see them through the small panes of glass throwing back their heads with laughter, and taking great gulps of their wine. It did not need Sherlock Holmes to deduce what they were so pleased about – and no doubt Mary's ears should be burning as they re-lived their successful spiriting away of the Scottish Queen from under her unsuspecting nose.

Mary clenched her fists. It wasn't just her ears that were burning out here in the dark; once again she felt her anger flaring up after being played for a fool.

There were other men drinking and chatting with them. Mary slowly unclenched her fists and counted a further six; all dressed in the fine clothes of merchants and gentlemen, but all with the broad shoulders and heavy build of fighting men. Each man was armed, with broad swords at their sides and poignard knives at their belts.

Mary slid slightly further back, putting herself deeper

into the shadow of the wall. One woman against ten men? Even if these were the only guards for the Scottish Queen and there weren't others in rooms she couldn't see, it was still scary odds.

She looked to the upstairs chamber. A pair of candles were burning in the window, their brightness making it difficult to see past them into the room. Maybe the magnification of the 'scope would help. She wriggled round to get the gun out of her bag, then decided she might as well load a cartridge into the breech, just in case. Settling herself into a comfortable position, she poked the barrel through the gate and sighted the crosshairs on the window. Now she could see into the room better, but her low angle meant that all she could see was the top of a four-poster bed.

She waited in case anyone moved inside, but nothing happened for many minutes, until suddenly the two candles were snuffed out, and heavy drapes were pulled across the window. If the Scottish Queen was in there, then she had retired for the night.

Mary turned back to the parlour, and focused on the men inside. She picked Rolleston in her sights, her finger hovering over the trigger as she kept him centred in the crosshairs. The small panes of thick, curved crown glass seemed to change the shape of his head as he moved, enlarging his chin and making his nose grow like Pinocchio.

The temptation to take the shot was strong, but Mary resisted. Not only was the thick glass likely to deflect it, but she would be giving up the element of surprise – her only chance to shorten the odds in her favour. If she took a pot at Rolleston, the others would immediately scatter, and no doubt hurry the Scottish Queen off to some place of greater safety, like the Secret Service around a US President. Then they would all spill out of the house to hunt down the lone assassin.

Better to deal with Roger bloody Rolleston later.

Mary followed him idly for a few more minutes, before spotting a woman coming into the room; well-dressed, grey-haired and looking around forty. She was carrying a large pewter jug and moved amongst the men, filling their glasses and chatting to each. She put a hand on Brooks's shoulder as she poured his wine – so presumably this was his wife. Mary moved her finger well away from the trigger as she watched Mistress Brooks finish replenishing the men's wine, before poking the fire, then leaving.

It was going to be a long night.

---0---

The dawn sun crept across Mary's face, waking her with a start.

For a moment she had no idea where she was. She stared bleary-eyed at a distant red-brick wall between the trees.

She was cold, she was stiff, and her neck was sore. Then it came back to her; she was outside Oak House, with the Scottish Queen hopefully still inside. As if a dream remembered, her situation started to become clear again. There had been the agonisingly long wait as the men laughed and drank in the parlour, seeming never likely to retire for the night. She had remained by the gate in the dark waiting for them to leave so she could do the same, until finally they had all yawned, scratched their chins and drifted off one by one until the parlour was empty.

Only then had Mary felt it was safe for her to try and get some sleep as well, so she had slunk over to the small, forested area a hundred yards back, where she had left Justice.

There she had found a small hollow filled with musty autumn leaves, and had crawled in, pulling the leaves over her to create some small warmth, and using her bag as a pillow.

And now it was morning. She stood and brushed off the leaves, then took a deep breath to steady herself. She was going to have to get moving if she was going to rescue her mission and stop the Queen of Scots from progressing south.

She gathered her bag and the gun, then glanced across to where she had tied Justice. At first there was no sign the horse, and for a dreadful moment she thought that maybe the previous owner had taken the mare back while she slept, but then there was a movement amongst the trees and Mary picked out the shape of a horse with her head down, eating some grasses. Nicely camouflaged.

She ran through the wood until she was beyond the gates to Oak House, then doubled back to a large oak. She had spotted it in the moonlight the night before, around thirty yards back from the gates. She looked at it again in the morning light. It seemed ideal – the perfect vantage point for the plan she had formed.

Putting the gun in the bag and securing it over her shoulders, she reached for the lowest branch and swung herself up. Then she climbed further until she reached a large wide branch. It was not too high, which gave her a good angle of fire, and had a number of higher branches hanging near, giving her some cover.

Settling herself onto the branch with her back to the trunk, she took out the gun and checked the chamber. The cartridge was still there, but she ejected it anyway, checked it over, then re-loaded it. She jiggled her hand in the pocket of her jerkin, and felt the reassuring smooth coldness of the other cartridges. Plenty of ammo.

Then she put the gun down on her lap, and waited.

38

CHAPTER THIRTY-EIGHT

It was around an hour later that the driver brought the carriage round to the front of the house. He stayed in his seat, as the six men Mary had seen the night before rode up, all armed with swords. They clustered around the carriage, their horses skittering about and raising their heads as the men chatted to each other. This seemed to make the pair harnessed to the carriage also skitter nervously, until the driver called out something that seemed to calm them down.

Rolleston and Brooks came out and conferred with the driver, then Brooks went inside, while Rolleston stood to one side of the carriage, glancing around. Maybe Mary was feeling vulnerable, but it looked suspiciously like he was deliberately noting possible hiding places.

She froze as he looked directly towards her tree.

Then he started to move in her direction.

Was he looking for her, knowing she might have followed them to Oak House? Was it her imagination, or was he staring straight at her as he walked? Surely he hadn't spotted her? Mary mentally shook her head. She was reasonably high up, the tree was at least fifty yards from the house, and she was sitting far back on the branch. She glanced briefly down at her sleeve. Her jerkin and breeches were made of dark serge and were covered in dirt after she had been wearing them for a day and slept a night in the open. She had even deliberately muddied her face with a liberal smearing of dirt, in addition to the darkening she had added the morning before to look like a man. So she should be nothing more than a vague shape blended into the distant tree itself.

But he continued to walk towards her.

Now he was close to the gate, still staring directly at the tree.

There was no other option; she would have to take him out if he came through the gate – and damn the consequences. She raised the gun slowly and put her eye to the sight.

Rolleston's face jumped into focus.

She centred the crosshairs on his forehead. It seemed as if he was looking straight at her, his piercing blue eyes under the heavy brow drilling directly into hers. Then he looked down. Mary dropped her sight to see what he was looking at. His hand was on the latch. He lifted it and started to open the gate.

She raised the sights to his head again, and settled her finger on the trigger.

Just walk through that gate, Roger, just you walk through, and I swear it will be the last thing you ever do.

Rolleston stopped, almost as if he had heard her.

She held her breath, as he turned his head and looked back. She glanced up and saw that Brooks was standing a few yards in front of the carriage, his hands on his hips.

"Roger?" she heard him call out.

Rolleston stopped with his hand on the gate and glanced back over his shoulder.

"Roger?" Brooks repeated.

With a last look at the tree, Rolleston turned on his heel and strode back.

Mary let out a long, slow breath and released her grip on the gun, bringing it down to her lap.

Rolleston got back to the carriage, and spoke urgently to Brooks, who nodded and hurried back into the house.

Just then Mistress Brooks came out with a tall red-haired woman in a plain grey gown.

Right. It was time to finish this.

Mary raised the gun again and took aim. Once more the Queen's familiar head jumped into her sights.

Mary slowed her breathing, keeping the crosshairs centred on the aristocratic profile, as she settled the trigger into the crook of her finger and started to squeeze...

The Queen's head suddenly disappeared from view.

Mary released the trigger and looked up.

Brooks was helping the Queen into the carriage, forcing her to bend down as she stepped in. Once inside, the Queen was only visible through one window, and then from the waist down.

Damn! Damn, damn, damn!

So now it would have to be plan B. Wait until the carriage comes closer.

Mary lowered the gun and tried to let her thumping heart settle as she waited for the carriage to move, but it seemed an agonisingly long time. There was plenty of comings and goings from the men and horses – one riding away then back with a costrel for the driver; another dismounting and running into the house before re-emerging with a bag for the Scottish Queen – but at the centre of this maelstrom of activity the carriage itself remained frustratingly still.

Just as Mary was wondering if she should maybe climb down and sneak up to the gates for a possible shot, the driver cracked his whip over the horses' backs. With a clatter of the wooden wheels on the cobbles, the carriage started to move; the riders all following close behind.

Giving a small sigh of relief, Mary lifted the gun again to her shoulder and took aim at the moving vehicle. As it turned towards the gates she was able to pick up the window in her sights, but the angle was still too sharp, and she could not see the Scottish Queen inside.

The carriage came up to the gates and one of the riders came forward, dismounted and opened them both up fully.

"Come through, Queen of Scots," Mary muttered. "Come on through so I can see you."

Once the carriage was past the gates, it turned slowly onto the track, so Mary had the open window more clearly in her sights, with the Scottish Queen's head in plain view inside.

Now it was time to make sure she finally finished the job.

But she did not take the shot.

There was a sudden whoosh, then a loud cracking thump that was so close it almost deafened her.

With a shocked scream she looked away from the carriage, and stared in cold horror at the arrow shaft that was now quivering in the tree beside her head, only a couple of inches from her ear.

As the gun slipped from her nerveless fingers and fell to the earth below, she heard a voice, worryingly close by.

"That was to show that I can shoot an arrow as true as I please," the voice said. "Stay still mistress, or I will put the next one through your eye."

A man emerged from the woods; an arrow held loosely in his bow.

It was Nathan the archer.

Mary had no doubt that if she made a sudden movement he would bring the bow up and fire within a fraction of a second. She raised her hands, noting as she did so that he still had one of his in a bandage.

"Aye," he said as he approached the tree, "as you see I still carry my injury from your musket, although it has not prevented me making such a nice shot this moment." He paused. "I was told by Master Rolleston to observe this tree most closely, and the Lord be praised; what do I find but Mistress Carter preparing to murder the true Queen." He chuckled; a dry, empty sound. "So I needs must fire a warning arrow to stop her in the attempt, must I not?"

He came closer and she saw him clearly, as if she was observing him for the first time. He was in his mid-thirties with sandy hair and a ruddy face, dressed in a green tunic under an armoured breastplate. His arms under the tunic bulged with heavy muscles, especially his right arm. "I could have pinned your ear to the tree from a furlong distant should I have wished, you understand?"

She nodded, her mouth dry.

"Good." He stopped a few yards away, while from the corner of her eye Mary saw the carriage disappear round a bend in the lane.

"Come down," he ordered.

As she was lowering herself from the final branch, he picked up the gun and was studying it carefully. "This is the firing weapon that put a hole through my hand as if driven by a burning stick?" he asked, staring at her with wide eyes. "By the Lord, where is the matchlock? The pan for the powder?" His face went white. "Belike 'tis the work of the devil, this?"

"I fashioned it myself," she stated, raising her chin. "It has nothing of the devil in it."

"So you say, mistress," he answered. "But I will have naught to do with it." He turned and threw it into the trees. As it landed, something must have caught the trigger and it fired with a loud crack. The archer crossed himself several times. "Christ in Heaven!" he exclaimed. "And you say there is no devilry in this, that spits out a ball without a human hand?"

"Whatever you say," she muttered, taking careful note of the tree where it landed.

"Now, tis no matter," he continued, "you will walk before me to the house, and there we will find out if there are useful things you know."

Mary made her way up to the gate, which was still open after the carriage had passed through. With her jaw clenched, she carried on up to the house. As she stepped into the hallway, the archer behind her said, "Up the stairs, if you please." At the top he said, "To your left, into the bed chamber."

She had barely had time to register the room with its brightly embroidered wall hangings and four-poster bed, when there was a blinding flash of pain in the back of her head, and the rushes on the floor suddenly came up to meet her.

Then there was blackness.

39

CHAPTER THIRTY-NINE

Someone seemed to be beating a heavy anvil in the back of her brain as Mary slowly opened her eyes and squinted up at the archer. He was standing over her, observing her with dispassionate curiosity like a scientist studies the object of an experiment.

She groaned and tried to rub the back of her head, but was surprised to find her right hand would not move. She tried her left, but that would not move either. With her breath starting to come in fast, shallow, panicky breaths, she moved her head painfully to both sides, and saw that she was lying on the bed with her wrists tied to each of the posts, so that her arms were spread out like a perverse image of Christ on the cross.

She tried to bring her legs up to kick at the man, but

neither leg would move either. She pulled at them with increasing urgency, but they stayed resolutely still. A sharp pain in each ankle made it clear that her legs were also tied up, presumably to the other two bed posts.

Mary stopped struggling and stared hard at the archer. "Let me go," she snarled.

"And why might I do that?" he asked with a thin smile.

There was no realistic answer, so she stayed silent, trying to ignore the throbbing pain in her head, now joined by the agonising tightness of the bonds on her wrists and ankles.

"Listen, woman," he said, his face becoming serious again. "I would know how much you can tell of your foul plot against the true Queen."

"And if I will not tell?" she muttered.

"Oh, in faith you will, I can assure you," he said. "The only question is how much pain you will endure first." Then he produced a short dagger, leaned over her and slowly, deliberately ran the flat of the blade down her cheek. "You will tell, mistress," he repeated, as the blade traced onto her neck and moved softly across her throat.

Mary tried to swallow the burning bile that suddenly came up. "Why ask?" she said eventually. "You seemed to have known it all anyhow."

"Belike we did," he answered, "but we would ensure there are no parts we have missed." He paused, "Parts that may prove most useful to our cause."

She shook her head, trying to ignore the dizzying pain. "Your cause has won," she said. "Your Queen is on her way to London, and I have no doubt she will gather support as she goes."

"Aye," he nodded with a real smile, pulling away the dagger. "Nottingham, Derby, Stratford, Oxford and many others besides – she will cleave each one to her side as she goes, with loyal Catholics emerging from the darkness of the bastard's heresy and embracing once again the true faith."

"Then let me go," she repeated. "I am no use to you."

He laughed; a bitter, twisted laugh with no mirth in it. "Oh, mistress, let me tell you what use you are to me." He leaned forward; his red face coming so close to hers that she could see the snot up his nose and smell the stale bread and ale on his breath. "You will tell me all, that is for sure. But before that, I would have payment for – this." He pulled back a moment, then his bandaged hand appeared in front of her eyes. Even though she tried to turn her head away there was no escaping the putrid smell of rotten flesh from the filthy cloth. He leaned back in. "Then, once you have given me all your secrets, you are right; I will have no use for you. So the only question is how I will dispatch you – mercifully and quick by a swift, deep sweep of my blade across your throat, or slowly by a small painful cut to the belly that could take days to bleed out."

"By Heavens," she said. "Your soul will face eternal damnation for this."

Unfortunately, this seemed to have little effect. "Nay," he said with a satisfied smirk, "you are a cursed heretic. Dispatching you will not only save my soul; it will ensure my everlasting place in Heaven."

She stayed silent.

"But I said first I wanted payment for your injury to my hand," he continued. He put it to his nose and grimaced. "It starts to fester, so that soon I will no longer have its use to pull my bow. And for that, woman, I would have you suffer greatly."

Mary could only look up at the man, her stomach twisting in dread as she waited to hear what particular payment he had in mind.

"I fancy I will take my payment from..." he looked down and paused a moment, then put the heel of his good hand up between her outstretched legs and rubbed slowly, "...from here."

Mary squirmed desperately as he rubbed harder – his eyes glazed and unseeing as his hand moved up and down. After what seemed like a lifetime he stopped, and his eyes focussed back onto her. Then he stood up and began to unbuckle his breastplate, before pulling down his breeches.

With a look of concentration, he turned to her own men's breeches and undid the lacing, then he pulled them roughly down as far as they would go, which, as she was spreadeagled on the bed, was not that far.

But unfortunately, it was far enough.

Mary thought she would be physically sick as she felt the air on her most private parts.

With an almost conspiratorial smile, as if this was some secret encounter that they had planned together, he climbed up onto the bed, and positioned himself over her.

"I would kiss you," he whispered in her ear, his breath making her skin crawl, "but I doubt I would find pleasure in it." Then he lifted his head up slightly as he arched his body in anticipation.

A kiss...

A Gorbals Kiss...

As the Alchemist had shown her...

The archer's jaw was right there above her...

With a force like a canon's fire, Mary brought her head up suddenly and directly into his jaw.

There was a sharp crack as she made contact; his head snapping back and his whole body jolting away as if she had hit him with a taser. Then his head hit the bed post and there was a second, even louder cracking sound, before he fell onto the floor with thump that reverberated around the house.

Mary dropped down onto the bolster, the pain in the back of her head now magnified to the level of a thousand hammers beating on a thousand anvils, and joined by an equal, if not greater, pain in her forehead.

The Alchemist had been right, and it did hurt to give a head-butt. It hurt like hell.

There was the sound of footsteps and a grey-haired woman appeared in the doorway.

"By Heavens!" she cried, "Who are you and what are you doing tied to my bed? What has passed here?" She walked over, and stopped by the archer's prone body. There was a silence as she took in Mary tied up with her breeches pulled down and her femininity on full display, with the archer beside the bed in a similar state of undress. Mary didn't suppose it would take a genius to work out what had been about to happen.

"Nathan is knocked out for sure," observed the woman, who Mary now recognised as Mistress Brooks. "For all he lives still. How came he so?"

"He was about to violate me," Mary said quietly. "So I used my forehead to hit his jaw. It was all I could do."

Mistress Brooks shook her head. "If had not seen it myself, I would scarce have believed it," she said. "And you are bleeding above your eye, which speaks further to the truth of this."

"Will you untie me and let me go?" Mary asked. "I will be most grateful."

"For sure," Mistress Brooks answered, and started on the nearest rope.

"Thank you," Mary said, with a relieved smile. As soon as the bonds were freed, she wiggled her fingers and circled her wrist to try and get some blood back into it.

But instead of moving round the bed, the other woman suddenly stopped and stood back.

"My other hand...?" Mary began, but the woman stepped further away.

"Wait! I know who you are," she said, colour draining from her face until it was as grey as her hair. "You are that Anne Carter that Antony talked of; she who would have killed our rightful Queen." She shook her head. "I would have freed you, and to do what? You would once more go about your evil heretic business."

"Please!" Mary asked, looking the woman directly in the eye. "Can you not see how I have suffered? That man would have raped me, had I not struck him first."

"That is as may be," Mistress Brooks said, her mouth now setting into a hard line. "But you are to remain tied up until my husband returns and says what is to be done."

"But that could be days or even weeks!" Mary cried. "I will be dead if you leave me here like this!" She used her free left hand to check her forehead, and found her fingers sticky with blood. "Will you abandon me here to starve or bleed to death? Have a pity, Mistress Brooks!"

"I have pity enough, but not for heretics." She grabbed at Mary's wrist and pulled it firmly back to the bed post, then re-tied the rope.

"And if that man awakes?" Mary said. "What then?"

"That is for God to decide." As Mistress Brooks stood back, Mary turned her head to look at her. As a woman she looked pleasant enough, and in different circumstances Mary felt she could have formed a friendship, but now was not the time. And indeed, time was the one thing she did not have. All she could think about was that carriage disappearing round the corner, taking all her hopes – and the future of the Elizabethan reign – with it. The longer she stayed tied to this bed, the less chance she had of catching it.

"I see you are determined on this, Mistress Brooks," she muttered. "I would you then leave me in peace to make prayers for my soul."

Mistress Brooks nodded, then went over to the door. With her hand on it, she turned back and seemed to be about to say something, then appeared to think better of it, and left without another word.

As soon as she was gone, Mary started twisting her left wrist to loosen the bonds. Mistress Brooks may have been a fervent Catholic, but, compared to Nathan the archer, she was very poor at tying knots. With a final few twists, Mary was able to slide her hand out. From there she made quick work of the rope on her other wrist; then she freed both her ankles.

Standing upright was not easy and she nearly fainted the first time she tried, but after a brief sit on the side of the bed, then using the nearest post as a support, she was able to stay on her feet. The next thing was to pull up and secure her men's breeches. "All my bits on display!" she said to herself. "I have *got* to get back into my women's clothes." She finished the lacing. "But first things first."

She took one of the four ropes, rolled Nathan onto his side and pulled his hands up behind his back. He started to groan as she secured his wrists, then his eyelids fluttered briefly as she ran the end of the rope down and tied it to his ankles. "There," she muttered as she pulled the last knot tight, "that will teach you."

His eyes opened and fixed on hers with a deep scowl. He tried to say something, but his jaw didn't seem to work well enough.

"Best not to try talking just now, Nathan," she instructed. "Just enjoy being tied up, eh?"

She knotted the other three ropes into one long length, which she secured to the handle of a heavy chest. Then she opened the window and threw the rope out, before clambering down and dropping lightly to the cobbles below.

Without looking back, she ran as fast as she could go to the gate, then to the tree where Nathan had thrown the gun. After a brief search among the leaves she spotted the steel barrel, grabbed it and ran to where Justice was still tied up, calmly chewing on some wild grasses.

Mary hauled herself up into the saddle, took a deep breath,

then gave Justice a small kick. "Come on, old girl," she said, "I hope you're feeling fresh. We have a carriage to catch."

---o---

When Mary got to the crossroads, she was almost falling from the saddle. Despite being an experienced rider, the combination of fatigue, stress – and being hit on the head twice – had left her as weak as a newborn puppy.

"Come on, Justice," she muttered, "we have to do this. We can sleep for a week, but only if we get it done." She studied the signposts. "What was it the archer said? *Nottingham.* He said the Queen would be starting to raise her forces in Nottingham." She wheeled Justice round. "Then that is where we will go."

Mary concentrated on two things as they cantered along the track; firstly, and most importantly, staying in the saddle as Justice leapt over ruts and fallen branches; and secondly, trying to work out how far behind the carriage she might be. Assuming she had only been unconscious for a few minutes – long enough for the archer to tie her to the bed posts – and that the attempted rape itself had only been say ten minutes, then together with her escape from Mistress Brooks, she was probably no more than half an hour behind.

Assuming she was on the right road.

She squeezed her legs into Justice's flanks. "Come on, old girl, this has got to be the right way. Let's keep it going."

But after a few miles she could feel Justice starting to flag, so at the next village she stopped and found the water trough, letting the mare enjoy a long drink. Then, when Justice was done, she led her over to a nearby tavern to have some hay in a stall, while she grabbed a quick meal of pottage and ale herself. She ate as fast as she could, then re-mounted and headed back onto the lane.

Just as she was about to kick Justice back up to a gallop, she saw an old man in a brown smock standing beside a gate. A thought occurred, and she wheeled the horse back and trotted over.

"By your leave, sir," she said, "I have become separated from my companions. Have they passed this way? A carriage pulled by a pair of horses and nine or ten riders accompanying." She smiled hopefully down at him.

There was a frustratingly long pause, and she was about to repeat the question a bit louder in case he was deaf, when he coughed and said, "Well, master, the carriage I saw a while ago was a noble affair, with many fine gentlemen riding beside," he looked her up and down and Mary was conscious that she must present a gruesome sight; a wild-eyed young man in filthy breeches and jerkin, with mud and dried blood all over 'his' face. "You became separated? Or in truth, they wanted you not?" He gave her a sickly grin. "Belike they threw you in a ditch and left you to wild dogs?" He touched his own forehead as if to remind her of the cut she had there. "For I cannot be seeing you as one of their company."

"Well, I do need to catch them up," she said. Then she added with what she hoped was a suitably passive-aggressive smile, "and I thank you for telling me that they passed this way."

She wheeled round again and urged Justice into a steady canter along the lane with a renewed sense of hope. For all that the old fellow had dismissed her as some sort of lying vagabond, he had confirmed that the carriage had indeed passed this way. If she kept up a reasonable and steady pace, with any luck she should catch up with them soon.

---o---

It was not long after she had left the old man that the lane emerged out of the forest, causing Mary to shield her eyes against the bright winter sunshine.

Ahead of her the path ran straight for what seemed like many miles across an open patchwork of fields: some bare and brown after the harvest while others lay fallow.

A flock of birds appeared and started swooping in formations above, creating a series of different shapes and patterns; calling and chittering so noisily that she could hear them clearly above the thudding of Justice's hooves and the regular jingle of her bridle. Then they flew away across the fields, just as another flock appeared directly ahead, and started making new formations of their own. It almost felt like they were choreographing their displays just for her entertainment.

Mary smiled at them, glad of some small diversion from the grim task she still faced. Maybe if she could concentrate on the birds, the winter sun and the joy of riding a great (albeit stolen) horse along the open fields, she could forget why she was chasing so hard after the carriage... and what she still had to do once she caught up with it.

The birds swooped low, bringing her gaze back to the horizon.

An unexpected movement suddenly caught her eye. A

loose, dark shape on the lane that did not look like part of the landscape; that seemed to shift and change.

With rising hope, she urged Justice forward to get a closer look. After a couple of minutes, the shape resolved itself into a central square that rocked from side to side, and tall, thin figures around it that moved up and down.

A coach and riders.

Got them," she said to herself.

Mary pulled Justice back and slowed to a brisk trot. Now she had the carriage in her sights, she was cautious about getting too close and being seen. Indeed, if she could make them out on the road ahead, it followed that they could just as easily spot her if they looked back. And judging by Rolleston's suspicions at Oak House that she was hiding in the tree – which he had presumably passed on to Nathan the archer – he would be ever mindful of the possibility that she was still following them.

But it was one thing to catch up with them; it was another to be able to take a further shot at the Scottish Queen and complete her mission. As she trotted along, keeping a good distance from the carriage, she explored possible plans in her mind.

It took a while, but eventually she nodded to herself.

"That's it," she said. "Got it!"

It was a plan that included not only resolving the situation with the Queen of Scots, but Mary's own escape thereafter.

And not forgetting Rolleston.

The plan included something extra special just for him.

40

CHAPTER FORTY

Mary kept well back while she studied the horizon for a forest that would give her cover to get past the carriage unseen, so she could then carry out the plan.

Eventually a long, low smudge of dark appeared along the horizon, and a few minutes later, she was close enough to see the crows and buzzards circling overhead and hear their calls as they swooped in and out of a deep line of trees.

The carriage ahead disappeared into the darkness of the forest, so she turned Justice off the lane and hopped her over the ditch into a field. Once they landed, Justice needed no urging to move smoothly up to a full gallop. With a shake of her mane, she put her head forward and fairly flew across the field, leaping over the ploughed ridges and dips with all the confidence of a Grand National winner.

In no time they entered the impenetrable-looking darkness, fifty yards or so across from the broad, well-worn path following the carriage.

For a moment it felt as if the lights had suddenly been switched off, so Mary eased Justice back to a steady canter. Over the next few minutes there were plenty of roots and branches to be cleared, trees to avoid and low branches to duck under, before a space opened up between the trees. She stole a quick glance to her right, expecting to be around level with the carriage by now. There was no sign of it through the thick trees. Mary only had a fraction of a second to feel reassured – if she couldn't see them, then they couldn't see her – before she had to drop her head down to Justice's neck as the mare took a flying leap over a fallen log directly under a low branch.

A few yards further on, another clearing allowed them to make even better progress through the forest. Soon after, Mary thought they must now be well past the carriage, so she decided it was time to head over to their right and pick up the lane again. Justice seemed happy with the change of direction, and they made good speed towards where Mary estimated the lane would be running through the trees.

It took a little longer than she thought, but then they jumped a root and Justice landed onto an earthy patch, before gathering herself and galloping across into the trees beyond. It was all so quick that Mary almost didn't register that they had reached the lane, but she was able to pull Justice up and trot her back to be sure.

Once she was certain it was indeed the lane, Mary cantered on in the direction of Nottingham, partly to check that she was not still behind the carriage – although at the speed they had been going, that was unlikely – but also to scout out the perfect tree for her plan.

She found it a couple of minutes later, then walked Justice a few yards further on and tied her up behind an oak.

Then she took the gun from her bag and settled herself to wait.

41

CHAPTER FORTY-ONE

It was quiet in the forest; the only sounds, apart from the soft thud of horses' hooves on the hard earth, were the jingle of bridles, the creak of leather on leather and the squeak of the wheels, as the nine men rode with the carriage containing the Queen of Scots.

Rolleston and Brooks were level with the driver, while the other six men formed a guard behind the carriage.

"I warrant we shall be in Nottingham within two or three hours, brother," Rolleston said. It pleased him that their mission would soon be moving to the next phase – getting the true Queen in front of her loyal subjects and ultimately, onto the throne in place of that heretic bastard, Elizabeth. It was a fitting reward for all the planning, subterfuge and dissembling needed to get them to this point – from his original pleading to that rogue Wychwoode in the Tower, to getting the Carter woman to play into his hands in Sheffield, to getting away from her at Oak House.

"Aye, brother," Brooks replied. "And we agree that we start with Francis Molineux of Haughton, who spends the winter in his town house in the city. He has stayed true to his faith and will be pleased to lead us to other noted Catholics hereabouts." He nodded. "So our movement will begin to build."

"Quite so," Rolleston agreed. "Francis is still most active for a man of... what is he... above sixty, I warrant? He carries some weight with the true believers of Nottingham." They rode on in an easy silence for a moment, then he added, "The Queen will be pleased to start meeting her subjects. Molineux will be an excellent catalyst to bring them to Her Highness's side."

"For sure," interjected the driver beside them, "And then there is Robert..."

But he never finished his sentence.

There was a sudden loud cracking sound from up ahead. Rolleston thought initially that it was a branch breaking, but then he saw that the driver had dropped the reins and brought his hands up to his chest. For a moment the man looked down in surprise at the bright red blood that started to pulse through them, then, with a small cough, he fell forward and lay still on the running board.

As Rolleston and Brooks stared in horror at the scarlet pool that began spreading out below the body and dripping down onto the path, a woman's voice rang out across the forest.

"Stop there, Roger, please."

A very familiar woman's voice.

Rolleston raised his head and snarled, "Anne Carter?"

"Hello Roger. You are indeed well met," the voice answered, sounding inappropriately conversational. There was a pause. "I said to stop the carriage, please, or should I once again use my gun?"

With a deep scowl, Rolleston put his hand to the bridle of the nearest horse and brought it to a stop. As he did so, one of the rear-guard men rode up.

"What has passed here?" he demanded. "Did I hear a musket..?" Then he saw the driver and turned to Rolleston with a white face.

"By Heavens," he said. "Are we under attack?"

Rolleston nodded. "Aye, Edmund, we are."

"I heard a woman's voice. Are we being threatened by... *that* woman?"

Rolleston nodded again.

"By the Lord's grace, I will have none of this!" Edmund drew his broadsword and started to ride forward. He had barely gone three yards when there was another loud crack from up ahead and he fell backwards out of his saddle as if struck by an axe, landing on the path with a heavy thud that reverberated around the forest. A few crows flew up from the tops of the trees, cawing loudly.

Rolleston's breath caught as he saw the neat red hole punched in the centre of Edmund's forehead.

There was a stunned silence, then Anne's voice came again. "Does anyone else want to try?" she asked. "I have more than enough ordnance here to do the same to each and every one of you. Several times over, in fact."

No-one moved.

"What is it you want, Mistress Carter?" This was Brooks.

"Oh, I think you can guess that, Master Brooks," she answered. "I set out on a mission to protect our true Queen by removing her Catholic rival, and I do not intend to fail."

"Then why do you not take the shot now?" Brooks gestured back at the carriage. "You have her at your mercy."

"Oh, I have no doubt that your heroic queen is presently lying out of my sight on the floor of the carriage. If I took a shot now, the best I could do would be to put a brand-new hole in the royal arse." There was another chuckle. "Anyway, why do you not ask Roger?"

"What you mean you by that?" Rolleston asked, feeling a small, cold chill of fear starting in his belly. Where was the she-devil going with this?

"Oh, come now, Roger, you know full well our plan. You can stop your lying now. These men will find out soon enough whose side you are truly on."

Rolleston felt the cold fear squeeze hard. "I am on the side of the true faith and the true Queen," he said

"Indeed you are, my friend," Anne Carter answered. "But do these men and the lady in the carriage know that means the reformed faith and Queen Elizabeth?"

"It does not," he snapped, feeling a cold sweat starting to run down his back. "And you know full well it does not."

"I know you are a consummate liar, Roger," she answered, her voice taking on a harder edge. Then she gave a bright, tinkly laugh. "But our plan has gone so well thus far, that in truth, I forgive you."

"Your plan?" Brooks growled, turning to Rolleston with a dark frown. "What plan was that?"

"Antony, my true friend," Rolleston said quietly, "surely you do not believe these lies? From a woman? A woman we have played all along for a fool?"

"I know not what to believe," Brooks answered. "But I do know you gained her trust on your journey north, so now I have a doubt that maybe you have conspired with her to bring us to this point? Belike she is no fool, and you have both been playing us?"

"By the Lord's grace, that is no way to address your oldest and dearest friend, Antony! Are we not as close as brothers? Have I not proved myself many times over?" Rolleston held his hands wide in a gesture of supplication. He turned round and appealed directly to the remaining men behind the carriage. "You will vouchsafe me, will you not? I have..." He paused, briefly distracted by the sight of one of them slithering into the undergrowth on his belly like a vengeful snake. "...I have been true to the cause from the start!" he finished, as the man's feet disappeared.

"As well as may be," answered Brooks, "but I fear I need better proof than just your word. This is the gravest matter, and even friends can turn their coats." He paused, chewing the inside of his cheek as he considered Rolleston. "I would you ride forward and capture the woman. Then I will believe you."

"Nay, do you take me for a fool?" Rolleston protested. "If I ride forward and am true to the cause as I say, then she will put a hole in my head just as she did with Edmund there. And if she does not slay me thus, then you will know I am false and you will want to do the deed yourself, brother or no."

Brooks was just drawing breath to answer, when the

woman's voice cut across them. "A fine exchange, gentlemen!" she called out. "And I am touched by this talk of brotherly friendship. But I am running short on time. Roger, we need to move on to the next part of our plan."

"There is no plan, woman, as well you know," replied Rolleston.

"Oh, indeed there is, and..." She broke off suddenly. "Oh! Hold on a moment..." Once again the cracking sound of the gun rang out across the forest. Some further crows flew up noisily from the tops of the trees. "Sorry about that," she resumed, once the crows had re-settled. "As you were. One of your men was trying to come up on me in stealth through the undergrowth. I think I got him directly through the eye." There was a further pause, and she said, "Now. Roger. As we agreed, please fetch the Queen of Scots from the carriage and bring her forward."

"You will do no such thing!" Brooks snapped.

"I have no intent to do so," Rolleston replied.

"That is indeed a shame," came Anne Carter's voice. "As it means I will need to put a hole in the head of your oldest and dearest, friend, who you call 'brother', Master Brooks. And then every other man here, until all are felled and the lady herself is at my mercy." There was a silence, then she added, "So belike the outcome is the same in any case."

"You would kill us all?" Brooks said.

"Most certainly. After your companion Nathan hit me over the head, tied me to a bed and prepared to violate me, I find my thoughts of mercy are somewhat strained." Then she added, "And I shall not weep for Mistress Brooks becoming a widow, for she would have left me to die after I had dealt with Master Nathan."

"You dealt with him?" Rolleston asked. "How so?"

"Well, let us just say that the cut I have on my forehead will heal soon enough, but I fear his broken jaw will take much longer. Now," she continued, her tone becoming more business-like, "do I need to count to three before I make Mistress Brooks a widow?"

No-one moved.

Brooks screwed his eyes shut and appeared to hold his breath.

"So be it," she said. "One – two – thr..."

The door of the carriage swung open, and Mary, Queen of Scots stepped out.

With a brief nod to the men behind her, she turned and walked stiffly up towards where Brooks and Rolleston were seated on their horses.

The two of them bowed their heads as she walked past, and Rolleston could see her hand was trembling.

The Queen walked on a few yards further, then stopped and spread her arms out wide.

"You, woman!" she called out in her strong French accent. "*Par Dieu*, you have won! If you want me, my chest is open to you, and this time I have no breastplate to stop the ball. So make your shot and then, *bien sur*, it is done."

There was a long silence in the forest, broken only by the occasional call of a crow and the rustle of the breeze in the tops of the trees.

Rolleston felt sick, expecting at any moment to hear again

the crack of the gun, and to see the Queen stagger and fall. Had it come to this, that just when he had been celebrating their success, Anne Carter had come in like an avenging demon to snatch away his victory? It would be the end of all his hopes and dreams, and those of every Catholic soul in England.

Nay, every Catholic in Christendom.

Yet the Queen stayed standing, until eventually she let her arms drop to her side.

That seemed to be the signal Anne Carter was waiting for. "Madam," she said, "it is true I have tried on two occasions to assassinate you, and both times I have failed."

Rolleston saw the Queen's head come up in a small gesture of defiance.

Then Anne said something he would not have expected.

"In truth, I find I no longer have the stomach to make the fatal blow."

The Queen turned her head slightly, as if she was looking back to Rolleston to explain this. "No," Anne continued, "I leave that to the man who you have trusted to set you on the throne, yet who has, all this time, been working against you in secret. Master Rolleston."

Now the Queen turned fully, and Rolleston felt the deep anger – and a hint of disappointment – in her piecing stare.

"Nay, madam, nay," he muttered. "It is all a lie. She is playing us..."

The Queen shook her head and turned back.

"So, madam," Anne called out, "I would ask that you kneel by yonder branch, with your chin resting upon it, and Roger, you may fulfil your destiny by being the man to make the final cut with your sword."

Rolleston looked across at the branch Anne had indicated, a short way ahead. It was sturdy-looking and maybe six inches in diameter, around three feet off the ground. There was no other branch above it, giving space for a swordsman to raise his weapon high. In place of a block, Rolleston could see it was a fair substitute.

"You win, Anne!" he called. "You win. I am sorry for all I did and all the hurt I caused you." He waited but there was no reply. "Does that not give you satisfaction, Mistress Carter?"

"A good try, Roger," she responded. "And in truth all was as we planned, so your apology is not needed. Now I know it is your deepest wish to be the final executioner, so I would you now go to it." Then she added, "I am counting the grey hairs of Master Brooks's beard in the sights of my weapon. Perhaps I will shoot them off one at a time."

Rolleston swallowed back the bile in his throat and drew his slim sword. "This rapier is too slight," he called out. "It will scarce pierce the skin."

"Then use the one from your fallen companion," Anne answered him. "It is broader and heavier."

"And if I refuse?" he asked.

"Then I will do as I promised, and end the lives of all here present, starting with Master Brooks and finishing with you, and then, if I must, the Queen of Scots."

He looked up in the direction of her voice, trying to see her among the trees, but failing to make her out. "You are a cruel and heartless woman, Anne," he said.

"No, Roger, I am not," she answered quietly, although her voice carried to them as clearly as if she had been standing in their midst. "I am an unfortunate at the mercy of powerful men and women, who forced me to act for their own ends, when I wanted nothing more than to live a peaceful life with my husband and family. It is all I have ever wanted, yet I have been wrenched away from them, jailed, threatened, nearly raped and made to become a spy and a cold-blooded killer. I have been lied to and manipulated. And do you know what Roger? I am sick and tired of being the victim in all this, and I tell you, I have really, *really* had enough. So yes, if I am being cruel and heartless, if I am barely able to control my anger, which is hard, Roger, let me tell you, and if I am killing people, it is because I am responding to those who would do the same to me." She paused. "Right now, Roger, I do not like myself. Not at all. Indeed, I do not even recognise myself anymore. But before I can become myself again and believe me there is nothing I want more than that, then we need to finish this thing." She paused again and her voice took on an authoritative tone. "So madam, I ask you please to kneel by the tree, and Roger, you are to perform the final act as we agreed."

"We agreed nothing," Rolleston muttered, but he picked up Edmund's sword in his left hand and tested its sharpness by running his right thumb down the blade, then he shook off the blood from the resulting deep cut and put both hands on the hilt.

The Scottish Queen walked slowly to the tree, then knelt by it with her hands clasped. As he went towards her,

Rolleston heard her muttering "In manus tuas, Domine, commendo spiritum meum."

Into thy hands, O Lord, I commend my spirit.

Then she said some more words to him, before placing her head carefully onto the branch, turned away from him, with her neck exposed.

He took a deep breath, then in one swift movement, raised the sword up high and brought it down with all his might.

As the Scottish Queen's head fell away from her body, there was an agonised howl from Brooks. He ran forward with his own sword raised. Rolleston turned with a look of surprise, almost as if he was not expecting it, then almost by instinct he came on guard himself.

"No longer play-acting, Roger," Brooks snarled as they faced each other.

"Nay," Rolleston answered, "For all Anne Carter was an accursed liar. I am still true to our cause."

"I judge a man by his deeds, not his words," Brooks said. Then he made a sharp flick with the edge of his blade, and Rolleston's sword dropped to the ground with a thud.

Rolleston stared blankly at the weapon now lying on the forest floor, then shook his head as he peered down at his right hand.

It was also on the forest floor, still grasping the hilt.

He held the stump up before his face, staring at it as the blood pumped out.

"I have removed the hand that killed the rightful Queen," Brooks said. "And now I will dispatch the rest of her executioner to Hell." He stepped forward and raised his bloody sword. "On your knees, traitor."

"I still say it was a lie..." Rolleston began.

"On your knees!"

Rolleston dropped down and bowed his head.

Brooks came up beside him, and raised his sword over Rolleston's exposed neck.

Rolleston twisted his head and looked up. "Would you kill me without hearing my defence?"

"Aye, I would!" yelled Brooks, and brought down his sword.

Then the other four men ran up. They all crowded around Rolleston's body with their poignards out.

Such was their focus on Rolleston, that none of them saw a horse and rider emerge onto the path up ahead. The rider stopped a moment to observe the scene around the body, then turned the horse towards Nottingham, and set off at a gallop.

42

CHAPTER FORTY-TWO

The afternoon sun was starting to set as Mary rode into Nottingham, throwing an orange glow across the timbered houses and creating deep shadows in the streets between. There was the usual urban bustle that she had come to expect; roughly dressed men and women scurrying in and out of houses and shops; yeomen and farmers in rough woollen jerkins shepherding pigs and goats, as well as the occasional nobleman riding on a fine charger while seeming to ignore the common rabble that swirled and eddied around his feet like waves around a rock. There was even a fine carriage pulled by two horses, which reminded Mary of the one she had left back in the forest with Brooks and his men. No doubt this was now pressed into service as a makeshift hearse on the return to Oak House, taking back the body of the man

Edmund whose sword had served so well as a headsman's axe, the other man who had tried to sneak up on her, and whatever was left of Rolleston.

As well, of course, as the head and body of the Queen of Scots.

This thought prompted the return once again of the horrible image of the Scottish Queen's head being severed from her neck and falling with a sickening thump onto the forest floor – an image she had been trying to block out, mostly without success, ever since it had happened. Indeed at one point she was forced to stop suddenly and run to a ditch to throw up what little she had left in her stomach, as a reaction to the horror of what she had caused to happen.

Would she ever be able to forget that sight? For all it was the objective of her mission, it was a true horror and gave her no satisfaction. Indeed, the only feeling she had as the scene played over and over in her head like a video on repeat, was of increasing disgust – with herself, with her situation, and with all the death and destruction she had caused. It made her feel as if she were a crab's shell that had been scraped clean; as if nothing remained of the living, breathing creature that once existed inside.

A sudden wave of dizziness made her sway in the saddle, and almost fall off.

She sat back and tried to regain her breath.

It must have been because she was hungry. When had she last eaten? It was hard to remember, given what had happened in the forest, but she finally recalled bolting down some pottage a while ago – that was all. So she had to get something to fill her empty stomach, before she fainted completely and fell from the saddle.

Then, once she had eaten, maybe she would be better able to think straight. And what she needed more than anything now was a clear head if she was going to plan how she was going to resolve the final, and seemingly most impossible part of this dreadful mission.

How to find and destroy Walsingham's coded letter before Brooks used it to blow the whole plan apart?

Mary gave a low groan of frustration. It seemed that ever since that fateful evening when Wychwoode had arrived at Grangedean with his men at arms, for every step forward she had taken two back, and this was just another in a long line of such setbacks to be dealt with. Added to which, she had taken two blows to the head and was finding it harder and harder to concentrate. For if she had been thinking straight, she would have found a way to get the letter off Brooks back in the forest, rather than letting the opportunity pass.

As she rode through the streets, it seemed as though the increasing blankness in her mind was like a heavy dark curtain, behind which a set of shapeless and nameless horrors were swirling about like so many demons, all fighting to get out. Whatever they were, they terrified her, so she had to keep the curtain firmly closed. Because that was the only way she could keep herself together, and keep going.

Another wave of dizziness made her grip her knees onto Justice's side in desperation, as she looked around for an inn.

"Must eat, must eat," she muttered to herself, as she stared hard at two people approaching her on horseback. "Because now I am hallucinating."

For what other explanation could there possibly be for seeing William and Olivia riding towards her in the streets of Nottingham?

---o---

Mary almost blacked out as William took her hand to help her dismount, then found herself slipping and sliding as if down a long dark tunnel that ended in his strong arms.

"Come now, my love," she heard him say as he caught her, holding her tight and stroking her head. "Oh, my love, my love, we have found you, we have found you, that is all."

She looked into his eyes and tried to say something; anything.

But no words came.

Instead his concerned face suddenly exploded into a thousand pieces as her eyes flooded with tears, then a great sob racked her body, followed by another and another, and then the heavy curtain was ripped back and all the demonic horrors flooded out; everything that had built up over the past few weeks and days, the endless procession of terrors she had suffered since being arrested; the threat of being tried and burned; the ambush in the forest by Brooks; taking the shot and escaping through Sheffield; discovering how she had been fooled; and finally, turning the tables on Rolleston so he had been the final executioner. They all flowed out with the force of torrential waters blasting through a breached dam, until she was nothing but a helpless, howling bundle, clinging onto her husband like a rock against the torrent because she needed to know deep down that he was real, and that this was not another cruel fantasy conjured up by her stress and hunger...

Time seemed to stand still as she held on to him, sobbing uncontrollably and squeezing him tightly. He held her for as long as it took for her sobs to thin out, until eventually with a few gasping breaths, they slowed enough for her to manage a few words.

"What..? How..? Why..?" was all she could say.

A hand touched her arm and she turned to find Olivia standing beside her.

"We knew you were in danger, so we came north to find you..." the girl began, but got no further. With a cry like a wounded animal Mary unpeeled herself from William and threw her arms round her friend, once again howling and dissolving into floods of tears.

"Oh my lady, my lady," Olivia crooned softly, holding Mary's shaking head to her breast and stroking her hair, "what has happened to you? What has happened?"

"We are here now, my love," William said, once the sobs had begun to slow down again, then eventually slowed enough for Mary to pull away slightly from Olivia. "We have come to take you back home," he said. "This nightmare is over."

Mary looked up at him and sniffed loudly. "No... no... it... is not..." she managed to gasp between further sniffs and gulps. "I... have... still... got... something... got... something... to do..."

"Well, by the greatest good fortune our paths have crossed," Olivia said, "so if there is aught we can do to help, then we shall."

Mary let Olivia go and staggered back.

"This is... trouble... of my own... making," she managed to say. "My own stupid fault... So I must... must... resolve... it my-self." Then she gave them a weak, watery smile. "Although... I am... very glad... to see you both."

"By Heavens, do you suppose we will abandon you now?" William exclaimed. "When we have done so much to find you, and have been blessed by God with the good fortune to come upon you here in Nottingham?"

"No... I... suppose... not."

"Then let us repair inside the nearest tavern, get some good, hot pottage inside you, then you can tell us what is done so far, and what is still to do, and we can decide how best to proceed."

"I... suppose... so," she stammered.

They found a tavern on the next lane, and Mary allowed William to half lead her, half carry her inside.

He made no demands for her story until he had ordered two large bowls of pottage and some bread, then watched as she ate her way through all of it. After that he ordered them a new candle for the table and a tankard of beer each. Then he waited until Mary had drunk half of hers, before leaning forward and saying quietly, "Tell us what you are able, Mary my love, and we shall agree what is best to be done."

Mary looked at each in turn and found that now she had some food and drink inside, her head was less painful and she was starting to think a little more clearly. William was look-ing at her with a mixture of love and expectation; the look of a man who still trusted her to make good decisions, just as she had for the last ten years as mistress of Grangedean Manor. Olivia was looking concerned and slightly confused, no doubt after having to comfort the woman who, the last time they were together, had comforted her.

Mary nodded slightly to herself. It was clear to her now, that her real loyalties lay with these two, not the men in London. Unlike Rolleston, she could totally trust them. She would not hold anything back. In truth, the more they knew, the more they could help.

Even if they knew the worst of what she had done.

"I was charged by Walsingham, Wychwoode and the Queen," she began, "to undertake a secret mission in return for my release from the charges against me."

"Even though Master Secretary Walsingham was deaf to your entreaties," Olivia asked.

"Nay, that was all false," Mary answered. She steadied herself with a deep breath. "It was all for show. In truth, Master Walsingham actually understood that my future knowledge would indeed be most valuable. He just play-acted."

"Then all the anger on the boat from Master Wychwoode was wholly unreal?" Olivia asked, her eyes wide.

"Indeed it was; designed to make me even more fearful of my fate as a blaspheming sorcerer, and therefore more likely to do their bidding."

"I shall never again trust that man," muttered William. "But what then?"

"I used my knowledge of the future to reveal to Walsingham all the events that are going to happen. I told him of the plots and Spanish war of invasion yet to come, that would all be centred around the life and death of Mary, Queen of Scots."

"And this mission?" William asked.

Mary took a breath. "In order to avoid such a future and to secure Elizabeth's throne," she whispered, "I was charged with assassinating the Queen of Scots,"

There was a long silence, during which Mary noticed William and Olivia exchange worried glances. Eventually, Olivia cleared her throat. "And did you?" she asked softly.

"She is dead, yes. But although I caused it, it was not my hand that struck the final blow." Mary paused, then added, "For all I tried on two occasions to kill her myself, and was unsuccessful."

"By Heavens, Mary," William said, "I would you tell us all, from the start, and with nothing omitted."

Mary nodded, took a gulp of her beer and indicated for the two of them to move in closer. They huddled either side of her, their eyes bright in the light of the new candle and their mouths open in expectation.

Keeping her voice low so as not to carry beyond the table, Mary said, "I will start with an apology to you, William, that I never told you the secret of where – or when – I am from. I am sorry that you had to find out the way you did." She gave him a small kiss on the cheek. "Were you angry with me? I will understand if you were."

He kissed her back. "I was much angered to start, for sure, but then I recalled what a constant wife and mother you are, so I forgave you." He paused, "Tom Melrose helped me see the truth of it – that where you come from does not alter the person you are."

"Well, sadly that is not how Wychwoode saw it," she said, "His arrest meant I had no choice but to undertake this mission – to use the Alchemist's special musket to kill the Scottish Queen."

"But we destroyed it in a forge on our return from York," said Olivia with a frown. "I recall it well."

"Yes, so I had to make a new one."

"You?" asked William. "In a forge? Like a common smith?"

She gave him a small smile. "Indeed, it was under the Alchemist's instruction, but yes, I made it."

"God's Blood, I would never have credited it!" His jaw dropped as he stared at her. "You are ever resourceful, Mary!"

"I had to be," she replied, "for there were times on this mission when it was most needed."

"So, tell us all," Olivia said as she and William leaned in closer.

"The start you know..." Mary began, and launched into the full tale.

---o---

The candle on the table was almost burned down to a stub as she drew her story to a close. She had not glossed over the parts that reflected poorly on herself – such as how she had been played for a fool in the ambush, how she had stolen Justice, how she had been tricked by Rolleston to give away too much information about the plot, and how she had then failed to stop him stealing the coded letter.

"...So you see," she had finished, "that letter, and its translation, are like gunpowder in the hands of this man Brooks. I could have resolved it in the forest, but failed to do so.

They were so busy murdering Rolleston, that it was too late to retrieve it – but I should have had Brooks destroy it while I had him under my control. The Earl of Shrewsbury will soon be in London with Frances Barwell as the Queen of Scots, and if they try to carry through the renunciation of her Catholic faith and her claim to the throne, then Brooks has only to produce the letter to explode the whole subterfuge. The Catholics will be emboldened and will almost certainly rise up; Philip of Spain and the Pope will then get involved and most likely put forward some puppet monarch." She had paused. "And Queen Elizabeth will once again face being deposed, imprisoned and no doubt executed." She swallowed hard. "I will have failed her."

William and Olivia leaned back and stared silently at her, as if they were unsure how to process what they had now heard.

Just as Mary felt that the silence had gone on long enough, William started to nod slowly. "That you have the courage to kill," he said, "we knew already, for we have seen it with our own eyes. That you have the wherewithal to plan and execute such a conceit as had this man Rolleston acting as the Scottish Queen's headsman, then have his own companions turn murderously against him – so much I could guess, for I have seen how you can bend any man to your will," he smiled briefly, "myself included." He leaned across and put his hand over hers. "Mary, my love," he said, his eyes unwavering on hers, "I bear you no ill-will for any of this, for even though you have come to us from the distant future and you have caused deaths and stolen property, I know you act from the purest of motives, and I would be sure that God sees the same good in you as I do."

Then Olivia placed her hand over William's. "I say the same," she said, "for I have seen how you care for those you love, and I know that it is as God wills it."

Mary smiled at them. "I thank you both for your understanding," she said. "I would not have wanted to do any of this, were I not forced to do so." She shook her head. "But all of what I have done so will be as naught, if we do not destroy that letter."

"I agree," said William. "So we must construct our plan of action, and carry it through together – the three of us." He paused. "As we did near York this spring."

"Yes," Mary said. "But we need to be well prepared." She looked at them both. "Starting with the gun. You both need to know how to fire it, in case you have to."

"But Mary, my love, are you sure?" William muttered, "I warrant that is your area of expertise."

"Come now, William," Mary responded. "What if I am not able to use it? What if I am injured..." she paused, "or worse?"

Her words hung in the air.

"Then one of us may need it," Olivia said quietly, but with more steel in her voice than William had shown.

"Exactly," Mary said, giving William a small smile, to re-assure him that she understood his reluctance to handle an unfamiliar weapon.

"I saw how you used it before," Olivia continued, "but I would have some more instruction, so I understand it fully."

"Then after we have finished here, I will show you both," Mary said, "so it becomes as natural to you as it is to me."

"Do we have time enough?" asked William.

"You are right, William. We will have to move quickly," Mary said. "I fired on the true Queen of Scots yesterday not long after midday. The Earl of Shrewsbury will most probably be travelling with Frances Barwell to Tutbury this day, and then on to London tomorrow or the day after, as the longer he leaves the deception, the more chance of discovery. If they ride hard they can be there in two days. Brooks will want to bury the real Queen, creating a shrine for Catholics to visit in future, but then he will want to set off to London as well, with the incriminating documents. So I think our best chance to find and take them is at Oak House tomorrow."

"But how to find these documents?" asked Olivia.

"I know not for sure," Mary answered, "but I warrant Brooks is most likely to keep them on his person. So we need to take and overpower him."

"How many men do they have?" William asked.

"There were nine originally with the Scottish Queen in the forest; Rolleston, Brooks, the driver and six others," Mary said. "I dispatched the driver initially, then one called Edmund, and another who attempted to come at me by stealth. And of course, Rolleston was killed by Brooks for treachery and beheading the Queen. So I make it that there are now five – Brooks and the four remaining men." She paused, "And at Oak House, there are Mistress Brooks and Nathan the archer, although I know not if he is in a condition to fight, after I broke his jaw. At least I think I did."

"By the Risen Christ, Mary," William said, "when this is over you will find life at Grangedean holds little excitement and adventure."

"But William," she said, leaning across and stroking his cheek, "that is my heart's truest desire – to live a quiet life of peace and order with you and the children, and not to be running through towns and forests as an assassin or spy." She paused. "Ten years ago I was just a girl living in twenty fifteen, with nothing more to concern me than pleasing my mother by finding a nice young man and settling down. Instead, I am now a cold-blooded killer, dispatching Her Majesty's enemies in return for the chance to save my own life, and live it with the nice young fellow I did eventually find." She stroked his cheek again, then dropped her hand. "Do you know, back in the forest this day I was even making jokes as I shot a man. Afterwards, I realised how much that sickened me." She sat back. "So we have one last battle to undertake – one last task to retrieve those documents. And either we succeed, and I never have to fight again, or maybe we die in the attempt." She looked at them both – her husband and her dearest friend. "So if you are with me, we do this together and risk our own deaths. If you would prefer to stay here and stay safe, I will understand, truly, and I will go alone."

She took a small breath.

"Are you with me?"

"We are," they both replied.

"Then let us make our plan."

43

CHAPTER
FORTY-THREE

The loud tick of a crude old carriage clock welcomed Mary, William and Olivia into the back room of the tavern, its second hand staggering round the dial like an unsteady drunkard.

Mary checked to ensure they were alone, then took the gun and a cartridge out of her bag and placed them carefully on the table. In the light of the flickering candles ensconced on the walls, she pulled back on the lever to open the breech, then held up the cartridge so that William and Olivia could see it more clearly.

"The breech opens to reveal the chamber, and the cartridge goes in here, like so," she said, slotting it into place. "Then you pull the lever up and forward to close the breech." She looked at them both in turn. "Now the gun is loaded and ready to fire."

"As the Lord is my witness, Mary my love," said William, his eyes glittering in the candlelight, "I would not credit that this wonderful piece of ordnance was made by your own hand." He shook his head slowly. "It is a remarkable thing indeed."

"Yes, but it was made under instruction from the Alchemist," she replied. "He showed me all the steps to take, and approved each one before I was permitted to move to the next."

"Then he is to be congratulated," William said, "for his ingenuity."

"Not hung, drawn and quartered, for his treason?" enquired Mary, now starting to feel sufficiently rested and well-fed to give him an impish smile.

William shook his head again. "I rather think not," he said. "I fancy he is even now aboard a boat bound for foreign lands."

Mary unloaded the gun and put it carefully down on the table with the cartridge, then she looked up at her husband. "Indeed?" she asked, her voice tinged with caution. "Wych-woode did offer him a way to achieve such a fate..." She left it hanging as a question.

"Mistress Melrose and I saw a man hung, drawn and quartered at Tyburn these few days past," he said, "and all who saw it would swear it was the one known as the Alchemist who met his end."

"But you think otherwise?"

"A well-clothed man who had the appearance of the Alchemist as you described him, and had the limp in his leg that would have resulted from the beating you gave him, led us to believe that the poor unfortunate upon the scaffold was in truth another fellow, put in his place and given his name. Then he told us he was bound out of the realm on a boat."

"And it was he who gave us the information that led us here," said Olivia. "He said to look for Rolleston, and also to seek one Anne Carter – the name you said you travelled under. He said we should head north. Had we not had such information to start from, we would never have found you."

Mary shook her head. "So Rick finally did the decent thing," she said, almost to herself. "Maybe there really was some good in him after all."

For all she would once have gladly hung the man, then chopped him into bits herself, now she felt nothing but relief that he had gone free. For they had parted, if not as friends, then certainly with an understanding that as fellow time-travellers and gunsmiths, they had some sort of common bond.

But would Rick survive in exile?

Mary nodded to herself. Of course he would; he was a natural survivor. No doubt once he had established himself in Germany or France or Holland or wherever, he would set himself up again as an inventor, conjuring up items that amazed the locals and made him lots of money, just as he had in Southwark. If only he could be content with that, and find someone who made pies as good as Mistress Somerville, he would live a long, and maybe even a happy life.

Mary was about to reply when she heard the sudden 'click-clack' sound of the gun being loaded.

Spinning round, she saw Olivia had lifted the gun to her shoulder and was pointing it at the opposite wall. Before she could say anything, the girl pulled the lever back and ejected the cartridge into her palm, then reloaded it in only a few seconds, lifted it and pointed it at the wall once more.

"Again," Mary said, glad of the chance to move on from the Alchemist and back to the matter at hand. "And this time point the cartridge in towards the gun as you load, so it locates into the breech more quickly."

Olivia nodded and tried again, this time taking maybe a second off the time to reload.

"Good," Mary said. "And again."

Olivia did so several more times, until she was as fast, if not faster than Mary herself.

"Now with your eyes closed," Mary said.

Olivia picked up the gun and the cartridge, closed her eyes and reloaded. It was much slower as she fumbled to locate the breech, but after a few more tries she was almost back up to the speed she had achieved with her eyes open.

"Truly excellent," Mary said. "I am most impressed, Olivia." She handed the gun and cartridge to William. "Now your turn, my love," she said, then added with a small knowing smile at her friend. "Show us how the man can better the womenfolk."

To give him his due, William tried hard. With a determined stare at both of them, he picked up the cartridge, snapped back the breech lever, then tried to slam in the cartridge, but missed the breech completely. With a grunt of annoyance, he tried again, and although this time it went in, he wasted time making sure it was seated correctly. After a few more tries he was consistently getting it in place, but not as fast as either of the women. Then he tried with his eyes closed, and after a few fumbles and dropped cartridges, he was able to achieve at least consistent loading.

"There," he said triumphantly. "It is a simple matter, and well-proven."

"That is deserving of praise, I agree," Mary said, "but you have two very competent women here, with smaller hands, who are both able to load and fire more quickly."

"Nonsense!" he barked, and tried several more times, shaving perhaps half a second off his time. But as he put the gun down, Mary felt he could do better, and decided to make it into a competition. "Marry," she said, "I will give each of you thirty seconds by that clock there, and let us see who does the most load, aim and unloads." She put the gun on the table with the cartridge next to it. "You first," she said to Olivia.

"Eyes open?"

Mary nodded, watching the clock. As the second hand staggered wheezily up to the hour, she counted Olivia in. On the command 'go!' Olivia sprang into action. She grabbed the gun and snapped open the breech, then slotted in the cartridge, slammed it shut and brought the gun up to the firing position. Then she unloaded and repeated, managing eight further sequences before the end of the thirty seconds.

"Well done," Mary said, as Olivia replaced the gun on the table and stood the cartridge next to it. "Now your turn," she said to William. He moved to the table and stood with his feet planted and his hands hovering over the gun, his fingers flexing like the wings of a bird.

"Now to show you both how a man moves with the speed of a lightning bolt..." he said.

"This I must see," said Mary, and counted him in.

When the thirty seconds was up, he put the gun down and stood back.

"How many was that?" he asked, with an expression that expected success.

"Seven," Mary and Olivia said together. His face fell. "For sure?" They nodded. "By Heavens!" he exclaimed, then stopped, and his frown turned into a broad smile. "Well, I warrant it was a fair contest. As a gentleman I needs must recognise when I am beaten – and by a woman!"

"There is no shame in that," said Mary, taking hold of his arm and giving him a kiss on the cheek. "You have speed, more than many would have in my time. It is just that we are a little faster."

"For all it galls me to say it, I can see that," he answered, "and I trust the Lord will not require me to take up this weapon when such speed is required."

"Then let us focus on our plan for the morrow," said Olivia, "And with God's good fortune, such a thing will not happen."

44

CHAPTER
FORTY-FOUR

Brooks, his wife and the rest of the men were breaking fast in the great hall of Oak House, a large room in the centre of the building with a high vaulted roof and brightly painted wood panelling. The roof was supported by a series of strong black oak beams running across the room between the tops of the walls, and it was these beams that had given the house its name.

It was the morning of the day after their return. The previous day had been filled with activity; beginning with them bringing a Catholic priest, Father Goddard, out of his place of concealment in a secret room behind the basement of a nearby tavern, then trying to convince him that they needed to hold a funeral mass for the Queen of Scots herself.

At first he had been deeply sceptical, and it had taken some passionate persuasion to convince him that this was not some trick by Pursuivants to lure him into the open and have him arrested.

Eventually he had agreed to view the body, which was laid out on the parlour table at Oak House. He stared at it silently for some time while Brooks and his wife watched, clutching each other's hand tightly. The Queen's head had been returned to its rightful place, with a small sack of flour underneath the neck to support it. If it were not for the ugly red gash running all round, she would have looked if she were merely resting serenely with her hands by her side.

Father Goddard studied the face, then moved round and turned his attention to the nearest hand. Then he raised his head upwards and moved his lips silently, while Brooks and his wife both held their breath.

Then he looked at them across the body. "Yes," he said, "God has told me this is indeed the true Queen." Then he had made the sign of the cross on the forehead, lips and chest, before placing his hands on either side of her head and leaning over it, his lips again moving silently. As he stood up, Brooks noticed that the Queen's eyes were now wet with Father Goddard's tears.

He had then gone out with them to view the burial site in the orchard behind the house, before saying the necessary words to consecrate the ground. After that the body was brought out in a shroud and lowered gently into the grave that had been dug, then covered over with soil.

It had been a moving service, with Mistress Brooks and

all the men gathered around with their heads bowed as the requiem mass was said, followed by Eucharistic prayers. Then Father Goddard had given a short homily.

"My friends in Christ," he had said, "it is with the deepest pain that we bury our sovereign lady, and with her we bury our dream of a quick return to the true faith." He paused, looking around. "This is a mass said by only a small number of loyal followers, when it should have been a royal service attended by all the Queen's devoted subjects. But my friends, our cause is like a candle that has its flame put out; the light is gone, but the candle itself is still there – and it is our duty as followers of the true faith to find a way to re-light it once again. As God is my witness, the fight continues, until the heretic usurper is removed from the throne she occupies against God's will, and a true Catholic sovereign sits in her place. I charge you to do all that is in your power to bring this to pass." He gave them all a hard stare then made the sign of the cross. "*In nomine Patris et fillii et Spiritus Sancti, Amen.*"

"*Amen,*" they had all said, then returned to the house for supper and to raise a glass of wine in honour of the departed Queen.

"I can still scarce believe the true Queen is dead," Brooks muttered as he broke a piece of bread the next morning. "All our plans coming to naught, because of that she-devil Anne Carter." He stuffed the bread moodily in his mouth

"So you have said many times over," replied his wife. "Saying it again does not restore the rightful queen to life, nor fulfil our obligation to continue the fight.

"I know, I know," Brooks replied once he had finished

chewing. "But it galls me nonetheless that we were thwarted by one such as her – a woman.

"We could have her arraigned by the Justices for murder," one of the men suggested. "Edmund, Richard and Samuel the driver were all slaughtered by her hand.

"Nay," Brooks replied. "Have you taken leave of your senses? She will be hailed a hero for causing the deaths of the bastard queen's enemies." He shook his head. "No, we must save our efforts for destroying Walsingham's plan to have the imposter queen renounce the true faith and her claim to the throne." He took out the two pieces of paper he had tucked into the front of his doublet. "With these papers we can still dismiss the false queen as a base conceit and cause a Catholic uprising. We may not have the Queen of Scots on the throne, but perhaps another of the true faith, as Father Goddard has said. Either way," he glared at each of them in turn, "either way, we have a realm restored to the Catholic cause, and that heretic bastard removed from the throne, which will be a blessed relief."

He was interrupted by a heavy thumping on the front door. "Pray, see who that might be at this early hour, wife," he said, putting the papers back inside his doublet.

Mistress Brooks went out, and returned a few minutes later with a tall blond man wearing a rough woollen jerkin, no hose and torn breeches held in place by a length of rough rope wound several times round his waist.

"Well, fellow?" Brooks demanded, as everyone stared at the man in silence. "What is your business here?"

The man took off his cap and twisted it in his hands.

"Please, sir," he muttered, "I come in haste to warn you of grave danger."

"Indeed?" Brooks asked, his voice showing only mild concern. "And what danger might this be?"

"I was in a hostelry in Nottingham…" the man began.

"And there should have stayed," one of the others muttered under his breath, but loud enough for all to hear. There was general laughter from all except for Nathan, whose jaw was heavily bandaged.

Brooks raised his own hand for silence. "Let us hear the fellow out," he said. "If he has come all the way from Nottingham on this freezing morning to warn us, he may have information of value. Come to the fire, man, you are blue with the cold."

"I thank you sir," the man replied and moved closer to the fire. "I was in the Prospect Inn last evening, and was seated near a group of fellows who, from their manner and conversation, I took to be Pursuivants. Their leader was one they addressed as Silas Taverner."

Now he had their full attention.

"I know this Taverner," Brooks said with a chill in his voice, "as it was he who arrested me once before."

"Aye, and he means to do so again, sir," came the reply. "I overheard them planning to raid your house again this very morn, so being a true Catholic myself, I awoke well before the dawn and rode up as fast as I could to warn you."

Brooks considered the man, his head on one side. "You have done well, fellow," he said. "What is your name?"

"Will, sir. Will… er… Bowyer."

"In truth, Goodman Bowyer, you are welcome this day,

and your warning is well heeded." He paused. "Did this Taverner say *why* he was planning to raid this house once again, perchance?"

"He did, sir, in his conversation with the others." Bowyer twisted his hat even more in his hands. "I listened hard, for all they talked quite softly, and it was to do with your apparent conversion to Protestant heresy after your last arrest. He has heard tell you have been once again hearing Catholic Mass."

"I see." Brooks looked round at his companions, then back at Bowyer. "And you say he is coming this very morning?"

"I would expect he is but a quarter hour behind me, sir."

Brooks stood and gestured to the men at the table. "Then I suggest we make haste away to Bridgeford. We should all go to the house of my Catholic brother, Master Cornell. Then there will be no person in the house when Taverner arrives."

"If I may, sir," interrupted Bowyer, "I would suggest you stay here. Taverner will be all the more suspicious if the house is empty and it looks as if you have flown. You and Mistress Books should stay and deal with Taverner without these other men here, to give him cause to see a conspiracy. You will be no more than an innocent man and wife going about your business as normal."

Brooks considered this a moment. "The fellow has a point," he said. "You all go to Cornell's place and wait for me there."

The men stood, then made their way out of the hall, heading for the back door towards the stables.

"You, Goodman Bowyer, take some bread, and be gone as fast as you can, lest you are found here and must answer questions from that louse Taverner."

Bowyer put on his cap and bowed. "I thank you sir, and I am glad I have been able to help a fellow Catholic."

"Indeed and we thank you. Now you had best be gone."

Bowyer selected a piece of bread, took a bite, then walked over to the door through which the men had just gone. But instead of leaving as bidden, he pulled the door shut and moved the bolt across to lock it.

As Brooks and his wife watched in amazement, Bowyer then walked to the open door on the other side of the room, and gave a soft whistle. A moment later a woman came in, dressed in black breeches and a tight-fitting black jerkin. She carried a slim tubular weapon that Brooks immediately recognised from the fake ambush in the forest. Bowyer closed the door behind her and stood with his back to it.

Brooks looked at the woman's face in amazement.

Anne Carter!

She smiled, then raised the gun and pointed it directly at his chest.

"Hello, Master Brooks," she said. "You are well met indeed."

Mistress Brooks made a small movement, as if she were about to attack Anne Carter. Bowyer stepped smartly across and grabbed her hands, pulling them up behind her back so tightly that she could not move any further.

"By Heavens, Carter," her husband snarled. "I would you were out of my life."

"Oh, I will be, believe me," she answered. "Just as soon as you give me the letter and note decoding it, that were taken from the Earl of Shrewsbury's desk."

"You do know there are Pursuivants coming..." Then Brooks stopped, as Anne Carter gave him a small smile. He nodded slowly. "I see," he said. "There are no Pursuivants; just you and this Bowyer fellow concocting a conceit, to have all my men put out of the way,"

"And it has worked, has it not?" Anne replied. "They are all now gone to, where was it...?" she put her head on one side, "Aye, the house of one Cornell. I mark it well, and will perchance let Master Taverner know that this Master Cornell is worthy of further investigation."

Brooks shook his head. "By the Risen Christ, you are the spawn of Satan, Carter." He looked at her with deep hatred. "And if I refuse to hand over the documents you seek?"

"That would be foolish, for it will be the last thing you do." She raised the gun still further, so now he was staring directly down the barrel. "This thing is close enough to blow your head clean off your shoulders. Will you risk that for a couple of pieces of paper?"

"Papers that will place a rightful Catholic king or queen on the throne of England."

"As may be," she said. "Put them on the table."

With a look that was now of pure loathing, Brooks reached inside his doublet and withdrew the two papers. Then he placed them on the table and stood back.

"Good, now you and your wife, sit in these two chairs, but put them back-to-back first." She indicated two high-backed chairs. Brooks placed them as directed, then sat in one. Bowyer pulled Mistress Brooks over to the other and pushed her down into the seat. Then he pulled the length of rope out from round his waist and tied their wrists to each other on either side, so they were immobile.

Anne Carter then picked up one of the papers – the one

that was coded in blocks of letters – and held one corner over the nearest candle. Brooks could just see a small black 'GX' and the numbers 3089 appear in the corner.

Anne Carter studied the code and her lips moved silently as she appeared to be doing a calculation in her head. "Yes, prime. It is the genuine letter," she said, then picked up the other paper and scanned it. "And this is the de-coding," she added. "I trust you have not made a copy of the coded letter, as it will be dismissed as a forgery if there is not a genuine code secretly written in the corner."

Brooks shook his head.

"Good." She moved over to the fire. "Then I have great pleasure in destroying these."

She put both papers into the flames, and as Brooks watched in sickened horror, they blackened, curled up, and eventually disappeared.

"There," she said, "my mission is accomplished."

Then Anne Carter gave the man Bowyer a triumphant smile. "Now, let us be away," she said. He nodded, and said to Brooks and his wife, "Fare thee well, Master Brooks, Mistress Brooks. I trust we shall never meet again."

As they turned towards the door, it opened.

A younger woman came into the room, also dressed in the same black clothing as Anne Carter. But she was not coming in willingly; rather she was being pushed in by a tall man holding her from behind with one arm locked across her ribs and the other holding a knife to her throat.

Anne Carter took one look at the man and put her free hand to a chair as if she was about to faint.

It was Roger Rolleston.

45

CHAPTER FORTY-FIVE

Rolleston kicked the door shut, then stood with his back to it, still holding his knife to Olivia's throat.

"I found this young woman lurking about the house in a most suspicious manner, for all the world like a bad odour," he said. "And while she is dressed most strangely, I fancy she might be quite comely if she were scrubbed and clothed correctly." He smiled at Mary, although it was more of a sneer. "I would say you are well met, Anne Carter, but it would not be the truth. The truth is, like another bad odour, you continually turn up when not wanted."

"I could say the same of you, Roger," Mary replied, looking at his right arm clamped across Olivia's ribs. It ended in a heavily bandaged stump where his hand had been. "When I left, you were about to be executed like the cur you are. I saw the sword come down, and the others move in with their knives out..." she paused. "Yet, here you are, somehow still living."

"Aye," he said. "Is it not remarkable what a single word can do to divert a sword from its deadly path?"

"A single word?"

"I was raised in the next house to this one. Antony and I grew up together, as inseparable as if we were brothers born. I simply reminded him of this, and called him 'brother'. It was enough to send the blow into the ground rather than my neck. The other men took their lead from Antony, and they all believed me when I then calmly explained to them that the evidence of my treachery came only from you, Anne Carter. They realised that we had all been the victim of your conceit, and I had not in truth betrayed my faith."

"Yet you killed the Queen."

"Indeed, but not by my will, rather by hers. You saw how she went gladly to her death. She was wearied of the frequent changes in her fortune, so here was a quick and painless way to achieve finality and begin her new life in Heaven."

"But this is your conjecture?"

"Nay, before she put her head on the branch, she said to me these very words; 'I find I am weary of life, Master Rolleston. I welcome death with open arms and the peace it will bring me. Go to it with my blessing.' So no, it is not conjecture."

He pushed the knife closer to Olivia's throat, causing Mary to give an involuntary gasp.

"Now, what is to do?" Rolleston asked with another sneer. "We seem to have something of an impasse here. I can dispatch this girl, whom I note seems to mean much to you, Anne Carter. Indeed I have a mind to do so, unless you drop your weapon immediately." He pulled the knife closer still, causing Olivia to flinch her head back, her eyes wide like a hunted deer. He nodded at Mary. "Go to it. Place it on the floor and kick it towards me."

Mary hesitated a moment.

"I said go to it, or your young friend here will feel the bite of my knife into her pretty neck."

Mary bent down and placed the gun on the floor, then kicked it towards Rolleston.

"Good," he said. "Now you, fellow," he said to William, "untie my brother Antony and his good wife."

William took a quick look at Olivia, then went over to the chairs and untied them as ordered.

"That is well done," Rolleston continued. "Antony, do me the favour of using this convenient piece of rope now to create two nooses, and throw them across yonder high beam.

Brooks nodded, used his knife to cut the rope in two, then created noose loops in each. He tested both to ensure the loop easily slid closed, then threw each rope over the nearest oak beam a few feet apart and secured them. The nooses were now both hanging around seven feet off the ground. Then he pulled two chairs across and placed one under each rope.

"You fellow, and you, Anne Carter, although in truth I doubt that is your real name," Rolleston said, "be so good as to stand on the chairs and put your heads in the ropes."

"Have you taken leave of your senses, man," demanded William, "to think we will readily comply?"

"Then you will see this pretty young girl here disfigured by my knife being pulled across her throat," answered Rolleston. "And when you have watched her pour out her life's blood and die in pain, if you still will not do as I ask, then I will try my aim on you with the remarkable weapon you have fashioned, Mistress Carter, to persuade you even more strongly." He smiled. "Although I doubt I will be as proficient with it as you are, so I will cause only pain and suffering with the firing now, leading to a death in time that is both slow and agonising."

Mary glanced over at Olivia, and noticed the girl look down at the gun on the floor, then back at her again. She did this a couple of times in quick succession, so Mary realised it was a signal. She thought she guessed what Olivia meant, so she said, "That gun at your feet? It is not about proficiency, Roger; you would not even be able to fire it."

"Perhaps not, but as I say, I am willing to try."

Then he looked down at the gun.

This briefly distracted his attention and enabled Olivia to make her move. She twisted her head in line with his movement and slammed it sharply back into his windpipe, causing him to gag and drop the knife. Then she made a quick turn of her body and slipped out from his grasp.

As she did so, Antony Brooks started to move to Rolleston's aid. Olivia dropped to the ground and in one smooth move, picked up the gun and fired a shot into Brooks's thigh. Mary's ears rang with the thunderous crack in such an enclosed space, as the shot tore into the grey-bearded man's leg. He screamed and fell to the ground clutching at the wound. Mary flipped a cartridge out of her pocket and threw it to Olivia, who caught it and swiftly reloaded. Pivoting round, she fired the next shot upwards at Rolleston, but she did not turn fast enough, and he was already moving sideways. The shot just missed him, instead blowing one of the antlers off a stuffed stag's head on the wall behind him.

As Olivia ran over to Mary's side and thrust the gun into her hands, Mary saw William diving for the knife where it had fallen. But Rolleston saw what he was doing and made a grab for it with his good hand at the same time. Together they fell to the floor.

As they grappled, Mary reloaded and tried to get a clear shot at Rolleston, but every time she thought she had the opportunity, William had his head in the way. So she held the gun ready but did not fire.

William managed to get two hands on the knife. Rolleston had his on it as well, and they rolled over a couple more times, ending with William on top. He had the knife in both hands and was trying to bring it down, but Rolleston's strength was the equal of his, and the knife stayed a few inches above Rolleston's chest. Then Rolleston brought his stump up and crashed it into the side of William's head; a move that would have made any normal man scream in agony. With a grunt of pain, William rolled away, allowing Rolleston to get back on top. Now the knife was bearing down on William's chest. It seemed to Mary that he was pushing back with all his might, but Rolleston was a bigger man, with his added weight giving him the advantage.

Mary continued to dance round trying to get a clear shot, but even though Rolleston was now on top it was still too risky; at this range any shot could potentially pass straight through Rolleston and hit William.

Then Olivia picked up the broken-off antler, and held it high over Rolleston's head to use as a dagger. But before she could bring it down, Mistress Brooks left where she had been tending her husband on the floor and ran at Olivia, snarling like an angry cat, and leapt at her, knocking the antler to the floor. Olivia put her arms up to defend herself as the woman then attempted to scratch out her eyes.

Mary looked back at the fight between William and Rolleston. She could see that the knife point was now only an inch off William's chest, and from his red face and bared teeth, it looked like he might be tiring.

Rolleston hunched his shoulders. "Die, fellow, die!" he yelled and thrust down hard.

Mary screamed as she heard William give a short cough, then she saw his eyes open wide, staring up at Rolleston.

Then his eyes closed.

"William! No!"

As she screamed, Mistress Brooks was briefly distracted from her scratching at Olivia, giving Olivia the chance to grab the antler and get a good swing into the side of the woman's head. As the weapon connected there was a grunt from Mistress Brooks, and she went sprawling into the wall. Her eyes fluttered briefly, then she was still.

Olivia struggled to her feet and leaped across to where Mary was trying to pull Rolleston off William, but for some reason he seemed to be dead weight. She came beside Mary and together they tried to roll Rolleston away onto his back.

Mary took a deep breath to prepare herself for the sickening sight of her husband with the knife deep in his chest, as she and Olivia finally managed to get Rolleston away.

Then they both gasped.

There was plenty of blood, but William's chest was clear.

No handle was sticking out.

A groan from Rolleston made Mary look across at him instead.

The handle stood proud just below Rolleston's ribs, surrounded by a widening pool of blood spreading across his doublet like ink on blotting paper.

Now there was a groan from William, and his eyes opened.

"Mary, my love," he whispered, "that was close." He struggled up on one elbow. "I had two hands on the knife, whereas he had but one. So I managed to turn it at the very last moment as he pushed down and he drove it deep into his own body." He gave a weak grin and rubbed his ribs, "For all I will have quite a bruise as the handle dug deep into me as he came down."

"Oh, William!" Mary sobbed, as she dropped to her knees and pulled his head up to her breast, cradling him like a baby," I thought I had lost you!"

"Oh come, now, my love," he said, with his face buried in her black jerkin, "it will take more than that."

She let him go and he struggled to his feet, while she picked up the gun. Then he went over and helped Olivia up. The three of them stood together, looking at Mistress Brooks out cold on one side of the room, her husband now passed out in a large pool of blood on the other, and Rolleston on his back with the knife handle standing proud in his belly.

"I would we get away now," William suggested, "before perhaps those other men realise they were deceived, or are still close enough to hear the sound of your gun, and make a return."

"Yes, we must," agreed Mary, "and now the documents are

burned, we have done what we set out to do." She looked at William, whose skin was now taking on something of a grey tinge. "Come, my love, you need rest, some wine and food, and to have your bruises tended." She turned to Olivia. "And you also, have scratches to your face."

"That woman was trying to take out my eyes." Olivia took hold of the back of a chair to steady herself.

Mary followed William out into the cool air. "I suggest we make haste for Nottingham first to get some rest and recovery, then make for Whitehall to report to Master Secretary Walsingham."

They walked to where they had left their horses.

"That woman put up a fight, did she not, Olivia?" Mary observed, as they started to untie the beasts.

There was no answer.

Mary spun round.

Olivia was not with them.

She looked at William, and together they both said the same thing.

"Rolleston!"

They ran back to the house and into the Hall.

Rolleston was standing and again had Olivia in his grasp, with the bloody blade of the knife once more held to her throat.

"Those nooses still await," he croaked. "I would you go to them, and I will not be so obliging this time."

"I am so sorry," Olivia said, her eyes wide. "He came up behind me and pulled me to him. I thought he was dead."

"That is the benefit of feeling no pain," Rolleston observed.

"Far from dying, I simply pulled the blade free and am sound in body once more."

Mary raised the gun and pointed it at his head. "Let her go, Rolleston," she ordered.

He moved his head behind Olivia, so she was almost completely shielding him – with just the smallest part of his head still visible. "Do you risk killing this girl?" he asked. "Or come any closer and watch as I make her die in pain." Then he whispered in Olivia's ear, but loud enough for Mary and William to hear. "It must be such a strange sensation, pain. I would you tell me how it feels when I cut your throat, but you will scarce have time." He paused. "Or the capability of speech." He looked up, "Come, Anne Carter, who this man calls Mary, and you, Will or William, step up to the nooses, and we can end all this."

For sure it was time to end it.

Mary took the shot.

Once again the report of the gun echoed around the room. The bullet missed Olivia by no more than half an inch and entered the corner of Rolleston's eye, then exploded out of the back of his head, killing him instantly. The force of the shockwave snapped Olivia's own head to one side making the knife cut into her neck. As Rolleston fell backwards, she fell back with him, then rolled off him and lay still on her side, as if she was a sleeping infant.

Even before Mary lowered the gun, William ran over to Olivia and was examining her. Then he picked her gently up in his arms and struggled to his feet, holding her as if she were a sleeping babe.

"She still lives," he said, "but she has a deep cut to the side of her neck."

Mary examined Olivia's neck, and breathed a small sigh of relief. "It is only a flesh wound," she said. "We should bind it up, so it will heal." As she said this, Olivia's eyes fluttered open.

"You will live," Mary said with a smile.

William carried Olivia outside. "Come," he said. "Let us make haste to Nottingham before anything else occurs."

"The Lord be praised," Olivia whispered to Mary as William carried her along towards to the horses. "He has saved me."

"I rather think the Lord had less to do with it than my aim being true," Mary muttered to herself.

46

CHAPTER FORTY-SIX

Mary shifted from one foot to the other as she stood outside Walsingham's study at the house on Seething Lane. The door remained firmly closed, as it had been since she had first been told to wait by a servant fifteen minutes before. She adjusted her gown for the hundredth time, smoothing the thick material down with her hands. Then she patted her hair again, making sure it was still in perfect shape.

Loud footsteps coming down the corridor made her turn. Wychwoode was striding towards her, his cloak billowing out behind him.

"Master Wychwoode," she said, as he came up. Then she added through slightly gritted teeth. "You are well met."

"And you, Lady Mary," he replied with a thin smile. "I am indeed most pleased to see you back, and also in good health. I believe you are here to report on the outcome of the mission?"

"I am."

"And you are to be congratulated," he continued. "All has turned out most satisfactorily. I trust you experienced no difficulties in the course of your endeavours?" Then he raised a hand. "But no, you must save your story for Master Secretary Walsingham. I shall not steal the thunder from your tale."

Just then the door opened, and Walsingham's head poked out, his dark eyes flicking across them both. "Lady Mary?" he asked, almost as if he was surprised to see her. "And Master Wychwoode, also? Good, then we are complete." He stood back and held the door. "Please step in."

Mary made her way to the table, and noted with a wry smile that her phone was once again sitting on top of some papers. She sat down and picked it up, turning it over in her hands, surprised at how the familiar touch of the smooth plastic brought back warm feelings of security and contentment. She pressed and held the 'on' button, but the screen remained resolutely black.

"I have spent some time familiarising myself with this amazing object," Walsingham said, making her look up. He gave her a conspiratorial smile. "I became particularly enamoured of the four young men who sing the song with the oft-repeated line 'Back for Good.' The words appear to be so much doggerel, but I found the melody quite pleasant. My wife Ursula has been most insistent that I cease humming it as I go about the house." Mary put the phone down, trying hard to process the image of the dry Elizabethan spymaster watching Take That videos.

"You are free to take this 'phone' device back, Lady Mary," said Wychwoode. "But we would have your assurance it will be kept securely locked away, or else destroyed. It would not be seemly for its existence to be made public, else we would have others react negatively to its powers, as we both did when we first saw it."

Something in the tone of his voice – almost the sound of a warm smile – caught Mary's attention. "I can take it back? Does that mean I no longer face the charge of blasphemy?" she asked.

There was a quick glance between the two men, almost as if they had been expecting this very question. Walsingham put his fingers together in the same 'church roof' shape as he had at their first meeting.

"I think you can rest assured that the charge of blasphemy has been dropped, Lady Mary," he said quietly.

"I see," she replied, trying hard to keep her tone measured. "And the charge of sorcery?"

"That too," said Wychwoode. "All charges have been dropped. It has been acknowledged that such charges were in truth, quite baseless."

Mary took a couple of deep breaths, then smiled at each man in turn.

All charges dropped...

All charges dropped!

What she really wanted to do now was to jump up, lean across the table, kiss them both, then throw back her chair and shout, 'Yes! YES!' while doing repeated fist pumps.

What she actually said was, "I thank you gentlemen. That is great news. It is indeed a relief to know I am no longer under such a threat."

Walsingham smiled. "I think, Lady Mary, that it is a

measure of the gratitude felt by our gracious sovereign, as well, of course by both of us here, that we must acknowledge the part you have played in her secret enterprise."

"Mistress Barwell was lately brought to London as we planned," explained Wychwoode, "and in the guise of the Queen of Scots, she signed an undertaking to renounce that queen's Catholic faith and her claim to the throne of England. It was done before Parliament, so it is fully in the public domain. I am pleased to report that no person there present questioned that it was the very Queen of Scots herself. The likeness was remarkable, and even those few that had previously met the lady in person were taken in by the deception." He inclined his head to one side and fixed her with his piercing blue eyes. "So the Catholics no longer have a focus for their seditious plotting, and we have the chance to secure a long-lasting peace in the realm."

"And we let it be known through some of our intelligencers that the assassin was believed to be a disaffected Catholic," added Walsingham. "So the change of heart by the Queen of Scots was better understood and no man thought to challenge it." He nodded. "It made good justification for the very public execution you performed, Lady Mary."

"Even though it was undermined by Rolleston and Brooks?" Mary asked.

"Perhaps," answered Wychwoode. "But the end outcome was the same, nonetheless. For which we have you to thank."

"Well, I am pleased it finally turned out so well," Mary said. "Mistress Barwell certainly impressed me when I met her in Sheffield." She paused. "What will become of her now?"

Wychwoode smiled. "She will continue in her role a few

more weeks, then it will be announced that the Queen of Scots has caught a serious chill and sadly, passed away. Mistress Barwell can then resume her previous life, and the deception will remain a closely guarded secret for evermore."

"I need hardly add that you are enjoined to keep the secret also," Walsingham said, his eyes suddenly very cold.

"Of course," Mary replied. "I have no wish to share it with any person. Besides," she added, "I hardly think anyone would believe it."

"I have no doubt you are correct," said Walsingham, sitting back.

Wychwoode said, "Those events you have told us that would have occurred, such as the plot led by one Anthony Babington, the original execution of the Queen of Scots and particularly Philip of Spain's attempt at a sea-borne invasion – all these will in every likelihood, no longer happen." He nodded in satisfaction. "You have changed the course of history, Lady Mary, and it is to be hoped, much for the better. It seems that Her Majesty is now more secure on her throne, and that is a most welcome outcome."

Mary did not respond immediately. That she had changed the course of history was something she had already accepted – indeed it seemed strange now how fearful she had originally been of the idea, and how keen she had been to preserve the history she had grown up with.

Although, was wanting to preserve it in truth no more than a selfish indulgence? It now existed only in her and the Alchemist's memories, so what was she protecting? A memory? Far better to let it go, and to focus instead on the benefits she had finally managed to deliver through this mission.

To focus on the lives she had saved and the plots that would now never happen. Whatever new history might now take place, there was a chance it could be a little less bloody and a little less deadly than the one she remembered. She should be grateful for that at least.

"I am pleased that the outcome was successful at the last," she said. "Although there were some difficult moments on the way, believe me."

"I am not surprised, Lady Mary," said Walsingham. "And we would very much like to have your report."

Mary leaned forward. "As you wish," she said, then paused to gather her thoughts. "Let me start by telling you that as I said originally, Roger Rolleston was not to be trusted. He was a Catholic all along, and a most dangerous one at that. He tried very hard to turn the mission against me, and he very nearly succeeded."

There was a long silence, then Walsingham whistled softly. "I had heard of this," he muttered, "but you have now confirmed it for sure." He did not look at Wychwoode as he said this.

Wychwoode appeared to be studying the table with great interest. Eventually he looked up at Mary. "I do most humbly beg your forgiveness my lady, for I genuinely believed him to be on our side in this matter." He reached across and took her hands in his own. "I would not have sent you with him if I had even had the smallest suspicion, believe me."

"What form did this treachery take?" asked Walsingham.

So Mary told them the full story, from the journey up to Sheffield, through to the final fight at Oak House, and even, with honesty, admitted to allowing Rolleston the means to work out the plot. They listened in silence throughout, apart from occasional exclamations of surprise or amazement. When she had finished, they sat still for some time. Then Walsingham got up and paced over to the fire, before turning back and asking, "This treacherous fellow Rolleston, he told you he was incapable of feeling pain?"

"Yes."

"And you saw the truth of this for yourself?"

"I did; in the forest when he and Brooks staged the counterfeit ambush, and on other occasions since. The last of these was when he pulled the knife from his belly in the Hall at Oak House."

"Ah, yes," observed Wychwoode, "Before you finished him off by the finest of shots; one that missed Mistress Olivia Melrose by a hair's width."

Mary nodded. Then Walsingham asked, "But if he had taken a knife in the belly, surely that was a mortal blow? Belike he was as good as dead already? You had only to wait a moment more, and he would have fallen?"

"I could not have taken that risk. As he felt no pain, he had no way of knowing just how badly he was struck. He genuinely believed he was recovered, and could thus have continued for enough time to have either killed Olivia or forced William and I into the nooses."

"So you took a shot that, had it been but an inch over, would have killed Mistress Melrose instead?" Walsingham's eyebrows seemed to climb halfway up his forehead. "Was that not foolhardy?"

Mary could not believe the man was asking the same question he had asked at their first meeting. "As I believe I explained before, Master Secretary," she said, trying to keep her voice calm, "I have every confidence in my ability to fire the weapon accurately. I did so when my son was close, and I repeated this with Rolleston as well. I did what was necessary."

"So it seems." He stared at her with his dark eyes, as if he was making his mind up to reveal something. Eventually he said, "It also seems from what you have said, that Olivia Melrose is equally competent to fire the weapon. How was she so able?"

"She had seen me do so, and I also gave her instruction while we were in Nottingham for just such an eventuality. She is quick to learn, and indeed, I warrant she is now faster than I at loading and firing the gun."

Walsingham put his fingertips together once more. "Good," he said, his tone measured, which made his next words sound all the more unexpected. "Which is why I have requested Her Majesty to release Mistress Melrose to my charge, so I can put her to work as an intelligencer."

"You have done *what*?" Mary asked, her voice rising.

"I have made her such an offer."

"And she has agreed?"

"She has indeed." He paused. "Olivia Melrose is a remarkable young woman; courageous, resourceful, capable with your gun and, I understand, utterly devoted to Her Majesty's cause. She is also very comely, and understands therefore how to bend a man to her will, as she did with Master Wychwoode." He paused, his eyes never leaving hers. "I already have missions in mind for her, which involve this remarkable weapon, so we will, regretfully, not be acceding to the Queen's request to have it destroyed. He paused. "I have scarce seen another intelligencer more fitted to such a role. Although," he continued, "I have in truth seen one other who is almost more suited." He was silent, clearly expecting her to respond.

"And that is...?" she asked finally.

"It is you, Lady Mary."

There was a heavy silence while Mary returned his stare, as if this had suddenly become game of high-stakes poker. "Almost?" she asked. "You said 'almost'?

"You made two errors in this mission," Walsingham replied, looking her direct in the eye. "The one; you allowed the secret of the plan to be discovered by Rolleston."

"And the second?" Mary asked, although she suspected what was coming.

"The second was that you failed in the forest to secure the destruction of the incriminating documents; the documents which were almost certainly on the person of Master Brooks, necessitating your near-fatal mission to Oak House."

"So, Master Secretary," she said. "What would you have me do?"

"Carry on in my employ, if you wish."

"Despite such errors?"

"Yes." He considered her, his dark eyes unsmiling. "For I warrant you have learned such a lesson from these errors that you will not make them again. So if you want to continue, then I would have you do so."

"I see." Mary scratched at a small itch that had started on the back of her neck. "You also know I will no longer have useful insight into events to come? As a result of this mission, the future I knew has quite gone. I now know no more than any of us."

"I understand, but it is of small consequence. I would have you more for the bravery, cunning, ingenuity and determination you have clearly shown these past days."

"I see. And if despite my bravery, cunning, ingenuity and determination, I do not want to continue in your employ?"

"Master Wychwoode here has impressed upon me your wish to live in peace with your family. I agree that you have earned that life if you want it." He regarded her thoughtfully. "I would also add that Her Majesty has expressed a wish that if you choose not to serve her as my intelligencer, then you regularly attend on her at Court instead. She says she values the calm and wise counsel that you offer, and particularly that you are honest with her, without looking for favour. Although," here he paused with a raised eyebrow, "she also asked that I pass on a singular message that means naught to me, but may have significance for you."

"Which is?" Mary asked, intrigued.

"She observed that she would only value your advice if it were based on sound thinking, and not on a sound carried by the wind." He smiled. "Does that mean anything to you?"

Mary felt her face flushing. Of all the things that Elizabeth had remembered, it was that she had been belching loudly from drinking that foul beer in the Tower.

"I have an idea, yes." Mary smiled inwardly. Perhaps this was the Queen's way of confirming just how much she wanted a totally open and honest relationship between them, with no false modesty.

Or maybe it was just her base sense of humour.

"Good," said Walsingham. "Then there are your options. Which is it to be?"

He sat back, and Mary looked from one man to the other. On one side the dark, brooding spymaster, fixing her with his hooded eyes and appearing to be calculating the odds on which way her decision would go. On the other side the old, white-haired lawyer, who had once been her friend and even something of a father-figure, and perhaps could be again if she forgave him for Rolleston and let him back in...

So, what was it to be?

Keep working for Walsingham as a spy and assassin, with all the adventure, excitement and action that would involve?

Or go home? Do nothing more dangerous than running Grangedean Manor and giving honest counsel to Elizabeth, while no doubt offering help and advice to Olivia so she could grow into an accomplished intelligencer instead?

Mary thought back to that ride through Sheffield, when the idea of a quiet life in Elizabethan England seemed so appealing. Indeed, her heart's deepest desires had been so clear as she rode through those oppressive and foul-smelling streets...

To be able to live at peace and fulfil her promise to Kat not to leave her again...

To be there to help not just Kat, but Ambrose and Jane as well – to enable them to become the fine young people they were now destined to be...

To grow old beside William, the man she had loved ever since she had first laid eyes on his magnificent portrait, before she had been thrown, a frightened girl called Justine Parker, into the confusing world of Tudor history; a world she now understood well, and indeed felt she was a valued part.

And to be there for Elizabeth – the woman not the queen – with her honest counsel...

But – and it was a very big 'but'...

How could she live without all the adventure and action, stuck in Grangedean Manor with nothing more exciting to concern her than the household accounts?

Would she end up a bitter, bored, dried-up old housewife?

What about all the obstacles she had faced and overcame on this mission? Could she live without such challenges?

Could she really just sit back and let Olivia have all the fun?

Mary picked up her phone and stood.

All things considered, there was really only one possible answer.

She stared down at both men, took a deep breath and said in firm, clear voice: "I have made my decision, sirs."

She paused as they looked up at her expectantly.

"I want to go home."

47

CHAPTER
FORTY-SEVEN

Mary stepped carefully down from the carriage. The trees around the Grangedean Manor park were almost bare, with a light silver coating of frost to match the tiny sparkling ice crystals that drifted through the clear air of the winter sunshine. She walked across the path and looked up at the façade of the Manor.

To her, the Manor was as warm and as comfortable as an old pair of shoes; every stone a familiar friend; every beam and every window as recognisable as her own face in the mirror. She smiled as she took it all in; the only place she had ever truly called home. The only place where her soul had ever truly lived.

She proceeded alone across the frosty lawn, then dropped slowly to her knees and gripped the cold turf in both hands.

"I make you this solemn promise," she whispered, "I will always live here, and I will always be happy here. Whatever comes to pass, whatever the future may be, I will never leave."

The Manor seemed to smile back, and the breeze in the trees give a gentle reply, "Always here for you, Justine. Always here, Mary."

As she stood up, Olivia Melrose came across the lawn and stood silently beside her.

"You have made the right decision to return here, my lady," she said softly.

"As have you, to seek new adventures," answered Mary. "I hear Walsingham has already briefed you on your first mission?"

"Yes."

"Then I wish you every success." Mary turned to study the girl's face. "Are you taking the gun?"

Olivia nodded. "I am up to fourteen loads in thirty seconds."

Mary smiled. "I expect no less." She reached out and touched the girl's arm. "Look after it please. I do not want to have to make another one."

Olivia gave a small laugh. "I shall." Then she became serious. "Will I be able to call on you for advice? I would very much value your wise counsel."

"Of course," Mary replied. "Any time, day or night." She turned to face Olivia and put both hands on the girl's shoulders. "I have no doubt you will face great dangers out there, Olivia Melrose, and I know you have the courage, resourcefulness and determination to get through. But if you ever need my counsel, you only have to ask. Any time you need me. Any time."

"I will." Olivia stepped back. "I must be away now, Lady Mary. The carriage is waiting to take me back to London, and I have much to prepare."

"You will not stay to see William and the children? I know they would be disappointed not to see you."

Olivia shook her head. "No, I will leave you to reunite together as a family."

"But you are as much a part of this family as any of us."

"That is kind of you to say," Olivia replied, "but this is your time to be with them, not mine." She leaned forward and enveloped Mary in a warm hug.

"I will miss you, Olivia Melrose," Mary whispered in the girl's ear. "You come back to me, you hear?"

"I will miss you too," Olivia answered. "I will, I promise."

They hugged a moment longer, then Olivia stood back. "On the boat those many weeks ago, when we thought you were facing execution, you asked me to give each member of your family a personal message." Mary nodded. "So now is your chance to give them those messages yourself. In person. As their wife and mother."

With that, she turned and walked back to the carriage.

Mary watched her go, then went up the steps to the main entrance. She gave three loud knocks, then stood back and waited for the door to open.

THE END

About the Author

Jonathan Posner is a novelist based in the UK, with a passion for the action and adventure to be found in Tudor England.

He has always been captivated by Tudor history, and has also been a lifelong fan of action-adventure novels. So when he decided to write a novel himself, it had to be the kind of adventure he loves to read; one with plenty of action, danger and suspense. And, of course, it had to be set in Tudor England - with a time-travelling heroine finding herself thrown into the deep-end of this fascinating historical era.

The result was **The Witchfinder's Well**, the first part of a trilogy. Book 2, **The Alchemist's Arms** is also available, and this book, **The Sovereign's Secret** is book 3,

Jonathan has also written **The Broken Sword** – the first of a series of adventures featuring an unconventional Tudor heroine called Mary Fox. More books about Mary's adventures are also planned.

Jonathan's other works include a book of short stories called **Once Upon an Ending**, a one-act play called **Private Eyes**, as well book and lyrics for three Musicals – **Spirit of History** which premiered in Old Windsor, **Hot, Mean & Green**, which premiered at the Rhoda McGaw Theatre in Woking, and **A Fine Time for Wine**, which also premiered in Old Windsor.

Jonathan is the father of two adult sons and lives in Exeter, UK. When not writing he is a regular presenter on local radio.

For more informaion and to **sign up for Jonathan's regular newsletter**, please visit Jonathan's author website at **jonathanposnerauthor.com**.

Jonathan's books are published by
Winter & Drew Publishing
winteranddrew.com

By the same Author

Part 1 - The Witchfinder's Well

The first book in the series tells the story of Justine Parker, and how she time-travels from 2015 to 1565, then outwits the witchfinder Matthew Hopkirk to become Lady Mary de Beauvais.

"A must for everyone who loves history and a must for everyone who wants to be whisked away to another time."

Part 2 – Alchemist's Arms

When Lady Mary de Beauvais she discovers there's another time-traveller from 2015, she sets out across Elizabethan England to find him.

But it's a search that leads her into dreadful danger - threatening not just Mary's own future, but the life of Queen Elizabeth as well. Can Mary face her fears and take control?

For further information and to **read the opening chapters**, visit **jonathanposnerauthor.com**.

The Broken Sword

Tudor England. When Mary Fox is ordered to marry a sadistic older man, she decides to strike out on her own. As a woman in a man's world, no-one expects her to survive, but Mary is determined to prove them wrong. Challenged to return the Broken Sword talisman and so break a centuries-old curse, she soon learns how to scheme, fight and outwit those who would drag her back to a life of servitude. And in doing so, she becomes more than a match for any man.

"Diabolically good! What makes this novel irresistibly readable is the emotional energy generated by the main character Mary Fox, her ups and downs, drawing parallels to our present times." *Gina Flyvholm*

"I would highly recommend this book for its entertainment, historical authenticity and value." *Philip Appleton*

**Jonathan's books are available on Amazon
or order through your local bookstore.**

For more information and to sign up for regular news, offers and sneak previews, visit Jonathan's website at **jonathanposnerauthor.com**